HUNTER
HUNTRESS

DARCY SCOTT

snowbooks

Proudly Published by Snowbooks in 2010

Copyright © 2010 Darcy Scott

Snowbooks Ltd
Kirtlington Business Centre
Oxfordshire
OX5 3JA
Tel: 0207 837 6482
email: info@snowbooks.com
www.snowbooks.com

British Library Cataloguing in Publication Data
A catalogue record for this book is available from the British Library.

ISBN 978-1-906727-47-5

Printed and bound by J F Print Ltd., Sparkford, Somerset

HUNTER
HUNTRESS

DARCY SCOTT

For Brad Daziel, sorely missed, who opened my eyes and heart to the joy of storytelling, and for my husband Cleave—kickass drummer and balls-to-the-wall sailor. Plus, he makes a wicked stir-fry.

Tantaene animis coelestibus irae?
In heavenly minds, can such resentments dwell?

—Virgil

NOVEMBER

No time to wonder, to protest; it was simply there—the car careening onto the blacktop just feet ahead. Surprised panic in place of fear, an arm thrown instinctively over to afford protection, a twist of the wheel to avoid impact before the world was remade in an explosion of bright light.

THREE YEARS LATER

ONE

She stoops quickly and, without breaking stride, picks the penny from the road and tucks it into the small inside pocket of her running shorts. That made three in as many miles. Out of the blue she remembers finding five all in a row and perfectly spaced in a dirt parking lot at a beach on New Castle Island. Last summer— no, the summer before. Before she met Peter. She'd thought about them for the rest of her rain-soaked run, and when she returned to the apartment over the donut shop, she'd placed them together along the sill of the bay window in the approximate configuration she'd found them—or as close as she could remember. GM had done that—put pennies in the corners of all her windows. Told Jamie it brought luck, old harpy that she was. She liked to call herself that—old harpy. Jamie never knew why.

She picks up her pace for the final mile, wiping the sweat from her forehead and eyes with a sticky forearm. It's still summer, third week of September or not, and the leaves of the oak trees lining this picture-perfect approach to town stubbornly refuse to fade. Irritated by all the perfection—the rich green lawns, the long row of quaint, weathered saltboxes—she pushes harder, smiling only when the familiar warning pains begin in her legs.

And pushes harder—concentrating on the pain now, on finishing the run and dropping the pennies into the smoky glass jar she began using once she'd crammed all the windowsills to capacity. She was still living over the donut shop the first time the jar itself became full, she remembers now; she'd taken it downstairs, bought herself coffee and a muffin and sat outside at one of the tables set along the sidewalk—the cool breeze from the harbor pushing off the heat while she watched the cars weave in and out of the small traffic circle feeding the marina. The trip downstairs clutching the jar of found money had a ceremonial feel that appealed to her, and she repeated it now each time the jar filled with coins—an oddly soothing ritual born of the running that had saved her life.

For a long time after the accident, she'd concentrated solely on this filling of windowsills, money found as she built herself up again. At first they'd said she'd walk with a limp; special shoes and various cane options were discussed. Then, when she'd proven them wrong about that, they'd warned her against running. To try, they'd reasoned, would be to risk all the progress she'd made. Now, three years later, she was back to running five miles a day, four or five days a week—pushing herself, like today, to the point of pain. It gave her something to focus on—the rhythm of her feet hitting the ground filling her ears, emptying her mind, while the windows filled with coins. GM had been wrong about the luck part, as it turned out, but she kept picking the change up anyway.

Her legs scream for relief, but she ignores them and thinks again of the cool, impassive faces of the doctors, the nurses who'd known too much to be comfortable in her presence. She remembers little else about the hospital. That whole first year had the feel of a vivid dream gone hazy and unreal upon waking—with just little bits coming back to her over time. She has only a dim recollection of moving into the apartment over the donut shop the summer following the accident—coming to herself finally, it seemed, amid the rich, yeasty smells that wafted up to her each morning before dawn. But always there was the running, the connection to her body immediate and reassuring. All this before she'd met Peter and had gone to live with him on the boat; before they'd been married—his agreeing, reluctantly, never to try for kids.

She rounds the final corner, skirting the edge of the traffic circle as she takes in the familiar sight of masts bobbing in the harbor, the keening of the gulls. Passing the donut shop perched at the circle's edge, someone else living in the apartment above it now, she slows as she reaches the wharf and the string of shacks hawking everything from rod and reel rentals to whale watch and sportfishing trips; walking its length and back while she cools off—hands on hips, breathing hard, the front of her t-shirt soaked in a sweaty half moon slung between her breasts.

The dogs pace anxiously in the cockpit while she stretches on the warm planking of the dock—Lucille wriggling her little sausage body in anticipation; Gus offering a wide, disinterested yawn from beneath a furry Airedale mustache.

"Hey, kids," she says climbing aboard. "Yes; okay, okay. Stop the licking. Ugh! Peter—call the dogs!"

"Yo!" His voice booms from somewhere below deck and Gus and Lucille are gone in an instant, scrambling down the companionway in a clattering of nails.

Jamie, lazy in a runner's soporific afterglow, sits for a minute fingering the coins in the pocket of her shorts. The constant small movements of the boat at first made it hard to find places where the sill pennies might sit, but Peter had solved the problem with pieces of double-sided tape, and now the lower edges of all the port lights winked with a coppery gleam. GM would be pleased, she thinks. She goes below and empties the shorts at the galley sink—dropping the pennies in the running jar wedged above the stove between two of Peter's cookbooks—and rinses cool water through the sweaty, worn baby sock she keeps tucked at the bottom of the pocket.

Peter's back is to her, his close-cropped head of sandy hair bent over a laptop. The aquaculture project at the Isles of Shoals, no doubt.

"Lori and Bake for dinner tonight, babe," he says, turning. The smile is tentative, apologetic. "Okay by you?"

Jamie shrugs, squeezing the little green sock and letting the water pool in her hand again.

He pulls himself up from the desk he's built into the bulkhead opposite the galley and comes to stand behind her—encircling her waist with his arms, nuzzling her neck.

"What are you doing?" she complains.

"*Just dropped in to see what condition my condition was in,*" he sings softly.

Jamie smiles into the sink as she squeezes the sock. "Kenny Rogers and The First Edition," she says after some thought.

He nods into her neck, planting kisses. "Before he got into country."

She thinks for a minute, letting the music take hold in her mind; then, traveling the arpeggio of triplets, the melody's turns and syncopated tempo of three against four—she hums the Largo section of the *Fantaisie-Impromptu*.

"Bach?"

"Chopin," she corrects.

"Damn," he says, rocking her gently now. "So it's okay tonight? Lori and Bake?"

She glances toward his collection of cookbooks: *Miami Spice; Biker Billy Cooks with Fire; Eat This; The Ubiquitous Shrimp.*

"Nothing too spicy," she reminds him. "Lori won't eat it."

"I'll do something Thai, but mild. Chilies on the side for those who want to go nuts." He hesitates, nuzzles her again. "Feeling punky?"

She turns and puts her arms around him, the little sock a sodden ball in her fist. "Better now."

"Well, before you start feeling too good, there's a letter from Philippe. I left it for you on the table."

It isn't until she goes to shower off under a generous stream of warm water, the letter still unopened, that she begins to shake. She'd almost made it, too. He'll be five tomorrow, she tells herself for the thousandth time since breakfast. Would have been, she amends. Would have been. This part even Peter doesn't know.

☙❧

The sun is almost down and still they linger in the cockpit—the growing chill settling into shimmering, translucent beads on the fiberglass combing. Before long they'll be spending all their evenings below deck, layered in sweaters and listening to the hiss of the coal stove, and Jamie isn't yet ready to give up sitting beneath a night sky full with moon and blinking with stars. She leans her head back against the warmth of Peter's arm and looks skyward, beyond the broad swath of the Milky Way, to the stars of the Pleiades and the hunter Orion—horny son of the god Neptune who, according to Peter, had a thing for unwilling virgins. She traces the belt, sword and legs of his constellation, then glances to the west where the deteriorating hulk of the old Wentworth Hotel looms from atop a far hill.

"It's the rudeness that gets you." Bake, on the opposite bench beside Lori, scratches the chin buried somewhere in his full, dark beard. "They hired another spare last week—little old lady, trained her myself. So, get this, last night she's in the toll booth next to mine, taking some guy's money, right? She looks down to thank him—being a retired schoolteacher and polite and all—and the freak's sitting there jerking off, watching her reaction. She's a grandmother, for Chrissakes—beaky nose, those long, dangly hairs under the chin. I mean, explain the appeal."

"You gotta get out of there," Peter tells him. "Road rage is endemic, my friend; toll takers are an obvious target."

"Toll attendant, please."

"And you working the graveyard shift—all those sickos passing through just looking for something to set them off. Evidence your flasher."

"He ain't my anything, Pete," Bake warns.

"I could use you on the fish farming project; the White Island mussels start coming in next month—pretty good pay, courtesy of NOAA. And you're the best systems man I've ever seen—pure genius when it comes to changing out an engine. There's enough work in this harbor alone to keep you busy. More than enough."

"Not in the winter, pal. And with Lori still looking..."

"I want something different this time," Lori announces—as though changing jobs was akin to picking out a new dress. "Something interesting, like Jamie's job. Development director for a symphony orchestra—wow. I'm, like, in awe."

Jamie recoils from the comment. She hasn't learned to read Lori yet, but the sucking up is getting old. The girl acting, when they'd first met, as if she'd never come across markedly patrician features on a woman before, or a tallish, lanky build matched with golden, almost tawny coloring—calling her green eyes haunting or haunted, something like that. Jamie can't decide if she's extremely young or just being shrewd, covering all the bases since her relationship with Bake is so new.

"It's not as glamorous as it sounds," Jamie corrects. "I spend my time trying to talk people into giving money to the arts. It's tiring, not to mention extremely frustrating."

"Don't let her kid you," Peter says. "She's more than tripled corporate support in the two years she's been here. The orchestra she was with in New York tried everything to keep her when she quit—huge raise, bonus—you name it."

This is veering dangerously toward a discussion as to why she'd moved to New Hampshire to take a job paying less than half what she was making in New York, so Jamie does what only moments before would have been unthinkable. "The new season starts in a few weeks, Lori. They've been looking for someone for the box office. I could find out where they are on it, if you'd like."

"Wow—I mean, yeah, that'd be great."

Peter turns a sly smile on Jamie. He's been baiting Lori all evening, but gently, and wouldn't do it at all, Jamie knew, if he thought Bake was serious about her. Never mind she's already living in the house trailer out in Lee; that doesn't necessarily mean anything with Bake.

Jamie considers the two of them, deciding the age difference has to be considerable. Bake, she knows, is thirty-three like Peter. His real name, Nicolai, is far more in keeping with his hairy lumberjack appearance—but he never uses it except when he reaches them on the cell with the invariable greeting: "It is I, Nicolai." She's never been told his last name. It seems extraneous with someone like Bake who, Peter once told her, was a professional hockey player in Canada until he bit some guy's earlobe off. Lori, with her chin-length auburn hair, long dark bangs and doe eyes, is probably all of twenty-five and right now is desperately trying to fit in.

"How far do you have to drive?" she asks, her gaze shifting from Peter to Jamie. "I don't have a really good car."

"Nashua—about an hour, " Peter says. "But you can ride with Jamie, right Jae?"

Jamie ignores him. "Let's start by finding out about the job, okay? It could be filled by now, for all I know."

"Anyway," Peter says, unwilling to let the subject drop. "There's some big arts conference in New York next month—their way of enticing her back, if only for a few days. All the bigwigs flying in from around the country to hear Ms. Jamie Lloyd reveal her secrets, teach them how to talk multinational corporations into forking their profits over for the cultural benefit of mankind—stuff like that."

Bake stifles a yawn with a pull on his Molson. "You're going then?"

Jamie shrugs. "Thinking about it." She turns to Lori. "Peter's putting you on. It's the annual American Symphony Orchestra League conference. It just happens to be in New York this year, and it has nothing to do with me. Really. I'm not even sure I'm going."

"Oh, she'll go," Peter says as the dogs begin barking from their customary after-dinner perch in the bow. "You couldn't keep her away." He turns to wave to a couple walking arm in arm toward the Morgan thirty-eight bobbing gently in the next slip.

Lori whispers something to Bake, who rolls his eyes. "C'mon, Lore. It's not a bathroom; it's a head. We went over all this, remember?"

"I just get it mixed up, is all."

Jamie feels a reluctant stab of sympathy for the girl—tossed as roughly into the world of boating lingo as she, herself, had been. The first time Peter took her sailing, she remembers now, he informed her there was no kitchen on a boat, but a galley. No bathroom, but a head. No front and back to a vessel, he'd said—by then enjoying her considerable confusion—but bow and stern. Left was port, right starboard. His bedroom—which she gained intimate knowledge of that weekend—was the forepeak; it had no bed, but a bunk. She imagines it's something like moving to a foreign country—strange language and customs, traditions so old no one could remember when they started or why. It took her months to get it all straight. And Lori, it's obvious, is simply no match for these two.

"Come on," Jamie says, putting her club soda on the bench beside her. "I'll take you down."

☙ ❧

She's reading in the bunk when Peter finally flips off the desk light and comes to her—stretching out fully clothed to rest his head in her lap. He cranes his neck to peer at the title of the article she's been skimming.

"Ten Deadly Mistakes in Direct Mail Campaigns," he recites. "Sexy stuff."

"Hmmm."

A sheepish grin. "She's such a dim bulb, Jae. I couldn't help it."

"I know," Jamie says, turning the page. "But we can't all be Ph.D.'s in marine biology. And Bake seems to like her."

"Yeah." She can tell by his tone he's stopped listening. "*Doctor, doctor, give me the news,*" he sings, sliding his hand along her thigh. "*I've got a bad case of lovin' you.*"

She puts the article down. "Robert somebody. You've done this one before, you know. You're starting to repeat yourself."

"Robert Palmer," he informs her, reaching above her head to shut off the reading light. "*No pill's gonna cure my ills—I got a bad case of lovin' you.*"

And then he begins, their lovemaking long and slow tonight— the papers slipping to the floor as she loses herself in the welcome oblivion of it, curling hard into him as he eases her gently past the midnight hour and into the first of the two days she's come to dread each year. The other three hundred and sixty-three she simply marks time, the hours ticking off toward their inevitable return.

TWO

She's up before six to walk the dogs. Moving purposefully through the day, she reasons, will get her past the worst of it. After the dogs, she'll run again. Sometime during the night she worked out a new, longer route in her mind—rural and more difficult—figuring it all of seven miles. She'll be forced to push herself, to pay attention to what she's doing.

The dogs clamber over the stern and shake themselves thoroughly on the dock; then Lucille takes her usual lead, waddling through the cool mist in the general direction of the deserted traffic circle—her vigorous interest in the variety of smells dragging them on a zigzag route from one side of the wharf to the other, Gus padding imperiously in her wake. The donut shop alone shows life at this early hour—the row of fishing shacks beside it closed now for the season—and the brightly lit interior draws Jamie, who releases the dogs to wander back to the boat on their own. Inside, the display case is already full: neat rows of the oversized powdered donuts the place is known for, then the muffins and various danish—raisin and pecan and fruit—and the sugary, crusty-edged palmiers GM had called elephant ears, pulling them hot from the oven on the wintry Sunday mornings of Jamie's girlhood.

She buys Peter two of the oversized Morning Glory muffins he loves—the warm, orange fragrance forever infused with the memory of the day they'd met. She'd only been living upstairs for about a month, then—had come down that morning after her run in search of coffee and a Morning Glory, courtesy of the found money cup. Still sweaty in her shorts and tee, she was skimming the paper at one of the outside tables when a bark of laughter drew her eyes along the sidewalk for her first glimpse of Peter and Bake, loping toward her from the docks. They seemed an oddly complementary pair, the one lanky and somewhat professorial looking—his clean-shaven face and close-cropped sandy hair in complete contrast to his beefy companion's bush of dark beard, hair that appeared to bloom outward along his shoulders and down his arms.

They stopped as one in front of the donut shop and without a break in conversation, crouched to remove two good-sized lobsters from a dirty aluminum bucket. Heads bent together with the intensity of five-year-olds, they each urged a reluctant lobster toward a key fob several feet away—arguing all the while about the lyrics of some rock song. Two dogs Jamie had seen hanging around the dock hovered nearby. The smaller one—a dachshund, she'd thought at the time—paced alongside, barking at the bluish backs of the slow-moving things while a mustached Airedale lay in the middle of the road, cleaning himself.

"Get the friggin' dog outta here, Pete," the hairy one complained. "She's spookin' the contender."

"Lucille, quit harassing the crustaceans." Peter's eyes moved casually over Jamie as he lifted a long arm to shoo the dog off, turning back to the race only to find his lobster making for the water. After a few futile attempts to urge it round again, he stood and walked past her into the donut shop, reemerging a minute later with three coffees. He put a cup down in front of her, sitting at the table without invitation and launching into equally uninvited discourse.

"*Homarus americanus*, in case you're wondering. Crustacean family. They're a kind of insect, really—related to the cockroach. Don't move as fast, though, as you can see. Amazing how much people will pay for them, considering." He turned. "Yo, Bake— coffee!"

"And where did you get them, if you didn't pay for them?" she'd asked over the top of the paper, unexpectedly drawn in by the unconventional topic.

"I keep a trap off the stern," he said matter-of-factly, cocking his head in the general direction of the dock, where maybe fifteen boats bobbed gently in their slips. Lucille began barking wildly, following Bake and the snapping lobsters he was carrying toward the water. "She gets like this when they've made their way into the trap, too—some sort of vibration traveling up the stern lines, I think. Drives her batshit."

Bake gave the lobsters an unceremonious toss and came to join them—not so much as glancing at Jamie as he drew his cup toward him from across the table.

"It was *Rocket in My Pocket*—I'm sure of it." His voice was deep and hoarse—reminding her strangely of Kermit the Frog.

Peter shook his head. "Nope. *Fat Man in the Bathtub*. Little Feat, 1978."

"Shit." Only then did Bake turn to her. "Is he right?"

Jamie looked at him blankly over the top of the paper, transfixed by all the hair—her eyes drawn to a thick circle of latticed tattoo just above the dark mat carpeting each arm to the fingers. "Excuse me?"

He swung his gaze away again. "Anyway, 1978 ain't fair, Pete. I wasn't but ten."

"That's the point of trivia, Bake—to amaze and impress with obscure facts most people would have absolutely no reason to know."

They left together after a few more minutes of haggling, during which time they took little notice of Jamie. Peter was maybe twenty feet away when he glanced back, almost as an afterthought. "How about a beer later?"

It was the first thing he'd said since sitting down that made immediate sense to her.

"About seven?" He nodded approvingly at the panicked look she felt taking hold. "Good."

Too stunned to react, Jamie had simply watched him head off with Bake toward the boats, her alarm at the thought of this man turning up at her door only slightly mitigated by the fact he hadn't asked where she lived. But he surprised her by arriving promptly at seven—cradling a six pack of Molson and making himself at home in a long sprawl across the worn, plaid couch that came with the sparsely furnished apartment. Jamie, stiffly formal in the single ladderback chair that completed the living room's furnishings, fought her agitation by absorbing the novelty of his energy flowing toward her across the bare floor. By the time he'd finished his first beer, he'd gone through most of the particulars of his life—that he was a marine biologist at the University of New Hampshire whose field was pollutants and their effect on shell fish; that he lived on a boat here in the marina; that the two dogs she'd seen that morning were his. And yes, he told her— twisting the top off his second beer—Lucille might be an odd, rather formal name for a dog, but it was the name B.B. King gave his favorite guitar and, well, he was the man. None of it meant much to her. She tended to sickness on boats, had never been much of a pet person, knew absolutely nothing about the music of B.B. King.

By the time Peter polished off his third Molson—never once commenting on the uncurtained windows, the bare walls, the lack of books or knick-knacks—he'd filled her in on the politics of a local salt marsh restoration project he'd become embroiled in. Jamie offered little about herself, having determined quite early on that she didn't much like him—her annoyance at his intrusion evident, she was sure, in her pointed lack of response. Still, when he finally left her at the door—the scrawl of a phone number stuffed in her hand—she was oddly reluctant to toss the empty bottles; left them on the floor by the couch for days until the stench of rancid beer became too much for her. It never once occurred to her that she was falling for a man who favored bright orange flip-flops and tended toward commentary drawn from rock and roll hits of the sixties, seventies and eighties.

Jamie pays for Peter's breakfast and returns to the boat. Knowing he'll be up and gone by the time she gets back from her run, she sets his muffins by the coffee pot and changes quickly—tucking the little sock into her shorts pocket as she steps off the stern.

She takes it easy at first, breathing deeply as she rounds the traffic circle, leaving the claustrophobic tidiness of the little saltboxes behind as she heads west into more open country.

Muscles looser now, she picks up the pace—emptying her mind of all but the soothing rhythm of her stride and the periodic contemplation of an occasional old farm house, stoic in its deterioration amid fields of autumn wildflowers. A sudden dip down and to the right reveals a small, rundown trailer set in a treeless lot, where a German shepherd chained to a porch rail sleeps in a puddle of early morning sun. Bits of trash blow across the drive, and Jamie catches sight of a flattened pack of Lucky Strikes dancing lazily with a few fallen leaves along the crumbling macadam—the box's crumpled, forlorn look reminding her for some reason of Philippe, who'd smoked unfiltered Gauloise.

His letter, briefly skimmed, lay in the trash. The third in as many years, it was somehow timed—as were all the rest—to arrive on Sam's birthday. Quite a feat, considering the vagaries of the French postal system. She has to steel herself for weeks before they arrive—his inevitable expressions of grief over the son they lost; a lingering regret for the way things ended between them. But this one had a forced, almost dutiful quality about it she found vaguely insulting—as if it were becoming harder with each passing year for Philippe to actually feel the loss, let alone scrape up the enthusiasm to communicate it.

Her sweeping gaze catches a line of oily drops on the opposite side of the road and she lopes over to check them out, running alongside as they become parallel lines of droplets, increasing in size and frequency until ending abruptly a hundred yards farther on in a large oil stain marking the demise of some car engine. Or a pickup truck. Engines and marriages, she thinks—both spring slow, almost imperceptible leaks, easy to overlook until it's too late, the sudden dumping of everything still somehow unexpected.

She pumps harder, pushing out her anger at Philippe during a long uphill climb. Strong now, no cramping in her legs at all—cruising on a runners' high that pulls her over the top of the rise. Her gaze tracks a low rumble to an unattended tractor idling just outside the open doors of a large graying barn. Beyond it, two horses—their heads bent to the grass, tails flicking—graze in a paddock that runs all the way to the stone wall fronting the road. Young ones, she thinks, based on their size, but as she gets closer and they make their way toward the wall—hoping to be fed, perhaps—she realizes both are not only old but sick, the larger brown and white in far worse shape than the smaller bay, and with a diseased eye that's clouded over and swollen. Just as she reaches them, he crowds the smaller one away from any possibility of a handout, indifferently pushing it into the rough rocks of the wall—all the while keeping his one good eye impassively on Jamie.

It reminds her of something, an uneasy connection she can't quite make, and she runs on faster now—pumping, pumping, as the animal's heavy, dull gaze follows her—past the dilapidated wall and the three unmarked mailboxes canting together toward the drive, pushing herself past another long stretch of field.

Here the pavement simply stops, the packed dirt of the road beyond narrowing to little more than a rutted path beneath tall oaks whose press of leaves block out the sun. Still she runs on—the occasional drop of an acorn into the dense underbrush echoing the soft slap of her shoes—and almost trips over a green and yellow garter snake stopped cold in the middle of the road. She slows, turning back to see if it will slither off after she passes, but it doesn't move. Dead? She wonders this without feeling—the casual consideration finally unleashing the dreaded heaviness at the back of her mind that signals the cascade of memory.

This is the way it starts, she knows—creeping up on her until some small, insignificant event triggers an avalanche of recognition, of smell, of small realizations that leave her breathless and shaken.

Engines dumping in the road.

She slows to a walk, pulling the tiny sock from her pocket and bringing it to her nose. His smell is long gone, but she can still sometimes catch a trace of the salty-sweet, little boy scent in the rounded contours of the heel.

His fifth birthday, she thinks, finally giving in to the reality of it. She runs the sock along her cheek, all softness until it offers the sharp, sudden realization that he's been dead now longer than he was alive. The awareness panics her—the three years since the accident feeling all at once like fifty—and for a terrifying instant she finds she can't remember his face. Grief comes in waves, they warned her. Go with it; wait it out. Such had been the expert advice of those who told her she'd need orthopedic support for the rest of her life. She quickens her step, concentrates on her breathing and tries to distract herself with thoughts of Peter, of their lovemaking the night before, of the work day ahead. Instead she finds herself trying to remember Sam's second birthday— just two months before the accident—but finds she can't. Or anything about how she spent what would have been his third. Not even if she was still living in the farmhouse in Connecticut then or whether GM had yet had the stroke that killed her. She can remember none of it.

Disturbed by the sudden cheat of memory, tired of the dimness of the woods, she turns and begins the return run, pitting speed against frustration, and hits the dock some twenty minutes later in a full sprint.

The only sign of Peter is a scattering of muffin crumbs on the lip of the galley sink. She goes immediately to their cabin, kicks the dogs off the bunk and reaches for the photo tucked in the bookshelf beside her pillow—losing herself in the details of the grinning face, the dancing blue eyes that hold no knowledge of what was to come. She feels again, as she always does when she looks at his picture, the impossibility of having produced and loved and cared for this little person, and it seems imperative, suddenly, that she immerse herself in as much of him as she can find—before she, like Philippe, finds it hard to remember, to feel. She's reminded then of the conference in New York. She could stay at the house in Connecticut, where they lived with GM those years between the divorce and the accident; take the hour-long train ride into the City. She should check on the house anyway, she reasons; the tenants have been gone for weeks now and she ought to go through the place before re-renting.

All right then, she thinks; a bit nervous at the thought but better somehow—more purposeful, and with an odd sense of hope.

THREE

Jamie opts for the stairwell rather than wait with the returning lunch crowd milling by the building's ancient elevator, determined to put off running into any of her old New York crowd as long as possible. Three flights later, she slips through the familiar etched-glass door, grateful to find the symphony's front rooms deserted. No one to feign surprise at her sudden appearance, thank God; the effusive greetings, the buzzing of cheeks barely disguising their curiosity as to whether or not she'll go off the deep end again.

A slight waft of cigarette draws her back along the narrow hallway, her gaze merely grazing the impressive brass nameplate at its end: Augusta Synden-Smythe, Executive Director. Resting her back against the door jamb, Jamie watches as her former boss stubs out the illegal smoke.

"Hello, Augie," she says quietly.

"Well, Jamie. I wondered when we'd see you." Augie nudges the ashtray back behind her computer monitor—a gesture more dismissive than guilt-induced—and runs a hand through her thick shock of graying curls. Beyond the European elegance—the high Scandinavian cheekbones, the Grecian nose—she seems in the same perpetually harried state as ever.

"We're going absolutely crazy with this conference nonsense," she continues, hunting through the mass of papers atop her desk. "Complete waste of time, if you ask me, but you know the board. Can't pass up the chance to host the damn thing—been talking about it for years. Orchestra business gets put on the back burner, of course, as if things could stop for a minute around here." She flips a long-fingered hand toward the outer offices. "I finally sent them all to lunch so I could get some work done." She rifles through the clutter on her desk for another minute, then looks up again. "Sit, sit," she instructs, motioning with irritation toward the chair opposite her. "Are you staying in the city?"

"No." Jamie sits as directed, placing her thin leather briefcase against the leg of her chair. "I'm at the house in Easton."

"I don't believe this," Augie says, still searching. "I had that contract in my very hand when you walked in. I thought you had tenants in the house," she adds in one of her legendary non sequiturs.

"It's been empty since Labor Day." Jamie glances around the familiar space where Augie reigns over the hundreds of people and performance details necessary to produce a symphony concert series in a major metropolitan area—every available surface covered with faxes, contracts, file folders; the bookcases flanking her desk crammed with back issues of *Symphony* magazine, the *Schwann Opus, Stern's Performing Arts Directory*. Jamie plucks a photo from the corner of the desk—Emanuel Ax leaning casually against a Steinway concert grand. "Manny's returning this season?" she asks, surprised. "What's the piece?"

"Aha!" Augie stands, contract in hand. "We're not sure," she says, skimming the page quickly before signing it. "Liszt, Rach-Two perhaps." She screws up her face.

"Don't be a snob, Augie," Jamie scolds affectionately. "The Rachmaninoff Second draws audience."

"So I'm told. I, too, love piano music—you know this—but the production is an absolute nightmare—tuning, tuning, tuning, and still no one is happy. Hardly worth the effort for something so shopworn. The Liszt would please me more." She retakes her seat, eyeing Jamie critically, but her tone has softened—as if the memory of their friendship has just kicked in. "You're playing again?"

Jamie laughs. "There's hardly room for a piano on a thirty-five-foot sailboat." She peruses the photo again. "What else is on the program?"

Augie shrugs. "Tchaikovsky Four if it's the Liszt. Mozart adagios, some Shostakovich." She sits back suddenly. "I'm sorry. I forget my manners. Things are so crazy—you remember, I'm sure. It's very good to see you. You are well? Happy with this new husband who keeps you in the frozen north?"

Jamie smiles. "Everything is fine. And Gaspar?"

"Gaspar is well."

"Composing?"

"Yes. The music, too, goes well, and he is happy. He speaks of you often." She pauses. "He remains appalled at Philippe."

Gaspar, as Jamie remembers, had been instrumental in Philippe's appointment as music director and conductor of the symphony—actually made a trip to Paris to convince him to take the job, and the two had quickly become friends. And when she joined the staff herself some two years later, Philippe gravitated toward her almost immediately—things happening quickly between them despite the thick, almost indecipherable French accent that made their first attempts at communication all but impossible. She'd been charmed, she supposed, by his comically outdated continental gallantry, his hopelessly lost approach to day-to-day practicalities. Their coupling had been embraced by

Augie and Gaspar and the attending, cultured European coterie who apparently felt Jamie's New England blue blood looks and Ivy League education the perfect fit for Philippe's frazzled demeanor, his almost constant need to be nurtured. GM, alone, had disapproved—never really warming to him. Funny how she knew.

Jamie, herself, had thought their marriage a fine one, if a little too focused on Philippe's career, until she found herself pregnant. At the time she put his growing restlessness down to nerves, the anxiety of impending fatherhood. Later she figured he'd probably begun the affair before Sam was even born, though it took him almost a year to leave her and marry the symphony's principal flute—moving them back to France almost immediately afterward, severing virtually all of his New York ties and leaving the orchestra scrambling for a conductor to fill the season's remaining obligations.

"The wife has given up performance," Augie continues. "There's no talk of a family, of course—history might repeat itself, no? It is said the woman wishes only to further his career. *Hohlkopf*," she adds under her breath. *Hollow-head*—the least offensive of Gaspar's seemingly inexhaustible supply of German epithets.

She sits back, draws another cigarette from the pack. "Anyone out there yet?"

Jamie peers around the door jamb, shakes her head.

"Good." Augie snaps her lighter at the cigarette's tip—exhaling a plume of smoke toward the ceiling. "There is something I must mention, Jamie, only because I'm quite sure you'll hear of it this afternoon." A pause, as if she's unsure how to open the subject. "The man responsible for your accident, Mr. Ryan—you remember him of course."

The sudden mention of the name freezes her, but she manages a dull nod—tries to remember to breathe. They've never actually met—not in the usual sense of the word—but this man who wasn't even a blip on the symphony radar before the accident nonetheless made a one-hundred-thousand-dollar donation not three months afterward. Jamie put her resignation on this same desk that very day.

"He continues to contribute annually, Jamie—seventy-five thousand each year, always in November."

November, Jamie thinks dully, her eyes casting about and finally coming to rest on a caricature of Augie and herself done the year *Symphony* magazine dubbed them classical music's dynamic duo.

Augie rolls the cigarette along the edge of the ashtray, studying it as she speaks. "Last week we received word that he intends to fund the new Steinway grand the trustees have been lusting after. That's a ninety-thousand-dollar piano," she adds, in case Jamie hasn't been keeping up with these things. "He's been asked to join the board."

Jamie's eyes remain glued to the drawing, afraid any movement might reveal the panic spreading through her. The photographer caught them grinning, she remembers now, because she'd just told Augie she was pregnant.

"No one else here knows of his connection to you, of course, but Debra will no doubt call the donation to your attention. She's under the mistaken impression it has something to do with her rather mediocre efforts."

From somewhere Jamie recognizes the name of the woman who replaced her as development director.

"It's such a shame, Jamie. You made quite a success here, built up so much support. It's not that Debra's so awfully bad, you see; she uses your funding proposals as templates so she can't go too terribly wrong, but she absolutely locks up if she needs to get creative, develop a new approach. Funding has not increased; there's been almost no growth in support since you left—except for Mr. Ryan, of course." She stubs out the cigarette and stands. "It's still hard for you, I know—this whole business. We'll have lunch, drink some wine, then make an appearance at the opening reception. You'll join us for dinner, of course; Gaspar is anxious to see you. You have a car?"

"No," Jamie manages. "I took the train."

"Too bad. Cabs are all but impossible this time of day."

"I need to make a call before we leave, Augie—check in with Peter."

"Of course; use my phone. I'll start down, see if by some miracle I can find us transportation."

Jamie waits until she hears the outer door close. Appalled at herself for what she's about to do, she nevertheless rounds the desk to Augie's computer and in less than a minute is scrolling through the donor database that she, herself, developed—rifling through proprietary information she no longer has any right to. Not legally, anyway. Still, she has to know, has to see for herself. And as her hands fly across the keyboard toward knowledge she's spent the last three years avoiding, she feels the heaviness come on her again—a stupefying, self-protective torpor working like some drug to slow her, confuse her, warn her off.

Suddenly, there it is—Michael O. Ryan's home address and phone number glaring defiantly at her from the screen; the reality of him sinking in, taking hold, leaving her as shaken as if he'd just walked through the door. Scrolling quickly over to his donor history, she notes the first donation—one hundred thousand dollars—made only months after the accident; another seventy-five thousand on November sixteenth of that year. She blinks at the date, then checks the next line. Seventy-five thousand on November sixteenth of the following year. Both gifts made on the anniversary of the accident. No time to consider this now—later, then. She copies the information quickly and exits the program, slipping the scrap of paper into her leather brief as she hurries toward lunch with Augie.

Bored by the small talk dominating the afternoon's reception and begging off from dinner with Augie and Gaspar in their West Side apartment, Jamie reaches GM's remote Easton farmhouse by early evening. Dragging her bags across the wide, empty porch into the fading light of the front hall, she takes only a cursory look around before heading back through the hallway toward the familiar thrum of the old refrigerator. The diamond-patterned wallpaper climbing the stairwell has long since faded from the colonial blue GM so loved to a dispirited gray oddly in keeping with the worn look of most everything here. Everything, it seems, but the Chickering—the baby grand that had been her mother's— its honeyed hues winking at her from the corner of the living room that opened onto the kitchen. Even this she ignores in her haste, throwing back the double bolt of the back door and stepping out onto the porch. All here exactly as she remembers—the field of tall grass, the small copse of pines off to the left swaying as one above the small family cemetery. The path is gone, of course, but she hardly needs it.

With silent apologies to GM, whose headstone she strides purposefully past, Jamie heads directly to the diminutive marble angel marking Sam's grave. Crouching before the serene, upturned face, the winged arms spread skyward in mute supplication, she reaches for her son, fights for some sense of him rising toward her from beneath the dense mat of decaying leaves and pine needles that choke the three lines chiseled into the cold marble base. Samuel Philippe Pasquier; September 23, 1995; November 16, 1997—the same words that drift unpredictably through her dreams as an undulating ribbon reveal themselves slowly as she clears away the dank vegetation, but give up nothing of his essence. After a time she looks beyond them, toward the worn headstone that bears both her parents' names, then beyond that to others—older ones of her mother's and grandmother's line— reciting the mantra of names and relations as she continues to groom the little grave.

It's fully dark when she returns to the house. Devoid of inhabitants, empty now of the busyness of living, it becomes again what it was for her at the very start—a seemingly ancient, reassuring presence which, at the age of nine and a half and still numb from the loss of her parents, she'd immediately and forever associated with the steady resonance of her grandmother's personality.

She leaves her bags where she dropped them and wanders the first floor, restless and distracted—her mind working to place the Fairfield address copied from Augie's computer. She works the circle from kitchen to living room to front hall and kitchen again—round and round, cleaning and rearranging furniture as she goes—drawn each time she passes it to consider the scrap of paper lying in the center of the otherwise empty kitchen counter. By the time she places the vaguely familiar address, figures out the location of Michael Ryan's home, she's returned most of the first floor to the way it looked just before the accident, when she and Sam and GM all lived here together.

She turns her attention fully to the kitchen then, attacking cabinets, shelves and floor with a thoroughness that would have impressed even GM, slowing only when the narrow utility drawer beneath the wall phone surprises her by refusing to yield. She manages to force her fingers in far enough to dislodge the jam and finds a large plastic bag of pennies—removed by the tenants, she realizes, from the corners of all the windows. Beyond it is the mix of odds and ends GM always kept there: a cracked plastic cup of rubber bands, garden string, old sets of keys, a pair of reading glasses. Buried at the very back she finds a framed photograph of Sam and herself lazing, little boy atop mother, in the tall summer grass she just passed through—a photo she'd forgotten about till now but remembers well. In happier days, they kept it on the mantel beneath the oblong mirror spanning the width of the fireplace, where Jamie could look up and see it, focus on it during her hours at the piano. Just how it ended up here is anyone's guess.

She stares, rapt, at Sam's bright blue eyes and at her own sleepy-eyed look of contentment as she lay with her arms wrapped around her son, a tousled mix of hair and grass tucked shyly beneath her chin. Memories wink at her from the smallest details—the wheaty smell of the long, parched grass; the tiny cricket they discovered in Sam's hair only moments after the shot was taken—something she'd been sure would frighten him but strangely did not; the feel of his wiry energy gone still for this one, blissful instant.

The growing hum of the refrigerator is what finally brings her back to herself—as if it, too, had stopped and held its breath for—how long? A few seconds? Minutes? Half an hour? She hasn't a clue, has even less of one as to how she's come to be standing in front of the mirrored mantel with a longing so intense it's made her mouth water. Tears, too, she realizes, swiping at it all with the back of her hand as she returns the photo to its former home beside GM's long-silent, seven-day clock.

It's well after midnight, after the clock has been rewound and the pennies returned to all the first floor windows, that Jamie suddenly remembers her promise to call Peter, who, she knows, would tease her gently about forgetting supper—though even he would have trouble pulling something together from these cupboards. She takes her cell phone to the back porch where she joins the full moon—lifelong robber of sleep—in its brilliant vigil above the field. Not wanting to wake him, she decides on the other number, and when the University voicemail routes her to his disembodied voice, she hums Debussy's *Clair de Lune* over and over until the machine cuts her off.

Only then does she lug her bags upstairs to the bedroom that has been hers, on and off, since the death of her parents—a place she's managed to land at every major turn in her life. She originally laid claim to the room because it was her mother's and because of the delicate pink rosebuds that climbed the walls and continued, arbor-like, across the ceiling. During her junior year at Yale, she painted each of the walls a different color, defiantly and without permission, right around the time her grandmother began signing her letters GM—some attempt at being hip, Jamie supposed. When she took the job with the symphony, she stripped the layers of paint and paper clear down to the original horsehair plaster, covering the walls with innumerable coats of the creamy peach that greeted her now. After she and Philippe split up she landed here again—this time with Sam—figuring it a good place to get her bearings, and painted his bedroom to match her own.

She draws an old blanket from the top of the closet and, without bothering to change, pulls it across her legs and back as she creeps onto the bed's bare mattress. She's exhausted suddenly, craves the oblivion of sleep, but her mind keeps working—each thread pulled from her life here worrying another. Something about the baby's room tugs at her now. When they lived here, she made a habit of picking it up each night as she readied him for bed—Sam so busy, busy, busy in his play that by the end of the day she'd have to wade through a mass of foam blocks and books and little cars just to get to his dresser. That's what it is, she realizes—the old pattern tugging at her now, telling her to get up and put things in order. Which is ridiculous; his things wouldn't be there any more. The tenants would have used that room for something or someone else. Some other little boy, perhaps—one with his own piles of toys. Suddenly she finds she can't remember what they did with any of Sam's things—those toys, the furniture, the baby swing she never got around to giving away. Had GM packed it all up? Or, God forbid, given it away?

Laying her arm across her face, drifting finally toward sleep, she sinks into a kind of waking dream of another self, another time—

feels herself moving through a forest of mythical proportion and lush, dripping greens. A solitary huntress shunning others of her kind, she avoids those she knows pursue her as she runs light-footed through the dusk along close, overgrown paths. Wary, alert, careful not to be seen, she climbs effortlessly upward along the gnarled trunk of an ancient tree—the ridges of its bark as familiar and welcome as the skin of a lover. Climbing skyward—a single star hovering above her. High above the forest floor now, she moves out along a heavy limb to the hidden nest of interlocking branches lined with pelts and thick furs and curls herself into their soft warmth—the supple boughs beneath rocking her to a safe, unseen, unreachable sleep.

From this height, as she drifts off, the old harpy appears unbidden—hovering just above her shoulder to whisper urgently about the wrath of the gods, while the sound of pursuing hunters passes yet again beneath her tree.

FOUR

It's a run of maybe three miles—six miles there and back, Jamie figures as she stretches in the early morning sun of GM's front porch. Her porch now, she reminds herself. A decent run, with a good number of hills to pump out the anxiety building in her chest. It's possible the stone wall could be gone now, of course; the tree that finally stopped the car on its sliding trajectory cut up and taken away. How to know the place then? The thought brings her up short, eats at this sudden determination to stand at the place Sam drew his last breath. But she throws the feeling off, intent on the fresh, urgent need to encounter his presence again somehow, meet it head-on as she did in the photo. Surely something of him remains in the spot where all life left his body—some relationship of place and spirit impervious to the texture of time.

She takes the first mile slowly, scanning the blacktop out of habit as she reacquaints herself with the long, curling stretches of road where she once spent whole summers pumping the reflective pedals of her Schwinn to the buzz of cicadas. Her nose tingles with the memory of sun-parched fields that no longer exist— the spiky grass, in those days taller than the combined height of girl and bike, tamed now into neatly groomed lawns studded with paved driveways pouring like perfect inky streams into her path.

Startled by the sudden, pulsing hiss of sprinkler heads rising from the ground beside her, Jamie picks up speed, driven forward by the same frenzied determination that compelled her to rifle Augie's computer. She pushes harder, pitting speed against her growing agitation, then harder again, focusing on the rhythmic swing of arms, the slap of feet on pavement, and is in a full-out sprint—legs screaming in pain—when she comes quite suddenly on the massive maple tree where her world exploded in the space of a heartbeat. Three days before Thanksgiving, she remembers quite suddenly; GM had already started on the pies.

Slowing, ignoring the sweat running into her eyes, the panic building in her blood, she walks past the tree—fingers going instinctively to the little sock curled deep in her pocket—then turns and walks by again, considering it from the opposite direction. After a few more passes, she approaches the sandy shoulder dropping off toward the tree and the stone wall just beyond. Heart pounding, her bulky running shoes slipping maddeningly on the graveled slope, she makes her way down and stands for a minute beneath the full canopy of rust-colored leaves. The long gashes in the trunk have scarred over in nature's ceaseless effort to restore itself and she examines these old wounds with both hands, runs her fingers along their lengths, feeling for something she can connect her longing to.

Nothing here. No sense of him at all. Flooded with disappointment, she makes to leave, begin the run home, but can't somehow—not yet. Instead, she turns to the stonewall and walks it slowly, scanning the rocks and the tangle of brown weeds choking the base. Only then she catches the flash of black and white so incongruous among the rocks and the faded scrub.

She stops moving, stops breathing it seems—a mix of excitement and dread climbing through her as she crouches to push the tangled brush aside, tease the thing from where it lay in a heavy crust of dirt and sand. Suddenly there it is—amazingly, miraculously, as if she'd known it all along—Sam's sneaker, the one she spent a good half hour looking for the only other time she'd had the nerve to come back here. It was snowing that day, she recalls out of the blue, and she was still on crutches, but she came here nonetheless, unable to live with the thought of this last little piece of him lying lost and vulnerable in the road. Staring down at it now—dirty, worn, impossibly small—she's helpless against the deluge of memory, the details of that morning dropping into place one by horrific one.

Sam, happy and compliant most mornings, fought her from the start that day—locking his bony little elbows against his chest when she pulled his sweater over his head, kicking his feet wildly against the need for shoes—and she'd wondered if he was coming down with something even as she calculated the odds of making her train into the city. Remembering belatedly the need to transfer his car seat to GM's old boat of a Buick, to drop the flat tire from her own aging Subaru at the garage on her way to the station. The Buick's back seat so seldom used that the belts had long since disappeared between the seat and backrest, which meant even more time spent wasted trying to finger them out. Sam in full-out tears by the open car door by the time she gave up, cursing, and found a way to make his seat fast in the front.

Her mind pauses over this last before stumbling on, remembering how much worse he'd been in the car—kicking his feet in teary frustration until he managed to work one of his sneakers off, the little green sock flapping against the tips of his toes about to follow it to the floor. She, herself, frustrated by this time, dreading the scene he'd make at day care as she reached over and snatched the sock, stuffed it quickly into the pocket of her coat.

The car came out of nowhere—some kind of dark BMW—cell phone glued to the driver's ear as it careened wildly out of a wooded side street onto the blacktop in front of her. Slamming her foot on the brake, instinctively swinging her right arm over to hold Sam against his car seat, she tried desperately to avoid impact and would have merely gone off the road and into the gully if it hadn't been for the patch of black ice that sent them rocketing into the tree.

The other car continued on—the driver later claiming he hadn't seen her, but just before she'd hit the ice, Jamie saw him glance in his rearview mirror and then accelerate as she veered off the road. The police would never have found him at all, she knew, if another driver coming toward them hadn't gotten the license plate number.

She remembers briefly coming to as they pulled her from the car, and catching sight of the little white-toed sneaker lying on its side in the middle of the road. Even in her shocky state, she'd felt a monumental dread, the desperate need to grab it up and cradle it to her chest.

Two weeks later, she was released from the hospital, along with a bag she found herself clutching when she reached home. In it was the coat she'd worn the morning of the accident and a few things recovered from the car: her half demolished briefcase, the stuffed bunny Sam called his bubby—and a single black and white sneaker stuffed with a green sock. It wasn't until much later that she reached into the pocket of the coat and found the mate to the sock, pulled from his foot just moments before the accident—the one she carried now whenever she ran. But the other shoe had remained missing. Until today.

She crouches on her knees in the grass and vomits; moves closer, picks up the shoe, and retches again.

Finished, finally, the shoe still clutched in her hand, she feels a sudden flash of the vividness and wonder of Sam's short life; it flies at her as if it's been hiding here—waiting for her all this time, then brushes her face and is gone, she's sure, forever. There's no question this is what has drawn her here. Anguish—raw and exquisite—sucks the air from her, leaving her breathless.

The airbag broke his neck—that much was clear from the autopsy. They said he felt no pain, but what else could they say to her, after all?

Jamie places the dirty sneaker on the counter next to Michael Ryan's scribbled address, showers and readies herself for the afternoon's seminars on fundraising and long-term planning—leaving the house early to allow for a detour that will take her past his home on her way to the train.

Twenty minutes later, she's winding her way along Morningside Drive—clearly one of the most exclusive areas in Fairfield—whose old, historic properties and sprawling grounds will never see subdivision. The oversized white mailbox marking the Ryan property sends her gaze up a long, crushed-stone drive to a meandering, gambreled New Englander set atop a low hill—a suitable home, she decides, for the man she heard described in court as a respected attorney, loving father, concerned citizen.

"So this is where you hide out," she murmurs, knowing firsthand how well he does just that. There was a time—those first few weeks in the hospital and then later, recovering at home as a silent GM tiptoed about her—when the only thing that kept her going was the certainty of his punishment. She spent long hours planning the things she'd say when they finally met face to face in court. How Sam's little-boy smell still lingered in the house—in his clothes, in the hollow of her pillow, in the shaft of sunlight that hit the kitchen floor where he played with his cars each morning. But as hard as these things were for her, she would tell him, what she truly dreaded was the morning she'd wake to find them gone.

She'd been a fool to think the bastard would actually show. Some conflict with his own court schedule, according to the harried-looking lawyer sent in his place armed with the technicalities that would ultimately exonerate him. The guy kept checking his watch, she remembers now—as if put out at having to go through the motions at all.

Jamie does a slow U-turn and drives by the Ryan place again—taking in the hundred-year-old trees, the manicured lawn. What bothered her the most, she decides—other than the actual verdict, which she still finds unconscionable—was the man's smugness as he left the courtroom, chuckling on his cell phone before he even hit the hall.

The words once saved for Michael Ryan visit her for the thousandth time, recast as a litany of cruel what-if's. What if she'd left the house just a few minutes earlier that morning? What if she'd simply taken the day off to stay home with Sam, as he'd pleaded with her to do? And somehow the worst of all—that perhaps she'd just been too busy to pick up on a little boy's confused sense of impending disaster.

Jamie, inexorably drawn now she's found him, detours past Ryan's place again that night on her way back to the house—pulling over in the growing darkness to watch shadowy figures caught up in the softly lit routines of evening. There—little ones slipping past windows warm with light. And again—left to right; right to left. One chasing the other, it seems. So there are children—a shame she can't tell sex or age from this distance. Still, they're little faces Ryan still sees every day, their forms so ingrained in his psyche he might just think he sees them in places they couldn't possibly be.

No, she decides; it's only when you lose them that they haunt you—especially those first months. Sam's face popping up suddenly in a tangle of children running through a playground, a fleeting glimpse of him in a car whizzing past her down the road—each sighting leaving her heart lurching, hands shaking for minutes afterward. Rounding a corner in the grocery one morning, she caught a glimpse of a little boy running off down the aisle—Sam's size, Sam's build, Sam's laugh—and was hit with the memory of the pure liquid energy of him, the wild squirming and giggling when she'd take after him and scoop him up from behind. She called his name that time—a hoarse whisper laced with bile that choked her.

She had the groceries delivered after that, worked from home, almost never left the house. The whole thing proved too much for GM, who grew increasingly listless alongside Jamie's terror, finally dying in her sleep one frigid February night. A stroke, they said, but Jamie knew better. The old harpy, tough as she was, had been felled by a broken heart.

It was three months before she went back to work in the city; God only knows how long afterward she spent simply sitting at her desk, staring at the pile of phone messages from people whose lives had continued without pause while hers bled away— their minds on the living; hers on the newly dead. Months later, when she heard the news of Ryan's first hundred-thousand-dollar donation, she gave her notice in a panic, rented out the house and moved to New Hampshire. Shut down and split town, was how Peter liked to put it.

So what about Ryan? Does he ever think about that unspeakable morning with anything more than some dark, secret relief at having gotten away with it all? And his wife—assuming he has one—does she actually swallow the rationale that because the two cars never actually collided, he wasn't responsible for what happened? It had been enough for the judge, after all. One-car accident; blame it on the ice.

Another, larger figure now, moving in the curtained light. Ryan? The wife? Rounding up the kids and sending them off to bed. Teeth to be brushed and stories to be told. How obscene that he should still have this perfect little family while she's forced to live life without Sam.

"I was a mother, too," Jamie says toward the house, suppressing a quiet curl of fury. "I had a little boy."

A police cruiser creeps past just then, its silent approach spooking her. She makes some pretense at rummaging through her bag, then puts the car in gear and pulls out behind it, following at a respectful distance as it continues, casually vigilant, past the homes of other Michael Ryans.

The call Jamie makes back at the house isn't to Peter, whom she meant to phone before he left for his evening seminar, but to the realtor—informing him of her decision not to re-rent the house after all. Somewhere on the road between Ryan's pampered life and her own empty existence, she's decided to keep it open, ready for her own use—her renewed awareness of the man working some change in her. How would he react, she muses, if she simply showed up at his door and demanded an accounting—this woman he's never spoken to, whose face he's never even seen except once, years ago, in his car's rearview mirror?

FIVE

Jamie's in her Nashua office, midway through a presentation on the status of the ongoing endowment campaign, when she suddenly remembers what she and GM did with Sam's things. It comes to her out of the blue, as if some part of her mind has been chugging away on the problem for the last three weeks and simply dropped the answer in all its full, vivid detail smack in the middle of her train of thought.

Alone after the meeting, she allows herself to call it up again—to remember the morning they finally packed up Sam's room and carted everything to the attic, even the dresser and crib which took them forever to dismantle and get up the narrow stairs. Knowing it's all still there, just waiting for her feels like an exquisite gift.

The phone startles her. "Jamie Lloyd," she says.

"Moon room's finished," Peter announces over the steady whine of a diesel engine. His tone's casual, but Jamie knows how pleased he is with the boat cover he and Bake have built to insulate them from the worst of the winter cold. This year's version—row upon row of fiberglass tubes running port to starboard down the length of the boat and shrouded in sky-blue tarps—allows for more headroom than last year's wooden A-frames, transforming the cockpit into a spacious, domed room filled with a soft, almost otherworldly light. From the dock, the whole thing looks more like some kind of space pod than a boat.

She envisions Peter in his oilskins and deck boots amid the diving equipment and ondeck bustle of the university's aging research vessel. "Heading out to check the mussels?" she asks against the amalgam of rock music and engine noise, the laughter of his students.

"Yup. And if this tub makes it back, the feed's on for tonight."

That means lobsters, of course, which explains Lucille's agitation, her pacing and yapping at the stern of the boat that morning—as if their presence in the trap some thirty feet beneath the surface poses a major threat. It also means Bake, Jamie realizes—his work on the moon room all but dictating he be included. Her heart sinks at the thought of yet another evening spent in company with Lori.

Peter counters her hesitation with a promise to have the boat cleaned up and cocktails ready by seven. When she reaches the boat at a quarter to, he's gotten as far as rearranging the CDs shelved above his desk and is in the galley, shirt sleeves rolled to his elbows, studying the lobsters thrashing in the sink—crusher claws clacking wildly as they maneuver for purchase.

"Thought I'd steam them first," he says not looking up, "then bake them."

"In this oven? They'll never fit."

"Sure they will. I'll stack them pyramid style, like we do at the lab." He's distracted, all business when it comes to his crustaceans—never mind this particular sample is about to become dinner. "I was thinking of a curried couscous."

He nods toward the well-worn copy of *Seductions of Rice* splayed open on the table. "Salad would be simpler, " she says. "I picked up some bread." She puts the French loaf next to the bottle of dark rum he's pulled out—noting the limes, the can of coconut milk. "Tell me you're not doing those blender drinks again."

He grins, finally moving to kiss her—his scientific demeanor dropping away to reveal the lover who'd seduced her for the first time on this very table. "Lori likes them," he murmurs, snaking his tongue into her ear. "Makes her wild. Bake always thanks me the next day."

They arrive just as Jamie is rigging the oil lamp over the companionway—lending the moon room an eerie blue glow. Cursory squeals of welcome come muted from somewhere on the foredeck, where Lucille and Gus are too busy exploring the swell of sail bags, lines and supplies piled beneath the dome to break for the usual pleasantries. Peter, just finishing the drinks, shoots Jamie a wink as he delivers two foaming glasses into Bake's hands and disappears back into the galley.

"Man, I need this," Bake mutters against a long slug of the icy drink, and only then does Jamie notice how subdued the two of them seem, how damp and red-rimmed Lori's eyes are.

Sighing, he loops a hairy, shirt-sleeved arm around her. Never mind it's November; Jamie's never seen him in as much as a sweater. "This one got herself a job waitressing at the Wildflower," he says, the admission clearly costing him. He takes another long slug to recover.

The hasty promise she made to look into the Symphony job for Lori comes back to Jamie now—though she has to admit that the Wildflower Cafe, with its omelet-based menu and whole grain atmosphere, better suits the girl's natural, dewy-eyed look. "That's great," she says, trying to keep the relief from her voice.

Lori's only response is a furtive swipe at her cheek.

"Great," Peter agrees, handing Jamie a glass of the blender concoction and pointing a bowl of tortilla chips at Bake. "Here. Start on these."

Bake grunts, unwrapping Lori to take the bowl. "Too high profile, you ask me, considerin' the guy that's been stalkin' her. I had a job all lined up for her at the tolls, but then the thing happened with the cat and she said she wouldn't work no place where they was throwin' baby animals outta car windows for the fun of it."

"What's this?" Peter laughs, finally coming to join them, pitcher of refills in hand.

"Some shithead tossed a kitten out a window at the tolls last week. Probably figured some trucker would run the thing down and save him a trip to the animal shelter. My booth, too—lucky I saw it. So now we got us a cat." He stuffs a fistful of chips into his mouth, chewing furiously.

"No, I mean the stalker."

Bake calms himself by emptying his glass, belches. "Some pervert she ran into at Walmart. She's in line at the register, right? So this guy behind her starts eyein' her up and down, makin' small talk. Guy's gotta be fifty, at least. Now, she's got my shirts in the cart, right? My socks? Any guy with half a brain's gonna know she's shoppin' for another man, but does this asshole back off? No way. Tries to get her to go for a drink, follows her out to my car—which was real bright by the way, Lore..." He throws her a glance. "So now he's got the plate number. Starts callin' the trailer..."

"It's no big deal." Lori's appeal is to Jamie and Peter, her eyes avoiding Bake.

"Don't start with that shit again," he warns as Peter refills the glasses. "I finally told the fucker what's what, but he's still callin'— only now he just breathes heavy when I answer, then hangs up."

"What kind of cat?" Jamie asks, hoping to defuse Bake.

Lori brightens a bit. "A little calico. We named him Highway, have to feed him every few hours with a bottle."

Just then a powerboat leaving the fuel dock throttles up, cutting through the channel behind them and setting the boat rocking madly in its wake. Jamie grabs the bowl of tortillas chips; Peter reaches the pitcher just before they lose the rest of the drink. *'It's only rock and roll but I like it, like it, yes I do,'* he croons.

"You gotta get after those assholes," Bake growls, roping Lori in with a hairy arm as she begins a long slide across the seat.

☒ ☖

Peter has stuffed the lobsters with bread crumbs, butter and crab—a few of which had been unlucky enough to wander into the trap with the lobsters—and the effect is stunning. Jamie suspects he's doused the mixture with a slug of rum, as well, the sweet dark flavor adding a new richness she knows he'll tuck into memory for next time. After they finish, Bake starts up again about the stalker so she slips below to do the cleanup, glad to have a few minutes alone. All evening she's carried the whereabouts of Sam's things like a delicious secret, an unexpected gift she's dying to unwrap—the thrill of it heightening her senses to an almost sexual buzz. The need to be alone with it almost overwhelming.

Moving about the small galley, she's acutely aware of how the tarped dome has changed the sound of everything, from the scraping of the dogs' nails across the cabintop to the mix of voices traveling down the companionway—louder and at the same time hushed—as though they were in some cave, where even a whisper will carry to the farthest corner. She catches a few words and frowns, not at all pleased to have become the topic of conversation.

"Major in music performance," Peter is saying. Bake knows all this, so she figures he's talking to Lori. "Some kind of piano prodigy as a kid—her parents were pretty famous in classical music circles before they were killed in a plane crash—then she went to live with her grandmother. Nutty old lady..."

Jamie runs the water hard in the sink, obscuring his words—almost hoping he'll poke his head down and bark at her about water usage. It annoys her when he reveals bits and pieces of her life like this, creating a kind of voyeuristic peek into her world for the various women who move in and out of Bake's life. He rarely thinks about what he reveals—the information only important for the reaction it provokes—the scientist in him poking, prodding. Thankfully, by the time she's finished with the washing, they've moved on to Bake's never-ending saga of life in the toll booth.

"Besides, I got eight years in now—full time," Bake says. "Another two and I've got health care for life. That's a pretty sweet deal. And what would I do otherwise—follow your sorry ass around all week?"

Peter's responses grow muffled and she knows without looking that he's stuck his head into the seat locker in search of something.

"Yeah, well," Bake grouses, "we all pay for our road through life, man—one way or another."

Finally, the galley clean and the coal stove stoked for the night, Jamie grabs a bag of chocolate chip cookies and heads back up to find Peter straddling the cockpit—a foot on either bench as he reaches to establish the four compass points on the dome with a magic marker. A roll of the bright yellow tape used for labeling the boat's wiring system protrudes from the back pocket of his jeans.

"And this," he announces—taking a long stride to the port side and applying a small bit of the tape, "is the North Star. Central to navigation."

"You mean like astrology?" Lori asks, nibbling a cookie pulled from Jamie's proffered bag.

"Well, astronomy—kind of the same thing. You know— planets, moons, stars?" Peter pauses to tear several bits of tape from the roll. "Over here in the east we have Orion, one of the better known constellations. You know the story? Myth of the hunter and the huntress?"

Lori shakes her head, lost again. Her eyes got wider when she was confused, Jamie was learning—as though expanding her area of vision might help her see more of what a person meant.

"There are several versions of the myth, actually," Peter tells them, dropping into his professorial tone as he reaches up over the companionway steps to begin the group of stars making up the belt and sword. "But they all revolve around this guy Orion's skill as a hunter, his devotion to the chase. He was the son of a god—Neptune, I think—and a real hunk, apparently. Bit of a dimwit, though. Violent, no self-control, drank too much. Liked to chase the women, too; raped the daughter of a king—chick by the name of Merope." He stands back to consider his work before starting Orion's club. "All this before meeting the huntress Artemis—a goddess as well, it turns out—and more than a match for him. She's quite the stalker of prey herself, spends her time hunting and running through the forest with her little nymph friends. She takes a liking to Orion, in a platonic sort of way, and they hunt together for a while—*mano a mano,* so to speak—but it doesn't take long before he gets the hots for her. Unfortunately for him, she's taken a vow of chastity, so he falls back on his old ways and tries to rape her. Any of this ring a bell?"

Lori giggles. "It kind of sounds like a soap opera."

Peter is polite enough not to comment. "In the Roman version, she's called Diana—daughter of Jupiter, sister of Apollo, goddess of the moon and the hunt." He pauses to tear more tape, then adds what Jamie assumes is the dog star Sirius—Orion's faithful companion.

"Okay, I'll bite," Bake says. "So what happens?"

Peter shrugs and hops back down for a cookie, which he waves in emphasis while regarding his work. "Well, she's pissed, of course, and the gods are understandably outraged. Soooo... she plugs him with an arrow; he dies. Eventually the gods take pity on him and turn him into a constellation. But even there he can't leave the chicks alone, it seems, and spends eternity chasing the Pleiades—up over here," he says with a flip of his hand. "A group of Diana's nymphs before they were turned into stars. In some versions of the myth, Diana falls in love with Orion and is tricked into killing him by Apollo. But I prefer the revenge version myself."

That giggle again. "So what's the moral?"

"Man who's led by dick gets arrow in heart," Bake tells her, passing up the cookies for more of the blender concoction. "Like that asshole's been stalking you. Please, God, give me five minutes alone with that fucker."

"See what I mean?" Peter grins. "Violence and revenge—the cult of the alpha male. Hardwired, I'm afraid. And just lying in wait under all this civilized demeanor." He fills his glass, polishing off what's left in the pitcher. "How about it, Bake—another batch?"

Lori giggles again and snuggles in harder, her earlier anger mellowed by the effects of blended rum and chocolate chip cookies. "Why do you guys call him Bake, anyway?"

"It has something to do with his propensity for consuming large amounts of alcohol, " Peter tells her. "Thus my question."

"Tell her *your* name, then, Pete," Bake says.

"Ah, well, that's different."

"Tell 'er Pete."

"Dr. Peter Apollo, since we're on the subject of mythology. You can imagine the jokes relating to astronomy and anatomy— all true by the way. The anatomy part, I mean. You can ask my wife—she's the one asleep there in the corner."

Bake turns to Jamie. "You *are* kinda quiet tonight," he observes.

She shrugs. "Long day."

Peter's tone, as he leans in toward Lori, is conspiratorial. "She's mad because I'm heading to Florida next week without her."

"Wow." Lori shoots Jamie a worried, commiserating look, which wins her a kiss atop the head from Bake.

"Lori, you gotta understand half what this guy tells you is lies. The other half is all made up. It's like a business trip—some kinda research or something."

"Whale tagging," Peter confides in that same tone. "Chasing them in a boat and shooting them with computer chips."

Lori's concerned look deepens. "Why?"

"To track them—learn their habits, their migration and mating patterns. The boat I'll be on is one of the few dedicated marine mammal research vessels in the world, kiddo. It's a big deal to be asked to go. Jamie will miss me, though."

"You think so," Jamie laughs.

"What did I tell you?" Peter complains, shooting her a wink Lori doesn't see. "Married not two years and already she's lining them up to replace me." The wink meant to remind Jamie of their conversation not two hours before, when she'd freed him of any guilt about this trip—despite its lousy timing. He'd have turned it down, she knows, if she'd balked.

"I'm sorry I won't be here this time," he'd whispered into her neck as she was changing, all too aware of the desperate low that gripped her every year on November sixteenth—that most awful of days. She'd hushed him with a kiss, assured him she'd be fine. It's been three years, after all, she told him. High time she learned to deal with all this. All it took then was another smile, another kiss, her promise that she really wanted him to go. In truth, she felt only joy at the thought of his leaving. It freed her to go home again—home, where memories of Sam, tucked away for so long, waited for her return.

The smile she shoots him is automatic, but it earns her another wink as he pins a cookie between his teeth and heads below for more of the blender concoction.

SIX

The door to the attic remains stuck—loathe, it seems, to give up its secrets. Frustrated, Jamie stands back and stares it down, ignoring her growing sense of urgency. There's a trick to it, if only she can remember—something she and GM used to coax it open on the rare occasions they made the trip to the cavernous space at the top of the house. Finally, with her heartbeat seeming to fill the narrow space of the stairwell, she gives the outside corner of the door a sharp kick while turning the knob, and the thing pops open.

Inside, the air is cold and musty as a grave—the room's single overhead fixture blown, but she hardly needs the extra light. Memory illuminates her way past things kept close by the door for easy retrieval—bags of off-season clothes waiting to be aired and returned to dresser drawers, a rocking chair she'd planned to re-glue, two boxes of Christmas decorations untouched since the accident.

Turning right, she moves in a crouch along the eaves, drawn by the darkened outline of Sam's dismantled crib leaning casually against the shadowy bulk of something else—his dresser, she realizes, its four drawers stacked haphazardly on top. Then there—the bags of clothes and toys, his baby swing, the blue oval rug she'd bought because the grinning little train traveling its perimeter had made him laugh.

She'd been at her worst the last time she saw any of this—the morning a startled GM walked into Sam's room to find her curled in a fetal position in the middle of that rug, the train chugging its cheerful path around her. Poor GM, she thinks now, remembering the tears streaming down those tissue-thin cheeks, the look of desperate determination as that tiny old woman snapped open a trash bag and began stuffing it with Sam's clothes. Jamie watching from the floor as she pulled open drawer after dresser drawer—grabbing and stuffing, grabbing and stuffing, pausing to swipe angrily at her cheeks before knotting the bag and dragging it into the hall. Managing to fill a second bag and a then a third before Jamie—finally coming back to herself—rose to help with the books, the miniature cars, the blocks, the stuffed animals. In the space of thirty minutes, they'd packed up Sam's entire short life and carted it all to the attic.

She drags the bags over to where the late afternoon sun streams as a single shaft of light through the room's only window, and for the next hour she sits reacquainting herself with the things that once populated her son's world. Here he still has life—in a few blond hairs caught in the wheel of a Matchbox car, the half-moon shape of his bite on a block, a powdery smear of something—milk, probably—where he wiped his mouth on the sleeve of his red turtleneck. She collects these treasures carefully, lays each aside to take back downstairs.

She's in the kitchen, plugging the new coffee maker in, when her cell phonerings—startling her. Has to be Peter. Panic, then, before she realizes he can't possibly know where she is.

"Jesus, you should see this boat," he says by way of greeting. "Get this: it's got two mini subs." A pause then. "Everything okay?"

"Everything's fine." She cradles the phone while she pulls coffee and light bulbs from one of the grocery bags littering the counter.

"Dogs okay?"

"Fine." And she's sure they are; the kennel she found for them has an excellent reputation, the pampering they're in for costing her half a week's pay. Still, she feels a stab of guilt at the half-truth, this breaking of their marital pact—total honesty, no matter what. Easier on him this way, though. He'd only worry—what with her being here, and alone, on the anniversary of Sam's death.

She pulls a handful of foam paint brushes from the sack, realizes she left vacuum cleaner bags off her list.

"I'd forgotten how muggy Miami gets—hits you as soon as you get off the plane," Peter tells her. "The boat wasn't ready for us, so we spent the night in South Beach. This place is nuts, Jae. We're walking back to the hotel after dinner, right? It's like twelve-thirty, and this guy in a thong whips by us on roller blades, carrying a window washer's bucket like it's the most natural thing in the world." He chats on as Jamie hunts through the bag for the box of nails she bought to repair the back steps. "Jae?"

"Sorry, what?"

"You sound funny. You sure you're okay? Why don't you call Bake, have dinner with them or something. I don't like the idea of you being alone tomorrow."

He thinks I'm on the boat, she reminds herself. And it doesn't matter where I am when November 16th rolls around—I'm always alone. "I'm fine, really—just a little busy. I'll call you in the next day or so."

"I better call you. You're in Nashua tomorrow?"

"No, I'm taking a few days off. Best to use the cell."

☙❧

After her shower the next morning, and with the coffee perking cheerfully in the next room, Jamie seats herself at the Chickering. Feeling thick with the desire to play—the old yearning settling on her in the night as the house creaked and shifted around her. An itch, a longing—lost, like so much else, when Sam was killed. Yet three years to the day and here it is, bubbling in her blood again like some long-dormant virus. She wonders vaguely at that, if returning to the house after so long has freed her to reclaim this thing that was once as natural and vital to her as drawing breath.

She adjusts her posture, the feeling of hands arched gently above the keys a little odd and at the same time so very familiar, and waits for the sense of strangeness to leave her. Finally she takes a stab at a few scales, surprised to find the piano perfectly in tune. One of the tenants must have played, she thinks—grateful to whomever it was for knowing enough about the quality of the instrument to keep it up. She gives herself, then, to the Chickering's rich tone, the hypnotic wave sensation of the scales—after a while varying the warm up with arpeggios, thirds, sixths, octaves. There was a time she felt the hard action of the keyboard almost too sluggish, but she's glad for it now; its resistance will work to strengthen her fingers, loosen her wrists.

She finds she wants Bach, but nothing too difficult, and settles after some thought on the little *Fugue in G minor*. Launching into the piece, eyes focused on the things she's dug out of the attic and placed atop the piano—the little car, the block, the milk-stained turtleneck—she's instantly reminded of how many times she sat like this when Sam was still alive, the quiet joy of having him here, safely under her gaze. He liked to stand before the fire, twirling to the music, she remembers now—twirling and twirling until he was flinging himself around the room in total abandon. The dancer becomes the dance. That was Sam. He might have grown to be one, too, given time.

She moves through a few Chopin *Preludes,* concentrating solely on execution, noting the tightness in her arm and shoulder muscles, the loss of finger dexterity. All control shot. Sighing, she pulls the old exercise books from the bench—her Cramer and Hanon, the dreaded Czerny exercises—and begins working her way through them, blocking out everything but the music, the forgotten coffee billowing into steamy clouds that flavor the air.

Around three-thirty, she's ready for the run. Though Ryan normally works into the evening, he leaves the office at four on Fridays to spend extra time with the kids—this according to the slew of articles she's found about him on the Internet, most written during his recent unsuccessful bid for state senate, when he felt moved to reveal more than he should have about his personal habits. The family man boasting about his easy commute: four miles, only ten minutes of drive time from those impressive red brick offices to his even more impressive home. If she times it right, Jamie figures, she may just catch sight of him.

The drive through Southport is the prettiest route, the road along the million-dollar waterfront of Long Island Sound with its massive, walled estates a slow curl through the land of old money. Jamie parks at a small, rocky beach she remembers from her teenage years—figuring it another two or three miles into Fairfield and Michael Ryan's Morningside Drive address. Briefly stretching against the bleached stones of the sea wall, she pulls one of Peter's worn caps over her ears and begins the run.

The road itself, recently repaved, yields little of interest in the waning light other than a small, round hummingbird's nest on the ground at its edge. Still whole and perfectly formed but disappointingly empty. Reminding her for some reason of Sam's bedroom, finally opened after ten minutes of pacing the upstairs hall like a nervous cat. A couple hours reminiscing at the piano, and she'd expected—just what exactly? That she'd open the door to find Sam sitting there on his rug, paging happily through one of his picture books? Nothing there, of course, but a few dust bunnies left in some other child's wake. A mere pocket of space like the hummingbird's nest—desolately empty, no longer of use to anyone.

She's pumping hard when she rounds the final corner and catches sight of the oversized, white mailbox. Slowing slightly, her gaze moving up the sloping drive, she catches sight of an uncarved pumpkin at the corner of the long front porch, a tricycle by an open garage door, the gleam of a bumper from within. Staring unabashedly, taking in every detail until a copse of pine trees at the end of the property cuts off her view, she loops around, crossing the street for the return run. Scanning the property so intently she doesn't even hear the dog coming up from behind until he's almost on her. Only then does she turn and see the jovial yellow Lab bounding toward her—its owner in pursuit of the leash bouncing along the pavement.

"He won't hurt you," the man calls as the Lab closes. "Loves people."

He's an enthusiastic dog—puppy really—equal parts curiosity and wet nose. A sweet animal, she decides, crouching to pet him. "Probably smells my dogs," she says, glancing up at the man who's managed to reclaim the leash. His suit is expensive, well cut; through its lines she senses the bulk of an athlete. A cashmere scarf is looped casually around his neck against the early evening chill.

He bends a dark, curly head close to hers as he strokes the dog, and she catches a whiff of expensive cologne. Late thirties, she thinks, maybe a little older, with the kind of chiseled features that only improve with age. And almost disturbingly handsome— the lips a little too red, the deep brown eyes sparkling almost unnaturally. The cold, she figures.

He gives the Lab a final pat then stands, cocking his head as he takes her in. "New in the neighborhood?" A special place, his tone implies—home of the chosen. The eyes crinkle in a smile. "I ask because I know just about everyone along this road, and I'm sure I'd remember you." He extends his hand. "Michael Ryan."

Jesus God.

She dares only a quick glance at the smiling eyes, lest he pick up on her absolute astonishment. Ignoring the outstretched hand, she returns her attention to the dog, working his ears now—the hair on her own neck bristling beneath Peter's cap. This is crazy, she thinks—a fluke. A glimpse was all she came here for—a face to put the name to—and now here he is, right in front of her, just a man out walking his dog. She has the urge to throw her head back and laugh but drowns the impulse in the thick ruff of the animal's neck.

"Diana," she says finally, choosing her middle name as alias as she smiles into the dog's eyes. "Diana Apollo," she amends, adding Peter's surname to complete the masquerade. Too late she realizes how ludicrous it sounds, wonders how much Ryan knows of mythology. She stands, irritated at the flush climbing into her cheeks.

The laugh is rich and deep. He's delighted it seems—by what she isn't sure. "How perfect. Diana—the goddess of the moon and the hunt—a runner." He watches as she begins the deep side-to-side stretches that will keep her from stiffening. "So do you live here with the rest of the gods, Diana Apollo, or are you merely tripping through our Elysian Fields on your way to the hunt?"

"A mere trespasser, I'm afraid, caught out by your hound." She begins a slow jog, needing to stay warm, buy time. She's at once horrified and perversely intrigued, wants to stretch the moment out, absorb all she can of his presence into her growing knowledge of him. She looks at him directly, then, daring him to recognize her, and it's clear he has no idea who she really is. Nor should he, she assures herself. For all that binds them together, they've never actually come face to face. She circles him, observing, savoring her advantage. The hair is a bit long for a lawyer, she decides, but this is a man who makes his own rules, as she well knows. A monster of a man, this one.

That laugh again as the dog strains on his lead to join her. "A trespasser, perhaps," Ryan says, enjoying the unusual repartee, "but a goddess nonetheless. This one," he says, cocking his head toward the dog, "always knows. Therefore, consider yourself welcome, Diana of the forest."

"Ah," she says, unable to keep the sarcasm from her voice. "To where you all have perfect lives."

"Absolutely—perfect lives."

"Careful, now," she warns. "The gods may take offense. Humility is wiser. There are the wife and children to consider."

Cocking his head, he considers her anew, the sparkle in his eyes more than just the cold now. "What makes you think I'm married?"

She begins jogging off but turns to call out. "The mailbox says M. O. Ryan, there's a tricycle at the top of the drive, and a woman is staring at us from your porch."

He doesn't glance toward the house right away—she gives him points for that—but sets the dog loose to nose his way into the yard. "You should have been a lawyer," he calls after her.

"What makes you think I'm not?" she shoots over her shoulder, speeding up quickly, then, to put some distance between them.

༄ ༅

Jamie spends the weekend working at the house—the physical activity an attempt at warding off her bizarre encounter with Ryan. Scouting for paint in the basement, she comes across a gallon of enamel labeled "kitchen"—a robin's egg blue she uses to brighten the worn cupboards between stints at the Chickering. She uses more of it on Sam's dresser after dragging it down the two flights from the attic—all the while reliving every word of their conversation, every nuance. Ryan's clearly a player—smooth, self-confident. As if he hadn't a worry in the world, as if three years ago didn't lurk in the back of his mind, ambushing him at odd moments as it did her. She's both repelled and drawn in—the reality of his life and family opening after all this time before her. How many kids, she wonders, and how old? If only he hadn't been on her with that damn dog before she'd had a chance to study the place, get her bearings.

She could always go back—a stunning thought that tingles through her. It's a public road, after all; who's to stop her? She mulls it over, growing excited as she gives the trim in Sam's room a coat of that same cheerful blue—enamel being just the thing to defeat greasy little fingers.

Still, it's Monday before she allows herself the same run again. No need to spook him, after all. An early morning jog this time, so she can catch them all at the start of their day. She parks at the beach again and by seven-thirty has Michael Ryan's place in sight, but a quick scan of the property reveals nothing—no wife, no children pouring from the house in a scurry of giggles to wait for the bus by the mailbox. She tries to picture Sam at five years of age, kicking his toe in the dirt as he waits for a bus of his own at the end of GM's dusty drive, but the picture fades at the sight of an enormous, dark SUV rolling from the Ryans' garage—the massive overhead door descending smoothly in its wake. It swings into the road without stopping and heads her way, the heavily tinted windows obscuring any glimpse of its occupants as it speeds past her, then almost immediately slows again. Averting her gaze, she hears a swish of tires making a U-turn, the lowering of a window as the vehicle pulls alongside her, keeping pace, revealing the Monday-morning version of Michael Ryan—freshly shaved, impeccably dressed, the same jaunty toss of that cashmere scarf.

"A bit early to be out stalking prey," he tells her.

"I prefer sunrise, actually, but the arrows needed re-tipping."
Where's the BMW that ran her off the road, she wonders? Back
in the garage? Traded in for this monstrosity?

"You're a puzzle, Diana Apollo," he says grinning. "No one
along this stretch of road seems to know you. Allow me a hint."

"I'm a goddess—you said so yourself. We don't give hints." She
peers past him into the vehicle's cavernous interior, but can make
out nothing. "Driving the kids to school?"

"No, my wife's in charge of the troops. If you're still casing the
neighborhood in, say, half an hour, you'll catch the mass exodus.
It's really quite something. She thinks I'm having an affair with
you, by the way."

"It's a shame she needs to worry about such things."

"Ouch," he says, the grin widening. "She bites." He considers
for a minute. "So tell me, is there a Mr. Apollo?"

"Of course."

"Children?"

"Yes." He's waiting, but she gives him nothing more, keeps her
gaze ahead, her pace steady.

"Not very forthcoming, are you? Then again, mystery has its
own allure."

She slows, stops—feels his eyes on her as she bends at the waist
to pry a stone from her shoe. What the hell's going on here? She
hears a soft trill from the cabin's interior. "Phone's ringing," she
informs him as she fingers the pebble from beneath her heel.

"Voice mail will get it. Meet me for a drink after work."

"That can hardly improve your position with the wife. Besides,
lawyers never ignore phone calls; everyone knows that."

He stares at her—flummoxed, it seems, by her unexpected
knowledge of how he makes his living. He doesn't speak again until
the phone has stopped ringing. "You have me at a disadvantage."

"I certainly do." This is taking it too far, but it's strangely
invigorating to have the upper hand after all this time. How long

could she string this out, she wonders—learning all she can about his life, what makes him tick—before he makes the connection, somehow traces her back to that horrific morning? Days? Weeks? And then what? She isn't sure, exactly—some kind of accounting, perhaps—an apology, the acceptance of responsibility. Right now, though, she has to keep him intrigued—keep him guessing.

"I used to live around here," she offers. "In Southport."

"That's it? That's all you're going to give me?"

"You seem to like a challenge, Mr. Ryan," she says. "I'm sure you'll come up with something." She makes a wide turn then, beginning the run back to the beach and her car, energized by the sudden thought that his obvious interest in her might just be the in she needs, that what initially seemed like some bizarre twist of fate may instead have been a gift from the heavens.

"I'd like to meet with Debra initially, take a look at her materials—the current corporate package, her annual fund letters, all of it."

"Of course." Augie is unable to mask her delight. "I'm pleased you've decided to accept our offer. It will be wonderful to have you back in New York."

Jamie stretches the old wall phone's cord as far as it will go, making a mental note to pick up another that will allow her to at least reach the refrigerator. "The offer was very generous. And I'm only consulting, remember—coming down once a month. Debra knows this, of course?"

"I think she's relieved, to tell you the truth. The board has been grumbling about the lack of growth since she took over your position, and she's feeling the heat, as they say. When will you be coming down?"

"I'm here already, actually—took a week off to do some repairs and painting at the house. I could come in this afternoon, if that works for you."

"Fine." Augie pauses. "It's going to be wonderful to have you with us again, Jamie, and I speak for the whole staff when I say this. We're doing some fabulous things next season—a Latin Pops thing with Dobrin to open; Midori, possibly, in the spring. We were on the line with her agent this morning, by the way, and he mentioned she'll be doing the Dvorak concerto with your little New Hampshire group in September. How did you ever manage that? Never mind—I don't want to know."

Jamie smiles into the phone. "Oh, it was that thing at Tanglewood five or six summers ago. I think my new boss hired me for my contacts as much as anything else."

"I doubt that. In any event, the Mendelssohn would be better for your crowd, I think. But don't ever tell anyone I encourage you in this."

Jamie laughs; she's missed this kind of thing with Augie. "I have nothing to do with programming, as you well know, but I'll pass the suggestion along."

"This is all right with everyone—you're sure? I ask this as your friend, of course. I know there is still much pain for you here." Augie laughs. "Listen to me. I've worked so hard to bring you back, and now I suggest you reconsider. Odd, is it not? I have the sudden feeling this might not be the right thing for you."

There'll be some flak from Peter, Jamie knows, but she's clear about this—clearer than she's been about anything in a long time. "I'll be fine," she says. "I have this feeling I was meant to be here."

SEVEN

Jamie, finally managing to get the Christmas tree inside and upright, takes a minute to catch her breath—giddy with pleasure at the nostalgic, piney smell of the blue spruce, freshly dusted with snow from its trip across the yard. Nearly too wide to drag through the doorway, its knobby top bent against the ceiling of the hall, she judges it by far the biggest they've ever had.

It's been years since Christmas, with all its excess and pageantry, has held any allure for her, but for some reason when she got off the train from New York tonight—catching sight of the families, the children running along the rows of trees beneath bobbing colored lights in the lot across from the station—something kicked in and she bought the largest one she could get into the back of her car, tipping the kid who loaded it exorbitantly.

Peter would think I've lost my mind, she murmurs—uneasy with the thought of him now that he knew she was spending time here, with the half truths necessary to keep the peace.

He'd been adding the belt of the Milky Way to the dome of the moon room when she told him about Augie's offer and her decision to accept it—explaining it as a chance to keep up her New York contacts, so vital to her line of work. And she was thinking about selling the house, she told him, but it needed painting and some repairs, and staying there for a few days each month would allow her to keep an eye on the whole project. She'd surprised herself with this last—not having given any real thought to selling the house at all—and she didn't think at this point she really could, but the part about the painting and repairs was at least true.

The Milky Way, a hundred billion stars tossed in a long swathe across the sky, required a multitude of tiny bits of silvered tape even for Peter's simple design—sketched, with his usual spontaneity, on a piece of paper toweling. He listened to her without interruption—tearing and sticking a cluster of stars to his shirt while peering alternately at his sketch and the constellations of the dome.

"Why?" he asked quietly.

"I told you why," Jamie said.

"No, what you gave me was some kind of hopped up rationale—the official Jamie Lloyd press release. What's happened that you'd suddenly want to go back there now, after all this time?"

"Augie's been after me to do this for a while, Peter—you know that."

He took a final look at his chart and stepped up on the bench. "Are you worried about money—is that why you suddenly want to sell the house?"

"No," she laughed. "Of course not."

He was quiet for a minute. "How long do you expect to do this?"

"A few months, probably. I can't imagine it taking much longer than that."

He nodded. She watched him place the stars—looking so serious and at the same time so silly—and felt a sudden flush of affection. He needed more, she knew—something to help him get comfortable with the whole idea.

"It's about my son, too, I guess," she said, wincing as she gave up the words. "I was running one morning—it was his birthday—and suddenly I couldn't remember his face. I feel like I need to be there right now, closer to him, to where we were together. I need to get that back."

He stepped down, stood back to compare the dome to the diagram. "Ah, the birthday thing," he said, picking up the roll of tape. "Each year September rolls around, and neither of us say anything, but we both know." He smiled at her look of surprise. "It wasn't hard to figure out, Jae. You get one letter a year from Philippe, always at the end of September. You're a mess for a few days, and then you stuff the whole thing down again. We've been together for a while now; you can trust me with some of this stuff, you know."

He began again with the tape, this time at the top of the dome, and was quiet for a minute. "So this is really a kind of personal odyssey," he mused, his words echoing outward across the celestial field. "I guess I can't argue with that."

She sat with him till he finished, neither of them saying much; then, afterward, because she couldn't tell him the rest of it, she made love to him—pulling him down onto her there in the cockpit. A quiet tenderness replaced their usual urgency, as though he were afraid to crush this newly exposed area of her heart. It surprised and moved her, but left her feeling oddly blue.

She shakes the feeling off now, gets a good grip on the tree and drags it to the living room, maneuvering it into the stand by the bay window fronting the road. If GM were here, there'd be all kinds of fuss: the ritual of the hot chocolate, the stringing of cranberries and popcorn, then the music—Nat King Cole roasting chestnuts and Bing Crosby dreaming of a white Christmas while they unpacked the boxes from the attic and hung the decorations, careful to keep the most delicate out of Sam's reach.

Well, she can do without all the ceremony. Too many memories—too much of her life as a mother to the one, a granddaughter to the other—lay in those boxes to ever consider opening them, exposing what remained of that life to one of such reduced circumstance. It occurs to her then to simply leave the tree as is. It's quite lovely, actually, taken on its own. And it's the kind of thing Peter would do. She smiles, having found a way to include him in the process, even in this minor way.

☙❧

She gives her heel a kick to clear the shoe of its icy crust, reminding herself that a bad landing in a snow-filled pothole means a sure trip to the Emergency Room—a place she's determined never to see again. She's run this route several times now, knows its dips and uneven spots, and is pretty sure that the three or four inches of unplowed snow hold no surprises. Still, she runs inside the path forged by a wide, heavy duty tire, keeping to the left so that the few cars willing to venture out on a stormy Saturday morning will approach head-on—this as a hedge against going without her reflective vest, the need to stay visible losing out to the desire to blend into her surroundings.

Decked out for the holidays, Michael Ryan's front porch has the look of a magazine cover—the snowy railings dressed with fir swags, the wide front door half covered by a huge holly wreath. Two of the three garage bays are standing open, and Jamie recognizes the dark SUV, notes the wide bulk of an expensive late-model station wagon—Mercedes, she guesses. Mommy about to go for groceries? Daddy heading off for a Saturday morning at the office?

The yellow Lab she met that first day trots out of the garage just then, heading purposefully along the side of the house, toward the back. She paces him, curious, then catches sight of two fast-moving sleds cutting through the trees at the rear of the property—a steeply sloping hundred yards or so from the back terrace to where the land flattens out by a stone wall fronting the road.

Jamie slows to a walk, drawn by the sight of the children sledding, all her trips here finally paying off. She counts four, then catches sight of Michael Ryan at the edge of the terrace, settling himself on a sled behind a crying toddler. She stares, mesmerized, focusing on the terrified child clinging to Ryan's neck, and is hit with the very physical memory of Sam's first run on GM's wooden toboggan—his initial fear, the way he went all stiff and turned a wide-eyed face up to hers when the sled began moving, then his sheer delight at the finish of the run. They had just that one winter—one without much snow, as it turned out—so only went out two or three times. The next year he was gone.

She's close enough now to see Michael Ryan's thick, dark curls atop the heads of the children towing their sleds back toward the terrace. Another sled sluices toward her, slowing as it reaches level ground and stopping mere yards away, despite the efforts of two giggling girls to urge it forward. The younger one—four or five years old, Jamie figures—smiles at her readily. The older girl, perhaps ten and already wary of strangers, averts her eyes as she hops off and begins pulling the sled back up the hill. Both have the same shock of dark curls barely contained beneath knit caps. All his, then. Busy boy.

The older girl stops, turns, drops her shoulders in exasperation. "C'mon, Meggie," she whines, clearly uncomfortable with Jamie's presence. "Help me pull." And the girl is up and running, tossing Jamie a final smile over her shoulder.

The Lab catches sight of her then and begins barking from the terrace just as Ryan purposely stalls his sled halfway down the hill, tumbling off with the now-laughing toddler still wrapped about his neck—the others running, shrieking, collapsing on them in a heap. Jamie turns quickly and starts off, praying he hasn't seen her through the falling snow. She runs an extra few miles before flipping, just in case, then keeps to the far side of the road on the return, but the sledding party has broken up by the time she reaches the house again, the SUV gone from its bay.

She's halfway back to her car when he finds her, the snow-packed road muffling the sound of the vehicle's tires until it's almost on her. She's been thinking about the smiling little girl, trying to imagine Sam at that age and finding she can't. Seeing the children was a mistake; finding them gone on her return has left her feeling deflated, torn from herself, strangely reckless. When she senses Ryan drawing alongside, she almost hopes he's found her out and has followed to warn her off his family. Put an end to this stupidity.

"You've got quite a brood," she says to the open window. She keeps her stride steady, concentrates her gaze ahead while her fingers search out the little sock.

"Word is we're not finished yet."

She throws him a glance, notes the sly grin, the heightened color of a morning spent sledding still in his cheeks and lips. "Congratulations. Is this a dynasty in the making?"

"I'm thinking more starting lineup—coed, of course. What's that—eight of them? Nine?" His smile is loose, playful. "My God, but you're fetching dusted with snow. Where have you been, anyway? I've been thinking about you for weeks."

She laughs lightly, suddenly invigorated. So the game is still on. "Not having any luck?"

"Luck?"

"The mystery of my identity."

He grins. "Still working on it. Tell you what; meet me for a drink tonight, and you can be as cryptic as you want. Promise I won't complain."

"And leave the wife to get the Little League settled in? Hardly seems fair." Still, she's tempted—drawn in by the chance to learn more about his family, those beautiful children. His obvious interest in her would make it easy. She looks him full in the face, then, as she accepts, and feels something drop away with the decision.

He's pleased, she can tell, and surprised; suggests they meet downtown at Tommy's. Jamie knows it; she and Philippe ate there the night he told her he was leaving her. Seems appropriate somehow. They agree on eight-thirty.

The place is dark and quiet, nicer than Jamie remembers—the lounge more upscale than the last time she was here. The five men seated at the bar all turn to give her the once over as she pulls the door closed behind her—professional men, dressed mostly in suits, despite the fact it's Saturday night. More lawyers, she figures, remembering the old line that if it weren't for all the attorneys in Fairfield, its bars would all go out of business.

She spots Ryan in a booth chuckling into his cell phone. Unlike the men still eyeing her from the bar, he's casually dressed in jeans and a dark blue cable knit sweater over a pinstripe shirt turned neatly at the cuffs. A stray hank of dark curl dipping almost to his left eye lends him an impish look—a little boy skipping school. He winds up the call quickly as she slides in opposite him.

"This isn't a problem for you?" she asks, glancing around uneasily. The fact that she might run into someone from her former life has only just now occurred to her.

"I bring clients here all the time," he says—meaning, she's sure, that no one will think it strange to see him here with some woman other than his wife.

He's drinking what looks like a martini on the rocks and has apparently ordered one for her, because the bartender delivers it almost immediately. It looks like a double. Michael Ryan, it appears, is trying to get her drunk.

He raises his glass. "To the goddess of the chase."

She takes a sip, the delicious bite of the drink tripping another memory even as liquid warmth overspreads her chest. Philippe insisted on Bombay Saffire with no more than two drops of vermouth. It was their Friday night drink—she and Philippe, Augie and Gaspar, out on the town in Manhattan. "I haven't had one of these in years," she says—more to herself than to him.

"Is that a clue?" He's grinning, leaning toward her over the table as if they were lovers. It hits her then that she's sitting here drinking with the man who took Sam's life and simply walked away—sharing a joke as if they were old friends with much in common. In a way, of course, it's true; they were both there during the last moments of Sam's life, even if Ryan was speeding away at the time. For Jamie, the connection is constant and fixed, and oddly compelling. It takes effort to look away.

Ryan is still grinning, as though her lack of response is meant to tease—no inkling of the horrific genesis of that long gaze. Lighten up, the look says; time to play. "I'm curious. How did you know I'm an attorney?"

"MacNamee Ryan Ross," she tells him. "Fairfield and New York City. Divorce and family law, for the most part. Some corporate stuff—especially in the city." He stops, mid-sip, to stare. "I'm obviously better at this than you are, Mr. Ryan. So which is it?"

"Divorce," he says, recovering enough to finish his sip. "Please God, tell me you're looking for one."

Jamie chuckles, relaxing enough to match his sip, fortified by anonymity. She's brought nothing with which she might inadvertently betray herself—no cell phone, no purse; she's even locked her wallet in the car, tucking a twenty-dollar bill in her pocket. Shedding Jamie Lloyd has been surprisingly easy, enabling her to conveniently sidestep the issue of Peter. "Tell me about your children," she instructs, nestling comfortably into the corner of the booth.

"Whoa—slow down," Ryan laughs. He tosses back the rest of his drink, signals the bartender. "So what do you do with yourself, Diana of the forest—when you're not out stalking our streets?"

Jamie considers a moment. "I work as a development consultant for nonprofits. Symphony orchestras," she adds on a whim—wondering how he'll respond.

His eyes travel her face. "How noble. I hope Mr. Apollo makes some money, though, because it's a sure bet you don't. Where is he tonight, if I might ask?"

"Busy. The wife?"

"Busy."

"Five kids will do that. They all look like you, by the way. So how old are they?" The drink arrives, and he settles back against the booth—weighing his response while the bartender drops another napkin and swaps out the glasses.

"Okay," he says finally, as if he's lost some battle with himself—breached some line he never goes beyond in these situations. "Let's see. Margaret is nine; Michael, Jr., seven; Meghan, five." He breaks for a sip from the overfull glass, as if the sheer size of his brood is too much to get through in one go. "Mia is four and Matthew, two. How about yours?"

"Just one—a son." She pauses, struck by the fact that Meghan would have been the same age Sam was when he was killed; that the wife got pregnant with their two-year-old about the same time. It stops her for a minute, complicating her take on Ryan, and she puts the knowledge away for later. "So what will you name the new one?"

He takes a long slug of the drink, a bit wary now. "What would you suggest?"

"Well, I've always liked Samuel—assuming it's a boy, of course."

"Which it is."

"Well, then."

"There's one problem; it doesn't start with an M."

"Ah, of course. The M-thing. How about the wife; is she an M, too? Margaret? Mary? Michelle?"

He leans in toward her again, chuckling as he moves his glass in wet circles on the table. Jamie locks onto the graceful swirls of fine, dark hair covering the back of his hands—the same hands that once steered a BMW into her path.

"This isn't the way the game is usually played, you know," he says softly.

She smiles at the hands. No wedding band, of course. "Ah, but you and I don't follow the rules, now, do we?"

He seems to like this idea. "Okay, then, more about you. Something else I can't possibly trace."

"Let's see. Parents died when I was nine—a plane crash on their way back from a concert tour. He was the conductor; she was the soloist—a pianist. I was her protégé. My grandmother finished raising me—over in Easton, actually." There, she thinks. That and the bit about the orchestra should give him something to chew on.

"You still play?"

"Not really." On a hunch she adds, " I had a bad car accident a few years ago; I haven't been able to perform since. Some kind of emotional block, they tell me." She shrugs.

He asks her about it and she tells him it was her fault—a stupid, careless thing—and that the guy really took her to the cleaners. All at once she has the strangest feeling that GM and Sam are near—the two of them hovering in the air above her like some kind of intergenerational Greek chorus. Be still, she admonishes. I know what I'm doing.

"Too bad I didn't know you then, " Ryan says. "I could have put you in touch with a guy who helped me out of the same kind of mess. Saved my ass." He points to her glass, but it's all Jamie can do to shake her head, too stunned by the comment to manage anything more. Bingo, she thinks, channeling her quiet fury into a blinding smile.

"I play a little, myself, " he tells her. "Cocktail party stuff, mostly, but my real love is the classical repertoire. I've got a vintage nine-foot Bechstein I'm quite proud of; picked it up at an estate sale on Long Island about ten years back."

Another surprise. Few of the old, classic Bechstein concert grands still exist, Jamie knows—almost of them in Europe. It's one of the very few pianos to rival the Steinway he's purchased for the Symphony, and if in good condition is most probably priceless. If he were anyone else, she'd have begged to see it.

"Anyway, my problem is I've never been able to sight read."

"That's the easy part," she tells him. "Simple eye-hand coordination—like typing."

"Yeah, well, I can't do that either—so there you are." He motions again to the bartender—two fingers this time.

"It's control you have to work for," she says. "Dynamics, for instance. And touch—learning to control the interaction of body and instrument. It gets fun when you can move beyond the written notes—forget your hands, your fingers—and feel it, hear it inside your head. It's like entering the music itself. You almost cease to exist outside it." She stops quite suddenly, appalled to find herself talking so unguardedly with this man.

He's grinning at her again, his face flushed and softened by liquor, his eyes an almost liquid brown. "Why don't you teach me? Liszt's *B minor Sonata*—now there's a piece I've always wanted to play. I'd pay you for lessons."

She laughs in spite of herself, envisioning the fierce, dark music—the double thirds, the leaps, the impossibly fast octaves.

"No good? Okay, how about the Mozart *Double Piano Concerto*? The Jersey Philharmonic did it last year, blew me out of the water. We could play it together. I'm not half bad once I memorize something."

His choice of the Mozart Double is hardly a surprise. If two pianos were having sex, she's heard it said, they'd be playing that piece. The mood, light and playful at first, growing into a kind of musical foreplay—the inner movement slow to develop. Tension then, an eagerness toward the end. She smiles into her drink. "Not a chance, if you don't sight read," she tells him.

The bartender brings two martinis this time, Ryan shrugging off Jamie's irritated expression.

"When I say no, that's generally what I mean," she informs him.

"C'mon...the evening's young. Besides, there's a full moon tonight—your element, if I'm not mistaken." He starts in with the compliments—tells her he loves the way she looks when she runs—like some long-legged animal set to leap off the ground—and that she's the first woman he's talked to in years that didn't bore him from the get go. Jamie sneaks a peak at her watch, surprised to see that ten o'clock has come and gone. He's apparently reached the point in the evening where he turns up the charm, hoping the woman will go for it.

GM and Sam are back, and this time she agrees with them. It's clear she's gotten everything she will out of Ryan—for tonight anyway. She takes a final sip of her martini and slides toward the end of the booth, relinquishing him for the night.

He breaks off his shtick—looking, she's surprised to see, rather hurt. "Hey, now, wait a minute. Tell me you're not leaving."

Jamie leans into the table. "You're drunk, Michael O. Ryan. Go home to your family. It's time to decorate the tree."

He scrutinizes her, decides she's serious, and quickly jots something on a damp cocktail napkin. "My cell number," he says, sliding it toward her. "Call me when you can get away."

She looks at the napkin for a minute before crumpling it into the palm of her hand, then grabs her keys and heads for the door. She's almost there when he calls out.

"Oh, by the way." His voice, instantly sober, travels easily above the increasing din. "There's no record of anyone named Apollo owning anything at all in Fairfield County—no land, no car, not even a phone. Not for the last fifteen years, anyway."

Jamie's cell phone, left behind on the hall table, beeps repeatedly as she lets herself in, signaling a message. He couldn't possibly have this number, she tells herself; still, just the thought is enough to send the adrenaline pounding through her. She punches the access numbers while she wanders to the Christmas tree, fingering the little blue matchbox car nestled in a vee of fir needles while she waits for the message. Staring at the familiar shape stupidly—the realization slow to sink in. A miniature BMW.

Jesus just left Chicago, an' he's bound for New Orleans; workin' one end to the other and all points in between.

Peter's voice, crooning the old ZZ Top riff, brings her back to herself. She dials the boat number, figuring he's out somewhere—probably with Bake—and she's right. The voice mail kicks in.

"I miss you, too, baby," she whispers, impaling the cocktail napkin with Michael Ryan's cell number on another branch of the tree.

EIGHT

Jamie's never seen Bake so down. Hunkered over a mug of coffee, he stares miserably into the inky fluid as if willing it to talk. The silence growing increasingly uncomfortable.

"And she never said nothin' to you?" he asks Jamie for the third time. Beside him, the coal stove issues a long, accusatory hiss.

"C'mon, Bake," Peter reasons, pulling the bottle of dark rum from a locker above the settee. "Jamie hardly knows her." He uncaps it and drops a healthy slug into Bake's mug, then his own, and they raise their cups in solemn salute. Happy goddamn New Year.

There were to have been four of them, of course—cocktails on the boat followed by dinner and fireworks in Portsmouth. Instead, Lori surprised them all by dumping Bake just that morning in favor of a cabin in Maine and the fifty-year-old lech from the Walmart. Only it seems he wasn't fifty, after all, or a lech—but a thirty-five-year-old accountant and Harley Davidson nut she'd apparently been seeing since that first day.

Having been through these things before with Bake, Jamie's braced for an evening-long discussion of Lori's shortcomings— angry, rambling complaints that Peter will sort through and somehow, by the end of the night, help Bake come to terms with. Experience has taught her to lay low, limit her role to the dispensing of food and drink—knowing that at times like these, Bake sees all women as part of the problem.

"She's been comin' home later and later all week," Bake tells them, finally getting to the heart of it. "And when I ask her about it, she gets all pissy like I'm checking up on her." He pauses to pour another slug of rum into his mug, declining Jamie's offer of more coffee. "So yesterday morning I'm on the pot, and I hear her cryin' on the phone out in the bedroom. Before I can get my pants off the floor and find out what's goin' on, she's halfway down the road, burning the rubber off them new tires I just bought her. I mean, what the hell? She can't take thirty seconds to fill me in?"

Peter maneuvers a shovel full of coal into the stove. "Bake, my friend, it no longer matters. She's not coming back. Remember Sherry? New horizons? Places unknown? Same thing."

It's not the first time Jamie's heard the name. The ghost of the Great Love, invoked in this way, usually brings Bake back—reminds him there was a time when he indeed felt lower than he does now. It seems to work; both men become wistful—thrown back to the earliest days of their friendship when, as Peter tells it, he first spied Bake, toolbox in hand, climbing aboard a brand-new, million-dollar Hinkley nestled into the next slip. Hours later, after he'd helped realign the auxiliary engine—wrenched out of position when the prop caught a net offshore—they shared a six-pack in the sleek, roomy saloon, discovering a mutual love of all things mechanical, a shared obsession with rock and roll trivia. Bake told Peter about life with the New Hampshire Turnpike Authority; how he worked weekends on boat engines, electrical systems and the like to pay off the diamond ring he'd just given his girlfriend, Sherry, whose computer genius of a boss owned the boat. More money than God, according to Bake, but not a clue how to maintain the thing, which he planned to sail to the

Caribbean for a winter's worth of partying. A month later, Sherry dumped Bake for the sun and fun of St. Barts.

Jamie extends a finger toward the kitten—orphaned, as far as Bake's concerned, when Lori walked out. Brought to the boat tonight in lieu of being skinned alive. He approaches her tentatively, the single bell on his collar tinkling as he raises his silky flank against her hand, oblivious to the growls emanating from the bunk in the darkened aft cabin.

Bake's glare is murderous. "Shoulda' just left the damn thing at the tolls that day, let some truck run it down. She was the one told me to bring it home, the one named it Highway. Every time I look at the fuckin' thing now, I want to throw it against the wall."

"If we take him to the shelter, they'll probably just put him down," Peter tells him. "Let's give it a few days, see what happens. Maybe Lucille will warm to him. Stranger things have happened. How about Chinese?"

Bake nods, leaning forward to fish the wallet out of his back pocket. "I buy; you fly?"

"I'll go," Jamie offers. "The dogs need to go out anyway."

🐾

Lucille takes the lead, heading determinedly back along the empty slips toward the granite boulders of the jetty, where just that morning Gus teased out the sandy, waterlogged body of a gull. Jamie pulls her coat tighter against the cold, the heavy clouds moving in from the west promising snow. She's perfectly happy with the change in plans, having attended too many New Year's Eve parties during her years in Manhattan to have a taste for them anymore.

She thinks of Augie and Gaspar out on the town, finds herself wondering what Ryan and his wife are doing this frigid New Year's Eve. Dinner in the city with friends, perhaps—the Symphony's

New Year's Pops afterwards where they mingle and preen. Pregnant, the wife no doubt abstains from alcohol. Then again, maybe not. She's married to Michael Ryan, after all; a few glasses of wine could go a long way in relieving that kind of stress.

In her fantasy, they beg off from some glittery post-concert reception—pleading the pregnancy and the five little ones at home—and speed up the highway toward this wealth of offspring tucked snugly in their combed cotton sheets.

Oh God, what she'd give for the feel of tiny arms wrapped about her neck—the damp, sweet-smelling breath of a child's sleepy kiss. With five, it would be so easy to take them for granted, so tempting to rush through the nightly rituals, the profusion of hugs and soft lips, the hushing of tentatively whispered fears.

The overabundance of such treasure is beyond comprehension—makes her heart literally ache with longing—and so she turns her thoughts instead to Bake, whose unwillingness to take any responsibility for the failure of his relationships complicates her otherwise warm feeling for him. Something he said tonight tugs at her now—some reference that's left her with a vague feeling of having missed something important, but what?

Lucille is hell-bent toward the body of the gull now, her breath coming in determined little gasps as she strains against the lead. Gus is less eager—having already nosed the thing to death—but good sport that he is, lends his pull to the cause. It's all Jamie can do to keep them on the dock and not veering off onto the slippery rocks of the darkened jetty, where one slip could mean disaster. She nearly panics when Lucille makes a quick lunge for the edge, the sudden emotional jolt clearing her mind of all but the connection she's been reaching for. Panic—that's it—Lori's frantic state as she sped off toward another place in her life so much like Michael Ryan on the morning of the accident. To be going as fast as he was when he cut her off—blindly shooting out of the side street like that—the man had to have been in some kind of panic himself. It's so obvious now; she wonders that she hadn't seen it before, that it never occurred to her to question why he was in such a hurry to begin with. One of a hundred details lost in the dark, cataclysmic void that became her life after Sam's death. Funny, all this time she simply assumed Ryan was a pathologically reckless driver—too self-absorbed, too intent on his cell phone call to pay attention to anyone or anything else. But that reading doesn't feel right now—seems too simplistic, too easy. It certainly doesn't jibe with what she's seen of him behind the wheel, coming and going from his home, when his driving seemed quite ordinary, if a little casual.

She begins picking her way cautiously through the emotional debris of that morning, feels herself once again in the driver's seat, something uneasy about the sense of Sam beside her—though she's careful not to turn, to look—so innocent and unknowing in those last few seconds before impact. The car careens wildly out of the narrow dirt road in front of her then, Ryan on his cell phone, and she slows the whole thing down, reaching for some sense of his state of mind. Yes, she's sure of it. Like Lori, he, too, was tearing off somewhere in a state of sheer panic. So where the hell was he going?

Guy saved my ass, he said the night she met him in Tommy's. Just what did that mean, exactly?

Something else bothering her now, too—something in the logistics of it all that makes no sense, and she works to track it down. They were on their way to Sam's daycare when it happened, she remembers—seven in the morning, almost no traffic on the back roads through Easton. Then it hits her. Michael Ryan was driving like a bat out of hell, the sun barely up, nowhere near his Fairfield home—not even in the same town. The question she should be asking herself, she realizes, is not where he was going in such a state, but where he was coming from.

The shape of that awful day begins to change in her mind—broadening, taking on more depth even as she thinks about it, and she's still considering the implications when she returns to the boat with the warm, sweetly fragrant bag of food in her arms—the sound of Bake's laughter rising above a long, bluesy riff from Peter's favorite Boz Scaggs CD.

NINE

Three times in as many days she's tried for a glimpse of them, but the weather has proven too bitter for outdoor play, and the sleds remain propped against the trees behind the house—the well-worn tracks through the snow icy and crusty-edged. It's as if they've all gone to ground, Jamie thinks—concentrating her gaze on the front door, willing it to throw itself wide and surrender its laughing, pink-cheeked profusion. Nothing. Not even the dog.

She turns, pushing herself into a hard run back toward the car and tries to redirect her thoughts toward the pile of work waiting at the house—the annual fund letter Augie needs faxed by the end of the day, her audience-building models, the new research on commercial fundraising websites—a feast of files and graphs and computer printouts set in neat piles like so many place settings around GM's cherry dining room table. But as if filling her mind with thoughts of Michael Ryan's family has somehow stirred them to action, the enormous SUV suddenly comes up on her from behind and slides past at a slow, measured pace toward the center of town.

Has to be the wife. If it were Ryan, she reasons, he'd have slowed to challenge her, ask why she hasn't called in the four weeks she's had his cell number. Elated at this change in her luck—the chance to see the children again, to catch a glimpse of the pregnant wife—she double-times it the final quarter mile to the car, skipping her usual post-run stretch to slip behind the wheel and head toward Fairfield's boutique-filled Main Street.

She finds the SUV almost immediately, by some miracle managing to grab a parking spot just two cars behind. It's not the wife after all, but Ryan standing on the busy sidewalk, his head tucked inside the rear door. She slips lower in her seat—eager and edgy as she waits, reciting the mantra of names and ages called up countless times since that night in Tommy's: Margaret, nine; Michael, seven; Meghan, five; Mia, four; Matthew, two.

The girl who smiled at her from the sled—Meghan, she figures— hops out first, dark curls poking from beneath the faux fur edges of a heavily quilted down jacket. Arms extended, she twirls on the sidewalk, flapping furry hands at the sky as Ryan pulls a snow-suited toddler from the car. Jamie exhales his name in a plume of frosty air—Matthew—eyes devouring him, stomach twisting as she notes his size, so much like Sam when he died. She's hit with the warm, wheaty fragrance of little boy hair, feels the clutch of pudgy fingers as he fights being lowered to the sidewalk. Two alternate versions of her own child stand before her now—Sam the toddler and the fully-aware five year old he'd surely be today— the years she's missed taking on a new heft, a tangible reality of their own, and she feels the weight of them settle irrevocably into her as yet another way to measure her loss. So mesmerized is she by the little boy, so intent on absorbing everything about him, she barely misses being seen, is only rescued from the possibility when Ryan takes both proffered little hands and heads up the street in the opposite direction.

She fights the urge to follow, instinct telling her they won't be long—running errands with the kids not being the kind of thing Michael Ryan would tend to dawdle over. Sure enough, she spots Meghan again in a matter of minutes, heading back to the car swinging a plastic bag emblazoned with a video store logo, followed by Ryan carrying several freshly dry-cleaned suits— Matthew nestled sleepily on his shoulder. He's all business, this guy; completing his assigned tasks as husband and father with efficient dispatch—ignoring Matthew's whines at being returned to the car seat, only half listening to the questions Meghan fires at him from the sidewalk. If only he knew how quickly, how unexpectedly life could change—a slippery road, the casual carelessness of a stranger—he might listen more closely, take a minute to kiss a forehead, run a finger along a sleepy-soft cheek.

They retrace their route, Jamie a few cars back and so focused on trying to get another glimpse of the children that when the SUV finally swings up the drive, she feels almost physically bereft—as though in these two she's discovered some vestige of Sam being wrenched from her yet again. Discouraged, her longing for him complicated now by a yearning tied somehow to Ryan's children, she heads home—her need for connection dictating a route that will take her by the scene of the accident, the nexus of three lives.

Coming on the spot, she notices a vehicle pulling out of the same narrow side street Michael Ryan had shot from that morning, and, as if out of nowhere, a possible way into the truth of that day reveals itself. Surprised it's never occurred to her to do so before, Jamie turns onto the rutted dirt road—a short cut to somewhere, she figures—hoping wherever it comes out might afford a clue as to Ryan's whereabouts that morning. The sign reads Porter Street—had she known that before? One of the thousand little details that washed over her in the tidal wave of those first weeks?

The road is a straight shot back through a thick overhang of leafless trees, dim even in the high sun of midday, and it's a good quarter mile before she comes on anything at all. Suddenly, through the trees, houses to the left. She notes what she can of each as she passes; a small, brown split level with a rusty metal swing set in the frozen front yard; another of the same early-sixties vintage, but a washed out blue with four tired-looking vehicles parked haphazardly in the drive; then another small home as well, but a quainter bungalow style with wrap-around porch. It's set farther back from the road than the others, blocked almost entirely from view by a small woods, and she'd have missed it altogether but for the mailbox at the head of the winding dirt drive directing her gaze back along its length. And with this, the road abruptly stops. Not a short cut to anywhere, then; just a depressing dead end street in the middle of nowhere. What would a man like Michael Ryan be doing back here—and at seven o'clock in the morning?

☙ ❧

The knock throws her timing off. Even so, it takes her a moment to register the dull rapping above the sound of the piano, the slow hiss of burning logs. She glances quickly at the mantel clock, surprised to find it's already past eight.

The knock again. Someone with car trouble? Peter popping down to surprise her? No, she thinks, rising and moving to the hall. Not his style. She switches on the porch light, leans against to the door. "Who is it?"

"Finally tracked the goddess to her lair." A comical attempt at a growl.

Michael Ryan.

Mind racing as she weighs her options—the chance to learn more about him, about his family, ultimately trumping caution—and she turns instinctively to the hall mirror, runs a hand through her hair. Too late to worry about what might be lying around the house, ready to give her away. At least the car, with its New Hampshire plates, is tucked safely in the garage against the prediction of more snow.

She opens the door to the smell of gin laced with the spicy cologne she's come to associate him with—not an unpleasant combination. "Well," she manages. "I'm speechless."

He leans casually against the door jamb—ballsy grin, sure of himself. Not drunk either, but just loose enough to be drawn to the utter outrageousness of a stunt like this.

"I've gone by this place five times in the last hour," he confides, looking past her into the hall. "So I know you're alone. Any chance I'm coming in, or are you going to keep me out here on the porch all night?"

She nods, debating with herself—both of them on the edge of something. "Wouldn't dream of it," she says, opening the door wide.

He steps into the foyer, surprising her with the way his bulk seems to fill the space, then stands for a moment unbuttoning his overcoat—eyes darting to her laptop, the mass of papers spread on the dining room table. Then he takes in the stairway, his nose picking up the pungent scent. "Fresh paint," he says, as if such a thing surprises him.

"My son's room," she tells him.

He nods and moves into the living room, eyes drawn to the dried-out Christmas tree she's neglected to haul out back, despite the fact it's lost fully a third of its needles to the floor.

Jamie curls into a corner of the couch, still more surprised than alarmed at his sudden appearance. She follows his eyes as they travel the room, taking in the details of her life, seeing it all suddenly as she knows he must—the open piano covered with scores and practice books, the embers of a fire she's neglected to feed, the rumpled couch cushions where she now sits littered with computer printouts and seed catalogues folded open to the perennials she's decided on for the front of the house. Taken together, they form a cozy afternoon's work that has stretched into evening, the breaks from her laptop filled with stints at the piano, wish lists of spring flowers. He takes it all in without expression, and her initial urge to turn him away retreats to a watchful place, replaced by a growing sense of irony. This is the man, she thinks toward her son. Can you believe he walked in here on his own?

His gaze returns to the tree and he reaches out, plucks the tooth-marked block from where she's nestled it into the crook of a branch. Then he notices the little BMW parked atop Sam's wrinkled red turtleneck draped over one of the upper branches. He shoots her a puzzled look.

"My son's," she tells him.

"Kids do the damnedest things, huh?"

She relaxes a bit at the comment, not sure yet what she's dealing with here but willing to play along. "How did you find me?" she asks, gathering the loose pile of computer printouts from the cushions around her—the negligible result of an hour's worth of Internet research into the Porter Street real estate records—and tucking them into one of the catalogues. Hoping it was the sight of her running this morning that's drawn him here, and not the knowledge he was being tailed.

He's begun a casual, exploratory stroll of the living room—hands tucked in the pockets of his open overcoat. "I followed you when you left Tommy's that night. Almost lost you, too; my luck I got stuck behind the only guy in Fairfield who refuses to run yellow lights." He pauses at an end table to run his finger along the edge of GM's favorite book of poetry, the rim of her old reading glasses—familiar things Jamie set out because they brought some of her presence back to the room. "I've been going by a few times a week since—before work, after work. Funny how you're never home."

She says nothing—thrown by the assumption of intimacy, his casual willingness to admit such a thing. Not to mention the patience this demonstrates—the route between their homes being a convoluted, slow going, eleven and a half miles. Exactly.

His eyes finally settle on the Chickering and the scores open on the stand. "I interrupted your practice," he says—no hint of apology in his voice.

"I was ready for a break," she lies, beginning to find his coolness, the casual, oddly proprietary scrutiny of her world unnerving. She wonders suddenly just how long he stood on the porch before knocking, if he watched her from the window first.

"Saw you running this morning," he tells her, "but I had my kids with me. Killed me I couldn't stop, especially as you have this habit of disappearing for weeks at a time."

"I saw your SUV pass me; figured it was probably your wife."

"She hates SUVs—thinks they're excessive. But she doesn't mind driving a sixty-five-thousand-dollar station wagon."

He's finally reached the piano—the destination, Jamie realizes now, of all his peregrinations—and peers down at the music on the stand. She's been working on the *A* sections of the *Fantaisie Impromptu,* and the open score is covered with scribbled notes. "You're very good, at least from what I could hear on the porch," he tells her. "I mean *very good*. How old were you when you began to play?"

"My mother started me on theory and harmony when I was five, I think."

He nods, distracted. "That's right. Your mother, the pianist." He turns a page of the score, examining her notation—then turns it back again.

So he has a mind for detail—so what? If he's trying to impress, he should really work on his tone. She considers calling him on the attitude when she suddenly sees the arrogance for what it is— nervousness, a defense against his admiration for her talent. Is he in such awe of her then?

"Molly's been pushing to start the kids."

The wife, Jamie realizes. "Meghan's about the right age," she says, moving to the piano. If he's surprised she remembers the name, he says nothing. "Start her on the basics now, and in a few years you'll know if she's got a feel for the music. If she still sees it as just a lot of black marks on a page at say, eight or nine, she'll be better off playing soccer. Happier, too."

"You felt it, though," he says quietly, watching as she settles herself on the bench.

"Oh, yes; right away—the emotion created by different keys, different chords. Even as a baby—or so my mother told me."

"But you never did anything with it. Why?" She doesn't answer, and he shrugs his own response. "Shit happens, right?"

"Something like that."

He's taking in the fireplace now, looking hard at the photo of Sam and herself in the field behind the house—the picture she rescued from the kitchen drawer that first weekend here. "Your son play?" he asks, finally removing his overcoat and draping it over the back of the couch.

She laughs. "No."

"Not interested, huh?"

"You could say that."

He bends and picks a log from the stack she lugged in earlier, tossing it on the fire, then adds another, larger one. After one or two jabs with the poker, the fire springs to life.

A sudden creak from the floor just above them—Sam's room, Jamie realizes—and Ryan glances up quickly, alarm in his face. "I thought you said no one else was home."

"Actually, that's what you told me."

He stares at her, the poker still suspended, and she laughs—takes her hands through a few preliminary chords. "Relax. It's an old house—shifts and groans constantly. Always has." She pauses. "Ghosts are another possibility, of course."

He replaces the poker without comment and comes to stand behind her, peering over her shoulder at the score of the Chopin. "Funny," he says. "You wouldn't think it was that hard."

"It looks deceptively simple." She withdraws her hands from the keys. "Here, for instance." She flips through the score till she finds the page she wants. "You're probably familiar with the largo section, the *I'm always chasing rainbows* part." She plays a few measures as he stands over her. "This occurs in the middle of the B section—not the key of B, but *ABA* in structure. Key changes here," she says, moving through the transition, "from four sharps to five flats. It's made up of an arpeggio of triplets in the left hand and melody in two or four, plus turns in the right hand. The largo gushes. It's easier to play than the *A* sections. What I like about it is that the tempo is three against four. It's slightly syncopated and often threatens not to come out, but with Chopin it always does. I prefer the *A* sections, though—*Allegro agitato*—because they feel so good. They lay under the hand very naturally—see here?"

Jamie flips pages again, and Ryan leans in closer, flooding her with the warm scent of cloves. She loves to talk music, and it's been a while since she's had the chance. Besides, she tells herself, if pulling him in like this will loosen his tongue, she'll play all night long.

"After the first twelve measures, a second theme starts up. The fourth or fifth finger emphasizes the melody in the sixteenth notes, but the rest of the right hand is busy with an understructure, like this." She begins to play again. "Very difficult, technically, but a great effect. It's always been my favorite part to play."

She's enjoying herself now, despite the recklessness of having him here. Suddenly she wants him to know just how good she is at something he's always wanted to be able to do, so she launches into the piece from the start, adding some extra fire. He says nothing, but moves again to the fireplace, staring into the flames while he listens—arm resting on the mantel mere inches from Sam's smiling face.

Jamie plays on, intoxicated by the music and this odd game they're playing, and transitions smoothly into another Chopin favorite—the *Nocturne in B*—as he makes his way to the kitchen.

"Anything to drink in this house?" he calls as she's finishing the piece. A dull thunk as the refrigerator is opened. "Ah." The pop of a cork, the chink of glassware. "Gotta tell ya, your hostess thing needs some work."

Jamie closes her scores somewhat reluctantly, shuts the piano. When she looks up, he's leaning against the doorjamb, tie loosened—a jelly jar glass of wine in each hand.

"Why are you here, anyway?" she asks—tired, suddenly, now that music has been taken out of the equation, and vaguely disturbed by the casual intimacy, how comfortably settled in he seems. "Shouldn't you be home tucking the kids in or something?"

"Does that mean you won't have a drink with me?" He walks to her and hands her a glass, and she's suddenly pulled into another awkward, large-seeming moment like that at the door—as if they're ticking their way toward some change.

He takes the easy chair where GM spent her evenings reading, not bothering to turn on the floor lamp beside him. "I like your place," he says. "Simple. Peaceful."

"By which you mean dull and unsophisticated," Jamie suggests, returning to the couch.

"My wife is a firm believer in sophisticated. Lots of friends, lots of entertaining. And only the best for the growing pile of kiddies. So fancy is what we do. This is more me," he assures her. He sits silently for a minute—enjoying, she thinks, the pop and hiss of the fire, the tick of the mantel clock. The absence, no doubt, of five children tumbling about. He relaxes into a long stretch, the thick muscles of his arms straining against his shirt as he raises them over his head. He's an enormous, sinewy thing—Herculean in his physicality, though it's more than that. Gregarious and self-assured, his presence simply looms large. A revolving door when it comes to women, she figures.

"Why is it you go all the way to Fairfield to jog?" he asks.

"I told you. I used to live in Southport. I miss running along the water."

"Uh-huh." He sounds unconvinced but doesn't pursue it.

"Why do you drive all the way over here to see a woman you hardly know when you have a house full of them at home?"

He leans out over his knees, clasps his hands. "I'm not sure. I just know each time I drive by and see that ridiculous, crooked little tree in your window, I want to stop and come inside, know your life. You intrigue me."

"What about your wife? She doesn't intrigue you anymore?"

He seems to like the in-your-face tone and grins. "Something happened a few years back that changed things between us. Irrevocably, I'm told. Nothing's been the same since."

The accident, Jamie immediately thinks—surprised once again at his candor and wondering just how far he'll let her go with this, where he'll draw the line. "Couldn't be too irrevocable; she's pregnant."

He couldn't look more stunned if she'd slapped him, but he recovers quickly.

"Oh, we still have sex—even Molly has the occasional need. But we never just have a good hard fuck on the floor, say, or the kitchen table. There's no sport in it at all anymore." Throwing it back at her; the new glint in his eye offering challenge, a dare toward explosive territory.

Crude, but she asked for it. How does Molly handle this feral side of him, she wonders; then wonders further if the woman might simply be burying herself in children; insulating herself against such brutish lapses with a surround of innocence. Has he hurt her then? Is this latest pregnancy the result of some fresh wound? My wife thinks I'm having an affair with you, he told her only days after they met. It seemed a throw-away remark at the time, the kind of icebreaker men often tossed her way. But in this case, it just might be true. And what about Matthew's birth—the year following the accident—same thing? Is this a woman who becomes pregnant each time something rocks her world—an imagined affair, a reckless morning drive that causes the death of a child her own daughter's age? A bit of a stretch, maybe, but close. She's sure of it.

He's still grinning—pleased, it seems, that she likes this sort of game. Arrested development, she decides, married to the natural magnetism of a born predator. Time to back off, keep him at arms length.

"Tell me what you'd be doing if you were home right now," she instructs.

He plays along, though obviously disappointed at the change in topic. "Tucking them all in, probably," he says. "They each have their own little rituals. Margaret—she's nine—she's the reader. She has to have a story. In bed and only with her mother—nobody else." He crosses his legs and leans back into the chair, warming to the subject. "Michael is our philosopher. He and I have to lie down together and talk. He worries about things—big things—political instability, world famine, things like that. No idea how he hears about them, but he's quite up on it all. And family stuff, some little problem he's picked up on between Molly and me."

I'll bet, Jamie thinks.

Ryan kills half his glass in a long gulp. "Meghan and Mia—they're just a year apart—so they share a room. Mia imitates everything Meghan does—big sister, little sister thing, I guess. She'd probably sleep right on top of her if we let her. I keep telling Molly we need to separate them, but she won't hear of it. Anyway, Mia will give Michael and me a few minutes alone, then she comes running in, and the three of us have this huggy, powwow thing."

"A snuggle," Jamie corrects, needing him to get it right. "It's called a snuggle."

He looks at her oddly for a moment. "Okay," he says, his tone almost kind. "A snuggle." He drinks off more of the wine. "Matthew's going through the night terror thing right now and insists on sleeping with us. Can't wait for that to end, I don't mind telling you."

Sam had just entered that stage when she lost him, Jamie remembers now—for the first time in his young life perceiving the world as the indifferent, terrifying unknown that it is. When she was really down, sucked deep into the ugly, dark maw of her loss, she imagines that in the second or two between their slide from the road and their impact with the tree, he felt abandoned to this reality.

"And Meghan?" she asks, veering from the pain. She envisions the girl with the dark chocolate curls who flaps her hands at the sky, the girl who will forever be Sam's age. "You skipped Meghan."

He finishes the wine in a long quaff, watching her over the rim of the glass. "Meghan," he says, rising and moving to the couch, "puts all her dolls and stuffed animals to sleep on the floor, covering them with blankets from head to toe like tiny corpses. It's a bit creepy, actually."

He looks at her expectantly, then, and there's a shift in the atmosphere—the very air seeming to grow thicker. Okay, I've played your game, he seems to be saying. Time to get past this talk of children, of things domestic. We both know how this is going to end.

Another creak of the floorboards just above them draws his gaze rather uncomfortably toward the ceiling. Jamie stands.

"I need to get back to the piano," she says, moving toward the hall. "And I'm sure Michael's waiting for his chat."

He gazes at her for a long moment, then stands and shrugs himself into his overcoat. He's silent until he reaches the porch, where he rests his back against a post, his eyes drilling into her. "Your husband doesn't live here with you." A statement.

"Doesn't he?"

But Ryan isn't having any. "Your son either. No food in the fridge, no toys spread around. Kind of obvious, Diana." He peers off into the dark. "My take? You're separated or divorced, your kid lives with his father for some reason." He turns to look at her again. "Maybe, like me, you find family life a little, well, stifling."

The arrogant ass. Reminding herself of the things she wants from him—an apology at the very least, her growing need for the truth—she merely shrugs. "Why did you follow me, anyway?"

"Why did you let me in?"

"I'm not sure."

He considers her words. "When will I see you?"

The guy's nothing if not direct. "I'm going out of town for a while."

He nods, his eyes searching her face. "Don't be gone too long."

She steps inside then and shuts the door before he can move to kiss her—certain he was about to try.

TEN

Traffic heading south stops dead just north of the Connecticut line—four lanes of Friday afternoon gridlock made worse by some kind of lane restriction up ahead.

"Damn," she mutters, knowing that if she'd left midmorning as planned, she'd be at the house by now. "Damn." She hurls this one toward Peter—responsible for the morning's late and decidedly ugly start, for the day's getting away from her.

An aging station wagon and a dented red pickup jockey for position, working together to squeeze out a Lexus merging into the right lane. There's a sudden flaring of egos—the blare of horns, aggressive finger gestures. She tries the radio, hoping for some classical music, a call-in show to concentrate on, anything to take her mind off the argument that has killed her enthusiasm for this trip, but shuts it off again almost immediately—too distracted, too rattled to focus on anything.

So stupid, telling Peter about the dream. Wouldn't have happened at all if her guard hadn't been down—that part of her that knew just how much to keep to herself still half asleep. She'd been upset, she reminds herself, crying out—her waking like a drowning, choking on tears. No way to keep that from Peter.

In the dream, she sits at the Chickering, the flowing triplets of Debussy's *First Arabesque* pouring from her fingers to the piano and back again into her soul, the melody building higher and higher in the in the bright, surreal light of late afternoon. The room seeming almost to breathe through sheer curtains billowing in the soft breeze of windows thrown wide; the tick, tick, tick of the mantel clock growing louder in air already thick with excitement, anticipation—as if something all-consuming were moving inexorably toward her.

And there was Sam, her beautiful Sam, as gloriously whole and real as ever he was in life—rapturous, transported, spinning round and round in the middle of the room before the high flames of the fire—laughing, laughing, laughing. And the old harpy—recast in death as a mere, subtle heightening of the unnatural light—floating above her, hovering like a bird on breezy currents of music.

She leans harder into the melody—stretching into the tempo rubato, then a repeat of the initial arpeggios—the individual frissons of energy exploding in her mind, her heart, her fingers. In the zone now. The music flowing faster and faster—racing as if toward something—Sam's frenzied whirling matched by the growing ferocity of the flames. A subtle shift in atmosphere, then—a sense of something wafting toward them through the open window, and Sam breaks off—the spell falling away as he runs giggling into the hall to tug at the door. Speaking—his voice just as she remembered, traveling back to her in a sweetly melodic rondo, a chant of pure jubilation. "Daddy! Daddy! Daddy!"

She's behind him then, even as she gazes back and sees herself at the piano, and when she turns again to the door, it's flung wide. Before them stands a man, briefcase in hand, his bulk filling the doorway—backlit by sun so bright she's blinded to his features. But it doesn't matter. Her heart knows him. He's home now, and she feels suddenly, astonishingly happy. Then he steps in, out of the light.

Michael Ryan.

Her choked sob had startled Peter awake, and he'd instinctively folded her in his arms—hushing her as they fought their way up from sleep, the tick, tick, tick of freezing rain hitting the tarp above the deck. "Shh, Jae—shh, shh," he'd crooned.

Laying against him, then—shaken and mortified at how deeply aroused the dream had left her. More than aroused—electrified. "Jesus," she'd murmured, hands covering her face.

"It's okay," Peter mumbled. "Just a dream." He kissed her head, and she felt him relaxing back toward sleep, his arms still wound around her as she began pulling away, moving off to recapture the musical sound of Sam's voice.

"No—stay," he said rubbing her back lazily. "Tell me."

The haze of her dream receded with the sound of his voice and she was filled, suddenly, with an inexplicable resentment toward this man—for loving her, for pulling her into his life, when all she wanted was the bliss of being mother to her son, to return to her sleepy vision of a boy still vibrantly alive. Here, awake and with Peter beside her, he was simply dead in his grave.

Arm draped over her eyes against the dawning light, she felt the music winding down, the buzz of it slow to leave her, and she grudgingly deferred to the woody smell of the cabin, the sound of water gently lapping the hull.

"It was Sam," she said, her voice still hoarse with sleep. "He was so happy, so alive. I was at the piano."

He swallowed, cleared his throat—the response so very Peter. "What were you playing?"

"Chopin. The *Fantaisie.*" A split second of recognition, deja vu. "I've had this dream before, I think—more than once."

At the sound of their voices, the familiar, sinewy knot of kitten uncurled at her feet—stretching, rising, making his way through the lumpy valley separating their bodies to resettle in the tiny hammock of blanket between them. Jamie ran a finger across his silky back, the gentle purr thrumming through the covers in response.

"Hum it for me," Peter said. "The Chopin."

And so she'd played the game, choosing part of the Largo section—right away making the connection with Ryan's visit to the house, their hovering over the music together. Relief flooding her at this obvious explanation for his presence in the dream.

"Oh, yeah," Peter yawned. "I like that one. Funny, though, your dreaming about the piano again after all this time."

"Not really," she told him. "I've been working on that piece a lot lately."

"You're playing again?" He was suddenly very awake. "Where?"

"At the house." Glancing quickly at his face, then—realizing too late what she'd done. "My Chickering's still there, after all," she said, scrambling. "Seems silly just to let it sit."

He'd propped himself on his elbow then—alarm in his face, in his voice. "You've been playing all these months and never said anything?"

"Why are you angry? You're always telling me I should relax more. The piano helps me unwind, gives me something to do at night."

"Jae—you're playing again." Enunciating each word, as if she were slow to get the point. "This is huge for you—you know it is—and you didn't say anything? Think about that."

He was right of course; the piano had loomed large in her life since childhood, a source of comfort in even the worst of times— the loss of her parents, Philippe's leaving her. The greater the pain, the more she'd played—pouring her anguish out, releasing it into the fluid depths of the music. It took a loss too great to expel to stop this flow, kill her desire to play. But this echo of her past was hers alone; it had nothing to do with her life here with Peter, where the focus was boats, dogs, the choice of wine for dinner. She looked up, willing him to understand all this, but the silence had grown heavy, carried some question she'd missed.

"I'm sorry. What did you say?"

"Have you put the house on the market yet?" he asked again, his tone impatient, demanding. "That was one of the reasons you decided to make all these trips back and forth, remember? To fix up the house and sell it?"

"I'm not ready to do that yet."

"You're not ready, or the house isn't ready?"

"Both." It was all connected, of course—playing the piano again, being at the house. But then that, she supposed, was his point.

He considered a minute, the scientist in him slow to let emotion seep into his reasoning. "You know, I've accepted the fact you don't want kids—that opening your heart to another child is something you just can't face. I don't like it, but I can understand it. I mean that, at least, makes sense. But this, this is..." He shook his head, crawled from the bunk and began pulling clothes on, as if he couldn't wait to get to work and throw himself into another bracing day of petri dishes and the dissection of bi-valves.

Obsession was the word he wanted, she knew—a word he's been careful not to use since the miserable, gut-wrenching fight that followed their disastrous visit to a support group for grieving parents a few months after they were married. Still, it hovered between them, the air all but crackling with it as he brought everything round to that night again—her unwillingness to sit through even one meeting, her refusal to try going back—tying it somehow to the growing secretiveness he felt in her. Evidence the piano. Any rebuttals had long since grown stale, even to her.

He zipped his jeans, buckled the belt. "You know, when you first brought this whole thing up—the job in New York, getting the house ready to sell—I thought, hey, this might be a good thing. Help you finally finish with all this. But it hasn't. You come home from these weekends exhausted, withdrawn; you have these nightmares. This isn't good for you. It isn't good for us. It has to stop."

Easy for him to say—this man who's not yet lost anything he loved to the blind randomness of life. How could he know what the house, furnished as it was with memories of GM and Sam, meant to her now? What would he say if she told him something of Sam still survived—a faint wavering presence in the atmosphere of the house itself, so subtle and tenuous that the mere mention of it might be enough to drive it off?

He looked away. "Do you know you've never once in all this time talked about this job in New York, or what you do at that house at night?"

"Well, now you know; I play the piano." She sighed. "Peter, this is ridiculous. We talk almost every day when I'm gone. Besides, you'll see it for yourself this weekend. Then you'll understand."

It was Augie who first suggested Peter accompany her to Saturday night's Valentine Gala—the five-hundred-dollar-a-head cocktail party and long-awaited unveiling of the new Steinway grand Michael Ryan had purchased for the Symphony. Jamie stalled for weeks, certain the Ryans would be there basking in all the gratitude. It wasn't until Augie assured her that he'd already declined—pleading, interestingly enough, his wife's difficult pregnancy—that Jamie agreed to attend. She'd been looking forward to a night in the city—dinner with Augie and Gaspar, the chance to introduce Peter to her colleagues and some of New York's social glitterati. It would be a quick trip—down for the night and back the next day, with a perfunctory stop at the house to satisfy Peter's curiosity. The chance of running into Michael Ryan all but nil.

"Well, things have changed," Peter informed her, his face tight.

Her heart dropped. No, she wanted to plead—come with me. Help me prove to everyone I'm all right now, that I'm happy.

"Glenn called last night after you went to bed," he told her. "The mussels are dropping off the seeding sock for some reason—parasite, probably. We're going to have to pull them this weekend, figure out what's going on before we lose the whole crop. So you're on your own, which is how you seem to like it, anyway."

This last, hurtful, swipe so unlike him. He just needs time, Jamie tells herself as the cars continue to inch forward. A few days alone and he'll come around.

☙ ❧

The room is almost exactly as she remembers—elegant, imposing, designed to heighten the feeling of exclusivity that major donors expect. The new brocade drapes framing the foyer's floor-to-ceiling windows are a nice touch; she likes the way the multitude of crystal chandeliers set off the phosphorescent shimmer of the material, spinning it into a room already ablaze with the glint of diamonds, the sparkle of beaded gowns, the ebony sheen of the new Steinway on the raised dais before her.

She isn't there five minutes, has managed only a quick wave to a harried looking Augie, before she's set upon by John Cohen— retired psychotherapist and octogenarian trustee whose tenure on the board predates her years as development director. As energetic as he is pedantic, he takes immediate command of her, procuring the requisite flutes of champagne as he steers her to a spot beside the piano. He wants first shot at her, it turns out—the chance to get her behind the proposed four-million-dollar capital campaign he's been pushing for.

"The board is close to giving its go-ahead," he assures her, voice raised against the swell of conversation, the four bored-looking musicians launching into an early Beethoven quartet. "But we need to know you're onboard for the duration." He leans in.

"Frankly, no one feels Debra Budlow has the horsepower for something like this. It requires someone with your contacts, your determination."

She smiles fondly at the diminutive man whose shining bald pate and trademark red bow tie offer welcome relief in a room of thousand-dollar tuxedos and designer gowns. Her staunchest supporter from the first, he could always be counted on to back her proposals when others on the contentious board found them too new, too risky. Funding the Steinway was another of his longstanding pet projects, and though they now stand mere feet from the spoils of that hard-fought campaign, he all but ignores its presence. Things accomplished, checked off his list, no longer occupied his thoughts.

It's a good sell, but Jamie already knows from Augie that any movement on the subject of a capital campaign is still years away. She smiles, nods, and begins trolling the wafting intellectual currents for anything pertinent—easy to do in a room this packed.

She catches the crackle of an inward draw of cigarette behind her, the rasp of a husky female voice. "I should think you'd be ecstatic." A quick exhale of smoke. "After all, Steinway is the best, is it not?"

A derisive snort, then, followed by an even haughtier British accent—Colin Bradbury, whose years on the board have been a lesson in micro-management for everyone. "Of course I know the reputation of the Steinway. What I'm telling you is the London Philharmonic prefers Bösendorfers. You draw your own conclusion."

Ridiculous, Jamie thinks, glancing again at the piano—its gleaming top open to the second position, the stick swung up in concert mode as if waiting for someone to take the bench, make it come alive. She knows firsthand the big tone, the tightly focused notes. The looser action of the Bösendorfer doesn't even come close.

Eyes working the room again, she manages to catch sight of Augie—signaling her urgently from amid a gaggle of garden society types. Grateful for any excuse to avoid the pompous Colin, Jamie takes firm hold of John's arm, smiling warmly as she picks up their conversation, and moves off chatting with him as they make their way toward her through the crowd—both of them focusing their attention on the floor to avoid being drawn into other conversations. It's a tactic they've used many times in years past—much to their mutual benefit—and it's comforting, somehow, to resume the association.

"My dear!" Colin has managed to follow their zigzag route after all, and rocks his rotund bulk toward her in a half bow—a flute of champagne clutched in one pudgy fist, a half-empty plate of hors d'oeuvres in the other. "Bloody marvelous, your being back. As usual, John has managed to snag you first."

"Afraid you've got it wrong, Bradbury. It's Jamie who's been steering me about the room while she holds court. Keeps the other men off her, you see."

"And no wonder." Colin leans in, buzzes both cheeks. "My God, but you look stunning." He plows on, offering her no chance to respond. "Augie tells us you've remarried. That'll put the bloom back in the cheeks, eh? Put all that horrid business with poor Philippe behind you? Fabulous. Any little ones yet?"

The flush is on her suddenly, triggering an almost desperate need to flee. John glares openly at the slip. Dear John.

"Well, you're young yet," Colin says. "Plenty of time for all that."

"For God sake, Bradbury," John hisses—turning to Jamie in a blatant dismissal of the man. "Augie is waiting, is she not?"

With that, they head off—Colin still somewhat in tow. Jamie's scanning the room for Augie's tousle of gray curls when John nudges her, nodding once in the direction of an angry-looking Adam Zorn—Debra Budlow standing flushed and awkward beside him. Is this what Augie wanted so desperately for her to notice? Their world-famous conductor being set upon by a fledgling development director?

Relief floods Adam's face as they approach, and he's quick to wander off with John and Colin toward the Steinway, leaving Jamie to deal with whatever damage Debra's done.

"What's happened? Adam looks absolutely furious."

Debra has regained enough of her composure to affect the defensive tone she's recently adopted with Jamie. "Nothing, " she snaps. "I merely suggested he think about bringing in a group like the Moody Blues for a crossover concert."

Jamie's incredulous stare brings an even deeper blush, a flash of defiance. She leans close. " Piece of advice, okay? Never suggest programming to the conductor. Putting aside the fact he's won two Grammy Awards and knows far more about music than you or I could ever hope to, he can have you fired at will. And he just may."

She turns away, then, leaving Debra to navigate this sea of competing egos on her own, and that's when she sees him. Ryan is flat-out gorgeous in an expertly tailored black tux—the thick curly hair, always just a bit too long; the full lips; the laughing eyes all marking him as an only marginally civilized bad boy.

Something dark and visceral moves through her at the sight of him, freezing her in place. She finally thinks to breathe, sucks in a breath and turns back toward Debra, who's spotted him herself now—seems actually to be trying to draw him with her eyes. Christ—where to go? Jamie looks desperately for John—even Colin to head toward before Ryan spots her, if he hasn't already, but the press of bodies is all but impenetrable. Besides, the look on Debra's face tells her it's already too late—Ryan's approach obvious in the color rising again to her cheeks. Nothing to do now but turn, pray the woman is too self-absorbed, too territorial to even consider a proper introduction.

If he's surprised to see Jamie here, he doesn't show it, his eyes simply registering approval of the sleeveless black sheath slit to mid-thigh, the double strand of pearls and matching earrings. He dips his head in a mock bow, then turns to Debra. "Ms. Budlow."

Debra leans into him almost possessively, her defensiveness replaced for the moment with an odd look of triumph, as if she's reeled this one in on her own—these exorbitant gifts of his the result of her efforts. Turning to Jamie, she says simply, "Michael is the one who donated the piano."

Jamie murmurs something innocuous and attempts to excuse herself, the woman's ill-mannered style a blessing for once. She's almost past Ryan when he takes her elbow, shooting Debra an apologetic smile.

"You'll excuse us, won't you? Pressing business."

Heart slamming in her chest, Jamie allows herself to be drawn away, guided toward the far side of the room, where the crowd has begun spilling into Symphony Hall itself—a surreal feeling settling on her as she glances back toward the Steinway. Only then does she finally catch sight of Augie. Their eyes meet for just a moment, Augie's earlier urgency—a warning, Jamie realizes now—replaced by a deflated look of apology. Not to worry, Jamie lies with her smile; everything is under control.

"You're certainly full of surprises," Ryan says under his breath—grinning and nodding as they make their way through the throng. "You never mentioned you were part of our little group— not that I'm complaining, you understand."

"I seem to remember telling you I consult for orchestras, Mr. Ryan." Her heart is beating so fast, she can feel its pulse in her neck, her temples. Still, she manages a playful tone. "The real question is what a lawyer from Connecticut is doing donating so outrageously to us when there are so many deserving orchestras in your own state—nineteen at last count, I believe."

They pause while he swaps their empty champagne flutes for

full ones offered by a passing waiter. The string quartet, tiring of the sedate, has switched to something edgier—Paganini? She's so rattled she isn't sure.

"Well," he says, retaking her elbow and steering her toward a quiet spot by one of the windows, "my usual response is that orchestral music represents some of history's most beloved cultural myths. I then go on to say that I feel somehow obligated to help keep those myths alive."

"How noble. But we both know that isn't the real reason."

He shrugs and drains most of his flute in one long sip. "There are others." Stepping very close, then—eyes resting on the pearls nested deep in her cleavage. "What is it about you?" he asks, tracing her bare collarbone with the damp lip of his glass. "You keep disappearing, then popping up again where I least expect you. Let's get out of here, go for a real drink, dinner—anything. Maybe you can explain why I can't stop thinking about you."

"You're babbling," she teases, fighting the pleasure the compliment gives her—the fight with Peter, his refusal to return any of her calls over the last day and a half having left her shaky and blue, oddly open to flirtation. Even with a man she loathes, maybe especially with him. Leaving quietly together might actually be a good idea, she thinks—get out of here now, before he finds out who she really is. Easy enough to shake him later.

The empty flute has come to rest on the pulsing vein in her neck. "You're quite nervous, " he says softly, then grins at her surprised response. "I make my living by being observant," he reminds her. "All those years in the courtroom."

"Ah, there you are, Ryan." Colin effuses, approaching with John. "You've met the star of our development team, then?"

"Not formally, no," Ryan says. "Though we've run into each other on several occasions."

Colin takes this as an invitation to introduction, jumping in before Jamie can think of a way to save herself. "Jamie, allow me present Mr. Michael Ryan—donor of the Steinway, among other outrageously generous gifts. Mr. Ryan, Ms. Jamie Lloyd."

Shit, shit, shit.

"Jamie was with us as development director until just a few years ago," John explains. "We've been lucky enough to retain her as a consultant. She's working with Debra Budlow, whom I believe you've already met."

Jamie follows the subtle changes in Ryan's expression as he works it all out—the name, the job, the timing—furious with herself for coming tonight, taking this risk. Of course he'd be here; he's the star of the show, after all. You couldn't pay him to stay away.

"Jamie's husband," John continues, "is Dr. Peter Apollo—a marine biologist affiliated with the University of New Hampshire. Quite the name in scientific circles, from what I understand."

Ryan nods a mild interest—careful not to meet Jamie's eyes—and tosses back the dregs of the champagne.

"Researches little bugs in fish or something, isn't it, Jamie?" Colin quips.

"Shellfish contaminants," Jamie corrects, affecting a light tone she doesn't feel—determined to keep her almost desperate disappointment to herself. Over. All over now.

"He's here this evening—your husband?" Ryan asks, looking around as if to spot him.

"Unfortunately, no," Jamie says. "Business kept him away. And your wife? We heard she was unwell."

"More unnerved than unwell, I think," he says, addressing John and Colin—as if he still doesn't trust himself to look at her. "She heard someone outside our living room window last night; it spooked her."

"How odd," John says. "A burglar, do you think?"

"More likely a peeping Tom. He took off through the woods when I went out to confront him. I doubt he'll be back."

"Listen, old man," Colin says, taking Ryan's arm in his pudgy fist—a chummy gesture he clearly dislikes, "I hate to drag you off like this, but the maestro has been asking for you. Seems he wants to thank you personally for that obscenely expensive piano. Look for me a bit later on, will you, Jamie?" he adds, heading off. "I want to discuss the audience-building model you submitted to the board. Wonderful work, by the way."

ELEVEN

Jamie fills most of Sunday morning working through the hurdles of the Chopin *B flat Minor Sonata,* waiting for Michael Ryan to show up. He has to confront her now, she knows; pride alone demands it. She's as certain of this as she is that she was fated to go to last night's gala alone; that Ryan would be there; that he'd find her out.

Slipping away had been easy enough once Colin dragged him off to find Adam, but it was hours before the adrenaline rush faded—before self-reproach dulled to disappointment and by morning, resignation. Their game, fruitless as it had been, over too soon; any truth buried in all that research on the Porter Street houses useless to her now.

She takes a break from the intricacies of the Chopin for the comfort of Bach and the solid little *Fugue in G minor*—making her way through the familiar piece in a state of almost preternatural calm. A part of her glad he knows, proud to have made a fool of him and his desire for her. Willing to wait all day and into the night for the chance to say the things she's wanted to tell him all along. And why not? No reason to rush back to New Hampshire, certainly. Peter's continued silence—so maddening yesterday—

seems almost providential now. She doesn't need his presence, even psychologically, in the middle of all this.

It's after three when Ryan finally turns up—striding past her into the living room without comment, unceremoniously tossing her bandanna onto the coffee table. "Yours, I believe." Face tight with anger as he looks her over. "You want to tell me what the fuck you were doing outside my living room window?"

She stares at the familiar material, grown strangely alien in his possession of it. An impulsive thing, going there—creeping around hoping for a glimpse of the wife, the children. The bandanna must have slipped from her pocket while she was backing away from the house, the dog having belatedly begun to bark.

She shoots him a defiant look charged with three long years of bitter resentment. For a smart guy, he really was awfully dumb.

"Hope you got your money's worth, at least." A sarcastic smile as he unbuttons his overcoat. "Best part was Molly's little tantrum, don't you think? One of her better ones, frankly—though I could have done without the Scotch tossed in my face. Bit overdone, I thought."

But effective. Drawn to the warm light pouring through a window, her approach muffled by snow cover, Jamie had surprised herself in coming almost face to face with the Ryans. Molly's petite, girlish figure was a surprise, but the red hair, the flashing, angry eyes as she paced before the dying fire some twenty feet away were not. No sign of the pregnancy beneath her beaded black gown, but then she probably wasn't yet four months along.

They'd been at it for awhile, from the look of it—a weary-looking Ryan weathering the tirade in one of two silk-covered wing chairs—tie loosened, fingers massaging his temple against Molly's agitated pacing, her anger-choked words. Jamie had to strain to follow the conversation—hard enough through the insulated glass of the window, all but impossible when Molly turned away.

"My God, Michael!" Turning away again. "————so humiliating! ————through this before————behind us!"

Her frustration felt oddly familiar—the indignation reminding Jamie quite suddenly of the fights she and Philippe began having when she, herself, was pregnant.

Ryan growled something indecipherable as he reached toward the coffee table for his snifter, but Molly was quicker, grabbing the drink and tossing it in his face—his shock, his mocking grin infuriating her all the more.

It was then Jamie picked them out—the two girls, limp and white-faced in the shadowy stairwell—one of them Meghan, the other almost certainly Mia. Shrinking away from their pain and confusion, she'd slipped away unnoticed—or so she'd thought.

"You showed up at my house first, if you remember," she reminds Ryan now, her voice laced with contempt. The thought of hurting him with mention of the girls is tempting, but betraying them leaves her strangely uneasy.

"How did you know I'd fall for it? That's what I don't understand." Hands jammed hard in the pockets of his overcoat, he paces a few steps, stops; paces, stops. A sarcastic tinge to his chuckle. "You must have had a good laugh last night, huh? There I was, gushing like some high school kid about how beautiful you looked, how good it was to see you. All I could think about was how to get you out of there and alone somewhere with me." He shakes his head in mock shame. "The things I've dreamed of doing to you, Diana. Not even your real name. Christ."

She perches on the worn arm of GM's easy chair and studies him—sensing danger in his mood and hardly caring. His humiliation like salve on a wound.

"It explains so much," he says sitting. "The way you disappear all the time, the long stretches when no one seems to live here. God, I've been haunting this place like a ghost, just hoping for a glimpse of you. I was half convinced you really were some mythical creature, sent here to taunt me."

Something seems to occur to him then. "Your husband never comes down here with you, does he?" He looks around, as if seeing the room for the first time. "This is where you were living then—you and that grandmother of yours, the boy. I remember now. No wonder the guy wants nothing to do with the place. Jesus."

He sits back, hands still jammed in the pockets of his coat—more comfortable now that he's getting a handle on it all. "So, what, you've been sitting up there in—wherever it is you live—planning how you'd come back and fuck with my head; is that it? Why now, after all this time?"

"There are things I want to know," she tells him.

He snorts a laugh. "And you're just now thinking of them? Like what?"

This isn't how it's supposed to go. She wants him furious, wants him to rant, to threaten her, demand she stay away from his family. Instead, he seems embarrassed at having been duped, hurt by the deception, maybe—but hardly wild with anger. Thrown by his cooperation, she hurls the first accusation that comes to mind.

"You never even bothered coming to the hearing—as if it didn't matter, had nothing to do with you. Were you that sure of yourself?" Confronting him, finally getting the words out, makes her strangely breathless—as if these thoughts have been too long inside her, have adhered somehow to the workings of her heart. It's a stupid question, of course; she knows this even without the amused disbelief registering on Ryan's face. *Think!* she tells herself, and then she remembers, sees it as a possible way in. A long shot, but worth a try. "Where were you coming from that morning?"

"What morning?"

"The morning you killed my son," she spits, forcing the words again.

"You're crazy," he laughs.

"You had to be in some kind of panic, the way you shot out in front of me like that. I want to know why." It won't bring Sam back, of course, but somewhere in all this is the reason he's no longer in the world and by God, she'll know it.

Ryan studies her for a long moment. "You have no idea what you're talking about," he says quietly. "Believe me, you don't want to get into this."

"Oh, believe me, I do," she mimics—her eyes blazing as he stands and walks past her into the kitchen. The sound of the cupboard, then; the refrigerator door; the pop of a cork.

He returns with two glasses cupped in one hand, a half bottle of white wine in the other. "It seems we have a situation." Standing over her, he pours first one glass then the other. "You want some things from me," he says, holding a glass out to her, "and I find I still want many things from you."

"You're incredible," she sneers, amazed he could continue this ridiculous pursuit of her now. "Knowing who I am doesn't bother you at all, does it?" And somehow she knows it's true; the inherent danger of the situation fascinates him. "You murdered my son and ruined my life, Mr. Ryan," she manages evenly, feeling betrayed by the flush of outrage creeping into her cheeks. "Even if you were as charming as you think you are, you would still disgust me." This last so vehement even she is surprised.

Something flickers behind his eyes. "Somehow, I don't think so." That appraising look again. "So this is what we do. We trade—a kind of quid pro quo. You want something, you give something in return. And vice versa, of course."

She laughs—incredulous at the suggestion, its lewd implications. Still, unbelievably, part of her is listening—recognizing this as perhaps her only chance to get at the truth. It might just be worth playing his little game, assuming she can set some basic ground rules. No guarantee he'll be honest with her, but she'll take the chance. "I won't sleep with you," she tells him flatly.

"Understood."

I'll bet, she thinks, but lets it go—reaching instead for the proffered glass in a tacit sealing of their bargain.

He removes his overcoat, tosses it across the back of the couch. "Okay," he says, sitting. "Shoot."

Jamie sinks into the reassuring embrace of GM's chair, the past three years of anguish, of what-ifs, distilled into this one moment, this one shot. Fighting the urge to rage at him for what he's cost her, she repeats her question—her voice stronger this time.

"Where were you coming from when you ran me off the road?"

He drains nearly half his glass before responding. "Just for the record, I didn't run you off the road; you hit a patch of ice and skidded into a tree—such was the judgment of the court, if you remember. Nevertheless, the answer to that will cost you. Ten minutes here on the couch. No touching, but I can say anything I want to you, be as explicit as I wish."

Jamie shifts uneasily, her anger rising. "We've covered this ground already, Mr. Ryan."

"Not really. There's quite a difference between eroticism and actual sex, Diana—something I have a feeling you're very well aware of."

He's baiting her, of course. And why that name, now he knows who she really is? "I'll pass, thanks."

"Okay, then, I have a question for you." He takes his time over another long quaff of the wine. "Did you know who I was the morning we met?"

Now it's her turn to set the terms for providing an answer. She thinks suddenly of the sad little houses on Porter street. It would merely be another way of asking her initial question, of course, but he might not realize she's made the connection or figure she can't do anything with the information, anyway. "If you tell me who you know on Porter Street."

He doesn't hesitate to nod his assent, willing to give up this apparently useless bit of information to learn if she actually sought him out, came looking for him.

"No," she answers truthfully. "I didn't know who you were." No need to elaborate—to tell him she found him through Symphony records, that she was already quite familiar with his house, the three car garage, the swing set in the backyard, before he appeared that morning and so conveniently introduced himself. She can see he's skeptical; it's too much of a coincidence, of course—her running by his house just as he was walking the dog. Well, let him draw his own conclusions.

"I had a client for some time who lived on Porter Street," he says—making good on his part of the deal without being asked, but, like her, not offering anything more than was absolutely necessary. And the answer made a certain amount of sense—as far as it went. But why meet with a client so early in the morning, and all the way out there?

This isn't getting her anywhere. Besides, he makes his living at this kind of intellectual sparring. How can she possibly hope to beat him at this game?

Ryan sips his wine while he waits for her next question, ignoring the sudden, muffled notes of his cell phone from somewhere in the folds of his overcoat. It's a tinny version of Rossini's *William Tell Overture*—silly, ridiculous sounding, but it gives Jamie sudden inspiration.

"You were on your phone when you cut me off that morning, Mr. Ryan," she reminds him. "Who were you calling?"

He waits out the music before responding. "You know," he says, sounding mildly irritated as he reaches back to dig out the phone. "This Mr. Ryan thing isn't working for me. I mean, considering everything we've been through together, don't you think it's time you began calling me Michael?"

The price for answering her question, she realizes. Simple enough. "All right, then."

"I was calling my attorney," he says, scowling as he reads the incoming number, then tucking the phone away again.

"Your lawyer? At seven in the morning?"

He reaches over and tops off her glass, though she's only managed a sip or two, then refills his own—concentrating on the pour each time, the final twist of the bottle expertly done. "You're implying another question, Diana," he says softly, his eyes only then rising to meet hers. "I don't mind going out of turn, here— but what is it you're offering in exchange?"

This time she doesn't flinch at the over familiar tone—panicked, suddenly, that he might be about to leave. She has to turn it around somehow, get him to react on a gut level. "I'll tell you why you make all these ridiculous donations to the Symphony," she says, unable to think of any other response.

Another amused look. "Please."

"It's obvious, really. Outwardly, it makes you look generous. For most people that would be enough—that and the gratitude, the adoration. But not you. You think throwing money at the Symphony gets you off the hook for what you did. Some kind of payoff to ease your conscience—assuming you have one."

"Guilt, huh?"

"Absolutely."

"You're incredibly cynical. I'm disappointed."

"It's not something I expect you'd understand. Your family is still whole, after all."

He nods. "Interesting concept, guilt—something I deal with every day, as I'm sure you can imagine. Not to be insensitive here, but since you brought it up, what about your own?"

"My what?"

"Your kid was in the front seat of the car, Diana." A pointed look. "Just a thought." He downs the last of his wine. "Well, it's been fun," he says, pulling his coat from the top of the couch, "but something's come up. We'll have to continue this fascinating exchange another time."

This is it, then: the end of everything. "That's hardly necessary," she says coldly, out of ideas now. And confused, strangely rattled by his comments. How dare he?

"Well none of this really is, is it? Humor me. After all, it is my turn to make a request."

Is it? With all this jockeying for position, she's lost track. "I'm leaving tonight," she says, having just at that moment decided to head home and make things right with Peter, whose steadiness and predictability suddenly seem very appealing.

"Next time you're down," Ryan says, shrugging into the coat. "A month from now, I've been told. We'll have dinner, continue our—what shall we call them—negotiations?"

Jamie grows still. Is it possible Augie has given him her schedule? No, she decides. Not in a million years.

The smile is warm, understanding of her confusion. "Colin Bradbury is a pompous ass, but he's incredibly forthcoming when it comes to you. According to him, you drive down once a month and spend a few days breathing life back into our flagging development team, regardless of how Debra Budlow might feel about it. She has none of your style, by the way. Worse—she knows it. I'd watch out for her, if I were you."

"How good of Colin to be so accommodating," Jamie says acidly, following him to the hall.

"He also told me you left your job here quite suddenly, citing personal reasons—he did have the good taste not to go into those—and that he secretly lusts after you in his heart." Ryan smiles at this—something about it striking him funny. "So," he says. "Dinner here, next time."

She calculates quickly, weighing a creeping sense of vulnerability against the desperate hope for truth. What could possibly be gained by exposing herself to him like this again? He'll never admit fault, not without some pressing reason to do so. Still.

"You bring the food," she tells him—knowing full well, as she reaches for the door, that absolutely nothing about this is a good idea.

"Fine," he agrees. "But get some decent wine, will you? Something red—French, preferably."

She says nothing further as she pulls the door open, surprised to see it's begun to snow. Sliding his hand over hers, Ryan closes it again softly. "Say my name," he instructs, his voice nothing more than a whisper. His hand is cool, dry; she can feel the throb of his pulse.

She hesitates, considering the tradeoff. That was it, then. In spite of all his training, the careful strategizing and tiptoeing through discourse, he's still a man, and he still wants her. That's how she'll win.

"Michael," she says simply and with little inflection—the new intimacy coppery tasting and unpleasant in her mouth.

A look of triumph in his eyes.

She smiles up at him, then—this hunter, this slayer of dreams. Fool, she thinks. I have you now.

TWELVE

Coils of sea smoke rise from the water, rolling toward her as she makes her way down the poorly lit dock—Bake's deep, hoarse-sounding laughter cutting the eerie gloom. His almost constant presence since the breakup with Lori has been getting to Jamie lately, but she's grateful for the company tonight—glad for the buffer between Peter and herself.

Closer now, she spies the homemade grill strapped to the stern—smoke shooting from the edges of its locked-down top, the sizzle and pop of fat hitting coals. Ribs, she thinks, stomach rumbling as she climbs aboard, ducks into the moon room. The CD is one she hasn't heard—something jazzy with a violin, punctuated with more laughter from below. Bake's growl of a voice mixing with that of an unfamiliar woman—one who's seen the inside of too many smoke-filled bars, by the sound of it. Gone forever, it feels like, and life here hasn't missed a beat without her.

Peter's back is to the companionway—the old, grease-spattered *Thrill of the Grill* splayed open across the narrow sink. Dirty rice, she thinks; his special two-day cole slaw waiting in the fridge, no doubt.

Dropping her duffel on the cockpit floor is enough to signal the dogs, who scramble off the aft cabin bunk in whines of welcome. Jamie perches on the top step and peers down into the warm, softly lit cabin. "Last time you forgot the cayenne."

"I didn't forget; we were out," Peter says, only half turning to her. His tone is relaxed, matter-of-fact—no hint of the tightly controlled anger that peppered their last conversation.

"You need me to run?"

"No, Bake brought some."

"Jay-meeee!" Bake greets her with a warm bonhomie, extending his arm in a hail-fellow-well-met gesture, a glass of dark rum clutched in his hand. Jamie spies a flousy bloom of red hair beyond him on the settee, the face beneath it buried in one of Peter's old copies of *Bon Appetit*. Stocky build, tight jeans, red plaid shirt.

"Jay-meeee!" Bake repeats almost languidly. He looks happy, relaxed—a different man than the Bake of just a week ago.

She can't help grinning back. "Evening, Nicholai," she says, adopting the formal tone.

The magazine drops abruptly, revealing a ruddy, chapped-looking face; the woman's incredulous cackle less laugh than bark. "Nicholai?"

Descending into the warmth of the saloon, Jamie deposits her duffel in the aft cabin, greets the dogs, touches Peter's shoulder lightly. "Hey, there."

"Hey," he says, turning away to rummage in the fridge. No smile, no kiss hello, though she'd have welcomed it.

"Enough for me? I'm starved."

"Yea, we got plenty," Bake tells her. "Pete said we'd probably see you tonight. This is Barb, by the way. Barb, Jamie."

"Barbara Ann," the woman corrects. "Howdy."

Grip like iron. Carpenter? Lumberjack?

"*Ba-Ba-Ba, Ba-Barbara-Ann,*" Peter sings, giving a brisk stir to the slaw. "*You got me rockin' an' a-rollin', rockin an' a-reelin', Barbara-Ann—Ba, Ba, Ba-Barbara-Ann.*"

Barbara Ann shakes her head. "Third time tonight."

"I got it now," Bake announces. "Beach Boys, 1965. That's pretty fuckin' ancient, Pete."

"But so apropos. I'm pulling the ribs."

ॐ ॐ

Jamie's hungrier than she can ever remember being. She tries to recall breakfast or lunch—comes up with nothing but a few pieces of toast, the wine she shared with Ryan. Michael Ryan—even his name feels different now that he knows who she is, what she wants from him. The events of the last two days crowd in again, rattling her, but she pushes them off, wants nothing more at this moment than to be right again with Peter.

"So, how was the party?" he asks, addressing her directly for the first time.

"We accomplished what we needed to, I think," she says. "Sponsors are happy; everyone got to ogle the new piano. I left early."

Bake reaches for the slaw. "Barb here's a musician," he tells her. "Drums, right baby?"

"Rock an' roll, hoochie-coo," she agrees, passing up the Merlot Peter has opened for another Budweiser pulled, dripping, from Bake's cooler. "All female band," she tells Jamie. "Me and a couple other lobstermen I know."

This explains the ruddy complexion, the muscular build. "How long have you been lobstering?" Jamie asks.

"Fifteen, sixteen years now. Got my own boat—a thirty-two foot Novi. Fished it with my husband before he died."

Peter, next to Jamie on the settee, reaches for the wine and refills both their glasses—the simple gesture a sign that things are on the mend between them. She's so grateful she could cry.

"You seen any changes in your catch over the last couple years?" Peter asks. "Latest studies point to the larval settlement being way down." He turns to Jamie. "Baby lobsters, " he explains. "Settlement has to do with the number that actually make it from birth to living on the bottom. Less babies, less catch."

She nods, thinking suddenly of their own lobster trap dangling off the stern—legal, strictly speaking, but local fishermen get pretty prickly about citizens catching their own food.

"Yeah, well, I'm not seeing it," Barbara Ann tells him. "My catch is almost double what it was five years back. I got almost two hundred traps out now, and my boys to help me. They'll be running their own boats when they're done with school; then we'll be pullin' in some real money."

"Only if the fishery lasts," Peter says, pushing the point. The fingers of his left arm, draped across the back of the settee, have begun scribing tight little circles on Jamie's shoulder—sending an erotic charge through her. "If it were me, I'd think about moving into aquaculture, get in on the ground floor. Fish farming is where all the action will be five, ten years from now."

"Spoken like one a them over at Marine Fisheries." The derisive edge to Barbara Ann's words only partly mitigated by her smile. "Government boy."

Peter shrugs off the mild insult, his eyes meeting Bake's for a beat. "World's gotta eat. We're just trying to find a way to make it work."

"Well, word is," she says, "the boys don't like them net pens you got out there at the Shoals. Hard to see 'em at night—keep from running them over, tearing them up on the way into the harbor. Accidentally, I mean. It's just what I hear."

"I appreciate the concern," he says lightly. "But the pens sit about fifty feet down, so there's not much chance of fouling them. Besides, the boys should be able to see the feed buoys, if nothing else, even at night—six feet across and lit up like the Vegas strip. Somebody's sure finding them. Unless the fish are filling them with bullet holes."

Guns now? Jamie shoots a look at Peter, who's neglected to mention this bit of news—has told her nothing, in fact, since the night one of his guys saw a lobster boat actually change course to charge one of the buoys, pulling it around for a while before tiring of the game and heading into port. Busting up the field an easy way of thumbing their noses at the Government.

"I don't understand," Jamie says. "The Shoals project is just mussels and whitefish. Why would lobstermen even care?"

"It's complicated," Peter tells her. "The different fisheries are all interdependent. If the state leases ocean bottom to aquaculture groups, it takes that much ocean area away from the lobstermen. Draggers, too."

"It's more than just bottom leases," Barbara Ann says. "You remember back when all them salmon escaped from that fish farm down east? Close to a hundred thousand juveniles, they figured—all swimming around, lookin' for food. If we get a hundred thousand cod loose out there at the Shoals, they're gonna decimate the entire fish population along this coast. Ain't gonna be nothin for nobody. That's when you're gonna see your friggin' larval decline." She takes a swig of the beer, shakes her head. "If you really want to do something about feedin' the world and all that, get Fish and Game after the lobstermen pulling egged-up females. I can't tell you who they are, mind you, but they're out there. If lobsterin' dies off down the line, that'll be the reason. Just takes too damn long to make baby lobsters."

"Can't be that fuckin' hard," Bake says through a mouthful of slaw.

Barbara Ann stops eating to glare at him. "It's a tough job, pal. You try creating life out of nothing. Females only produce eggs once every couple years, and they carry their young as long as people do. You do the math."

Jamie's surprised Bake takes this, but he shoots a grin at Peter— busy burying a smile in a sip of wine. Then she gets it. Bake's not generally known for his subtlety, but apparently even he can tell when a subject needs to be changed. She can't resist. "How did you two meet, anyway?"

"The tolls, " Bake says, preparatory to a long belch. "One night this shitbox truck comes through, loaded to the fuckin' gills with lobster traps. Middle of the night, too, so it's real slow. This one's sittin' there, grinning at me, so we start shootin' the shit, flirtin' a little—an like that, an like that." He reaches across the table, snags another pile of ribs.

"Shows how much you know," Barbara Ann says. "Girlfriend a' mine told me about you—the one works at that biker bar down in Portsmouth. So I called the tolls and got some guy to tell me your shift. Lucky I got the right lane. Would've been a bitch to go around again with all them traps."

"Well, God damn," Bake says proudly. "Picked up in a bar, and I wasn't even there."

Peter nods. "Every man's dream."

For the next hour, Peter and Bake roll seamlessly through everything from the politics of the university system and the New Hampshire Turnpike Authority, to diesel engine repair and the physics of projectile vomiting—Barbara Ann holding her own all the way. It's almost midnight when she finally rises to leave, Bake stumbling up the companionway in her wake, and Jamie slips from the settee to begin the clean up. She's just managed to clear the table when Peter pulls her down beside him again.

"The maid will get it."

"You gave her the night off, remember?"

"I had ulterior motives." He slides the shirt from her shoulder and plants a kiss, the moist touch taking her breath. He pulls her closer, goes for her mouth.

"Peter, listen—about..."

"Ssh...ssh...," he croons, slipping an arm around her and pulling her to him. "My fault. I overreacted." He plants a kiss on her head, and they turn to sit facing the glowing coal stove, his arms around her as they rock gently with the motion of the boat. Forgiven then, thank God. She sinks back against his chest in the familiar evening ritual. This is why she married him, she remembers now—the soothing predictability, the established routines of their life together.

Peter is the one to break the silence. "So, what do you think of Bake's new lobster-lady?"

Jamie smiles up at him. "She can take anything he throws at her; that's for sure. But Bake and kids? You think he has a clue what he's in for?"

"Wouldn't know—never having had any myself."

Please God, not another tortured discussion about having children. Her nerves still raw from the face-off with Ryan, she craves only peace on the home front, reaches for something neutral that will take them out of danger. "She held her own pretty well during your little dissertation on aquaculture."

Peter's hand, wandering beneath her shirt, slides up to cup a breast. "I was testing her. But there are things I'm sure even our Barbara Ann doesn't know. It's a little known fact, for instance, that a female lobster won't mate with a small male."

"Small in what way?" Jamie asks, turning to face him as she searches with her own hand.

"Whoa—careful now," he says, sucking in a breath. "Or we're not gonna keep this pony in the barn." He shifts, allowing her to unzip him.

"Did you miss me?" Stroking, kneading him—the familiar, delicious feeling of arousal overtaking her.

"I slept on your side of the bunk," he admits, starting in on her neck again. The simple admission is all she needs, but he pulls back after a moment, searches her face. "Sorry I didn't call," he says, tenderly brushing hair from the edge of her face. "I needed time to think it all through."

"This hasn't hurt us, has it? I don't want it to hurt us."

He shakes his head, love coming into his eyes as he pinches her nipple lightly, then again hard, and flicks his tongue at the edges of her mouth—forestalling any further discussion.

She wakes at three, jolted from sleep by something Ryan had said about being on the phone with his lawyer when the accident happened, only now making the connection between this and some earlier conversation about that day. When was that? Wide awake now, a sated Peter snoring softly beside her, she slides from beneath his arm and crawls from the bunk, wrapping a blanket around her as she moves to the chilly quiet of the moon room. Settling herself on the cushions beneath the blanket, knees pulled to her chin, she traces the comment to the night she met Ryan for drinks, baiting him with some story about a car accident she'd supposedly caused—just to see how he'd react. He mentioned a lawyer then, too—one who'd gotten him out of the same kind of mess. His exact words. It seemed an obvious reference to the accident, but were the two things related? No, she decides; timing's all wrong. Might have been the same lawyer—how many could he have, after all—but they couldn't have been talking about the accident, because it hadn't happened yet. What then?

All at once, a piece of memory drops into place. Ryan wasn't just talking on his cell phone that morning; he was yelling, almost screaming. The thought brings it all back—a flash of him in the car, the back of his head moving so violently he could only be shouting. What had him so wild?

It could mean everything, or nothing at all. Suddenly it all seems so hopeless—so pointless. She should give it up, she knows; forget about Ryan and what he's cost her. There's danger here; the last thing she wants is to screw things up with Peter. If only she could throw herself completely into his warmth, his love for her, the joy of nights like this. She has the sudden urge to slip the boat from her moorings without a word to anyone, trade in their mired-up lives for the simplicity of life at sea— navigation across a thousand miles of open ocean, eating what they can manage to catch, making their way from port to port with only the boat, their wits and each other. She tries the feeling on, imagines Peter's initial, enthusiastic embrace of it until he feels its heft, trades the spontaneity of the whole thing for the need to plan, arrange, wait—when she feels only a desperate need to flee while the freshness in their relationship still wafts of possibility and before whatever it is she feels gathering above her breaks.

Still. Still.

She stares up miserably at the dome—the taped constellations eerily backlit by a bright disc of moon from which she tries to draw meaning, answers, some kind of direction. With the moonlight on her face, she drops into half-sleep and the familiar fantasy of that unencumbered, essential self—running lightly along the forest floor beneath a tall canopy of trees, the moist padded earth beneath callused feet, the dried tips of arching fronds brushing against her as she slips along the path. A few of the hunters have grown bolder, it seems—breaking from the others to track her— and she feels them near. Veering from the trail, still following the lone star that guides her, she dips into the close growth of lush greens to lose them, moments later reaching the tree that soars skyward. With a glance over her shoulder, she shimmies quickly up the ancient trunk, toward the safety of her pelt-lined nest, the rough bark scraping her naked thighs as she climbs. Vine tendrils clutch at her in a twining embrace of feet and toes—the tree receiving her in its roughness—and she snakes her legs around it in response, watching the ground below where the hunters slow, listen, then move on—fanning out far beneath her in search of her trail.

THIRTEEN

Ryan's due at eight-thirty, so she does six miles in the late afternoon to quell the tension, figure out how to turn the tables on him and come away with the truth this time—this one last time, she's assured herself—the troubled compromise helping to focus her.

Spring has begun a slow return here—scores of earthworms floundering on the puddled macadam, the inexplicable sight of tiny, perfectly formed frogs belly side up in the road. She pounds out the miles in the struggling warmth of the mid-March sun, blood screaming through her as she works on a strategy that will compel the man to come clean about that morning—shock, threaten, seduce him into revealing whatever it is he's hiding. Somehow, somehow. She considers, decides, tosses out first one then another of her ideas as too simple, too complicated, too transparent.

Back at the house she showers, pushes off the utter craziness of the situation as she picks up the living room, runs the vacuum, lays a fire. Setting the stage for whatever is to come.

It's just eight-thirty when she hears his knock, wonders as she pulls the door wide if he's gypped the children of their bedtime rituals for this. Before her, leaning casually against the edge of the door jamb, stands yet another version of Michael Ryan—relaxed looking in chinos and a bulky fisherman's knit sweater—cradling a large bag from one of Fairfield's numerous gourmet groceries, a long loaf of designer French bread poking out the top. Dismissing her initial plan to don sweats and an oversized turtleneck, Jamie has instead dressed in a blousy silk top, suede pants and low heels—her tawny hair pulled back in a simple clip. Casual chic, she's heard it called—understated, but sexy. A little distraction, she's decided, might just work in her favor.

She inclines her head, her greeting cool. "Mr. Ryan."

"Lovely to see you again, Diana," he says pleasantly, moving past her, into the hall. Chipper, enthusiastic, man on a mission. And still throwing that damn name in her face.

She's stuck for an opening, some blithe way to work into this, but he breezes through the awkward moment as if such things were common for him—handing off the bag while he shucks his overcoat, drapes it over the banister. Reclaiming the food, he heads back toward the kitchen and begins immediately to unpack the bag—olive oil, head of garlic, sirloin tips, fresh Portobello mushrooms.

"You're cooking?" This is a surprise; she figured him for upscale take out—Thai food, maybe, or Italian from Tommy's.

"Not only that, I'm making you my specialty—steaks tips à la Michael." He continues pulling from the bag—mesclun greens, pine nuts, rice vinegar—then grins over at her. "You know what they say—food, music, and sex: the three great pleasures. Not necessarily in that order, of course. You bought wine?"

She points to the bottle of Chateau Larose-Trintaudon on the counter. Medoc is too heavy for this meal, of course, but she couldn't care less.

"One bottle?" he laughs. "You're no fun at all." He's orienting himself now—opening and shutting drawers, poking around in the cabinets. His broad shoulders seem to fill the kitchen, and all at once she's acutely aware of how out of date, almost primitive it is—no dishwasher, the stove and chatterbox of a fridge verging on the antique.

"Knives?" he asks. "I'm going to start on this if you don't mind. The sauce takes a while."

Is he kidding? What about this doesn't she mind? Stepping to the counter, she pulls open the nearest drawer then shuts it again as soon as he reaches in, almost catching his fingers. He looks up in surprise, and her gaze holds his. "Don't ever phone me in New Hampshire again, Mr. Ryan."

That damn grin. "It's Michael, remember?"

"I remember," she says. "And I want you to remember. What we do here stays here. This is not negotiable."

It's the only way she can do it, she's decided; what's more, she needs to be sure that when she stops this whole business, he won't try to contact her at home. She hadn't planned on meeting him at all, of course—had convinced herself, at least for those first blissful weeks after making up with Peter, that she'd blow him off if he tried to contact her again. But hearing his voice when she picked up her phone in the Nashua office had rocked her—the impulse to hang up on him abandoned in favor of the faint chance he might have decided to come clean—if only to get her off his back. Their conversation had been short, cryptic— the presence of other staff in the room necessitating a kind of code that, disturbingly enough, they both understood. And so she found herself agreeing, despite the risks of meeting him again.

"Are you always that touchy at work? Jesus, I thought lawyers were intense." He selects a knife, closes the drawer, glances quickly at her. "Come on, lighten up. How else were we going to arrange all this?"

He's opening cupboards now—gathering bowls, pans, a round platter for the meat. It bothers her that he seems so at home in her kitchen, that he's doing something as domestic, as intimate, as making her a meal, but all this hostility isn't going to get her anywhere, so she reaches for the wine, retrieves a corkscrew. She's opening the bottle when she recognizes the round platter he's chosen as the one she used for Sam's birthday cake just weeks before he died. Her skin goes cold at the sight of his hands moving carelessly over it.

"Kiddies all tucked in?" she finds herself asking, rubbing the sudden goose bumps from her forearms.

He's doesn't miss a beat. "I'm at the office tonight. Molly's got it covered."

She wrests her eyes from the plate and opens another ill-fitting drawer, painted over so many times it barely closes, and tosses him one of GM's old aprons. "Yeah, well, better put this on. You don't want Molly wondering how you got olive oil on your pants while you were sweating over some poor guy's divorce."

She tries watching him for a few minutes—her back against the refrigerator, wine glass in hand—but the whole thing is just too weird, so she moves off to the Chickering, figuring it will relax her, maybe even win her some points. She begins with some Debussy to calm herself, then lets the mood take her. Ernesto Lecouna's *Malagueña*, because she's been messing around with the modulation lately; bits of Mozart and Chopin, some of Cobb's *Russian Rag,* just to keep things light—a piece of this, a movement of that—the rhythms and patterns helping her focus, remember how she wants this to go. She follows his comings and goings out of the corner of her eye, makes a game of selecting music to accompany his movements about the house—a Rachmaninoff prelude when he wanders from the kitchen to feed the fire and stands for a moment staring off into the flames; a sampling of Beethoven sonatas when he's back working in the kitchen, all the while using the music as a stop against conversation, a setting of mood. She segues into Debussy's *Clair de Lune* when she hears him pulling plates from the cupboard. Takes it to the end. Painful. Exquisite. Full of the strange longing she's begun to feel.

He closes the drapes in the front window—paranoid about being seen, she figures—and if he notices the long stretch of pennies lining the sill, he says nothing. They eat al fresco—he on the couch, Jamie nestled deep into GM's reading chair—and say little during the meal, as if the music has pulled them both deep into thought. Even the house has gone still around them, its usual creaks and unexpected thumps gone silent for once—as though the dead have new ears for the affairs of the living.

"Not bad," she says, reluctant to compliment him at all, though the meat is nicely rare, the flavors in the silky sauce rich and complex. Still, most people can claim at least one dish they do well.

Putting his plate down, he laces his fingers together over his head in a long stretch. "Gotta say," he announces, "it's nice to have a peaceful dinner for once. Lately, supper at our place has been a series of battles—one protracted battle, really—over whether to send Meghan to public or private in the fall. Kindergarten. Her best friend will go to public, and Molly wants them kept together."

She was wondering how he'd start, her gut telling her to let him be the one; still, this sudden dip into his home life is a surprise.

"I take it you want her in private school, like the rest?" It's a guess, and she keeps her voice neutral, a polite inquiry—the tone costing her. All the while she's thinking how this explains why, in all the mornings she's kept watch, she's never seen any of them get on or off a school bus. That, and how this could be her way in, talking about the kids. Start with the girl and lead him around to the little boy, the toddler Sam's age—well, the age he was then. Of all of them, this one intrigues her the most. "What does Meghan want to do?" she asks.

He laughs, gathering the dishes and starting for the kitchen. "She's just five years old, for Chrissake. All she cares about is whether or not they'll have chocolate milk."

He continues in this vein from the kitchen, apparently finding nothing at all ironic in lecturing her on a parent's responsibility to ensure the best educational start for a child. Once again she's thrown by the thought that Sam, too, would be starting kindergarten in the fall—her mind wandering to the lunch box she'd have bought him, the buddies he'd no doubt have by now. She can't listen to this, so she returns to the piano, counting on the combined effects of the wine, food and music, his unloading about the family, to lull him into complacency. Once again she chooses Beethoven—one of his favorites, she's noticed—and after the dishes he brings out what's left of the wine, dividing the bottle neatly between their two glasses before sitting down with her on the bench.

"Second movement of the *Pathetique*, right?" He shrugs off her look of surprise. "I tortured myself trying to learn this once."

She nods. "I've always loved his sonatas—the technique is just incredible. An amazing composer."

"Brilliant and misunderstood—all that horseshit, huh?"

Jamie smiles. "Actually he was an impatient man—demanding and volatile. Kept falling in love with women he couldn't have." Suddenly she's reminded of something from S. J. Perlman—*I tried to resist his overtures, but he plied me with symphonies, quartettes, chamber music and cantatas.*

"Oh, yeah; the Immortal Beloved thing. I saw the movie. I prefer Tchaikovsky, actually. The *Fifth Symphony* gets me every time."

"Doesn't surprise me you like him. He was trained as a lawyer, you know."

Ryan's eyebrows shoot up. "No kidding? Well, then."

"He hated it, though. Too sensitive, too emotionally honest for the law."

The comment appears to go over his head. "A ladies' man, too, I'll bet, " he says. "All those guys were."

She can't resist. "He was gay, actually. Killed himself when it came out, rather than face the public humiliation—times being what they were."

He thinks for a minute, then lets it drop. Talk turns to jazz. He brings up Art Tatum; she tells him Rachmaninoff was a great fan of Tatum. He tells her Rachmaninoff is very overrated. She asks according to whom, but the sparring is getting old. There's no way he can beat her at this game; she's been studying this stuff pretty much since birth. Things go quiet between them, as if they've talked their way around it as much as they can—have finished, finally, with this requisite sharpening of knives.

"You owe me a question from last time," she says lightly, her fingers moving over the keys. "You mentioned you were talking to your lawyer on your cell phone that morning. What were you talking about?"

He shakes his head, eyes glued to the fluid, intricate movements of her hands. "Can't tell you; attorney-client privilege."

"You're telling me you were talking to your lawyer about one of your own clients?"

"In a manner of speaking."

Porter Street, she realizes. He mentioned before that he had a client on Porter Street. It keeps coming back to this. "So who's the client?"

"Can't tell you that either."

This is just a game to him, she thinks bitterly, this hiding so conveniently behind rules he probably breaks every day. So what's holding him back now—ego? Fear? She realizes she's stopped playing; her fingers rest heavy and leaden on the keys, all music gone from them now.

He smiles as if he really wants to help. Mister Nice Guy. "C'mon, I'll throw in a freebie. But make it a question I can answer."

She closes the keyboard lid softly and faces him, deciding on another tack. "Why didn't you stop when you saw me go off the road?"

A snort. "That one's simple. I didn't see you." But she's learned to read him, knows now when he's lying. "Look," he sighs. "It was a long time ago. It's too bad it happened; it's too bad your little boy died, but dredging it all up again isn't going to change anything. Won't help him, and it won't help you. Just tell me what it is you want here. Money? Is that it?"

Trivializing her, trivializing Sam. She looks down at the hands in her lap, curled into each other like fetal twins. They seem the hands of a stranger suddenly, each gripping the other so tightly the knuckles have gone white. She's never hated anyone before, not like this. Never thought herself capable of it.

Rising from the bench, not quite sure where to go, she turns, heads for GM's reading chair; then stalls numbly before it—wanting to throw him out, needing to get to the truth. He's motivated by things you don't understand, she reminds herself; backed by a system that's already exonerated him. He owes you nothing.

"I saw you look in your rearview mirror just before you forced me off the road," she tells him. "It's the last thing I remember, and I remember it very clearly."

Ryan, too, rises from the piano. "And if your son hadn't been in the front seat..." He runs a hand through his hair. "I mean—okay. Airbag broke his neck, right?"

Jamie blinks, sits.

"See—I know." A pause. "And you gotta ask yourself about that."

"It wasn't my car," she says toward her lap. "Mine had a flat." Her voice trailing to a whisper. "I couldn't get to the belts in the back."

The unfairness of it. Sam always, *always* rode in the back in her car. Car seat strapped in so tight he looked glued to the seat. It was just that one day. One day.

"Look, it's just us here, okay?" he says, moving toward the couch. "I mean, you were in a jam—anyone can understand that. You fucked up, is all."

Why did I tell him that? Jamie wonders, only half listening now. All that about the cars, the belts—things I've never even told Peter. Marveling at this, trying to figure it as her hands return to their fetal curl.

"And I never said anything about it—not even to Molly," he assures her, relaxing onto the couch. "Told my lawyer to back off, too—leave it alone at the hearing. I mean, there you were in a wheelchair, for Chrissake—just lost your kid. Gotta blame somebody, right?" A pause, as if he expects thanks. "I'm trying to be a nice guy here, okay? It's over. Let it go."

Silence while she absorbs the crushing words, stuck forever with this forced intimacy now he's drawn her here—a dark burrow of insinuation, confusion, doubt. Room for just the two of them. Fighting to control her voice when what she really wants is to jump up and pommel him for gut-punching her like this. "Well, if it's so over, Michael," she says quietly, reasonably, stressing the use of his name, "how can it possibly hurt to tell me what really happened?"

"The problem," he says leaning toward her, "is that you keep asking for things I can't give."

This last reminding her of just why she allows him back here, what she needs from him. Aware now that none of this is going anywhere unless she backs off, comes up with another way in. She hits, then, on the idea of using the children as a way to keep the door open, comes alive at the thought of getting some time with the boy, little Matthew. So much like Sam when he was taken from her. Maybe too much so—Ryan was sure to sense some kind of threat. He's far more likely to agree to Meghan, say—opposite sex, different age, a mere glimpse of the inquisitive child Sam would no doubt have become. Getting time with the girl was a necessary first step in gaining access to the boy. If Ryan will only go for it.

"All right then," she says. "I want to meet Meghan."

A glint comes into his eye as he weighs this. Is it an out he sees? Something she'll take in lieu of the truth? "Only if I get those ten minutes on the couch."

Ah yes, it's about time he trotted this out again—this tendency to counter with a sexual request.

She shrugs as if it's nothing to her. "Ten minutes for ten minutes. You'll keep your hands to yourself, of course."

His smile is slow, but there's no masking the sweetness of this victory. "Meghan's sick right now," he tells her. "Some flu or something. I'll set it up for next time. I'll need your cell number."

She wants to protest, sensing another intrusive tactic that's sure to come back on her, but it's this or he'll call her at work again, so she heads to the kitchen and jots down the number, carries it to the couch, where he's waiting to claim the one thing he's wanted from the start.

Handing him the number, she sits down close to him—a foot, she's decided, would work—and smiles. Surprise at first, a wariness, then he begins to relax against her as if he senses the clock ticking on his prize.

Before he can begin unloading whatever twisted fantasy he's been nursing, Jamie reaches to the end of the couch, pulling forward the hand-embroidered pillow GM spent an entire winter completing. "I want to show you something, "she says, bringing out the quilted blue baby book she found during the morning's exhaustive search of the attic.

He's not paying attention, too busy nosing the stray curl he's entwined around a finger—mumbling something about her smell, his loneliness. Breaking the rule against touch, but she doesn't care. She turns to him, their faces mere inches apart, and flashes the warmest smile she can muster.

"We've talked so much about your children, I thought I should show you something of mine. Won't take much time. He didn't live very long." It's her ace in the hole—something she wasn't sure she'd have the nerve to use, but knew would break things loose one way or the other, if nothing else worked. Suddenly she's calmer than she's been all day.

Tacked to the inside cover of the album is a photo of herself at full term—radiant and swollen-faced, leaning huge-bellied against the same counter where Ryan had chopped mushrooms and carefully marinated his steak. She flips through a few pages of birth photos, the requisite family trees, lists of baby gifts. She's gone through the book twice already today, so her tears are spent, her smile serene as she slows to touch Sam's hospital bracelet, the hank of impossibly fine, almost translucent hair. Candids then—nursing at a month or so; crawling grinning and drool-faced along the hall floor, a blurry shot of his first tentative steps.

Ryan has grown still and tense beside her, so she knows he's looking, couldn't turn away if he wanted to. She suppresses a smile, turns the page. First Christmas—the photo taken in this very room—an infant Sam in GM's arms in front of the same window whose drapes Ryan pulled closed only an hour before. A shot of dimpled hands plunged deep in the icing of his first birthday cake. And here—one of her favorites—chin tilted up, eyes closed as he catches snowflakes on his tongue; then a real party when he turned two with his friends from daycare—cake, ice cream, hats, the whole bit. Everyone crammed into the little kitchen, goofing for the camera.

"His name is Sam," Jamie says quietly, running a finger over the last shot. He's dressed in jeans and corduroy jacket here—a real little boy, now—mouth wide in a burst of laughter. "I took this one the week before he died."

She turns to Ryan then, damning and triumphant—unprepared for the caved-in look of his face, the unexpected anguish in his eyes.

He shakes his head, stands, goes for his coat in the hall. Recovering, she follows, clutching the book to her chest—her words bitter and choked. "Is it something I said?"

He chuckles a you-got-me kind of laugh then looks toward the door for a moment and sighs—nodding slowly, almost reluctantly, as he wrestles with some decision. She barely registers his turning before he's on her—grabbing her hair and forcing her back against the wall, pinning her hands above her head as he mashes his mouth against hers. Sam's baby book slips from her hands as she struggles to fight him, terrified suddenly of his immense strength, the thought he can do anything he wants to her now. His tongue demands entry; a sound in his throat as he forces through, tastes, swallows, goes for more. Hard, painful—teeth biting and cutting—not caring that he's hurting her, keeping it up until his anger ebbs. She waits him out, utterly immobilized; watches him draw back, look at her for a long moment with a kind of surprise, then move in for another kiss, a real one this time—passion tinged with something approaching tenderness.

He leans in for more, and suddenly, unbelievably, she's responding—hating herself even as a nipple springs up against a hand that has wandered there—and she opens her mouth to him. Pain, fury, regret—all of it—pulled into this single moment of intense hunger, as if she would devour him. Behind closed eyes she sees the look on his face when she showed him the book— wounded into vulnerability, as if he only now understood.

His breathing is hard as he whispers her name—over and over—not Jamie, but Diana, always Diana, the name that makes her his. The thud of their heartbeats echoes in her ear, filling the empty hallway as he breaks from her, head resting against the wall mere inches from hers; then he steps back, finally releasing her as he turns away—all business as he buttons his coat, rakes his hands through his hair. Tears roll down her cheeks as she watches him.

"Why?" she manages—her voice pained, incredulous.

He's opened the door and stares off now into the dark, considering. The look he throws back over his shoulder is a twisted mix of triumph, anguish, desire. Then he's gone, slamming the door behind him—something in the living room crashing to the floor.

Jamie drops to her knees then—gathers Sam's trampled and ripped baby book to her chest and cries. Cries for herself, for Sam, for Peter—oh God, Peter! Rocking back and forth on the hallway floor, she huddles over the precious book as if it were Sam himself, until all at once she's flooded with GM's presence— the dear old harpy enveloping her like a mist—soothing, calming, flitting about her in whispers of the hundred ways the fates might take their revenge.

FOURTEEN

"He did what?" Her voice is sharp, trembling—the stress of the last week uncurling in a fast burn. She has to fight the urge to throw her cell phone through the car window.

"I know, Jamie. I can hardly believe it myself." Augie is at once jubilant and apologetic. "It happened at last evening's board meeting. John was making his usual, tired pitch for the capital campaign, and Michael surprised everyone by suggesting we weren't aiming high enough. He said we really should be looking for ten million instead of four, and right there pledged the first million himself. You should have seen John."

The drive west over Route 101 toward Nashua is bogged down heading into Manchester. Jamie curses herself for not getting an earlier start, for falling all over herself to make Peter a real breakfast for once. And now this.

"But there's a caveat," Augie is saying. "He insists you oversee the entire campaign. If you're not on board, he withdraws the offer."

Somehow Jamie manages to slide across three lanes of traffic, barely missing a fast-moving pickup, and is shaking by the time she pulls to a stop in the narrow breakdown lane.

"I'm sorry, Augie," she says against a growing sense of panic. "I promised Peter I'd wind up the consulting by summer. A campaign like this will take two, maybe three years. I simply can't do it."

"You can write your own ticket on this, Jamie. I want you to know that."

"Money isn't the issue." But then, neither was Peter—not really.

"Well, there's a history here, of course. I realized when I saw him with you at the gala that he knew of your involvement with us, but does he know who you really are? I mean..."

"He knows," Jamie says, her voice flat. She leaves it at that, doesn't mention the promise of this donation is almost certainly connected to all that has come before—not just three years ago, but to whatever it was that happened last week at the house in Easton. If she'd told Augie about it—impossible, of course—they wouldn't even be having this conversation.

"I don't know what to say, Jamie. Michael has seen the tremendous strides we've made since you've been back, of course; it may simply be that he's impressed with your abilities, wants to be sure the right person is spearheading the campaign. If anyone can get the job done, you can. We all know that."

It's not like Augie to push, and Jamie resents it now, doesn't care how much pressure she's under to make this happen. Suddenly she wants to tell her all of it—dispel this notion of Michael Ryan as knight in shining armor, no matter that it might cost her Augie's friendship, not to mention her job—then immediately dismisses the idea, the repercussions too unpredictable, too dangerous. He'll have prepared some response to the possibility of confrontation, of course—an initial look of incredulity, the sheepish admission, when pressed, that the wine had gone to their heads, and they may have slipped a little, shared a bit of kinky fun in the hall as he was getting ready to leave. Unfortunate and embarrassing—unprofessional, certainly. But nothing more.

Trapped into silence, she rockets between rage and guilt—the sense of having betrayed Peter in some complicated way she's still getting a handle on. Telling him what happened is out of the question, so there was breakfast, the promise to quit the job. Small concessions. Guilty concessions.

"Debra will never put up with it," Jamie says. "She'll quit first."

"Perhaps." Augie chuckles. "She certainly isn't happy about it. She's gone so far as to imply there might be something, well, unprofessional between the two of you—ridiculous of course, as you and I both know—and I warned her against ever voicing such an opinion again. Should word of such a thing reach me, I'll fire her myself."

Jamie leans back against the headrest and shuts her eyes against all of it, fights the vision of Michael Ryan that's infected her dreams since that night, of being with him in some cramped, shadowy space—their joining desperate, feverish, strangely unsatisfying.

"May I at least tell the board you're considering it?" Augie asks, as if even the possibility of Jamie's cooperation will win them both some time.

☙ ❧

Jamie checks the cell phone at lunch to find the voice mail icon winking at her. It's a little early for Peter. Augie again?

"Get back to me. I have a proposal for you." The hair on her neck prickles at the sound of that voice—so brusque, so matter-of-fact—and she erases the message before he can finish rattling off his cell number, berating herself for having given him hers.

It rings again on the ride home, and she flips it open without thinking, assumes it's Peter with news of where they're to meet Bake and Barbara Ann for dinner.

"Hello, Diana." The voice shoots through her like electricity—his haunted look, the hungry feel of his mouth on hers coming to her unbidden. "Augie tells me you're hedging on our offer." No mention of that night. Of what he did. What he forced on her a violation of everything dear.

Anger, confusion, an icy fury as the words hiss past her lips. "This is so transparent. You think throwing money at the Symphony can ever make up for the unconscionable things you do? You can't possibly think I'd agree to this now."

"Why not? It makes complete sense. You're the best person for the job—the only person, as far as I'm concerned." A heartbeat later he adds, "I've arranged for you to meet Meghan, by the way."

"What?" And then she remembers: Meghan as booby prize, an offering made in lieu of the truth. A connection to Matthew—her heart aching at the very thought of him.

"A deal's a deal. You'll have to come to the house, of course."

"Are you crazy?"

"If you're worried about Molly, don't be. I told her I've contacted a woman to appraise the Bechstein. She's wanted to get rid of the thing for years. I figure you'll have about an hour."

It takes Jamie a moment to catch his meaning. "I know nothing about appraisals." It's all she can think to say. Cocky son of a bitch, blind-siding her like this.

"She won't know the difference—believe me."

Smart, this offering up of a child to tempt her—but then he has so many. Access to the Bechstein the sweetener. She should be concerned with just why he'd do this, she knows, but the thought of the children, of legitimate entree into a home defined by the busyness of all those little lives—his home!—is far too tempting to permit much scrutiny. The possibilities unleash an almost physical reaction, her rage quieting to something keenly, intuitively opportunistic. Watch and wait, its motto; the truth alone, it whispers, is no longer enough. Not now.

"Only if you're not there, and only if I get some time on the piano," she snaps, determined he shouldn't know the depth of the draw this has for her.

"Goes without saying."

The whole idea is nuts, she thinks—even as she feels herself going for it. It's just an hour, after all. Just an hour and she's out of there.

∅⅀

He sets it up for the next time she's down—eleven o'clock on Saturday morning. He'll arrange to be called to some conference at the office, he tells her—just before she arrives. She's on her own once she gets inside.

Jamie's beyond nervous when she turns up the drive, the lawn on either side bursting with the nascent green of early April. The yellow Lab appears out of nowhere, barking and bounding alongside the car as she pulls to a stop at the top of the hill, parking beside a shiny red tricycle sitting at the edge of an empty garage bay. At least he's kept his promise to be gone, she thinks— glad now that after all her waffling that morning she actually got up the nerve to come, never mind the masquerade.

Grabbing her briefcase and opening the door to an enthusiastic nosing of legs and crotch, she makes her way along the flagstone path toward the wide steps of the front porch. She notes a pair of small, flowered gloves and a gardening trowel tossed together between long flats of cosmos and petunias in the flower bed fronting the house; miniature jeeps and trucks and an assortment of action figures abandoned mid-battle in the dirt at the base of the steps. The dog trots ahead, ignoring a noisy flock of sparrows who've descended on the huge maple tree above them; then he inexplicably takes off at full bore around the side of the house, leaving Jamie to mount the steps alone.

She has to knock twice before she hears anything from within, wonders for the thousandth time as she waits just what kind of woman has married this man, borne his children—her well rehearsed line of introduction flying out the window as a bolt is thrown, the door swung wide to reveal a bluejeaned, barefoot Michael Ryan. She stiffens and stares, a flush climbing into her cheeks now that she's face to face with him again—all that happened that night charging the air between them.

She turns to leave, but he steps forward—takes her arm. "Diana, wait."

Just then a little girl appears from somewhere behind him, Michael dropping his hand as the child curls into his side—snaking an arm around his thigh and resting her head comfortably against it as she peers from beneath an unruly bush of dark curls. Liquid brown eyes turn on Jamie—curious and alert, but wary. Too wary.

The sight stops Jamie in her tracks—something about the child striking her as unusual, almost mystical. Meghan? Can this be Meghan? So petite, almost reed thin. She swallows her bitter words, the urge to unload on Michael. No need to confuse the girl, upset her by making some scene. "Mr. Ryan," she murmurs, her smile tight. "What a surprise."

"Relax," he says, his hand resting on the girl's head. "Couldn't be helped."

"Mattie put Mia's beads up his nose again," the child offers, as if she for one has had enough of his high jinx. "Purple ones. He only likes purple."

Sam did the same thing with peas, Jamie remembers suddenly—a smile of recognition on her before she can quell it.

"Does it all the time," Ryan tells her, the hand stroking his daughter's head now. "Second trip to the doctor this week. A mere father can't be trusted with the mission, of course. Believe me, I tried." He squats down, slides an arm around the girl. "Meghan, this is Diana Apollo. She's here to see the piano." He smiles up at Jamie. "Isn't that right, Diana?"

It takes her a minute to get it. Matthew's not here; Molly has taken him to the doctor. All this waiting to see him for nothing.

She could balk—just turn and leave and be done with it, but her heart is set on seeing him. She wonders how long they'll be gone, how long she might stretch this out without Michael's growing suspicious.

"So," she says, smiling down at the girl. "Where's this piano?"

Meghan leads the way along the rich, cream-colored carpet, past the wide stairwell with its ornate, polished balustrade—an answering machine blinking urgently from a side table on the wall beneath it—past the arched entrance to the living room opposite the stairs, where Jamie spied the girls the night of the little drink-tossing scene. A determined column of three—Meghan, then Jamie, with Michael close behind—they file through the large, sunny kitchen, then down one hallway and another. Left, left, right: a course Jamie memorizes in case she needs to navigate her way out of here in a hurry. Finally, Meghan comes to a halt before a massive oak door. Grasping the bulky brass knob with both hands, she turns and pushes with easy familiarity, and all at once they're in what can only be Michael's study—the nine-foot piano covered and crammed into a corner of the room.

Jamie parks her briefcase on the edge of an oversized cherry desk angled to face out a broad expanse of curtainless windows, while Michael moves to uncover the Bechstein. With a quick glance she notes an open laptop at the center of the black leather blotter, stacks of files, a multi-line phone and fax. She takes a minute to orient herself—decides they're at the very back of the house, the west-facing view that of the sledding hill. It's a nice enough home—comfortable and rambling—but hardly grand. Surprisingly unpretentious for someone able to drop a million dollars on a whim.

Meghan, their audience of one, remains propped against the doorjamb—one leg bent stork-like against the other, the floppy end of a purple sock dangling from her raised foot. She draws a thumb into her mouth as Jamie unzips the briefcase, pulls a yellow legal pad and ball-point pen from the otherwise empty interior. She might be clueless when it comes to appraisals, but she does know pianos, and as long as this one is watching, she's going to play the part.

The smooth ebony finish appears undiminished by age, though the design clearly puts it pre-1925. A trill of excitement, of possibility—despite the ridiculous circumstances.

"Open the lid to the second position, please," she instructs curtly.

Meghan cranes her neck, following every move as Michael lifts and then props the lid, and Jamie begins a check of the case—slowly running her hands along the gleaming black sides looking for cracks, crazing, warping—taking her time along its curves so as not to miss anything. Next she ducks beneath the lid and examines the soundboard for cracks. Finding none, she starts at the rear of the board and makes her way forward—bass bridge, hitch pin, long bridge, wrest plank, tuning pins. She checks the wear of the strings, the hammers and damper felts—finds all in remarkable shape, considering. Finally, she pulls the bench away and kneels to examine the pedals—finding the damper a bit stiff but nothing more. Only then does she see the little family of dolls spread about under the instrument—a few covered head to toe, another eating at a little makeshift table, one propped up in a doll-sized car.

Replacing the bench, she sits, opens the keyboard and examines each of the eighty-eight keys for chips and cracks, and finding only some minor staining. She tries a few chords, a run or two, adjusting her touch to the light action. "This was just tuned," she says, unable to keep the surprise from her voice.

"Yesterday," Michael tells her, displacing a diapered doll as he settles in the wooden swivel chair behind the desk. "I wanted it ready when you arrived."

"What do you know about it?"

"Not much, I'm afraid. It was made around 1910, if that helps."

She continues with the scales, senses Meghan's interest pick up. "Debussy once said that piano music should be written only for the Bechstein. Brahms and Liszt preferred them as well." She decides on Schumann—something simple, soothing. And so she begins, the longing of the piece a perfect match for the gentle tone, the warm sonority of the instrument.

"Nice," Michael says. "Very Home-Sweet-Home. I've heard it before. What is it?"

"Robert Schumann. *Träumerei*, from his *Scenes d'enfants—Scenes from Childhood*. Seems appropriate," she mutters as an afterthought.

The music is working its magic on Meghan, but Jamie's careful not to look at the girl as she moves closer. Sam, she remembers, often shied from people who showed an obvious interest in him; found those who ignored him absolutely fascinating. She segues into Beethoven's *Für Elise*—the first piece she, herself, fell in love with as a child—extending the repetitive lead notes of the first section a little more each time, then breaking off to shoot the girl a quick, conspiratory grin. She's rewarded with a shy smile before picking up the music again.

Meghan is beside her when she finishes. "Are you going to take the piano away?" she asks, brow furrowed. My piano, the eyes say. My secret, glorious play space.

She's just a slip of a thing—the hair and face all Ryan, but with her mother's petite build. Jamie smiles. "Wouldn't think of it." Reaching over, she buttons the top of her sweater—a tiny pink ceramic heart, the corner chipped so it slips through again almost immediately. Then softly, so Michael can't hear, "But be careful of the pedals when you play under here, okay?"

Meghan nods, eyes glued to the keys.

Jamie considers her for a moment. Can't hurt, she decides. Besides, it'll help kill the time. "Come on, hop up. I'll show you." Meghan is beside her in a heartbeat and Jamie glances quickly at

Michael, rocked back in the chair now—hands clasped behind his head as he takes in this little show. Amusing himself with what he's set in motion here.

"I could use a cup of tea," she snaps, pleased to see his composure slip a little. "Meghan, too, as she's assisting me." The girl glances up—wide-eyed—but Jamie says nothing more until Michael's closed the door behind him. "Let's see...what kind of music do you like?"

Meghan shrugs, puts a long finger on a key, looks up at Jamie as if for permission.

"It's okay. Let me help." She lifts the girl onto her lap, the warm smell of those luxurious, unruly curls rising between them. The heft of five years old—the heft of Sam, had he lived. Pushing the thought off as she arranges the little fingers into a simple C Major chord, noting their length and spread, then covering them with her own. "Push the keys down all at once, like this," she says, pressing gently. "Now you try." The resulting sound is clear and full, nothing at all tentative in the girl's touch, and Meghan grins up at her—surprise, elation, pride.

"It feels like the music is coming up through your fingers, doesn't it? That's one of the best parts. Now, what's this?" Jamie begins the simple tune, the same one she played for Sam whenever he crawled into her lap like this. This is who he'd be now, she realizes—the same curiosity, same eagerness to learn.

"*Twinkle, Twinkle Little Star!*" Meghan crows delightedly, putting her hands quite suddenly atop Jamie's to feel the movement of her fingers.

"When I was your age, I used to think pianos were magic," Jamie says, still playing. "There was one in my bedroom—not a little piano like babies have, but an upright. I thought it could protect me against anything."

She begins the *Träumerei* again, careful not to dislodge Meghan's hands, and closes her eyes, imagining that it's Sam—his weight in her lap, his hands on hers. She plays to the end of the piece, rolling seamlessly back to the beginning—round and round, loathe to give up the feeling of a child in her lap once again, the little fingers on hers.

She has no idea how long they stay this way—could be five minutes, could be fifteen—but when she looks up again Michael's back in the chair behind the desk, watching intently as he sips from a mug. Steam wafts from two others set on the edge of the desk.

"So what do you think?" he asks.

"I can see why your wife wants to start her," Jamie tells him. "The hands are right."

He smiles. "I mean about the piano."

She shrugs. It should be illegal for this man to own such an instrument, but then he has so many things he has no right to. Starting with the one in her lap. "It's fabulous, probably priceless in this condition. But you already know that. Get a good humidifier in here right away. An instrument like this needs steady humidity, gradual temperature changes."

He nods, sips from his mug—his gaze on Jamie's hands. Only then does she realize she's stroking Meghan's hair, combing it back with her fingers into a ponytail as the little girl continues to plunk away on the keys.

The slam of a door, then—a clattering of dog's nails on linoleum, and Jamie's heart lurches at the thought of the boy. More sounds—children's voices, excited and louder by the second; the dog lapping water; little feet pounding down the hall until another, slightly smaller version of Meghan bursts into the room, followed moments later by Molly carrying two-year-old Matthew, whose almost comical spikes of red hair mark him as the sole child to have inherited his mother's fiery coloring. Jamie is riveted at the sight of him, his set on his mother's hip so reminiscent of Sam on her own. Hungry for every detail, she examines, gauges, compares.

He seems smaller now, she thinks—has less bulk without the snowsuit that covered him the first few times she saw him. Was Sam really this little when he died? Surely not.

Molly's initial look of surprise turns to a quick flash of something darker as she takes it all in—Meghan seated in Jamie's lap, Michael at the desk, the steaming cups on the tray. Two older children spill into the room behind her, then immediately turn and race back through the hall for the phone, which has started ringing.

From the chair, swiveled now to face his wife, Michael says, "Molly, this is Diana Apollo; Diana—my wife, Molly, and our daughter Mia." He grins at Matthew, squirming to be set loose. "And Mattie the Martian—he of the beads up the nose. Hey Mol—Diana here has good news for you. Looks like this beast might pay for a college education or two, after all."

Not on Molly's immediate list of priorities, it seems. After a quick, cursory nod in Jamie's direction, she addresses her husband. "There were four this time," she tells him, boosting Matthew to the other hip and revealing a rounding of the abdomen where child number six is fast blooming. "Right nostril. Paul was amazed he could still breathe."

So this is Molly; Jamie thinks—incredibly trim for a woman who's borne five children. The same bloom of red ringlets, the same flashing eyes she remembers from that night a few months back, but she's dressed today in a green, designer sweat suit as attractive in its own way as the beaded, black cocktail dress Jamie first saw her in. She's easy to read—everything right there in her eyes—and in a flash Jamie knows she's dismissed her initial suspicions as too monstrous for even her husband.

Molly gives in, finally, and sets Matthew down—both women's eyes following his every move as he makes a beeline for Michael. All raw energy and determination—all boy. Jamie doesn't have to heft him to know exactly how he feels.

"Mommy, look at me. I'm playing the piano." Meghan is beaming.

"Listen, little man," Michael grins, poking Matthew playfully in the chest. "Nothing more up the nose. I mean it now."

Meghan is pounding away. "Look, Mommy."

Mia turns her face up to Molly, imploring. "I want to play it too."

"I don't suppose you've given her any lunch," Molly accuses, running a hand through Mia's dark, springy curls, so much like Meghan's.

Michael looks sheepish—rocks the chair forward, checks his watch.

"Didn't think so. Meggie, let the lady work and come have lunch. Matthew, Mia." She shoots a grim smile at Jamie. "Good news about the piano," she says. "Now we can finally sell the blessed thing and be done with it."

Meghan scrambles off Jamie's lap, face flushed, eyes flashing—no hint of the reticent child who hung by the door—then she, too, is gone. Funny the sense of lightness, of emptiness, once the warm weight of a child has left the lap.

Jamie's temple is throbbing with the start of a headache—as if the sucking of all that energy from the room has created some imbalance in air pressure. She sneaks a peak at her own watch, shocked to find it past twelve-thirty—too late for the promised call to Peter, who will be dismantling the boat cover with Bake by now—an annual rite of spring involving copious amounts of beer and chili, and, for some unexplained reason, a torturous dunk in harbor waters. Something else to apologize for. Seems that's all she does lately—apologize.

All at once she feels simply part of Michael's dirty little game; co-conspirators, they, in this fouling of the nest. She closes the keyboard lid and rises, refusing to meet his eyes even as she reclaims her briefcase from the desk.

"Bravo," he says softly, chuckling behind her as she heads for the door.

Molly's too busy tending to lunch, the children too busy laughing and squabbling and scrambling around, to notice Jamie slipping through the kitchen on her way back through the house. Closing the front door behind her, she's met with the self-important fussing of the sparrows in the maple overhead. Settling in, starting their nests. She should shoo them off, she knows, warn them not to make their homes in a place so poisoned with deception, lest their babies sicken and die.

Michael finds her as she's climbing into the car, stands stubbornly by her window until she lowers it.

"Thanks," he says smiling. "I haven't seen Meghan that animated in weeks."

Thanks? Suddenly she's furious that he's brought her here, that she's been forced to witness this cozy little family scene. All she's missing laid out in front of her like that—all she's missing because of him. "Tell me something," she says. "Just what was it you got out of this little performance?"

A shrug. "I've dreamed about watching you play my piano, though I must admit you weren't wearing nearly as many clothes. But, hey—all things come to he who waits. Besides, it was part of the deal."

"The deal," she says flatly, slipping the key in the ignition and starting the engine. "As in that night at my house? You just don't quit, do you? I should have called Augie right then, blown your cover."

"And tell her what, exactly?" he laughs, arm resting casually on the roof of the car, his face so close now she can see her reflection in the deep brown of his eyes. "That I cornered you in the hallway and kissed you? That you just about came right there against the wall?"

He taps the roof as he backs away, flashes her a big, friendly smile. "You stay in touch, now."

FIFTEEN

At first she's simply speechless.

"Look, it's all Meghan's talked about since you left," Michael says. "She's been kind of listless lately, and Molly thinks lessons might perk her up. She'll come to your place, so you'll have her to yourself." He lets that sink in—no doubt flashing to the cozy little scene at the piano, the sight of Jamie's hands moving casually through the girl's hair. "Two hours each time. We'll pay whatever."

Not yet twenty-four hours since she left his house and already he's at her again, treating her like some domestic he's considering taking into service. It's beyond insulting. She wouldn't be talking to him at all if it weren't for the boy—the nagging desire to see him again, to hold him. That and this perverse need for the truth, the lure of it stubbornly dragging her forward.

"I'm not the person to do this," she tells him. "I wouldn't even know where to start."

"But your mother taught you, didn't she? You must remember at least some of it."

True enough. And hadn't she sensed the girl's interest? A thirst almost, not unlike her own at that age. He knows this, of course, is probably counting on it. Still, throwing her together with his wife on a regular basis seems awfully dangerous, considering. Why, then—some macho game he's playing with himself?

"Besides," he says. "Molly wants you. Meghan's something of an odd kid—kind of distant. Fragile constitution and all that. She doesn't usually take to people the way she did you."

Now she gets it. "She'd have to practice every day; is she ready for that?"

"Absolutely."

"On the Bechstein." Playing with him now. No real intention of teaching the girl at all but enjoying the fact he needs something from her.

"That's a bit more than she can handle, don't you think?" Sarcasm in his voice. "We could easily rent something a little smaller, a little less—valuable."

"What for? You have one of the finest pianos in the world right under your roof. And she's more than half in love with it already, in case you haven't noticed, so she'd be more likely to practice." Too bad, really, Jamie thinks. Someone should be getting some use out of the thing, and she rather likes the idea of giving the girl some legitimate access to it.

"Hey, if that's what it takes..."

So smooth. Convinced he's got her, damn him. "There's absolutely no reason I should do this for you," she snaps—shocked to find she's actually considering it. Despite his manipulation. Despite everything.

"You won't be doing it for me," he reasons. "You'll be doing it for Meghan."

She has to keep reminding herself it's the girl he thinks she's interested in. Stupid man, really. "Uh-huh." Letting him know she isn't falling for it. "I'll think about it, let you know." She hangs up then, dismissing him mid-plea.

The plan comes to her over lunch. Augie's taken her to a toney French place off-Broadway that she and Gaspar have just discovered—expensive, busy, a bit out of the way for the symphony crowd. A clear indication any subjects raised are not to be discussed elsewhere.

They chat over menus, discussing the recent NEA survey of symphony orchestras and their conductors, the possibility that Adam Zorn might be considering other offers. Their golden boy looking to jump ship.

"We know Cincinnati and Seattle have already approached him," Augie tells her, eyes scanning the menu with the same cut-to-the-chase intensity Jamie has seen her apply to the finer points of soloist contracts and production detail. "And with the rumor that James Levine might be leaving the Met for the Boston Symphony, the board is very nervous."

"Understandably." They've lost other conductors with fewer than the four years Adam has put in, Jamie knows—most notoriously Philippe. She offers her usual refrain—no less passionate for the innumerable times she's voiced it. "We've been over this ad nauseam, Augie. We have to set ourselves apart somehow—modernize the programming, market ourselves as a haven for up and coming young composers—both things Adam has wanted from the start. We'll lose him otherwise—it's just a matter of time."

"I agree." Augie pulls a cigarette from her pack, snaps the lighter at its tip and sits back—her look deadpan as she meets Jamie's eyes. "But this takes money, Jamie—a lot of money."

Of course, Jamie thinks, wondering why she didn't see it coming. The capital campaign—a subject she has yet to broach with Peter. Something else occurs to her then, and in a flash she knows why they're here. "Let me guess," she says, her tone gone flat. "Adam's been told about the million dollar pledge."

Augie nods. "Michael phoned him personally." She smiles at Jamie's incredulous look, leans toward her over the table. "You must remember he's a board member now, my dear—entitled to do such things. In any case, you can imagine how excited Adam is at the prospect. We would be sure to keep him."

"Assuming the campaign is a go."

"Assuming the campaign is a go." Augie, who rarely drinks at lunch, is nonetheless nursing a martini. Jamie could use one herself just about now.

"So," Jamie says, "if we don't go forward, he'll start looking around. Assuming he isn't already."

"The last thing I want to do is pressure you," Augie tells her, "but this thing is taking on a life of its own, as you can see. I need to know if you've made a decision."

Jamie sidesteps the question with one of her own. "What if we proceed and Michael doesn't make good on his pledge?"

"The paperwork has already been processed, the only caveat being your participation, of course. A series of two-hundred-and-fifty-thousand-dollar donations, one each year for four consecutive years—all bills and receipts to be sent to his office, not his home." She takes a long sip from her drink, her eyes holding Jamie's over the wide rim of the glass.

"His wife knows nothing about it, then."

"It wouldn't be the first time such a thing has happened," Augie says. "In this case, however, it concerns me." She draws on her cigarette, exhaling languidly toward the ceiling. "We've never met the wife, you know. You'd think she'd have come to at least something in all this time. No," she insists, stubbing out the cigarette. "There's some problem there. I only hope they don't divorce anytime soon. That's the one thing that could put a kink in all this—assuming you're onboard, that is."

Jamie laughs. "That's what I love about you, Augie—your single-minded devotion to your work."

"Not so single-minded," she says softly, and if she's noticed the slight flush to Jamie's cheek at the conversational turn toward the Ryans' marital woes, she says nothing. "I didn't mention this before, but Michael has made it clear he expects direct involvement with you on the campaign. I put my foot down, of course. I had to wonder, though; it seemed such an odd request—especially considering the history between the two of you. So I made a few calls, discovered he has a reputation of, shall we say, inappropriate behavior with professional associates. Above all, I will protect my people from such things—million dollars or no million dollars."

Lunch arrives, allowing Jamie time to absorb all this, the feeling of having been ambushed by Michael and his strange resolve to keep her around. Augie's suspicions aside, the trouble in the Ryan marriage is hardly news—not to her. A quarter hour spent peering through their living room window told Jamie everything she needed to know about those two. Such fury, such bitterness in the toss of that icy drink. And Molly's breezy coolness toward Michael yesterday—all of it evidence of that irrevocable rift he mentioned, the loneliness murmured into her hair just before she showed him Sam's baby book.

Suddenly everything about this screams of opportunity, the potential of turning it all around on him. And why not? She gave him the chance to come clean, offer up the truth on his own, and look what that got her. Now, incredibly, thanks to these foolish lessons, he's about to provide access to the only other person who just might know the real story of that day. The wife—and an angry one at that. Two hours for a piano lesson was ridiculous, of course; a child Meghan's age might be good for half an hour, which would leave lots of time for conversation. Jamie envisions tea with Molly to discuss the girl's progress, long chats designed to gain the woman's trust.

And then there's Meghan herself. Who knows what she might have heard when she hid in the stairwell the night of that little drink-tossing scene? What other information she's gleaned over time—information that might be coaxed from her gently, patiently, unknowingly.

There are other ways to get at the truth of that day, Michael Ryan—other ways to settle the score. And you've just handed me two.

"I'll talk to Peter about staying on," Jamie says, though she knows convincing him won't be easy. "I'll need another week or so to work it out."

A light comes into Augie's eyes as she drops her napkin on her plate and sits back, drawing another cigarette from her pack. "Will he agree, do you think?" she asks, flicking the lighter at its tip.

"If he knows it's important to me."

Augie regards her as she exhales. "One thing, Jamie. I'm told Michael is not a man to be crossed, that he can be very vindictive. The board doesn't care about any of this, of course; they see him quite simply as the answer to their prayers. But I'm beginning to get an odd feeling about all this myself. Promise me you'll be careful, no matter what you decide."

∅ ꙮ

The chance to broach the subject with Peter comes just days before she's due to head south again, a few days before Meghan's first piano lesson.

It's finally warm enough to be up on deck in the early evening, and they take a bottle of Chardonnay and steaming bowls of Peter's shrimp-laden jambalaya to the cockpit for an early supper—the dogs wandering to their usual spot in the bow for an hour's perusal of the comings and goings of the harbor. Peter's been grousing on and off since Jamie got home about the political games the government's begun playing with his aquaculture funding, and he starts in on it again now.

"So anyway, the Feds have been hitting fishermen pretty hard lately—what with all the new regulations, catch limits. They have to give them something, I guess." He glances down, picks a greasy slick of rice from the front of his faded UNH sweat shirt. "Looks like I'm it."

"But they believe in your project at the Shoals—you've said so yourself a hundred times. You think they'd really cut the funding?" Loss of the grant means the project would be shut down—both of them know this. Five years of Peter's life down the drain.

"Probably not. This is the only offshore aquaculture project in the world, remember—every other country into farming fish uses bays or other interior bodies of water. It's a real feather in our cap, much too important to just cut off. What they really want is for me to make nice and accept new project guidelines—changes in buoy placement, the marking of the nets—things like that. The whole field will be less defined, of course—more easily sabotaged." He stands, picks two of his small, potted herb plants from the cabin top and places them carefully on the companionway steps. "Hand me the rosemary, will you?"

Jamie passes him two more pots, then keeps the hand-off going—basil, oregano, thyme, mint—until all seven in his spring crop are back in the warm safety of the cabin. Another week or so and they'll be hardy enough to stay on deck at night, draped with a dishtowel; another month, and the leaves will start turning up in her food. Such a farmer, this guy.

He finishes with the herbs and returns to sit beside her, sliding an arm along the fiberglass combing just inches beneath her shoulders—his warmth against her reassuring. "It makes no sense, Jae—that's the thing. These feed buoys, they're built by MIT; very high tech and very expensive—sixty, seventy thousand dollars apiece. They have to be placed in a particular configuration to be of any use at all. Letting the fishermen tell us where they want them is ludicrous. We're just inviting more damage. But, hey, that's what I love about the Federal Government." He taps the side of his head. "Nobody home."

"So what will you do?"

"Nod and smile, kiss ass—do whatever I have to do to keep the funding. 'Course, the pisser is I still have to deal with the fishermen. Would help if I knew just who was pumping holes into my buoys," he muses.

Jamie's reminded of the night she met Barbara Ann—the only lobsterman she really knows—and recalls the sudden tension when talk shifted to Peter's project. She tries to picture Bake's girlfriend braced in the stern of her boat, cackling with glee as she takes aim at one of Peter's buoys. "Why not talk to Barbara Ann?"

"You nuts?" he laughs. "She won't tell me anything. Thing to do is set up a meeting—an informational session about the project, show them what we're trying to accomplish. Maybe if they understand the whole thing a little better, they won't feel so threatened. I have to make them see how important this is, what it means for the future. How can a few people stand in the way of something like that?"

It hits her then that this is it, the opening she's been waiting weeks for. Even as she nods—knowing he needs her to listen, to empathize right now—she sees through to the end, knows if she lays it all out just right everything will fall into place. And hating herself for it.

"I've got the same kind of situation in New York right now, actually," she says, trying for a casual tone. "Some big donor dangling a million dollars in front of us for a new capital campaign. Only one problem: he insists I stay on to head it or we don't get the money. Two years—maybe more."

She sips the Chardonnay, letting her words sink in. His look is one she'll always remember—blank at first, then brows knitting together as he realizes he's caught; that any protest on his part would seem inconsistent, self serving. She moves on quickly, ignoring the sick feeling of having duped him, of hitting him when he's down.

"I'd have to go down more often at first—twice a month, probably, at least for a while. But if I can just get the whole thing rolling, someone else could easily take it over." Inventing this compromise on the spur of the moment. "He can hardly withdraw his pledge then."

Suddenly Lucille appears on the cabin top above them—nose twitching busily as she sniffs toward the stern. Barking then, loud and insistent—interesting enough activity for Gus to rouse himself and saunter over. Lobsters in the trap, it seems. Peter rises slowly, lifting the bowl of chow to Lucille's feet to distract her, then spends a minute kneading her ears until she decides the food is of more interest than the vibration of the trap line.

"Feels odd not having Highway around," Jamie says, her reference to the kitten an attempt to lighten the impact of her news. No big deal, this—mere suppertime chitchat.

"You know Barbara Ann's crazy about him," he says distractedly. Gus, too dignified to submit to anything as familiar as ear rubbing, accepts a few quick head pats before Peter moves to the line, uncleating it. "Besides, he'll have more room at her place." He starts with the questions then: why the woman who's taken her place down there can't handle the job; why they can't just bring in someone else—all things Jamie expected, has well-reasoned answers for. He grows quiet then—as if still trying to figure out exactly what's happened here. He's too good, loves her too much to ever suspect he's been set up, maneuvered into accepting something they both know he doesn't want.

"So, what do you think?" she asks.

"Don't know." Pulling the line in slowly now, hand over hand. "Does this have anything to do with Matthew?"

She grows still, hopes she hasn't heard him right.

"Jae?" Glancing over his shoulder at her.

She smiles. "I'm sorry. What?"

"Last night in your sleep you were talking to someone named Matthew."

Shock, shame, a damp trickle of fear all combine in a light laugh. "A little boy I met in Connecticut—same age my son was when he died."

He nods as he pulls seaweed from the line and tosses it back toward the water—the flinging motion attracting a group of gulls who bicker and keen above them for a handout. "Something about pianos, too." Pulling on the line again—long, measured movements. "Do you realize I've never even heard you play?" His tone thoughtful, a little sad.

She's crossed some line here and hates herself for it—but deflects the guilt with the absolute necessity of besting Michael Ryan. The realization she'll be face to face with him again in a matter of days sends a cool shiver along her spine.

"Let's go down," she says, rubbing her sweatered arms briskly. "It's getting cold."

SIXTEEN

Three nights later, she's back at the house—wired, unable to sleep though it's well after midnight. Wandering the circle of rooms, kitchen to hall to living room, dark now but for the wide shaft of moonlight striking deep through the front window. Round and round for what seems hours, and still the steady presence of the house does nothing to calm her. A clammy stillness has instead taken hold, as if GM has bolted in disgust, withdrawn her spirit to the complacency of death. How stupid to have agreed to this—putting everything on the line, and for what?

Another circuit of the rooms and another—past the Chickering, the moonlight bursting brilliantly on the honeyed wood of its case; through the kitchen, whose bouquet of smells is as much remembered as new. The hallway then, with its faded wallpaper and worn stairwell—fouled now with a darker energy that disturbs her, drawing her increasingly with each trip around. Pausing this time, giving in to it, she flattens herself against the wall—arms thrown wide as if pinned—and finally allows the memory of that night, the feel of Michael's mouth, her own response. His presence in her mind constant now, like a dull throb, a headache she can't shake.

Sometime later the cell phone rings—startling her from a restless half-sleep on the couch. Awake at once, she rummages on the floor for her bag.

"Peter?" Sleep in her voice, a stifled yawn.

"I woke you." Michael's tone is a liquid challenge, as if her memory of that night in the hallway has likewise stirred him, prompting the call. "You're in town?"

It has to be after two—all the world asleep but for the two of them. "You don't trust me. How disappointing."

"Wanted to check; make sure you hadn't changed your mind. Meghan would be devastated, as would I."

Change her mind? She's only thought to do it a hundred times. Still, here she is—prepared to play the teacher, to use his wife and daughter against him any way she can. Make use even of his seeming desire for her, if she can manage to put all that's happened out of her mind. Rising, moving to the window, she stares off toward the road, picks out a small red fox trotting casually across the moonlit expanse of lawn. "We haven't discussed my fee."

"Whatever; just send the bills to Molly."

No mention of the capital campaign, the fact she's accepted the board's offer despite the blood wrung from her marriage. "It's rather a poor use of your energy—all this finagling to keep me here."

"Worked though, didn't it?"

"Oh, I'd have stayed on for the campaign anyway, if only out of loyalty to Augie. Tell me," she says, watching as the fox slips quite suddenly into a blanket of shadow at the edge of the woods. "How much does Molly know about the money you've promised the symphony?"

"Absolutely nothing. Why do you ask?"

"Just curious. You should know that my involvement's going to cost you—make quite a dent in that first installment of yours."

"Oh, I'm not worried about your salary; I plan to pay for you over and above."

"Well, good; I'll be sure to double it, then."

He's still laughing when she disconnects, tossing the phone toward the couch as she heads for the stairs. Knowing she can sleep now; his call somehow breaking the tension that had her strung so tight.

The night is a puzzlework of fractured dreams, and she wakes with the lingering image of a five-year-old Sam sporting Matthew's spiky red hair, echoes of the little voice that used to call to her as morning stirred with light—the sound so real again, so immediate. "Sammy up! Mommy, Sammy up!"

She rises, the dream still echoing through her, and pads down the hall to his room—just as she did each morning while he waited for her to fetch him back to her own warm sheets—half thinking that if she opens his door before the feeling has faded, she'll catch his shadow there, the room looking just as it did every morning of his short life. Cotton blanket kicked into a ball at the end of a mattress fragrant with his smell; Winnie the Pooh grinning from a poster tacked to the peach-colored wall behind the crib; the blue oval rug with its smiling train.

Instead she's hit with the lingering smell of paint, the drawers of the dresser still gaping wide, pouring their emptiness into the hollow-sounding room. No crib at all where Sam, all tousle-haired, would be grinning and reaching for her now. Biting her lip, she sighs—relieved, embarrassed, disappointed. What had she expected after all?

∅ ∂

A car door slams, and moments later Jamie hears the knock. A fast-moving front has blown in overnight and she opens the door to a chill, gentle rain—the misty landscape behind Michael and Meghan rendering the full green of early June almost iridescent.

No Molly. Christ, why hadn't she seen this coming?

Ignoring Michael, she scrutinizes the upturned face beneath the plastic, cornflower blue rain hat—sizing the girl up against an unexpected hostility. Reluctant, suddenly, to bring another child into this house. Don't think of her as a child, she tells herself—think of her as a connection to Matthew, to Molly, a start toward unraveling the why of that awful day.

"I thought you'd just be dropping her off," she says, stunned by the sight of Michael shucking his coat and giving it a shake, draping it over the banister.

"I can't imagine why." Standing behind Meghan now, placing his hands on the shoulders of her matching plastic raincoat—the get up comically large for the girl's delicate frame. "Remember your manners, Meghan, and say hello." But Meghan is tongue-tied, it seems, her attention riveted to something off in the living room. He gives the little shoulders a squeeze. "She's been antsy all week, waiting for this. She's just a little nervous."

Maybe so, but she's absolutely still right now—almost catatonic, she's so subdued. Cold from the rain, perhaps, and white as a sheet—not at all the talkative little girl Jamie was hoping for. Not that it matters anyway; no chance of learning anything at all from her with Michael around.

He stoops and removes her hat, begins on the coat buttons.

"I can do it, Daddy." Meghan, back from wherever she was just a moment ago, is full of sudden energy—the little fingers moving deftly along the line of large, round buttons.

Jamie refuses to meet Michael's gaze as he stands, has no intention of revealing how rattled she is by his presence here after what happened last time—not just physically, but emotionally, the agony he unleashed with his twisted version of the accident. She'll never forgive him for that—never.

Leave, she thinks—hurling the thought at him as she takes charge of the wet things, ushering the girl back toward the kitchen. Go to the office, take a drive, get lost.

She hasn't given much thought as to how this is going to go, figuring she could easily bluff her way through the lessons without Meghan catching on. Molly, even, if she'd been here. Scrambling now to come up with something authentic enough to satisfy Michael, who'll no doubt be watching her every move. Best make use of him, she decides; that way she can at least keep an eye on him. Figure a way to get rid of him later.

"Can she read?" Jamie calls over her shoulder.

A snort of laughter as he trails them into the kitchen. "She's not in school yet, remember?"

"In that case, you can help by watching what we do." Instructing him in a clipped, matter-of-fact tone as she drapes Meghan's wet coat and hat on the glass doorknob to drip their hearts out onto the linoleum. "In case she has questions at home later. Just stay out of my way—you can take a chair from the dining room and sit to the right of the bench."

Meghan seems not at all interested in any of this; she's too busy staring past Jamie toward the Chickering, the gleaming side of its wooden case just visible through the kitchen's arched doorway. Comparing it to that magnificent other, no doubt; unaware she's already seen more quality in these two pianos than many professional pianists see in a lifetime.

The unruly tumble of curls has been gathered at her neck today, corralled with a purple butterfly clip; the pulling back of all that hair revealing the bony state of her shoulders, the long, thin arms looking painfully insubstantial in the cotton folds of her purple turtleneck. But the dark eyes are just as intense, just as curious. A beautiful, solemn child.

"Warm enough?" Jamie asks brusquely, and Meghan nods, eyes glued to the piano. Still, she gives the thermostat a nudge as they leave the kitchen, motioning for the girl to take the bench while she opens the lid of the Chickering to the first position.

Michael has placed the chair as directed but stands before the mantel, rolling back the cuffs of his blue denim work shirt as he scrutinizes the photo of Sam and herself. Studying it, now that he knows who this boy actually is.

"Understand," Jamie says quietly, snatching the picture and turning it face down. "This is just a trial. If I don't sense any real interest or talent, it will be her only lesson." Not wanting to do this at all, anymore; wanting them both gone, no matter what might be lost. Out of her house, out of her life.

Michael shrugs, as if it's all the same to him, slipping his hands in the front pockets of his jeans in a gesture of nonchalance.

Meghan, in the meantime, has risen to stand on the bench and is craning her neck to peer into the open piano—a mesmerizing array of wires and pins and oblong wooden hammers that somehow combine to make music. A way into the situation occurs to Jamie then and she takes the bench, directing the girl to watch what happens inside when different notes are played. The jump of the hammers hitting the strings called for in *Twinkle, Twinkle, Little Star* brings a giggle and a quick glance back toward Michael, who's chosen this moment to scroll, frowning, through the numbers on his cell phone.

Jamie continues with the tune as she works to reclaim Meghan's attention, strike some tone she can carry off for the next hour. "The real name of the piano is the pianoforte, Meghan. In Italian, piano means soft and forte means loud. But the name was shortened to piano."

"Like a nickname."

"Like a nickname," Jamie agrees.

The girl is much more animated after scrambling back down to sit beside her—less intimidated, it seems, now that some of the mystery has been explained. Jamie checks her height at the bench, which seems okay, but the feet are left to dangle high above the floor. Glancing around, she decides on the oversized atlas which she has Michael fetch from the stand beside GM's reading chair, and it bridges the gap perfectly.

"Music is a kind of language—just like words," she says, playing a progression of chords meant to soothe.

Meghan's look is skeptical, as if Jamie were trying to trick her. "Pianos can't talk!"

"Well, in a way they do. Think of it as like having a conversation with someone, only each time you say something to the piano with your hands, it answers you in music." Her own mother once told her this, and it's stuck with her all this time—has much to do, she thinks now, with why she's always taken such comfort in playing. She's offering a gift in the observation, she realizes, and despite herself feels strangely pleased to do so.

She begins with the basics: that music has an alphabet, just like words—one that goes from A to G—with all of the keys, both black and white, taking the name of one of those letters. Finger numbering follows; the thumbs number one on both hands, fanning out to the pinkies, which are number five—a concept she herself had trouble with at first because the left-hand fingering is so counter-intuitive. But Meghan gets it right away.

Michael's chair remains empty, but Jamie no longer feels his eyes boring into her. Shifting slightly, she catches his reflection in the window overlooking the back yard—gazing out across the field of summer grasses just now gaining some height. Just beyond his line of sight stands the copse of pines shading the barren little plot where her son lays, and Jamie imagines Sam turning his head slowly toward the window in recognition, drawn to the sight of the one who put him in that cold place.

Returning her attention to the lesson, she points out the repeating pattern of black notes—two, three, two, three—all the way up the piano. Has Meghan play all the paired twos— left hand if they're below middle C; right hand if they're above, then all the sets of three in the same way. Some of this she's pulling from memory, but most she's simply winging. It doesn't matter anyway; Michael's barely listening. Instead, he's begun a casual circumnavigation of the living room, killing time as he peers indifferently at things that have peopled her world since childhood—GM's collection of antique Hummel figurines, her shelves of old books—some of them first editions, the long line of photos on the table behind the couch. Meghan seems oddly disturbed by this—keeps throwing him glances—and Jamie has the sudden flash that she's not used to having him to herself in this way, longs for his undivided attention now that she does.

The music stand is empty but for a small, unused notebook unearthed from beneath Jamie's old practice books in the piano bench—one in which she's begun jotting the work she wants Meghan to practice. Give her a study book, she figures, something to carry around. Suddenly she's sorry the flimsy little notebook isn't something more substantial, that she hasn't filled the stand with impressive looking scores and sheet music to make the child feel these lessons are important, that she herself is important.

The soft trill of the cell phone claims Michael's attention, and he pulls it from his pocket, flipping it open as he moves to the table by the front window.

"Cup your hand as if you're holding a ball," Jamie instructs Meghan over the sound of Michael's voice, showing with her own hand how it renders the fingers all the same length. "And keep your wrists level—like this," she says, then has her repeat the finger numbering exercise with her hands held just so, pushing the notes down with each finger. But the girl seems oddly deflated now—tired or disappointed, or both—her concentration and enthusiasm gone. Out of nowhere comes a memory from the earliest lessons with her own mother, and Jamie tells Meghan to pick out some of the black notes—any order, just make something up, and play them with the correct hand. As a child, she thought her mother must be reading her mind when they did this, but she's long since come to understand. As Meghan begins, Jamie fleshes the single notes out with chords made up of white notes and suddenly they're making music. It's a trick of harmonics, of course—a slight of hand to bring the girl back, remind her what it is about this that so intrigues her.

Meghan is thrilled into laughter, real laughter—a lovely, tinkling sound Jamie hasn't heard before. If nothing else, this should get Michael's attention. Sure enough, when she glances over, he's turned a surprised look in their direction. Her gaze drifts down to his hands, then—his fingers busy flipping through the pages of the day planner she's left open on the table.

"Close that, please," she says pointedly, glaring at him over Meghan's head—the girl thankfully oblivious, plunking away in complete abandon now.

She's sure he's heard her; still he continues flipping through her days, talking as he peruses the details of her life. A question into the phone then, a soft chuckle as he turns yet another page.

The incredible nerve. She considers, then decides she'd gain nothing by making a scene—would surely lose what little ground she's gained with Meghan, who's just now easing out of her seemingly constant state of hyper vigilance.

Thankfully, the day-by-day minutia of her life quickly bores him, and, phone still in hand, he moves through the hallway to the dining room, where she's left her strategies for the capital campaign splayed out across the table, her briefcase open on a chair. Nothing too personal there, beyond her cell phone and a couple of receipts tucked in a side pocket; still, she's glad now she finally tossed all that research on Porter Street—Michael's casual mention of a client who lives there having come to nothing in the end.

He takes his time in the dining room and when he finally reemerges, tucking his cell phone in his pocket, she's adding a final note to the study book.

"You've done well, Meghan." she says, struggling to keep the anger from her voice. "That's enough for today, I think."

Michael's head snaps up as the girl scrambles from the bench. "That's it? We haven't been here forty-five minutes. She hasn't even played anything."

"Well, of course she has."

"Christ, you know what I mean."

Jamie closes the keyboard lid, freezing him with a look. "It's her first lesson. I thought we'd save the knuckle-busting techniques till next time—that okay with you?" Then rising, plucking the little study book angrily from the music stand, she follows Meghan and her assorted rain gear through the kitchen to the hall.

"How did you do that, by the way?" Michael asks mildly as he shrugs into his coat—as if he hadn't just spent the last fifteen minutes casually rifling through her belongings. "That thing when the two of you were—well, it actually sounded something like music."

"Harmonics of the penta scale," she says, pushing the study book at him. "Has to do with the way the white notes are arranged between the black." She watches him stuff the notebook in his pocket, wondering if he'll even remember he's got it once they get home. "Someone needs to sit and go through that with her when she practices—a half hour each night, repeating each of the things we did today. One night off a week is all right, but it should be the same night each week." Nothing like the three hours each evening she, herself, struggled to put in under her mother's tutelage, but enough to keep the interest up—keep Meghan coming back. Which is the point, after all.

"I have no time for this sort of thing."

"Oh, sure you do," Jamie tells him, pulling the door wide. "This was your idea, remember?"

"Molly's idea, actually—not mine. Hey," he says, catching the collar of Meghan's coat as she attempts to slip out onto the porch.

"Hat, young lady. And no splashing around, getting your shoes all wet, okay? "

A steamy mist is rising from the stone walkway, and the eaves are still dripping—but the rain has stopped for now, despite the rumble of thunder in the distance. Jamie crouches beside Meghan, who's looking longingly toward the puddles dotting the drive. Time for the first salvo in the war for heart and mind. "Tell your dad it isn't raining anymore, in case he hasn't noticed," Jamie says in a stage whisper. "And that puddles are good for the soul."

Meghan looks up hopefully, opens her mouth to speak.

"All right, okay," he says, giving in. "Go on to the car; I'll be there in a minute." A grin and she's off—down the porch steps in two hops, landing both feet hard in a puddle. "Terrific," he says. "Teaching her to defy her father."

"And you thought I was just going to teach her piano." Their eyes meet and hold for a moment before Michael looks away. "One more thing," Jamie adds. "Your presence distracts her. In the future, I'd prefer Molly drop her then pick her up after the lesson."

Michael keeps his eye on Meghan as he pulls the door partially shut. "Nice try," he says, "but if you think I'm going to leave you alone with my kid, you're crazy."

"You're worried about me? That's a laugh." Any lingering discomfort at being alone with him gone now, replaced by incredulity—anger at this casual, proprietary usurping of her time, her life. Crossing her arms, she cocks her head toward the dining room. "Find what you were looking for in there?"

A smirk as he glances down again, fiddling casually with the doorknob. "You know," he says, "life's funny. You spend years getting things set up just the way you want—think you know how everything's going to go from this point on, then something totally unexpected crops up."

So slick, this guy—sliding over the accusation, admitting nothing.

Turning the bolt now, fingering the lock assembly. "Take us, for example—you and me." Glancing up, he shoots her a megawatt smile that somehow contains little warmth. "There's got to be some element of fate in all this—don't you think? It's as though I was meant to be thrown into your path that day, that this has all happened for a reason."

The implication is so outrageous it takes a second for Jamie to get it, and when she does her heart heaves so hard the room seems almost to shift—all thought crushed beneath the suggestion that Sam was somehow destined to die that morning. An inexcusably monstrous thing to say, even for him, and for a minute she's so stung she can't even breathe, let alone respond; can only watch as he absorbs her shock.

"Well," he says, still smiling, pulling the door behind him as he's leaving. "We'll be on our way. Till next time, then."

SEVENTEEN

"A fight?" She can't quite take it in. "Is he all right?"

"Yeah, he's okay," comes Bake's growl. "Arm's wrenched pretty good, but at least it's not broke. Got it in a sling, which you know he ain't never gonna wear once we get outta this dump."

In the background, against the hollow, flat sound of announcements echoing down a hospital corridor, Jamie can hear Peter's voice—tired and irritated. Suddenly she knows it was Bake who wanted to call her, not her husband. "Put him on, okay?"

A shuffling, then Peter's voice. "I'm fine, I'm fine. It's no big deal."

"A fight? Peter, what..."

"Yeah, well, more of a scuffle, really—a misunderstanding after the meeting this morning."

Had he told her about this? One of the things he'd mentioned while she was packing to head south again?

"The fishing co-op," he says patiently. "The talk I gave explaining the Shoals project to the fishermen?"

"Right, right. I remember now." Not really, but it doesn't matter. "Someone hit you?"

"A shoving match between a guy from NOAA and a couple of testy lobstermen; I just happened to get in the middle. Barbara Ann and Bake broke it up before it got out of hand. It's no big deal. Bake shouldn't have called you."

"I can be home later tonight."

"No need. Listen, they're about to spring me from this place with a mess of drugs guaranteed to knock me on my ass. Can't wait. Hell of a way to get a day off, but you take what you can get." Softening his voice now. "Don't worry about me—really. I'll see you when you get back. Oh, Christ. Here comes little mother again."

"Mr. Tough Guy," Bake says, taking the phone. "He tell you he's got a pretty good shiner too?"

She can't even imagine, doesn't want to think too hard about it or the guilt will drive her crazy. "Make sure he gets some rest, okay? I'm serious. Take him by the ears and make him listen to you."

"I ain't no babysitter, Jamie. Besides, I got work. You need to get home."

Meghan is due any minute, and nothing short of life-threatening disease will get Jamie to cancel now. She's waited weeks for another chance at the girl, the chance to make a start with Molly, and she's determined on her plan, despite Michael's vicious comments having pitched her into a depression the likes of which she hadn't seen since just after Sam's death. If anything, his callousness has worked to focus her, harden her intent. "I can't possibly be back until tonight," she tells Bake now.

Silence. "Yeah, well, we all have our priorities."

"Come on, Bake. I have obligations here."

"Whatever." A click and she's holding a dead phone, anger and guilt warring inside her. Peter will be fine, she tells herself. He'll go back to the boat, take his medication and be out like a light before she could even get on the road. If she left now, she'd just be hanging out, listening to him snore all afternoon. She'll call Augie later, explain the situation, be home sometime after dinner. But first she'll have her time with the girl and, hopefully, Molly—no matter how Bake feels about it.

Fifteen minutes later, she opens the door to an earnest looking Meghan, arms crossed against the practice book clutched to her chest. Taken literally to heart, it seems—the name *Meggie* drawn— no, painted—on the cover now, the final "*e*" trailing off into a pool of glittering, silver stars. Beautifully, lovingly done. Must have been Molly. Well good, then.

Her heart drops at the sight of Michael coming slowly up the path, scowling as he follows through the open door. Damn, she thinks. Where is this woman? Isn't she even a bit curious?

"I have to take off for about an hour," Michael announces gruffly, clearly uncomfortable with the prospect. "Client having a meltdown." Shooting Jamie a warning glance, he turns and studies Meghan, who's struggling with the small wooden buttons of her cotton sweater. Strands of dark hair, alive with static electricity, float above her shoulders as he lifts her chin with a finger. "Remember what I told you, Meghan," he says sternly. "I don't want you bothering Mrs. Apollo with all your chatter. You're here to learn." He pulls a card from his wallet, places it on the hall table. "I'll be at my office," he says flatly. "Number's on the card."

Jamie can hardly believe her luck. Closing the door left wide in his wake, she fights the urge to simply abandon the lesson and draw the girl into conversation. Bad idea, she decides. Michael will surely ask about it later. Best to play it safe, keep to the plan.

They've only just taken the bench when Meghan turns to her. "Margaret told me not to smile at you that day because you were a stranger, but I didn't care. I knew you were nice. Sometimes I know that."

"When was this?"

"When we went sledding that time."

"I remember that." Jamie raises the keyboard lid slowly, wondering if the girl has told Michael she saw her watching the children. Still, he knows she runs past the house; he's seen her himself any number of times. She waits to see if Meghan will offer anything more on the subject, but she clams right up again—as if she just wanted to get that one thing cleared up.

Before them on the stand are the twin red volumes of Bastien's *Primers for Young Beginners* and the first book of the Burnham Preparatory series—picked up just that morning in her determination to be better prepared. No need to buy the advanced exercises; by that time, she figures, she'll have gotten everything she can from Molly and the girl. Canceling the lessons should be easy enough then.

They begin with a review of the alphabet concept and quickly move on to the naming of the white notes nestled at the base of each double pair of black keys: C, D, E; C, D, E all the way up the keyboard. It's clear Meghan's been practicing, which is a relief, and in no time they're on to basic rhythm—the difference between quarter and half notes, the division of notes into measures, counting beats. Less than thirty minutes into the lesson, they've finished with proper hand positions and Jamie's beginning to wonder if she's underestimated the girl's talent, should be moving things along faster. She decides to try out the first of the Primer's short three-note songs.

"Do you have any kids?" The little face, lit with curiosity, is turned up to her now.

She'd forgotten this about children—their sudden, breathtaking turns toward the unexpected—and she tries stalling, flipping purposefully through the primer as she scrambles for some innocuous response. But Meghan's gaze is steady and unflinching. Nothing gets past this one; she's sure to smell a lie a mile off.

"I had a little boy," Jamie says carefully, praying she won't have to explain the whole concept of death to an uninitiated five year old. "But he died."

Meghan's nod is one of recognition. "I had a kitten one time. His name was Zoom, but he died, too." She pauses then—as if, like Jamie, she's considering what to reveal. "Mikey said God took him back because I was bad."

Ah, Jamie thinks. Seven-year-old Michael, junior—in training, it appears, to be just like his father. "I don't think God would do that," she tells Meghan. Though of course, you can't be sure. An inscrutable thing, this God. Not at all bothered by the untimely death of innocents, as she herself has come to understand. "Listen, why don't we take a break? I think I have some hot chocolate around here somewhere." And with that they're off to the kitchen, Jamie calculating she might have maybe half an hour before Michael returns—thirty minutes to get a feel for what, if anything, Meghan knows.

She reheats the kettle, still warm from her morning tea, and pulls mugs and the box of cocoa packets from the cabinet. Time to start keeping some cookies in the house again, she supposes.

"I found these over there," Meghan says, opening her hand to reveal several pennies. Jamie glances toward the window above the small kitchen table, noting the gap.

"Hmmm," Jamie nods. "My lucky pennies."

Closer scrutiny of the coins then, looking for some evidence of this promised power beyond the mere monetary.

"My grandmother believed putting pennies in window sills brings luck," Jamie explains. "So that's what I do when I find one." Pulling the kettle from the stove, she fills the cups and mixes the chocolate, tosses in a few marshmallows—watching Meghan out of the corner of her eye as the pennies are carefully returned to the window. Probably figuring Jamie's luck needs all the help it can get—what with a dead little boy and all.

They choose the table by the door for the sipping of their chocolate, and while Jamie tries to figure a way into the subject of Michael and Molly's relationship, Meghan sits kicking her feet and peering about the room intently—trying for another stash of magic coins, perhaps.

"Meghan..."

"My mom calls me Meggie. It's a nickname," she informs Jamie. "Like you said about the piano."

Right. Okay then. "Do you want me to call you Meggie, too?"

An emphatic nod. "Daddy's the only one who calls me Meghan. He doesn't like nicknames much. Except for Mattie, but that's because he's still a baby."

Matthew. Maybe she could start with Matthew. First things first. A dark chocolate mustache has formed above Meghan's upper lip. "Here," Jamie says, handing her a napkin. "For your mouth."

A scrape, then a thump from somewhere above draws Meggie's eyes toward the ceiling. "I think he's playing up there," she giggles.

"Who?"

Looking at Jamie as if this were obvious. "Your little boy."

"He died, Meggie," Jamie says, reaching over to hook an errant curl with her finger, then tucking it behind the girl's ear. "You do know what that means, don't you?"

Another emphatic nod. "But maybe he didn't really die," she reasons. "Like on TV. Maybe he's just invisible, so you can't see him." Another thump. "I think he's up there jumping on his bed. Just having fun jumping." She seems to like this idea, attacking the cocoa with new relish.

Jamie envisions the white enameled crib resting in pieces against the wall of Sam's room—the five bulky sections, plus mattress, which only last night she manhandled down the steep attic stairs. One of them slipping slowly to the floor, no doubt.

"This house is pretty old," she tells Meggie. "It makes funny noises sometimes. When I was a little girl, I used to hear strange ticking sounds while I was going to sleep, and for a long time I thought it was my grandmother, knitting in bed all night while she watched over me. But it was really just the heater in the hall making noise as it cooled down." Now where did that come from? she wonders. I haven't thought about that in years.

Meghan looks chastised, as if she's made the mistake of blundering into yet another unimaginative adult. Idiot, Jamie thinks—talking down to her like that. After all, who brought up the idea of magic pennies? She struggles for a way to make it up, take away the sting of her words, but the moment has passed. Meggie has pulled into herself again, saying nothing more about the sounds stubbornly continuing from the second floor.

They return to the piano, but the girl has grown listless now—only half listening to Jamie's explanation of the basics of notation, the concept of chords. Useless to try to teach her anything more today. She's noting everything in the study book, Meghan beside her on the bench kicking her feet, when Michael reappears at the edge of the living room. No knock, no greeting; he's simply there when she looks up. Beyond him, the front door yawns wide. *Born in a barn?* GM would have snapped.

"Meggie, your dad's here," Jamie says indifferently, taking her time with the notes before joining them in the hall. Michael, who hasn't moved, appears bored as she stoops to help Meghan with the wooden buttons of her sweater. Interesting. Perhaps this little game is proving less entertaining than he'd hoped, and he'll hand the whole thing off to Molly after all.

"How did your little boy die?"

Michael's head whips around, the heat of his gaze boring into Jamie as she finishes the last button, gently smoothes the front of the sweater. She glances up then, watching with satisfaction as the color drains from his face. Eyes steely, full of a quiet dread.

She has him now, she knows—could hurt him irrevocably with just a few simple words—but it would mean hurting Meghan as well. Quite unexpectedly, she finds she can't. Not this way.

"He was killed in a car accident," she says. "Now—here's your study book; practice hard, okay?" She stands then, staring Michael down—daring him to say anything to her now. Anything at all.

But he remains silent, assessing. She can all but see the wheels turning—the quick, lawyerly weighing of options. Finally, he takes the little hand and moves off toward the SUV idling in the drive.

She'll have to work fast now, she knows. He must surely sense the danger, may already be pumping the girl about what they talked about, how the subject of Sam's death came up in the first place. Even as she smiles, returns Meghan's wave, she's planning the call to Molly, praying she can reach her before Michael gets home with some trumped up excuse for canceling the lessons. If she loses access to the girl and the wife, Jamie knows, she's lost it all.

Playing to Molly's maternal pride is the way to go, she decides. What mother could resist such praise, after all? A friendly call from the teacher, a kind of progress report to rave about Meghan's innate talent—certainly no stretch there. Jamie smiles then, thinking she might just add a little something disturbing about Michael himself—a vague discomfort at his insistence on staying through the lessons—allow her tone and Molly's imagination to fill in the blanks. Help nudge the woman into bringing Meggie herself from now on.

You want to throw guilt around, Michael? I'll give you guilt.

She shoots them a final wave and shuts the door, chuckling at the thought of the interesting evening the Ryans are about to have—already scripting the conversation with Molly as she heads for the phone.

EIGHTEEN

Things are still strained between Jamie and Bake on the ride into town—the three of them wedged into the grimy cab of his Ford F150, where the smell of oil, sweat and old burger wrappers hangs heavy in the air. Once in a while a piece of furniture shifts in the overloaded truck bed, and Bake peers in the rearview mirror, leaning into Jamie as if she isn't there. But then that's the point. There's no one like Bake for carrying a grudge.

"I'll bet I could do it in under ten minutes with the Zodiac," he claims, looking past her to make his point with Peter. "Can't be more than a couple miles."

"Depends on the tide," Peter says, glancing out the open passenger-side window at the crowds of tourists packing the streets of downtown Portsmouth for the long July Fourth weekend. At least from this angle, Jamie's spared the sight of his bloodshot eye—the blackened orb faded now to a sickly yellow-green patch covering much of the right side of his face. He's begun cradling his arm again, though; overworked it, probably, with this business of moving Bake into Barbara Ann's.

"I'd never go this way," he grouses. "Too much traffic; we'll be stuck for twenty minutes if the bridge is up. Should have taken the interstate."

"Bridge goes up on the half hour; we've got three or four minutes at least." The challenge of making the old lift bridge across the Piscataqua River into Maine without mowing down a pile of sightseers has Bake grinning. "Anyway, Barb's Zodiac has a fifteen on it. I figure if I shoot straight across to Prescott Park from her place and hug the shoreline out to the Coast Guard station, I can be at your boat in Little Harbor in under ten."

Peter cocks his foot on the dash and considers this. "Awful choppy in the main channel there, with the current and all that ship traffic. If the tide's right, you could duck under the causeway bridge at New Castle, cut through the spur and come out just behind the slips in the marina. You could do it in ten minutes that way—no big ships either."

They just make the bridge, and Bake leaves off debating the route to lean across Jamie again—pointing and shouting to Peter above the whine and rhythmic whap, whap, whap of tires hitting the mesh deck, that Barbara Ann's place is just there, somewhere beneath the blur of trees on the far side.

A sharp right just off the bridge and then another—Bake's tattered collection of belongings shifting wildly in the back of the truck with each turn—and suddenly they're dodging potholes on an unmarked street the width of an alley. A dead end street, it appears, dipping sharply down to the water and curling around a small cove filled with maybe fifteen lobster boats—the homes here a grouping of weathered capes perched along the shore, each with its own dock, ramps and floats loaded with fishing gear. Picturesque until you catch the smell of old bait, rotting seaweed, slimy ocean life drying out on the lobster traps that fill the driveways and minimal yards.

Barbara Ann's place is the last on the street, where the relatively protected waters of the cove meet the swirling current of the back channel. It looks to be the largest of the bunch; one of the few with a good-sized lot, as if it were built before the others, when land along the river wasn't going for a hundred thousand an acre—even land like this, sitting smack beneath the metal trusses of the bridge. They pull into the drive and come to a stop behind another pick-up even larger and dirtier than Bake's—a bait truck, Jamie figures, based on the smell that hits then as they open the doors.

Bake is fumbling with the ropes securing the worn leather recliner he's refused to give up when a screen door slams, and Barbara Ann comes around the side of the house, clothed in jeans and a faded blue t-shirt. Ready to take him on—it would seem, though Jamie still can't quite believe he's giving up his place to join her here. Two teenage boys trail behind—Billy and Drew, eighteen and fifteen, Bake has told them on the ride over—tall and coltish, not yet grown into their hormone-juiced bodies, covering their shyness with a spate of mutual shoving and mock punches.

Half an hour later, the contents of the truck a hodgepodge in the middle of Barbara Ann's living room, Jamie stands alone, nursing a beer on the deck spanning the back of the house. Surprised by how nice it is here overlooking the little cove; what with the bridge and the boat traffic along the river, it's quite a view. And on a holiday weekend like this, complete pandemonium—the channel before her choked with a sensory overload of powerboats, jet skis and inflatables, all screaming past the no wake sign bobbing at the entrance to the cove.

Elbows propped on the rail, her gaze returns to the dock some thirty feet below where Peter stands with Bake—his foot resting on the gunnel of Barbara Ann's lobster boat as it rocks and pulls on its lines. Both of them taking pulls of beer while they shoot the breeze with Billy, who's scrubbing the skids in the stern almost angrily—cigarette parked in the corner of his mouth. Suddenly Bake erupts in laughter—flipping a hand against Peter's arm as he gestures expansively out across the river.

Peter glances up just then and grins, as if sensing Jamie's eyes on him, and she raises her bottle in mock salute. But it's the dog that's drawn her attention, really—a yellow lab asleep on its side beside them, oblivious to the mix of laughter and music and engine noise, the grinding screek of the metal ramp leading from dock to deck shifting with the movement of the water. Some neighbor's, most likely, but a dead ringer for the Ryans' dog, and an uneasy reminder of the call to Molly, the fallout she feels inexorably heading her way.

Their conversation had been cordial enough, though shorter and more restrained than Jamie would have liked—Molly's initial surprise at hearing from her and the pride she'd voiced at her daughter's progress fading quickly when the subject shifted to Michael and his odd desire to be present at the lessons. Jamie stressing the word *odd*. Even over the phone, she could feel the woman bristling, growing edgy; knew she'd found her mark when Molly cut the call short, dismissing her with a terse thank you and an even colder goodbye.

Oh, to have been there when an unsuspecting Michael walked through the door. I understand Meggie's doing very well, Molly might say—smiling down at the girl, no doubt running her hand through that thick shock of curls. A natural at the piano, Diana tells me, wants her twice a month now. Pride in her voice, and praise. Michael growing still at this—wary, then furious that Jamie has pre-empted him—doubling her contact with Meghan when he was looking to cut it off altogether. Molly's alert for any reaction, of course—Jamie's veiled implication of something unseemly in her mind, but it's only later that night, alone together in their room, that she demands an explanation from him. Why this insistence on staying for the lessons, she wants to know—something she'd clearly been unaware of. Tears, then—a litany of accusations, past transgressions. Jamie envisions Michael standing stony and silent before his wife and a delicious rush runs through her at having reached into their lives like this, stirring it up between them. Well worth whatever payback is headed her way.

A slam of the screen door and Barbara Ann is suddenly beside her—a plate of raw burgers in one chapped hand. She nods toward the cove, pointing with a bent metal spatula toward the boat where Billy has taken a final pull on the cigarette, flicking the butt to the water before turning the hose on the cockpit floor.

"You know I can count the number of bikinis on the river by how long he takes to clean that boat?"

Jamie smiles. "Your other son doesn't help?"

"Drew-boy?" Barbara Ann heads to the massive, winged Weber grill by the door. "No," she laughs, lifting the hood to release a puff of greasy smoke, "cleaning the boat's Billy's thing—took it over when his dad got sick. Won't even hear of help."

The silence is full of questions Jamie won't ask, can't ask.

"Six years ago last month," Barbara Ann says, depositing the burgers, "and I can't even say the sea got him." The line has a practiced, almost flippant tone—a bridge for the uninitiated picking their way across chasms of unimaginable loss. She shuts the hood, lays the plate on top. "The man smoked his whole life, you see. Most of 'em do—keeps 'em warm on the water." She settles herself in one of the white plastic chairs facing the railing and plucks a Bud from the cooler at her feet. "Hell of a way to die," she says with a twist of the cap. "I can tell you that."

Jamie quickly does the math—Billy would have been twelve, she realizes; Drew, nine when their father died. Must have been awful—beyond awful.

"Bake told me about your little boy—that car accident and all," Barbara Ann says. "Man, that's gotta be the worst. It'd drive me nuts to lose one of mine."

He didn't just die, Jamie wants to say; he was taken—his life snatched away. But this moves her toward freshly tortured territory, and she offers nothing of it—no easy, rehearsed entree into her own pain; regrets now having stepped inadvertently into Barbara Ann's. Not for her, this mutual serving up of heartache.

She glances again at Billy—just a kid, really, for all his posturing and the bold smiles flashed toward preening girls sprawled on the foredeck of a passing speedboat. There were long years when she was sure that losing parents was the worst possible pain a person could feel, but that was before Sam. Different kinds of pain, she knows now; different regrets.

"How do you ever get over it?" she muses—less question than observation, really—vaguely wondering as she watches the speedboat bounce a good three feet off a wave why no one has insisted on lifejackets.

"You don't." The response, blunt and soul-baring, surprises Jamie into turning, and she meets Barbara Ann's gaze—knows then just why it is we wear our pain on the inside. Keeps others from going blind.

"Grief gets all over you like a smell," Barbara Ann says. "Makes people uneasy after a while—believe me, I know. There comes a time you have to just put it away."

Jamie shifts against the railing, uncomfortable with where it sounds like this is heading, but Barbara Ann's attention has shifted. A lobster boat has broken from the stream of traffic to swing into the cove, slowing as it passes the dock on its way toward a mooring. A kid about Billy's age in a dirty t-shirt and orange coveralls stands in the open stern scraping down the skids—rock music from his radio mixing with the keening of the gulls, the whine of a lawnmower starting up a few houses over. A graying, stubble-faced man leans from the wheelhouse to shoot Barbara Ann a wave. Arms like Bake's—thick and powerful. Once she would have seen him as just another lobsterman, part of a mysterious and colorful segment of New England life, but no more. One look at Peter's face has changed all that.

"What really happened at that meeting about the Shoals project?" she asks. Barbara Ann returns the wave, eyes on the lobsterboat as it makes a slow turn back toward them. Backing down over its prop wash as it pulls alongside Billy, the man shouting a greeting.

"Everything was fine at first," she says. "Pete and this government guy talked about the pens out there at the Shoals—how fish farmin's the way of the future an' all like that. Told 'em it's another way to work for yourself out on the water but with a guaranteed catch—you know how he goes on about it. A couple of the guys got testy—just wantin' to bitch about all the restrictions, how this is just another government ploy to drive us all out of business, but Pete handled it okay. It wasn't till they brought it outside and the government guy took off that things got outta hand. It's just a couple of 'em, you understand. Wanted to make sure Pete knew they wasn't gonna just roll over for this."

Jamie's blank look follows her back to the barbecue. "He wasn't just caught in the middle, then? Somebody actually went after him?"

Barbara Ann barks a laugh as she flips burgers. "Is that what they told you? Come on, you see what he looks like. That make any sense?"

Something's happening down on the water, where the lobster boat has drifted back closer to Peter and Bake. The talk seems friendly enough—what they can catch of it, anyway—but Barbara Ann has grown suddenly vigilant.

"You gotta understand," she says—eyes glued to the dock, "some of these people been fishing for two, three generations. It's not just a job to them; it's family." The hood of the Weber flips back down, and Barbara Ann comes to stand by her again. "A guy calls in a mayday—he's in trouble somewhere outside the harbor, say—you'll get twenty boats steaming outta here before the Coast Guard even knows about it. You get a couple of them pissed off, you got the whole lot on your case." She pauses. "Pete's messing with people's lives here. You can't go messing with a man's life and not expect a reaction."

Jamie nods, knowing somehow it was Barbara Ann who convinced them all to come to the meeting in the first place, that she was probably the one who kept them from hurting Peter even more than they did. "And where do you fit in all this?"

A shrug. "Pete is Bake's friend, so I'm tryin' to keep a lid on it, but I'm part of that family too. You need to know that."

Jamie catches it first—an escalation in rhetoric. The guy in the wheelhouse talking directly to Peter now, a nasty edge to his tone. So he's recognized him, after all—her Peter, who's only ambition in any of this is to help feed the world. Suddenly Bake goes all stiff, his hands balled into fists at his sides as he spits invective— Peter trying to defuse him, hold him back. Disbelieving laughter from the boat. A grinning Billy watching quietly—hands tucked behind the bib of his orange coveralls.

"Oh, Christ." Barbara Ann puts two fingers to her mouth, lets out a whistle to rival anything on the river, even as she starts down the ramp. "Yo!" she calls. "Grub's on! Get your asses up here!"

✍ ৡ

Jamie pushes through the screen door, carrying bowls of pasta and potato salad destined for the wings of the Weber—Barbara Ann behind her with a bowl of chips.

"No," Peter says patiently from the deck chair beside Bake, his leg propped on the rail. "What I'm saying is there's no possible way a forty-foot sailboat can go that fast."

"Yeah, and I'm telling you the thing was doing twenty knots if it was moving at all." Bake takes a pull on his Bud and glares off over the water, his mood soured from the aborted confrontation on the dock. It's this side of him Jamie's never had any patience for—all bravado once the adrenaline starts pumping, unable to back down from the most untenable of positions. He'll be in a black mood the rest of the day unless someone can turn him around.

Peter rises in a long stretch, then makes his way to the grill. "Laws of physics are against you, my friend. Hull speed's defined as one point three times the square root of waterline length. A forty-foot sailboat—wood, fiberglass, or fucking kryptonite—can do eight, eight and a half knots, tops, unless it's going downwind in a goddamn hurricane." He licks a mayonnaise smear from his thumb. "Great potato salad. There's basil in here, right?"

"Fuck it, "Bake says, scowling now. "I know what I saw. Hey, baby," he croons, wrapping an arm around Barbara Ann's waist as she settles in his lap, hands him a plate loaded with burger, chips, salads. A peace offering of sorts, Jamie figures, since diffusing the situation on the dock hadn't won her any points. Bake fights his own battles, period.

The screen door slams, and Barbara Ann's boys head to the grill; a silky, black streak—Highway, Jamie realizes—slips out behind them to skitter off the deck and around the side of the house. Billy grabs a burger and moves back inside, the door slamming again behind him. There's the sound of a television—laugh track blaring till he thinks to turn it down.

"Hey, my band's got a gig in Portsmouth tonight," Barbara Ann announces a little too brightly. "How about you all come into town, check us out? Some group up from Boston gonna be at Johnny-O's on the beach, too."

"Jamie don't like your kind of music, baby," Bake tells her. "She's into all that fancy, highbrow shit—symphonies, opera, crap like that."

"What's the name of your band?" Jamie asks, ignoring the dig.

Barbara Ann cocks her head toward the Weber. "Ain't got one yet. Drew here suggested *Boat Bitches*. Nice, huh? Fifteen years old."

Drew grins as he ladles potato salad onto a cardboard plate close to collapsing beneath the weight of his meal.

"And you," Bake grouses, turning his black mood on Barbara

Ann now. "Just so's you know, I don't need no woman defending me."

"Course you don't, baby. It's Pete, here, I was worried about. Course you had one foot on Wally's boat, fixing to beat the crap outta him for callin' Pete out, and he's one of the few men I know could probably take you on."

Peter laughs. "It's not Bake he wanted. He was just dying to finish what he started at the co-op meeting. He's not convinced the lobster population is decreasing, but if it is, by God—it's gotta be my Shoals project that's screwing things up."

"Yeah, well, Wally's always been a hot head," Barbara Ann tells him. "And you don't really know it isn't something going on out there that's killin' off the lobster babies, do you? I mean, assuming what you're sayin' about all this is true."

"Can't be us," he says. "The problem isn't just here; it's all along the New England coast. The theory is it's something oceanographic, some ecological shift—changes in current flow, maybe—that's creating unfavorable conditions for larval settlement."

Barbara Ann scrutinizes him. "You have me half-convinced, you know—otherwise Wally woulda gotten a real crack at you down there on the dock."

He laughs. "I'm sure."

"In fact, me and Bake and some others are headin' to a powwow with the Feds down in Connecticut end of next month. About that mess in Long Island Sound. Gonna give us the results of all their tests. Months and months they been doin' this. We could use somebody like you to sniff out the bullshit."

"Are we talking about the huge lobster die off?" Peter asks.

Barbara Ann nods as Bake grabs another couple Buds from the cooler, hands her one. "Eleven million pounds in one year," she says. "Pesticides. Malathion, probably—used for mosquito control."

"Might be," Peter says neutrally, "but the jury's still out, from what I hear. The amebic parasite theory actually has the best correlation with mortality statistics."

"Parasites my ass, " Bake says, popping the top. "The only parasites are the government guys tryin to cover their asses. Think about it. They spray all this shit around, and suddenly a couple hundred lobstermen ain't got no jobs? No wonder they want us to think it's just some Mother Nature thing. Sue their damn asses off otherwise."

"It happens like that sometimes," Peter says. "Some mysterious way of balancing things out—nature, fate, whatever you want to call it. We might never find the reason for a die-off like this, but it usually happens when a species is out of balance with everything around it. Besides, I don't think the government would have wasted two-point-five million studying the problem if they were trying to put something over on you."

A snort from Bake. "Why not? Gives 'em another excuse to waste our money."

"I mean it, Pete," Barbara Ann says. "We could use you down there. You could be our expert; make sure everything's on the up and up. Would give you a chance to make some points with the boys, too."

Peter laughs, shakes his head. Still, Jamie can tell he's pleased.

"Reminds me I gotta call my aunt down in Bridgeport," Barbara Ann says. "Make sure she's got room for us." She turns to Jamie. "Isn't that somewhere around where you are? That house you have from your grandmother?"

Jamie nods, glad for a way into the conversation that keeps her clear of Bake's ire. "Over in Easton—along the old road to Fairfield. The house is pretty secluded—off by itself, a mile or so from anything else, set back from the road."

"Wait a minute. Big white place? Used to have an old tire swing hanging from a Maple down by the mailbox? I know that place!

We used to drive out that way when I was a kid visiting in summer. Best way to get over to that reservoir for a swim.

Jamie grins. "Devil's Den. My grandmother used to take me there for picnics. Wouldn't let me swim, though. Said it was too deep."

"It was. Some kid drowned there one summer. I remember that."

"Danny Entwhistle. He was in my class."

"You're shittin' me."

The sudden, odd connection has them both grinning, which seems to only worsen Bake's mood. Still pumped, needing a fight—some outlet for all that excess adrenaline. "Yeah, that's just what I need," he grouses. "Some road trip to fuckin' Connecticut with Wally and them. With me lookin' out for Pete's ass the whole time. I'll end up punchin' somebody's lights out for sure."

"Look," Barbara Ann says, the playfulness gone from her voice. "We talked about this. You want to be part of things around here, you can't be stirring it up. Might be a good thing if the government does shut down Pete's fish pens for a while. Give all you hot heads a chance to cool off."

It takes a minute for Jamie to get it, then she turns a pointed gaze on Barbara Ann. For a moment, the two women simply regard each other.

"Oh, swell," Barbara Ann says, glaring at Peter. "You didn't tell her this either? Christ, don't the two of you ever talk?" Disgusted, she turns to Jamie. "Pete here told us the Government might put a lid on the fish project for a year or so. Placate all us fishing types."

Jamie stares at Peter dumbly. "You'll lose your job if they pull the grant."

Bake snorts derisively, swipes a napkin across his mouth. "No shit."

"So his plan is to get all these hot heads together again, work it out," Barbara Ann continues. "And it ain't a good idea—not right now. What Petey-boy here needs to do is keep a low profile. Low, low profile."

Jamie's still staring at Peter. "You didn't tell me this—why?"

Another snort from Bake, a swig of beer. "Probably cause you ain't here half the time—too goddamn busy down there in Connecticut or New York or wherever the fuck it is you're always running off to."

"Knock it off, Bake," Peter grumbles—rubbing his arm now, as if all this testiness has triggered a sudden flare up of the injury.

Bake ignores him. "And even when you are here, you're starin' off into space half the time. Someone says something to you, and it's like, hello? Anybody home?"

"I was four hours away when you called from the hospital, Bake—you know that."

"Yeah, well, whatever it is you got goin down there is interfering with what you got goin up here—you know what I'm sayin'? I ain't the one should be drivin' this guy around whenever he gets hisself beat up."

Okay, enough. "I don't know why not," she shoots back. "Since these new buddies of yours are the ones who did it."

This draws a hoot from Barbara Ann. "She's got you there, baby."

"Cool it, you two," Peter grouses. "Look, Jae, nothing's definite, okay? Shutting the project down is just one possibility—probably won't happen anyway." Glancing from one to the other now. "So. Let's all just drop it, all right?"

But Bake won't let it go. "You know, I told him you were bad news that first day we saw you—sittin' there at that table, reading your goddamn *New York Times*, lookin' down your nose at us wharf rats. But would he listen? Christ, you were all he talked about for weeks. *How quiet and sad you were*," Bake says in a prissy little tone. "Catatonic is more like it. Strangest fuckin' woman I ever met."

"Jesus, Bake," Jamie protests—color flooding her cheeks as the sting of his words hits home. Wondering if any of this is new to Peter; knowing, of course, it isn't.

"I said can it, Bake. What's with you?" A new edge to Peter's voice; he's had it now, too.

But Bake's already up, heading for the side of the house. "I'm goin back to the trailer for another load," he says with a glance back at Peter. "You coming or what?"

Barbara Ann is clearly astonished. "Christ, there's more? Just where do you think we're gonna to put all this crap?"

"Okay, okay," Peter says. "Give me a minute." He walks to Jamie, enveloping her in a long, slow hug she doesn't return. "Come on, Jae," he laughs. "This is Bake we're talking about. He'll be all over himself apologizing by the time we get back. You'll see." He plants a kiss on her forehead—Bake gunning the engine of the F150 now. "Yeah, yeah, yeah," he mutters, starting off. He's halfway across the yard when he turns, jogging backwards as he calls out to her. "By the way, who's Michael Ryan?"

It's a struggle to keep her face blank with her heart leaping so. "Who?"

"Michael Ryan," he says. The sound of the horn then—three impatient bursts. "Called my cell this morning. Something about trying to reach you but not being able to get through."

"Oh, Ryan," she says lightly. "One of the board members working on the capital campaign down in New York. Something must be up. I'll call them." Them, she says, hoping this makes the call sound less personal. The lying coming so easily to her now. "Thanks."

"Yeah, well, better get your phone checked."

She nods, knowing there's nothing at all wrong with her phone and hugs herself to keep from shaking as he jogs off toward the drive. Turning back to the water, then—hoping she's managed to pull it off. Stands to reason he'd go for Peter; how stupid not to have seen it coming. But Peter's cell number? How in the hell...

And then she gets it. A flush of heat as she remembers the long minutes Michael spent in the dining room during Meggie's first lesson, her cell phone right there in her bag. He must have scrolled through the menu till he found the number. His real message the simple fact he'd called. You reach into my life; I reach into yours. Drawing the proverbial line in the sand.

"He's got to be crazy," she mutters aloud. After all, he has so much more to lose than she does. And none of the incentive to risk it.

"Testosterone poisoning, close as I can figure," Barbara Ann says, starting in on the grill with a wire brush. "I can just see those little hairs poppin' out on his chest now—*ka-ping, ka-ping.*"

Moments later the cover of the barbecue screeches shut and Barbara Ann is beside her, swiping palms on the front of her jeans. "Hey, come on, " she says, sliding an arm around Jamie's shoulders. "It ain't you—he's just worried about Pete—all this mess goin' on. You know men; they see something needs fixing, drives 'em nuts till they set it right."

NINETEEN

Dripping sweat, her moist fingers fumbling with the key, Jamie finally manages the door—making her way back through the oppressive heat of the hallway to the kitchen and the shrill, insistent ring of the old wall phone. Trying to remember just who she's given this number to. It could hardly be Peter at this time of day—his classes start too early. Besides, he always calls her cell. She checks her watch, still panting from the final quarter-mile sprint. Barely eight o'clock.

"Hello, Diana? It's Molly Ryan. I'm sorry—you're obviously in the middle of something."

"It's okay, Molly—hi." She pushes damp tendrils of hair from her face in an odd attempt to appear presentable, taken off guard by Molly's friendliness as much as the call itself. Gone is the cool, guarded tone of their last conversation. The new Molly is perky and solicitous. Jamie's friend. All her warning bells are going off.

She reaches for a glass—the bulky receiver propped on her shoulder as she draws cold water from the tap. "Everything's all right, I hope. Meghan still on for ten o'clock?"

"Well, no, actually; that's why I'm calling. Michael had an early appointment at the office, and I'm stuck here with a toddler who woke with a temperature of a hundred and three. I'm afraid we're going to have to cancel."

"Ah." Damn, she thinks. Damn, damn, damn.

"Meggie's heartbroken, of course. Insists she's going to walk." A soft chuckle. "Can you imagine?"

So, Jamie thinks, Michael gets his way after all. It's tempting to imagine his hand in all this, but even he can't arrange for a sick baby on cue. Still, she's loath to let it go. His being stuck at the office means she'd have Meggie to herself again—which is the point, after all. She considers, decides—knowing it's sure to make points with Molly, who's the other person in all this she needs to impress. Besides, it's the perfect way to thumb her nose at Michael—something that has its own rewards.

The words slip out before she has a chance to change her mind. "I'd hate to disappoint Meggie, " she says. "How about if I just swing by, pick her up?"

ॐ ॐ

Molly greets her at the door, holding a flushed and feverish Matthew—all apologies as she struggles to keep the dog from planting his nose in Jamie's crotch. Grabbing him by the ruff, she drags him back through the entryway toward the insistent whistle of a kettle, tossing an invitation to follow over her shoulder. Jamie gladly complies, giddy and disoriented by this unexpected chance. And jazzed, if she's honest, by the danger of it. She tries for a closer look at the listless lump of boy on Molly's shoulder, but his face is tucked deep into her neck—the little arm draped above it fisted with the coppery curls that match his own red shock of hair.

As they pass the stairwell, a small, plastic figure plunges from between the balusters, landing in a pile of others on the thick carpet. Molly pauses to glare toward a platoon of action figures poised for battle along the edges of the upper steps.

"I know you're there, young man," she says. "Come down and get these before someone trips on them. Then tell Meggie that Mrs. Apollo is here. And Mia is to come down and pick up her markers. Now, please. Your grandmother will be here any minute."

Molly finally sets the dog loose in the kitchen and pulls the kettle from the stove—an industrial-sized stainless steel thing with eight gas burners and two oversized ovens, an enormous range hood hovering above it. None of which Jamie remembers from her piano-appraising visit, but then she'd been too overcome by self-loathing to notice much as she was leaving. After a brief, suspicious glance in Jamie's direction, the animal pads toward the back door and a bowl of water set beneath a large bay window whose mullioned panes look out over the rolling lawn and graceful, sloping drive.

Warm, buttery smells linger here in the Ryan kitchen. The long harvest table at the center of the room—seating for ten or twelve, at least—is littered with pulpy-rimmed juice glasses, bowls of half-finished cereal, a pile of Crayola markers lying uncapped and forgotten on an open coloring book. Breakfast, it appears, is just over. Weekends were like that, she remembers now—slow and easy. Tucked amid the soft whir of the range hood, the dog's wet lapping, the sound of little feet pounding overhead, are memories of Sam in her lap at the table—lots of time for hugging, tickling, a second or third cup of coffee while still in her robe and slippers. The life she should have had. Would have had.

Cheek resting on Matthew's head, Molly pours water into a mug trailing the string of a tea bag and replaces the kettle. When she turns again to Jamie, the swell of her abdomen is fully revealed beneath the sleeveless, yellow-flowered sundress. Six months along, probably—water gain evident in her face, the hand she puts to Matthew's forehead. He coughs in response, nuzzles a snotty nose into her neck, and she adjusts his position, settling him on her hip this time—his leg crooked in an unknowing caress over the mound of his nascent sibling.

"Excuse the mess," Molly says, settling her back against the counter. "My mother's due soon; she lives to tackle my kitchen on Saturday mornings, help ferry the kids." Blowing across the top of her mug, she gives the tea a tentative sip—her green-eyed gaze sharp and steady. And amused by something, apparently.

Jamie retreats from her scrutiny, turning instead to scan the photographs covering the massive stainless steel refrigerator to her left. Everything about these people is epic in scale, it seems— the rambling house, the oversized appliances, the ever-increasing number of children whose pictures, taken in clutches of two and three, loom at her now. Hundreds of faces—laughing, pouting, cutting up. She lights on a recent one of Meghan and Mia, the inseparable sisters—arms wrapped gleefully around each other as they mug for the camera. Another of little Michael, barely tolerating the presence of the newborn propped awkwardly in his lap. The three girls together in matching dresses—Margaret, the oldest, looking imperious, almost disdainful. The five of them dressed up and sitting in a row on the couch—Easter baskets in hand. And still she scans. It's Michael she's looking for, she realizes—photos of the father with his children, something to use to whip up her pain, sharpen her focus. There, finally, toward the bottom where the photos are worn and shoe-scuffed, Michael sits cross-legged on this very floor attempting to engage a toddler of indeterminate sex. Her heart catches in her throat at the set of the little body, the shape of the head before she registers the unfamiliar clothing, the glint of red hair. Not Sam, then. Well, of course not, she tells herself. For God's sake, get a grip.

Matthew is fussing again, and Molly shifts him to the other hip—a hefting Jamie can feel in her very bones. She considers offering to take the child; even a solid "*no*" would break the silence, give her an excuse for conversation. What did she think, that simply coming over here meant she had a right to familiarity, to questions? A cup of that tea? It's then she spies the plate smeared with egg yolk on the counter beside Molly, a mug inscribed *World's Best Dad* abandoned beside it. Both stark reminders of her trespass—this slipping past Michael, into the soft underbelly of his family. A rare chance, this. No guarantee she'll get another. And so she struggles for a way in, grasps finally at the obvious opening—intrusive as it is. She smiles. "When's your baby due?"

"Late fall," Molly says before taking another sip of the tea.

Jamie nods, sneaking a peek at her watch and wondering how long she's got before Michael returns. "Boy? Girl?"

Molly smiles. "Boy, actually." Another pause, only slightly less awkward than the last one. "Any kids of your own?"

Jamie shakes her head, relieved that whatever tale it is Michael has told Molly about their acquaintance didn't include anything about a son—alive or dead. Still, after their last meeting, he's no doubt added to his tale—something to stir misgivings.

"You know, I'm wondering," Molly says. "When you called a few weeks ago, you told me you believe Meggie's quite talented. Can you really know something like that after only two lessons?

"I ask," she says, eyes trained on Jamie, "because Michael seems to feel we should discontinue them."

"This is the first I've heard of it," Jamie says, feigning surprise. "Does he say why? Perhaps he'd prefer a different teacher?"

Molly regards her for a moment, then shakes her head. "That's not the issue—at least, not that he's said. It has more to do with selling the piano, it seems."

"You've had some interest in it, then?"

"Hardly." She smiles. "He's made no effort to sell it since the appraisal. I didn't think he would, frankly. Suddenly, though, he's hot to sell it for some reason—but can't, he tells me, because you've decided Meggie should use it for practice. So in order to get rid of the piano, I have to cancel her lessons." She meets Jamie's eyes, holds them. That hint of amusement again. "Which I won't do, of course—she loves them far too much."

Jamie returns her attention to the fridge, fighting the urge to like this woman.

"My husband is an excellent attorney," Molly continues. "It suits his rather aggressive style. But I find I have to guard against his embroiling the children in his various battles."

As if on cue, a rumble along the stairwell announces the arrival of several of the children. A moment later, Meggie all but tumbles through the doorway into the kitchen, practice book under her arm—Mia and Michael junior in her wake.

"Hi," Jamie says brightly. "Ready to go?" Needing, quite suddenly, to get out from under Molly's scrutiny, to sidestep whatever's in play here.

Little Michael has a pained look on his face. "Mom," he whines. "I can't find my goggles."

"Well, I'd suggest you find them soon; Grandma will be here any minute to take you to swimming." Molly shifts her gaze to Mia, points to the table—even as she loops her free arm around Meggie, halting her progress toward the back door. "Your markers, Mia, if you have any hope of gymnastics this morning." Bouncing Matthew higher onto her hip now. "And you, young lady," she says to Meggie, gathering that bloom of hair into a hastily pulled ponytail. "You'll sit in the back and wear your seatbelt—no argument." She corrals the hair with a fuzzy green band produced from a pocket of the flowered sundress; even so, a few long curls evade capture to lie in corkscrews along Meggie's neck.

"I can drop her off after the lesson, if you like, " Jamie suggests. "I'm heading into town later, anyway." Liar, she thinks, but she's determined to have the girl the full two hours, and it would be best to forestall Michael's reaction to this visit as long as possible. "Twelve-thirty all right?"

☒ ☒

The whine of cicadas in the brittle, sun-bleached grass seems even louder as she slows for the turn onto the narrow dirt road— heart pounding, knuckles white on the steering wheel. The idea only came to her as they were leaving Michael's, and she feels wild now with the outrageousness of it, the potential. This despite a clammy nervousness at having a child in her car again—in her care—for the first time since, well, that day.

The car bounces once as it leaves the macadam and she glances quickly in the rearview mirror, but Meggie—belted in as tightly as Jamie could manage—remains quiet and introspective, head down as she doodles on her practice book.

More jouncing as the tires struggle to meet the deeply rutted surface of the road, and Meggie's head pops up—her face brightening with interest as she peers around. "Where are we?"

"Just a little side trip." Jamie smiles over her shoulder. "Don't worry—won't take long."

Despite the August heat, Porter Street is dark and cool beneath a full canopy of leaves, the dim light adding to the dreary, wrung-out feel of the place—as bleak and cheerless as when she cruised it's length last winter looking for clues to Michael's whereabouts just before the accident.

She tries for a conversational tone. "Actually, your mom told me you might know someone who lives down here." Not true, of course. The idea was all hers. "Maybe we can figure out who."

"Like a game?"

Jamie nods. "Like a game." Brushing off the dirty feel of the lie before it defeats her determination. "Here's the first house," she chirps as they slow, cruising past the brown split level with the canted, rusty play set in the front yard. "Recognize anything?"

Meggie studies the property briefly before shaking her head. "Nope." Then, perking up, "Hey, they have swings!"

Jamie grunts in response. One of the chains holding the a narrow metal swing to the crossbar above it has broken since her last time here—leaving the seat dangling disconsolately above a dusty oval of dirt. Nothing any mother in her right mind would allow a child on. She tries to recall what she learned about this place when she did all that research on the Porter Street houses and their occupants—all of it tossed when it offered no insight into Michael's whereabouts the morning of the accident. This one, she remembers now, owned by the same couple for more than ten years—the children who'd once used the swing set teenagers now. The second house—another aging split level—perpetually rented out to students whose cars, parked haphazardly, fill the driveway just as they did last winter. Neither place with any obvious connection to Michael—not as clients, anyway. Her new theory, possibly just as dubious, is that the Ryan family is somehow familiar with whomever Michael saw here the morning of the accident—assuming he saw anyone. Short of trotting Meggie up to each door and asking the occupants if they know her, Jamie's only hope is that she'll recognize one of the houses or remember a car that occasionally comes to visit. Pretty thin, but it's all she's got.

"My Grandma has a bumpy road like this," Meggie says now.

"Hmmm." Jamie's mind stumbles over the words, then backtracks. Grandma—as in the grandmother showing up to clean the kitchen and ferry Michael to swimming? And Mia, she realizes now, to gymnastics? Then it hits her. If Grandma is doing all this ferrying, she could easily have delivered Meggie for her piano lesson. So why the call this morning, unless Molly was counting on Jamie's offer to fetch the girl herself? Manipulating things in order to size her up? The amused glances, the cryptic commentary—if she hadn't been so nervous at the house, she might have picked up on it. Gotten the message that had been the real point of it all. *Whatever game it is you two are playing, keep my children out of it.*

Still, it's obvious she's passed some kind of test; she was allowed to leave with the girl, after all. Strap her into the back seat and just drive away. And it's clear now that without some compelling reason to change her mind, Molly plans to allow Meggie her lessons every other Saturday at ten. There's that, at least.

"This place is creepy," Meggie announces—her upturned face anxious in the dim light of the car as they cruise past the second of the drab looking properties.

Jamie feels it too—an almost palpable gloom, the meager whispers of breeze able to penetrate the thick overhang laced with a kind of perpetual longing. "You're right," she agrees, realizing as well that the longer they linger here, the more likely it is Meggie will mention this little detour at home. She turns, smiles reassuringly. "This was a silly idea. I say we get out of here."

She does a three point turn in the last drive—one leading to a place set too far back in the trees to get a decent look at, just as before. One sold right around the time of the accident, if Jamie remembers correctly—the new owners a young couple mortgaged to the hilt. No obvious hit here either; no burst of recognition from Meggie. This whole thing a bust.

Suddenly, she's fighting the urge to hurry—gripped by an irrational fear that Michael will appear out of the blue and find her with his child—here of all places. Absurd, she tells herself; still, her heart pounds wildly as she accelerates toward the comforting blaze of light at the end of this dark tunnel of trees, a thick plume of dust rising in a cloud behind them.

TWENTY

Jamie pulls the bag of cookies from the cabinet above the sink, only half listening as Meggie struggles through the arpeggio—*C-E-G* with the left hand, *C-E-G* with the right—a tortured pause as her left crosses over reaching for that next *C*. Even with the sound of the piano, the sense of another body taking up space here, the house feels hollow and empty—almost unnaturally still after the bounding activity of the Ryan home. Having to recast Molly as a woman not easily fooled—one, it appears, she's going to have to be very, very careful of—has put Jamie in a dark mood. Worse, she feels guilty now for having dragged Meggie to Porter Street, as if she's crossed some line with this that even she couldn't have envisioned.

"Okay," she calls. "Time to give the fingers a rest."

The routine she's hit on—thirty minutes of piano work followed by a break; another thirty minutes of music, another break, then a final review—leaves lots of time for talk, but so far today it's been like pulling teeth to get the girl to say anything at all. At times she seems so knowing, so self-contained—much like herself at that age, Jamie realizes; the expectations of her parents on her already, like so much outsized clothing. Still, Meggie is only five years old—of an age, certainly, to appreciate a plate of cookies and a cold glass of lemonade. And, Jamie is hoping, the innocent trading of secrets.

Today, instead of coming straight through to the kitchen from the piano, Meggie loops back through the living room and the front hallway—the sound of her footsteps coming to an abrupt halt by the stairs. A pause, the scrape and rustle of cardboard. It's then Jamie remembers the box.

"Hey, you have toys!" Meggie crows—astonished to have stumbled across such a thing in this of all places. "Can I play with these?"

Stepping into the hallway, a sweating glass of lemonade in each hand, Jamie watches her drag the half-opened carton from the second step. "I suppose." She'd have preferred going through it herself first, of course—as she has with others pulled from the attic—savoring the fix of bittersweet memory that hits her each time she rediscovers something of Sam in the house. Then again, there's Porter Street to make up for.

"They were my son's," she says. "Too young for you, probably—but sure, go ahead. If you wait a second, I'll help you."

But Meggie's already got the box halfway down the hall, a determined set to her face as she forces it over the threshold and into the kitchen.

Placing the lemonade on the table, Jamie crouches beside her—chest tightening as the girl pries open the flaps and lifts an oblong basket of small metal cars from the box. The heart recognizing them before the mind—brightly colored pickups and jeeps, some dented, others scratched, a few with missing wheels—as those they'd kept by the hearth once Sam began using the grouting between the bricks for roads.

"There's a plastic garage around here someplace," she mutters, vaguely considering a trip to the attic to look for the thing as she fingers a miniature school bus with flaking yellow paint. Next time maybe. There's also a Sit 'n' Spin up there, she remembers now, a bucket of fat crayons—if they haven't congealed in three years of summer heat—and a plastic tool set she'd bought to give Sam for Christmas. The Christmas that never came.

"Hey—books!" Abandoning the cars to Jamie, Meggie maneuvers a stack of Sam's cardboard picture books from the box. *Good Night Moon, Where the Wild Things Are, Pat the Bunny.* "We have these," she chirps, piling them into Jamie's lap. "And look!"

The girl's attention has moved on to something else, but Jamie is still with the books, staring down through them at Sam crawling into her lap with *Pat the Bunny* in his pudgy hand. Settling in, then flipping immediately to the page with the father's stubbled face—stroking that little piece of sandpaper cut in the shape of a man's cheek over and over. She hunts for the page now, but a drop of something—jam, she thinks—has glued several of the pages together. Still sticky. Imagine.

"See?" Voice triumphant, Meggie lugs the molded plastic piano from the bottom of the box to the floor. Sky blue, single octave, with a handle so Sam could carry it around. The piano he never touched, never had any interest in. Funny, considering.

"That's it," Meggie says cheerfully, as if they've just finished some chore like folding laundry or unpacking the groceries. No real desire to play with any of it, apparently—just wanted to see. Packing it up again now in reverse order: piano first, the books—though Jamie's still picking the jam from *Pat the Bunny* and will hold this one out—the basket of cars. Something about this odd mix of things, their being packed together like this in a box only half-full, nags at her as Meggie folds the lid shut and scrambles onto her knees. "C'mon," she says, already sliding the box back toward the hall.

"What? Where?" Even to Jamie, her laugh sounds tinged with panic. She knows where, of course—without exactly knowing how. "Wait, now." Feeling the weirdness of it, needing a minute to slow things down.

"If he has his toys to play with," Meggie reasons, "he won't have to jump on his bed so much."

Ah, yes, the noises from the second floor—sounds that all along Meggie has assumed come from a room she hasn't been told even exists, the room of a little boy long dead. And finding nothing strange in this. She's still young enough to go with her instincts, not having lived long enough to see them lead her astray.

Suddenly, the desire to share this part of her life—a part everyone else has long urged Jamie to forget—is so overwhelming she feels herself folding to Meggie's will. After all, where's the harm in simply poking their heads in the door, returning a box of toys to its rightful place? Some part of her needing these rationalizations, another part not caring about reasons at all—just wanting this, the sharing of her life with Sam. Besides, it's clear Meggie finds nothing strange in the keeping of a room for a dead child, that she won't balk at the sight of a crib made up for a boy who will never sleep there. A dresser full of freshly washed summer clothes arranged as they'd once been—clothes Jamie will swap out for warmer ones in the fall. Simply because it soothes her to touch them again. To wash them and fold them and put them away.

Oddly enough, it's Jamie, putting the box down gently just inside Sam's door, who finds herself suddenly shy in the face of Meggie's open interest. Watching her gaze travel from the newly shampooed rug with its grinning train, to the twin posters of Winnie the Pooh on the wall behind the crib, to the blue race-car-emblazoned lunch box resting on the corner of the dresser—the price tag still dangling from its plastic handle.

"I thought he'd like it," Jamie explains, rising. "He'd be starting school this fall, like you." Watching the girl carefully. Any sign of discomfort, she tells herself—any at all—and they'll head right back downstairs. It's then she feels it, as she so often does, the way the room seems to settle softly around her—as if part of Sam still hovers in this place. A comfort, usually, but it feels different today—alert, watchful.

"We have a baby room too," Meggie says, stooping to open the box. "It's getting ready for a new one now."

Jamie smiles, touches the crib lightly, lovingly—smoothes the sheet as Meggie pulls the toys and books from the box, finding homes for them around the room. Suddenly she realizes just why this particular combination of things felt so familiar down in the kitchen. These were the toys Sam had on the first floor those last weeks; toys still there when they left for day care that last morning. Hurriedly boxed up by GM, no doubt, before Jamie and her hospital bed arrived home to face them.

"Wait a minute!" Meggie cries, and in a flash she's up—charging off and down the stairs before Jamie can manage a reaction. Pounding back along the hall toward the kitchen, from the sound of it, and pausing only seconds before retracing her route. All of it so sudden, so astonishingly loud and full of life in a place long gone silent.

"Here," she pants, opening her hand toward Jamie. "We forgot the luck."

There, nestled in her palm, are two copper pennies—borrowed, apparently, from the kitchen window.

"Luck," Jamie whispers, and together they place the coins in the corner of Sam's single, uncurtained window.

☙ ❧

"How do we get music?"

They're back at the piano when Meggie poses the question, Jamie feeling strangely rattled—the stupidity of what she's done in taking the girl upstairs finally dawning on her. She's torn between suggesting that they keep the whole thing a secret and just getting on with the lesson. The damage is done, after all; why draw even more attention it?

"What do you mean?" she asks.

"How do we get it?" Meggie asks again, pointing to the well-worn volume of Debussy's song-cycles lying open at the edge of the stand. "How do we make it?"

"Ah." This Jamie understands; this she can explain. Relieved to be back on solid ground, she reaches for the score, centers it before them on the stand. "We write music, the way we write stories—but using notes, like the ones you're learning now, instead of letters and words. It's called composing; the people who write music are composers."

Meggie nods, captivated it seems by the intricate notation, by Jamie's comments—scribbled like hieroglyphs in the margins.

"This music was written by Claude Debussy," Jamie continues. "He was more than just a composer, though; he was a fabulous pianist, too." She has an idea, begins flipping through the music for something she hasn't played, she realizes now, since before Sam died. "He was about your father's age when he wrote a series of songs for his little girl," she says, smoothing the spine against the stand and praying this will be enough to distract Meggie from the idea of the toys, their little trip upstairs. Enough to keep her from blabbing about it at home later, anyway. "It's called *The Children's Corner* and there are six pieces…"

"What's her name?"

"His little girl? Claude-Emma, but he called her Chou-Chou."

"How old is she?"

Jamie turns and considers her. "When he wrote this music? I'm not sure." No need to mention that this child, too, is long dead.

It hits her then that this sort of thing—the playing of real music, the discussion of composers—should be part of every lesson. Will be part of every lesson. After all, a child as intuitive as Meggie needs more than just the notes, the simple mechanics. If given the chance, she, too, might come to feel the music, learn to grasp the composer's intent.

"Debussy wanted this music to paint pictures and feelings in Chou-Chou's mind," Jamie explains. "As if he were telling her stories with notes instead of words." She adjusts her position at the bench, having already decided on the brief, highly visual fourth piece, and begins the rhythmic teasing out of the introduction. "This one's called *The Snow is Dancing*," she says, fingers tickling lightly along the upper keys. "Can you hear it?"

Meggie nods, eyes fighting to keep up as Jamie's hands move faster and faster, frenetic and intricate patterns now; a confusion of movement creating the sense of a growing storm—intense but lyrical—which quickly peters out to the twinkling of flurries that end the piece.

"There." Jamie smiles down at her. "World's shortest snowstorm."

"My dad plays the piano sometimes," Meggie announces. "I hear him through the door."

Jamie feigns disinterest as she flips a few pages, segues into the jazzy, lighthearted cadence of *Gollywog's Cake-walk*—her heart pounding wildly. Meggie has never before mentioned Michael; certainly not like this. "Do you go in and watch?"

"No, he locks it. I knocked once, but he didn't answer." Kicking her foot now, something she does, Jamie's noticed, when she's thinking something through.

"How about when you practice?" Jamie asks quietly, conversationally. Reminding herself to hold back, go slow. "Does he play for you then?"

Meggie shakes her head. "He sits at his desk and talks on the phone a lot."

She's dying to ask what it is he talks about, if he closes the door then as well, but her instincts tell her to let the girl take the lead, not to force this sudden flowering of trust.

"He talks mad sometimes," Meggie tells her. "One time he hit the desk really hard and spilled his drink. He said a bad word then. I told Mommy after."

"Hmmm," Jamie says noncommittally. She's reminded suddenly of the coffee mug on Molly's kitchen counter. *World's Best Dad*, my ass. "Sounds like your father's pretty busy. Maybe your mom could help with your lessons instead."

Meggie shakes her head, the foot kicking harder now. "She says that's daddy's job, and he should pay attention to me, not his work. But he says the kids are her job, and he's just trying to find a way to pay for them all."

It takes Jamie a minute to realize she's hearing the blow-by-blow of an actual argument. It's more than she could have hoped for so early in the game. She should be elated, but somehow she's not.

"He's mad about the new one, too. Enough is enough, he says. Mommy doesn't care, though. She laughs when he gets mad, but I get scared. Then I run under the piano."

Jamie stops playing, though her hands remain poised on the keys, and when she finally turns, she finds Meggie's quiet face lifted to her own. Looking for—what, exactly?

"You don't have to be afraid, you know," Jamie says softly—feeling suddenly quite out of her depth, unprepared for the girl to need something from her. Something like this, anyway. "You don't have to be afraid," she says again. "Not with your mom there."

Meggie nods solemnly. "She's brave."

"Who's brave?"

They both start at the sound of his voice, the sight of him standing there in the doorway—Michael, who hasn't bothered knocking, who has once again slipped into the house silent and unnoticed. And, it appears, royally pissed. His eyes, steely and cold, bore into Jamie from across the room. Molly's told him, then. Well of course she has; she probably planned to all along.

Meggie, stricken, stares helplessly at her hands.

"We were discussing the songs Debussy wrote for his daughter," Jamie lies—voice calm, eyes on the books she's now closing. Willing Meggie to understand, to realize Jamie will not betray her. Suddenly her hand, of its own volition, slips down to find the girl's—her heart wrapping finally and irrevocably around the child in less time than it once took to arrange those small, willing fingers into a C Major chord. "Some of the music can be little frightening," she says coolly. "But we're finished now, aren't we, Meg?"

Satisfied with the small nod, Jamie finally raises her eyes to Michael—her gaze defiant as she holds his. Berating herself for the knocking of her heart, the heat she feels moving into her face.

"Meggie," she says calmly, closing the score on the stand and gathering the practice books, "I'd like you to work on the key of C for next time; as well as the arpeggios we went over today, okay? And," she adds, reaching for the Bastien as an afterthought, "see what you can do with the first song in this book as well, all right?"

Meggie's head snaps up at that—her sudden grin full of surprise—and she scrambles from the bench, books clutched to her chest as she all but skips toward her father; the fear of a moment ago dissipated by this one small gesture.

"Go on to the car," Michael says, his eyes trained on Jamie. "I'll be out in a minute."

Shutting the keyboard cover, Jamie rises from the bench—forcing herself to move casually beneath his seething gaze toward the hallway. She can hear the car now; he's left it idling in the drive, and through the window she sees Meggie beside it, tugging at the passenger door. An odd sense of relief washes over her.

Michael grabs her arm as she passes him. "Who's brave?" he asks again in his clipped, cold, don't-fuck-with-me voice.

"Your wife," Jamie all but spits, squirming to get loose. "For putting up with you, I should imagine. Let go of me," she says yanking her arm free and squaring off against him. "You could have saved yourself a trip. I'm sure Molly told you I was going to drop Meggie off later. She was probably on the phone to you the minute we were out the door—if only to feel you squirm."

"One of the little things she does to enrage me. It's a game she plays."

"Oh, the things we do to keep a marriage alive."

He ignores her. "I thought I made it clear you were to stay away from my home. I hardly thought it necessary to mention that you were not, for obvious reasons, to drive my children around. I was apparently too subtle. That could change."

Turning the knife in that freshly opened wound.

"Oh, please," Jamie says, recovering. "Whatever you might say to Peter is nothing compared to what I could tell Molly. She asked if I'd be willing to pick Meggie up, by the way—she must have forgotten to mention that." A bit of a stretch, though there's no longer any doubt in her mind that Molly finessed the whole thing.

The smallest flicker of doubt as he considers this. "Bullshit. Not her style. To her, you're nothing more than the hired help."

"I hardly think so. We're pals, Molly and I. I'm Meggie's teacher, after all—part of your inner circle now." Her lips curl in a nasty smile as she starts toward the door. "Get used to it."

But he grabs her again, moving them out of range of the window before pulling her up hard. "You think I don't know what you're doing? One word from me..."

"One word from you—and what?" Jamie sneers. "Molly will stop the lessons? Go ahead—you think I care? You're the one who threw Meggie at me to begin with—dangling her as some kind of incentive to keep me around. The real question is why? Besides, we both know the only thing that could turn Molly against me is the truth. And what a conversation that would be."

"Oh, trust me, " he hisses. "It will be. You lied to me from the start about who you are; remember that. All I have to say is that I found out it was you playing peeping Tom outside our window last winter; that you've been stalking us for months. She'll grab her babies and run for the hills."

Jamie throws her head back and laughs. Even she knows Molly would never take such a thing at face value; the irony being, of course, that it's true. "Oh, come on," she admonishes. "This whole thing was your idea. You're the one who brought me to the house in the first place. Molly's never going to believe you didn't check me out first; that you didn't know who I was when you entrusted your daughter to my care. No, you started this little charade; you're stuck with it."

"Think so? Your word against mine? Shall we try it?"

"Hey, I'm game. You have far more to lose here than I do, though—remember that. Don't think I won't tell Molly how you've been trying to keep me here, how you attacked me in my own home..."

He pulls her closer still, his fingers digging into the flesh at the edge of her t-shirt, and she grimaces—jolted back to that night— the cool, fragrant smell of him, the feel of his solid bulk moving against her. When he speaks again, his voice is hoarse with rage. "Back to our little adventure in the hall, are we? I have to admit I was surprised when you responded like that. We'll have to try it again some time."

Jamie's face floods with loathing—for him, for herself, for the current still charging between them despite everything. Willing it away. "Screw you," she hisses.

"Promise?" He pushes her off then, moves to the doorway. "One more thing. You say another word to my daughter about your kid, and I'll tell Molly everything. And I mean everything. I don't care what happens. So don't fuck with me. Do not fuck with me." He turns then and is out the door, moving quickly to the car.

Her arm is on fire; still, she forces herself to stand in the doorway long enough to return Meggie's happy wave—the small face receding as Michael reverses down the drive. Knowing it's all over if the child isn't smart enough to keep quiet about Porter Street, their little visit to Sam's room. It's only after the SUV has disappeared that she finally shuts the door, lays her forehead against it. She tells herself Michael is only bluffing, that he won't risk everything with the truth. Still, time is running out. She's getting too close, squeezing him now, and he's feeling it. Something will have to give, she knows, and soon.

TWENTY-ONE

"The first two concerts are going to kill us with instrumentation—you realize that, of course." The toss of the salt and pepper curls, an impatient tap of Augie's cigarette on the edge of the hidden ashtray as she scowls into the phone. "No, absolutely not. Cutting back on the strings will only destroy the sound. Adam will never allow it." Another impatient pause. "Well, that and five percussion. And we need two harps for the opener. I also see a celesta here; we're paying cartage for that as well, I assume."

Augie hates these conversations, Jamie knows—this haggling over the instrumentation for each concert of the coming season; the thrashing out of musician lists and contract negotiations. She offers a smile of support from across the desk, then returns her attention to the notes for their meeting on the launch of the capital campaign.

"All right, then," Augie sighs. "Let's move on. For *Bolero* I see three saxes or clarinets—double. Um-hmm. Well, I'd rather pay doubling fees than for an extra body on stage. You've heard that union fees have jumped again?"

Jamie's replacement breezes in just then, Debra Budlow's

sleeveless red sundress and high-heeled sandals a nod to the stifling heat gripping the city. Taking the chair next to Jamie, whom she blatantly ignores, she crosses her legs and checks her watch—crinkling her nose disapprovingly at the smell of Augie's cigarette. She's brought no briefcase or files for their meeting— no notes at all, it appears—simply a blank legal pad which she parks in her lap. No sign of a pen. Augie gives her a curt nod and continues into the phone.

"Both *Faune* and *Orpheus* require timpani," she says. "Well, of course it's a problem; you're forgetting our timpanist is in Europe that month—vacation. No, he won't; he's put it off twice already." She rolls her eyes at the ceiling. "Yes, I know it's summer and the city is deserted, but I'm still here, as are you. Make some calls. Find someone." She covers the mouthpiece with her hand, tells them she's just about finished here.

"Yes, yes, the hunt for a rehearsal piano. Yes, I do know about that one, but it's very second-hand—with the all the issues such a thing involves. Discussion for another time, I'm afraid. I have people arriving for a meeting on the campaign. Yes, Wolfie—I'll give Jamie your best."

This brings a frown from Debra, who re-crosses her legs, flipping the heel of her sandal off and on in obvious irritation. And still ignoring Jamie—some imaginary slight, no doubt. She's a big one, Jamie has learned, for nursing such things. It would be almost comical if it didn't remind her of Bake's continuing grudge and the bombshell Peter dropped during their discussion of it two nights ago.

"Maybe I should talk to him," she'd suggested over the dishes Wednesday night. "Apologize for being a lousy wife or whatever. Maybe then he'd stop avoiding me." No reason she should care, really—except that she did.

"Will you stop making such a big deal about this?" Peter had laughed, sliding the last of the pots into the sink. "Nights he's at the tolls; mornings he fishes traps with Barbara Ann. He's just been busy."

Thin excuse—considering the endless trail of sunglasses, ball caps, and packs of gum Bake was always leaving onboard continued unabated. Apparently it was only when Jamie, herself, was here that he had this little problem with time.

Peter stood at the edge of the counter, balancing himself against the rolling wake of a powerboat as he popped the remains of a dinner roll in his mouth. "Besides," he said, "they're in Connecticut till Sunday. Another protest about the fishing restrictions on Long Island Sound or something. I'll get them over for dinner next week if it's that important to you. Assuming they can fit us in."

Bake as political animal—it was a concept Jamie still had trouble with. A firebrand, too—as Bake never did anything halfway— with all the zeal of the newly converted. Spurred on by Barbara Ann, of course, who was busy refocusing everyone's energy on the fiasco on Long Island Sound. The brouhaha over the Shoals project put on the back burner for now. There was that, at least.

Peter parked his back against the counter behind her. "What would you say to a change, Jae? A big one, I mean—Hawaii, maybe or Spain? Both places are heavy into aquaculture—poised to take it offshore. They'd kill for my kind of expertise."

She turned, soapy sponge in hand, and stared. "You mean move?"

"We could take a few months off and sail the boat over—make it a real adventure."

"What about all the time you've put in at the University?" His fondest wish, she knew, was to turn the one-off project at the Shoals into a full-fledged university program—with aquaculture farms spread up and down the coast. It was what he'd been working toward all this time.

"Five years," he said, "and I still can't get anywhere with these people. They refuse to face the fact that the whole East coast has been over fished to the point of depletion; that the only way they're going to have any fish to sell ten years from now is if they farm them. That's the simple truth. Which is inconvenient, I realize." He reached deep into the pocket of his jeans and pulled out his army knife, began picking at a splinter lodged in the tip of his thumb. "And if I can't bring them around soon, convince them this is all in their best interests, then I may as well hang it up." A sad smile as he repocketed the knife. "I don't know— maybe it's time to cut my losses, move on."

No, she'd thought. Not now, not when I've finally gained Meggie's trust. Just the thought of the girl was enough to shock her yet again with how close she'd come to blowing the whole thing. What had she been thinking, dragging her over to Porter Street like that? Allowing her up in Sam's room? Stupid was what it was. Stupid and reckless.

She drained the small sink; wiped the counter down. "I just can't see you picking up and leaving," she told Peter, somehow managing a neutral tone. "You love it here—you know you do— your students, being out at the Shoals. Why would you want to start it all somewhere else?"

Slipping his arms around her waist, burying his face in her neck, he became her Peter again—lighthearted, upbeat—lapsing into song in lieu of explanation. "*Cause I'm a wanderer; yeah, I'm a wanderer; I wander 'round an' 'round an' 'round an' 'round.*"

She'd been feeling out of sorts all day; wasn't in the mood for his jokes—not now, not about this. "I have no idea. Fabian maybe."

He gave her neck a loud peck. "Close. Dion. Beach boys did it later, too." He released her then, resuming his position against the counter. "Oh," he said, sounding suddenly peeved. "I forgot. That guy Ryan called again this morning."

She was still reeling from his little bombshell about work, and now this. She shrugged in a way she hoped looked nonchalant, but her thoughts were on Meggie—what the girl might have said; what Michael may or may not be calling to tell her. "Apparently he's figured out if he can't get me, he can at least get you."

"Well, tell him to piss off. I don't like his attitude. Too chatty, like he's fishing for something."

"Seriously?" Remembering how they'd left it the last time, or rather not left it—the confrontation ending in a kind of stalemate, leaving her blind with fury and churning in disbelief at how easily she'd been taken in by Molly. Quite a pair, those two.

"Yeah, like he's keeping tabs on you or something."

"Well," she said, "if you'd dropped a million dollars on a capital campaign run by a woman you barely know, you'd probably want to keep your hand in too."

Peter grunted. "He's the one, huh? Doesn't surprise me; he sounded like a guy used to having his way." Then he laughed. "When he first said his name—Michael O. Ryan—so businesslike and all, I thought he said *Orion*. You know, like the Greek god, the hunter—the one that got in that pissing contest with Artemus, a.k.a. Diana." A pause. "Your middle name, too. Freaky, huh?"

She nodded. A sudden urge took her and she moved to him, resting her head on his chest. The beating of his heart steady and strong beneath her ear. "He was in love with her, you said."

"It was complicated, but yeah, basically. Before things got really nasty."

"In the end, she won, though, didn't she?"

"If you can call it winning. She lost a lot, too." He lifted her chin, a playful look on his face. "When I heard his voice I had a vision of this brainless, muscle-bound jock with a crush on you."

"Brainless he's not," she said turning back to wipe out the sink. "And you can forget about the crush part. This guy is all about money and power."

"He was rattling on about some lesson this weekend."

"Ah." She took her time with the sink, then turned and tossed the paper towel in the garbage. "What did he say, exactly?"

"*Have her call me about the lesson this weekend.* Just like that. You know, God-Has-Spoken kind of thing."

She'd actually been considering telling Peter about the lessons—knowing if he found out about them on his own he'd wonder why she hadn't said anything. Leave it to Michael to force her hand. "He's been after me to give his daughter piano lessons the Saturdays I'm in town. He's probably just looking for an answer." More likely yanking my chain, she thought—determined to avoid the other, even less pleasant possibilities. Well, hell with him. He'd get no call from her—about the lesson or anything else.

Peter's eyebrows shot up. "You doing it?"

"What?"

"The lessons," he laughed. "What else?"

She shrugged noncommittally. "It would help fill the time."

"Well, you don't want to piss him off if he's the money man. How old's the kid?"

"Five," she said. Like Sam is. Would be.

He'd nodded then—satisfied, apparently—and reached into the cabinet for the chocolate chip cookies while the dogs yawned and stretched at his feet, whining for their after-dinner walk among the summer tourists roaming the dock, the music and food smells wafting from the visiting boats. Fingering a few cookies from the bag, he'd kissed Jamie's head and grabbed the garbage before bounding up the companionway—the dogs clattering up after him.

Jamie's still thinking about all this—wondering how wise it had really been to tell Peter about the lessons, and weighing the odds that Meggie would actually show up again tomorrow morning—when Augie finally hangs up the phone, resting her palms against her eyes a moment before changing gears.

"Another word about that damn rehearsal piano and I'll scream," she says.

"I take it this is the same baby grand Colin's wife has been trying to unload for the last year?" Jamie asks.

Augie nods, snubbing out the cigarette and sliding the ashtray back behind the computer monitor. "Three thousand dollars and it's ours."

"And we'd spend another twenty-five hundred renovating it. I know for a fact the soundboard's cracked, and God only knows how many times it's been repinned. We'd be better off with a new Yamaha C-Five."

"Indeed. Unfortunately, costs are already out of control. Now I have the two of you telling me we need new database management software; marketing is demanding real-time ticketing for the web site, and if Wolfie reminds me one more time that we need two Steinways on stage for the Mozart double concerto, I'll slit my wrists. Which," she sighs, "brings us to this capital campaign. Frankly, it couldn't come at a better time. Contributions, as we all know, are way off."

Debra's sandal begins flipping again at this. Her continuing failure to make the fundraising goals that she, herself, established has put added pressure on everyone. She sighs impatiently, shifts in her chair, re-crosses her legs.

"A few days ago, I approached Michael Ryan with the idea of the press conference we discussed," Augie continues. "Unfortunately, he's declined any and all participation. In fact, he wants to remain an anonymous donor from this point on—disappointing, to say the least. It was a good idea, but we're going to have to rethink a number of things, I'm afraid. Come at this from a different angle."

"Frankly, I think we're better off without him," Debra says dismissively.

Jamie turns an amazed look on her. Not only has she watched the woman throw herself in Michael's path at every possible opportunity, he's literally all that stands between her and the unemployment line. How can she not know this?

"The man's in love with himself," Debra continues. "Besides, I've done some digging and found a few things that could backfire on us if they came out. A car accident a few years ago, for one thing. A little boy was killed. Not his fault, apparently, but people won't care."

Jamie freezes, the familiar warmth coming into her cheeks as she waits for some indication Debra knows the rest of it, but there's no sign she's dug deep enough to connect Jamie to the accident. For once, she's glad for the woman's ineptitude.

"He's hardly a political candidate, Debra," Augie says. "No one is going to delve into his past simply because he's made a large donation to our orchestra."

"There's more. Some questionable use of client funds. Pretty juicy stuff. Five or six years ago he became legal conservator for some family friend. An artist by the name of Susan Archer— eccentric, apparently, and with a pile of money. From what I read, she was having a hard time managing her finances, so she asked him to oversee things for her. Anyway, somewhere along the line he loaned some of her money to another client without her knowledge. And get this. Part of the loan was used to pay the other guy's outstanding legal bill with Michael's firm." She lets that sink in. "To top it off, the guy never repaid the loan."

Augie shoots her a look, eyebrows raised.

"It gets worse," Debra says with undisguised relish. "The woman filed a complaint against Michael, and he was reprimanded by some legal grievance committee over the whole thing. It's..."

Augie holds up a hand. "Enough," she says tersely. "Our trustees—the people you and I and Jamie all work for, Debra— would not be pleased to hear you've been digging up dirt on one of their own, not to mention the fact that he's our largest donor. So let's keep all this to ourselves, shall we?" She turns to Jamie then—their eyes locking for a moment. "Moving on," she says, "I still like the idea of a press conference. The Mayor has agreed to participate; he suggests next week."

Jamie shakes her head. "End of July is a bad time to launch. Everyone who possibly can has left the city."

"Exactly," Debra says, turning a how-could-you-be-so-stupid look on Jamie. "There'll be no competition for media coverage."

"And wasted effort, because no one will be paying attention," Jamie tells her, returning the look. "Timing aside, the launch of a capital campaign is hardly considered news in this city—not unless there's a big name involved, big money. A few multinational corporations. And unless I'm mistaken, all we have right now is one donor who's decided to remain anonymous." She turns from Debra's furious gaze. "You know, Augie, marketing should really be in on this."

"Screw marketing," Debra says, still glaring at her. "And screw Michael Ryan."

This draws an astonished look from Augie, to whom Debra now shifts a pained expression. "Are we just about finished here?" she asks. "I'm due across town in thirty minutes—meeting with a potential sponsor." She flings a look Jamie's way. "Multinational corporation."

Augie nods, lips pursed. "Feel free." She pulls another cigarette from her pack pensively, lighting it as the click of Debra's sandals recedes down the hall. Leaning back in her chair, she tosses the lighter onto her desk and sends a plume of smoke toward the ceiling. "Incredible."

"What was that all about?" Jamie asks. "Only a month ago, the man could do no wrong."

"Yes, well." Augie teases the ashtray out from behind her monitor. "I'm told she rather threw herself at him a week or so ago and that and he turned her down. Which rather surprised me, actually. Word is he used to be something of a serial philanderer."

Jamie's laugh—ironic, bitter—escapes of its own accord. The only surprising thing in any of this is that Michael seems to have suddenly developed scruples.

"And it wouldn't surprise me," Augie continues, "if Debra resents his determination to have you involved in the campaign. I'm sure it's not lost on her that there would quite possibly be no campaign at all if you hadn't agreed to stay on and run it. But this new hobby of hers—digging up the past, trying to discredit him—greatly disturbs me. It could be dangerous—to all of us. Of course, the decision not to tell the board about his earlier connection to you was mine; something I alone will answer for, should it come out."

"Do you think she knows?" Jamie asks quietly.

Augie shakes her head. "She'd never keep such a thing to herself; it's far too perfect an opportunity to embarrass you."

"She might plan to use it elsewhere."

"She's not that subtle," Augie assures her.

"This doesn't sound at all like Michael," Jamie says. "From what I've seen, he enjoys the limelight too much to be interested in being an anonymous anything."

"Doesn't want the publicity, apparently; other groups approaching him for money—that kind of thing. At least that's what he told me. I suppose this legal trouble, if true, could be part of it. He would hardly want the whole thing brought up again."

"I still think there's more to it. His wife may not know about the million dollars, for instance," Jamie says, remembering the night Michael told her this very thing over the phone. Proud of it, too, it seemed.

Augie nods. "A possibility you and I have already discussed." She pauses. "In any case, I'd be careful in my dealings with Debra, if I were you. It would be wise, as well, to avoid all contact with Michael in case she gets it in her head to look for some connection between the two of you." There's gentle accusation in her eyes, the look of an old friend aware she's being kept in the dark. That unerring instinct Jamie has come to value working against her now.

Jamie sighs, uncomfortably aware that with this, Michael has officially wormed his way into every part of her life—her job, her marriage, her friendship with Augie. She thinks again of Peter, his growing awareness of Michael. The first phone call had simply made him curious. Now he's annoyed. Next time he'll start asking some very pointed questions.

She opens her mouth to respond, but Augie stops her with a raised hand. "It's best I don't know, Jamie. Whatever it is, I'm sure you have your reasons. Now," she says, standing, gathering her cigarettes and lighter, tucking them in her purse. "There's a great new lunch place just around the corner. I hope you like Thai. I have to admit I never have—though I'm quickly becoming a convert. Anything to avoid the eternal hunt for a cab."

TWENTY-TWO

They're late, a good half hour now, but she'll be damned if she's going to call. Another of Michael's games, she thinks—ignoring the trickle of doubt. It was risky, not calling him back about the lesson, but she's learned to take cover when he's after her like this; her strategy this time is just to stay out of sight, keep shaking him off till it's too late to cancel. Sounded good at the time. Only Meggie's not here, is she?

Reaching nervously toward the music stand, Jamie rearranges everything yet again—her notes for today's lesson, Meggie's theory book, the score of Robert Schumann's *Scenes from Childhood*. Their composer of the day, so to speak; chosen not merely because he and his pianist wife Clara produced eight children—and she can engage Meggie, Jamie's learned, with stories about the children—but because theirs was a stormy home filled with Robert's fits of temper. A good way, she figures, to bring the subject round to Michael and Molly again. No need to mention that Schumann had himself been going mad at the time.

The house, already steamy and oppressive when she woke, breathes the odor of freshly baked cookies. Stupid idea in this heat. As if baking something for the girl would be enough to conjure her here. A psychic crossing of the fingers, like telling

Peter about the lesson when he called early this morning—as if speaking of it out loud would cause a rearranging of probabilities, shift the realm of possibility in her favor.

Where are they, damn it?

It's a waste of time just waiting around like this. Sighing, she plows through the scores for something that requires real concentration and digs out Chopin's *Nocturne in D*, though she feels little enthusiasm for the music today. Her fingers feel fat and sluggish as they make their way through the appoggiaturas of the initial eight-bar phrase. Still she pushes on, through the introduction of the minor harmonies, the doubling of the melody in thirds. Head down, eyes closed, the intricate cascades of figuration finally begin to take her, the exquisite longing Chopin was going for working its magic once again.

Her head comes up slowly with the knowledge that Michael is near; she can feel it—like the closeness, the heaviness in the air before a storm. No Molly, then. Damn. Hardly surprising, though. She'd gotten her look at Jamie, after all; already made her point. Still, it means Meggie is here, which means she's said nothing to anyone about last time. Thank God.

Jamie's heart leaps at the slam of a car door and then another, but she forces herself to continue playing—through the end of the thematic statement, the final continuation in parallel thirds— not even bothering to look up as the front door opens and she senses them at the edge of the living room. The resolution into cadence at the beginning of the coda then, the meditative farewell.

Finished with the piece, finally, knowing she's never played it as well, she draws her hands to her lap and looks up—for once not even caring that Michael has simply walked in as if he owned the place. Nothing matters now but that Meggie has come.

The child is in a pink, flowered sundress today, delicately smocked across her birdlike chest. One of the straps, tied at her shoulders, slips down a slender arm.

"I learned the whole song," she blurts proudly from halfway across the room, even as she's heading toward Jamie—the books clutched across her chest. "Want to see? Hey, I smell cookies."

Michael, who's made no pretense at a greeting, is leaning back against the archway—hands deep in the pockets of his pants as he stares out the window. The music has disarmed him, it seems—made him pensive, forestalling whatever verbal volley was surely headed Jamie's way. Still, when his eyes come round, they're loaded with all the fury of their last meeting.

"Today is my son's eighth birthday. And because I couldn't reach you," he says pointedly, as Meggie scrambles up beside her, "Molly changed the date of his party for this." He flips his hand dismissively toward the piano. "But then, you probably already know that."

"Nope," Jamie says cheerfully, snagging a loose curl and looping it around Meggie's ear. More trouble on the home front, she thinks—what a shame. "Do you want to play the song for your father once before he goes?" Jamie asks the girl—hoping Michael will get the hint.

"I've heard it a thousand times already," he says, moving toward the window—his gaze having caught on something. "Meghan's been putting these all over the house," he says, nodding his head toward the pennies nesting in the corners of the sills. "Now I know why. What is it—some kind of hex thing?"

"No, Daddy," Meggie giggles. "It's for luck."

"Luck, huh?" Michael, smiling as if at some private joke, draws his hand from his pocket and glances at his watch. "Yeah, well, I've got a deposition in twenty minutes. It'll take me about an hour. Have her ready when I get back; I won't want to wait."

Not much time, but then that, she's sure, is the point. Still, she doesn't want to push it—has the feeling he's on the edge as it is.

Once he's gone and with Meggie plunking out the notes to *Rain, Rain, Go Away*, Jamie moves to the front door and throws the bolt against the chance he might decide to come back early. There'll be no wandering in unannounced this time.

They start with an introduction to simple time signatures, the concept of whole and dotted half notes. With so little time, Jamie's decided, they'll forgo a break, put off the overview of the pedals. Save the cookies till the end in case Michael cuts their time short. She has maybe forty minutes of usable time—forty minutes to see what she might draw from the girl.

"Play that song for me again," Meggie begs as they're finishing with the notation. "The bouncy one."

"*Gollywog's Cake-walk*? Tell you what. I'll play it for you at the end of the lesson. Right now, I want to play something by Robert Schumann." Jamie flips to the score of the gentle, soothing *Träumerei*—a kind of comfort food for the ears, chosen in hopes it will relax the girl and get her talking. She may or may not remember it from the day they met—the afternoon of the faux Bechstein appraisal.

"What's *his* little girl's name?" Meggie asks.

Ah—Chopin and daughter Chou-Chou revisited. "Schumann had eight children, actually," Jamie laughs. "Quite a few of them girls."

"Eight?" Meggie's incredulous. "That's even more than Mommy!"

"True," Jamie laughs. "He had a few boys, too—though one died as a baby." Only afterwards does she realize what a stupid thing it was to say. This was not the way she'd wanted to start. And indeed, Meggie's foot has begun its little kick.

"Why did *he* die?" she asks, as if dead children were popping up everywhere.

"He got sick. It was a long time ago, Meggie," Jamie explains. "A hundred and fifty years or more. They didn't have a lot of medicine back then. Not like today—today we have medicine for almost everything." She's almost babbling in her effort to undo the damage, keep the girl talking. If she shuts down now, that'll be it for the day.

Meggie considers. "Then why couldn't they fix your little boy?"

Jamie immediately goes still, her hands sliding from the keyboard to rest in her lap. Well, she wants to say, there's not much you can do for a broken neck. She sighs. "It's complicated Meggie. They just couldn't. He was too...hurt."

Meggie nods—no doubt accustomed to this kind of vagueness from adults; then cocks her head thoughtfully, pushing first one then another of the keys down slowly—too lightly to make anything more than a soft thud. "I saw him last night in my dream," she says with a chilling nonchalance. "Your little boy."

Jamie pauses, unsure. "How do you know he was my little boy?" Her tongue, gone suddenly leaden, stumbles awkwardly around the words *my little boy*.

"Because he told me." Cocking her head the other way now—eyes still on the keyboard. "He said his name was Sammy."

Had she told Meggie his name? She can't remember now. She certainly wouldn't have said *Sammy*—a name she'd only used when they were snuggling, the name he called himself.

"He said you shouldn't be sad anymore." Flashing Jamie a brilliant smile. "He's happy."

This is nuts, Jamie thinks—fighting the sudden, almost desperate need to take the girl seriously. Creative children, she reminds herself, often blur boundaries between the real and the imaginary. In the end, though, she has to ask. "What did he look like?"

"Shiny—like a star."

Like a star. Despite the heat, Jamie's arms are covered in goose flesh. Out of the blue, she remembers the single brilliant star lighting her way through last night's dream as she ran full out along the forest floor—veering as always from the trail into the lush undergrowth toward the safety of her ancient tree. The light all around her diaphanous and otherworldly. Only a single hunter left now, the only one she hasn't managed to shake off—his pursuit dogged, patient, more dangerous than the others, because he knows of the burden that slows her. Something she's carried all along, it seems, but is only now aware of. The changeling grasps and clings to her back, thin arms twined about her neck and arms—as watchful and keenly alert as a little gnome. And in danger, it's clear—of a mortal kind. Because this, she somehow knows, is what the hunter is after. Bearing down effortlessly, certain of his success. And so she turned to face him. And woke.

Meggie's gaze is intent, almost expectant—as if tracing Jamie's very thoughts. If only it weren't so hot in here. And the room almost unnaturally bright—as though all her ghosts were suddenly in shimmery attendance. Air. What she needs is air.

"What do we do with things when they die?" Meggie asks, her gaze still unnervingly intent.

Jamie sighs. "Well, it depends, I guess." She pauses. "Are we talking about people here?" And she knows before Meggie even nods what it is the girl wants—what she, herself, is going to do. "We bury them, Meggie," she says softly, almost sadly. "In the ground."

They make their way through the tall grass behind the house, Jamie in the lead to knock down the new growth—the whine of cicadas all around them. It's better out here—still hot, but with a newly freshened breeze stirring the dry, wheaty-smelling shafts that bend and whisper alongside them. The path to the small graveyard is packed and worn under all the vegetation and as they approach the copse of pines, a large flock of crows lifts as one from the up-most branches, cawing their displeasure.

"You okay?" Jamie asks, turning toward the girl—knowing she should call this off, head back to the house. And yet she doesn't, though thoughts of Michael and his threats dog her with every step. Meggie nods, saying nothing, and continues her clomping gait.

It's almost cool beneath the trees—the air dank and heavy with the smell of damp earth and decaying leaves. There are maybe a dozen headstones back here, and Jamie continues past several till she reaches the small marble angel marking Sam's grave. She pauses a moment before crouching to free a leaf caught between the fingers of a winged arm. Wishing she'd thought to bring something to clean the little cherub with; sorry that Meggie has to see it covered with dirt and ringed with spider webs.

"What do the words say?" Meggie asks, kneeling beside her.

"Samuel Philippe Pasquier," Jamie recites, using a stick to clear an intricate web from the angel's face. "September 23, 1995; November 16, 1997. He was two years old," she adds, without knowing exactly why.

"Mattie is two," Meggie offers.

"Yes," Jamie says quietly. "I know." It's then she notices the girl has begun clearing the plot of leaves and pine needles with her hands. The black earth of Sam's grave already lodged beneath her fingernails. "Oh, Meggie—don't," Jamie says. "You'll get all dirty." She pauses, considers. Knows what she must do if she has a prayer of seeing the girl again after this little stunt. "Listen," she says, "you know what secrets are, right?"

"Yes." Her tone offended. "I'm not a baby, you know."

"Then can we keep a secret about coming out here today?"

"Why?"

"Well, I'm supposed to be teaching you to play the piano, Meggie—not taking you on walks through old graveyards. Your parents might not let you come anymore if we tell them about it."

The face Meggie turns to her is smudged with dirt. "I won't tell," she says earnestly, spontaneously sliding an arm around Jamie's neck. "I promise."

Jamie simply nods and goes back to grooming the little plot, trying her best to ignore the slender arm whose weight seems to press right to her heart.

"Who are those other people?" Meggie asks, pointing toward the headstones deep beneath the trees.

Jamie rocks back on her heels and considers. "My parents are buried back in there," she says. "And we passed my grandmother's grave on the way in. The others are great aunts, great grandparents—people I never knew. This house has been in my family for a long time."

"Can we go see?"

Meggie covers her dolls at night—head to toe, like little corpses. The thought comes to Jamie out of the blue—Michael's very words that first night he came to the house. She's suddenly and unexplainably anxious, almost nauseous with it. The wind, chilly now, whips about them, stirring up pine needles and grit; above them the sky has gone dark and squally-looking, the trees beginning to bend.

"We should get back," she says, oddly relieved to have a reason to wrest the girl from this place.

Meggie appears transfixed as she stares up at the branches swaying above them. "I'm not afraid, you know," she says, the hair whipping about her face. "Sammy said I shouldn't be afraid."

They take the plate of cookies to the front porch after the shower blows through, and are ready for once when Michael pulls into the drive. Meggie, her practice books on the step beside her, pops the remains of a second cookie in her mouth and hops up, swiping her hands against the sides of the flowered sundress. Jamie opens her mouth to remind her again about keeping the secret of the graveyard, but changes her mind and simply smiles as she hands her the books.

All at once she's engulfed in the enthusiastic crush of a child's hug—the warm smell of that skin, those curls, the sharpness of the bare shoulder beneath her chin. She closes her eyes against its warmth, but it's reached her already, flooding her core unchecked—her head, her chest, her very heart—and when she opens her eyes again it's to the sight of Michael—head cocked back against the headrest—staring impassively from behind dark glasses. Only when he reaches back, angrily flinging open Meggie's door, does Jamie pat her back, plant a quick kiss on her cheek. Cool and dry like paper, the skin of an onion.

"Okay, then," she says quietly, smoothing the hair from the girl's face. "Best not keep your dad waiting."

She remains seated on the step, watching Michael reverse angrily back down the drive, and hates herself for the deceit, the manipulation—deciding right then and there to change tacks, go after Molly now instead of later. Work on building that rapport, but subtly and without Michael's knowledge. What Jamie has to tell the woman could give her the upper hand for years, but it will come at a price. Truth for unvarnished truth. Still, just how much information Molly will be willing to part with is anyone's guess.

Time to get her here and find out.

TWENTY-THREE

Hours later, Jamie's into the final mile of her run—sprinting through the deepening dusk when the familiar SUV pulls alongside and the front passenger door is flung wide.

"Get in!" Michael spits—fury in his eyes, in the tense folding of his body over the steering wheel. "Now!"

She bends for a moment, hands on knees as she catches her breath. Heart sinking, she approaches the vehicle and slowly climbs in. As if complying will make any difference at this point.

"Are you crazy?" Michael all but screams before the door is even shut. "Are you fucking nuts? Taking her to your kid's grave?"

She turns to face him, strangely indifferent to his indignation. "It's just out back," she says reasonably, wiping a rivulet of sweat from her eye. "She asked to see it."

"Why the fuck would she ask to see it?" he demands, barely glancing in the side mirror before squealing out. He whirls on her, then, as she's attempting to buckle herself in. "This was the plan all along, wasn't it? To fuck my kid up, lay all this on her because of what happened three goddamn years ago."

Jamie shifts her gaze to the passenger window and the fields of tall grass quickly flying past, not even caring where he might be taking her. All she can think of now is that it's over. The whole thing—over. "I wouldn't do that to her."

His laugh is dismissive, disbelieving. "And just where the fuck do you get off telling her to keep a secret, any secret, from us? I thought something was funny when I picked her up today, but by dinner she was so twisted up about the whole thing she couldn't eat—finally spilled her guts to Molly an hour ago. Been crying ever since, afraid we're going to cancel her precious lessons. Who is this woman, my wife asks me, that she tells my daughter to keep secrets from me?"

Jamie winces inwardly. The poor kid; if only she could see her, assure her none of this was her fault. "She wanted to go out there, all right?"

"You expect me to believe that? A kid as passive as Meggie just out of the blue asks to see a grave? How stupid do you think I am?"

"She seemed to sense Sam in the house somehow. There are times when—well." No use trying to explain. "She was just curious, I guess." She sighs. "So now what?"

"I'm pulling the plug—that's what. You've screwed yourself this time, lady—I didn't have to do a goddamn thing."

"Get her another teacher, at least. She really is talented. And she loves it so."

"She'll get over it."

"You don't even know her," Jamie snaps. "It's too bad, really, because she adores you. She's terrified of you, but she adores you."

"My daughter? You're telling me about my daughter?" His laugh bitter, laced with rage. This is the Michael she remembers from the morning of the accident—out of control, speeding recklessly through intersections in a blind fury. His eyes only minimally on the road as he turns to bark at her. "Well, fuck you. You're never going to see Meggie again. You're never going to see any of them again—not Meghan, not Molly, not Matthew—none of them. And that's straight from Molly herself. So much for being part of the inner circle."

Matthew. How ironic; she hasn't thought of him in weeks. "You want me out of your life?" she asks, shifting sideways to face him. Out of the corner of her eye, she catches the shape of a car seat strapped in behind them, a few stuffed toys in the shadows behind his seat. "Then I want the truth about the accident, why my son had to die." Reaching instinctively to her pocket, fingering the little sock. "You tell me that, and I guarantee you'll never see me again."

"Your son died, lady," he hisses, "because he was in the front seat of the car. Who the fuck puts a kid in the front? Everyone knows an airbag will break a child's neck."

Sam was fussing, she wants to scream. She couldn't get to the belts in the back. She had to make the train. A thousand things come to mind. Stay focused, she warns herself. Don't let him distract you. This just may be your last shot.

"If you hadn't been in such a goddamn panic, forced us off the road," she reminds him, "he'd be alive today." She leans in, wishing she could simply will the information from him. "You owe me the truth!"

"I don't owe you a thing," he spits. "I never did."

A wild laugh escapes her. "Oh no? Then why all those enormous contributions to the symphony? You weren't even a blip on our radar before the accident—I know; I checked the records—and suddenly you hand over seventy-five thousand dollars on a whim? And another seventy-five thousand each year on November 16th—which just happens to be the day my son died? Then there's the Steinway. Not to mention this million dollars you apparently haven't bothered telling Molly about. You know, I might just give her a call—see if I can manage to fill her in before she hangs up on me."

"Too late, " he laughs, his features ghoulish in the purple glow of the dashboard lights. "Debra Budlow beat you to it."

Poor, foolish Debra, Jamie thinks, wondering if she has any idea yet how vindictive these two can be. "A woman scorned, eh? What must poor Molly think—beset by all these women with axes to grind?"

He reels on her.

"Oh, everyone knows about Debra coming on to you. We're only surprised you said no."

"I bet you were all over it, too," he sneers. "Because—since you're so obsessed with *truth*," he says, all but spitting the word, "the *truth* is you liked what was happening between us in the hall that night. You were as attracted to me as I was to you. Admit it. Where does that little fact fit into your notion of the *truth*? Hey, and since we're baring our souls here, let's talk about what really happened that morning, shall we? I mean, we both know your kid's safety wasn't a priority, but what about yours? Were you even buckled in?"

She glares at him, her mind racing—figuring this for yet another of his traps. Of course she was. She must have been. She always does.

"Because according to the police report, you weren't. So it's obvious your overall judgment as to safety was somewhat impaired that day. If I really wanted to be a prick, I'd reopen this whole thing and file a friend of the court brief, sue you for negligence on behalf of your kid. It's been done, you know."

Jesus God. There was a time, maybe even until this very moment, when he might have gotten away with an explanation, an apology, some acknowledgment he'd been wrong to walk away without a backward glance—if nothing else, then for Meggie's sake. Not now. Not after this. She thinks, then, of Molly. The crack about calling and filling her in had been just that, really. Only now, she decides, she really will. Call her up and lay it all out—start to finish. Won't even ask for anything in return. Ready to accept that she'll never get to the truth of that day, willing now to exchange it for the satisfaction of ruining his marriage, seeing his perfect little world torn apart. She has a wild urge to lunge at the wheel, wrench it sideways and send them both careening off into some field. With any luck, she'd kill the both of them. It hardly matters anymore.

But he's already begun easing up on the accelerator, pulling over abruptly at the edge of a large meadow she vaguely recognizes but is too disoriented to place. "Now get out."

She glares at him as she steps from the SUV onto the gravel scrim, miles from where he picked her up—not a house or a light to be seen. Adding probably five miles to the run she thought was just about over. She has to scramble back to avoid the gravel spit by the tires as he tears out again.

"Get her another teacher!" she yells after him, the rectangular red lights of the SUV receding in the darkness.

TWENTY-FOUR

Bring them on; why not? Truth is, she couldn't care less. She's so heartsick over the mess she's made with Meggie that nothing else can touch her—not even Molly's refusal to return any of her calls. Michael's orders, no doubt. The two of them closing ranks, circling the wagons.

Jamie deletes Augie's voice mail from her cell phone, gets back with a quick message agreeing to attend the seven o'clock executive board meeting. Some emergency having to do with Michael; Augie didn't elaborate. With any luck, he's run that damn SUV into some wall, saving Molly the trouble of taking one of her fancy kitchen knives to him. Jamie smiles at the thought and lets it go—knowing it's far more likely he's complained about Debra's call to Molly—that or someone has finally uncovered the tie between Michael and herself. Might even be that in the two weeks since he dumped her at the side of the road, he's come up with some way to have her fired. Her attendance required tonight so they can do the deed in style. Well fine; let them fire her, then. Frankly, it would be a relief.

She checks her watch—just before six. Thankful to be in the city already at least—having spent her entire Saturday reworking the next round of appeal letters rather than sit at the house, thinking about Meggie and the lesson she should have had this morning, would have had if Jamie hadn't so stupidly indulged her own almost desperate need to share little bits of Sam with someone—anyone, apparently. Pathetic.

Sighing, she pulls her attention back to Debra's latest appeal letter and the paragraph she's been reworking for the last fifteen minutes. Minor editing, she finally admits, won't do it this time. The whole thing needs to be rewritten. It's bad even for Debra.

Raising her arms in a long stretch, she catches sight of the woman herself leaning casually against the doorjamb. Her first thought is that Debra, too, has been called here for this sudden, unexplained meeting—a possibility she immediately rejects. It's almost unheard of for even senior staff like herself to receive such a summons. Besides, Debra is in chinos and sneakers, a sleeveless red t-shirt. Hardly proper attire for a board meeting.

"Looks like neither of us had anything better to do this evening," Jamie says, mustering a smile as she tosses her pen onto the desk.

Debra's eyes move to the letter and flicker briefly in recognition. There's no avoiding it, Jamie knows. Might as well get it over with. Maybe she'll be smart, take the thing home with her for a weekend rewrite.

"I'm sorry, Debra," she says, and strangely enough she really is. "I can't let it go out like this."

She's expecting anger—that or the woman's biting sarcasm—but Debra merely crosses her arms, cocks her head in an enigmatic smile. "What's wrong with it?" Oddly bemused, as if she doesn't really care.

"It rambles; doesn't go anywhere; there's no call to action—take your pick." Jamie sighs and picks up the letter. No need to be nasty about it. It's Saturday, after all; the woman is here on her own time. "Look," she says, holding it out across the desk. "Why don't you just take it with you, work on it at home?"

A short, derisive laugh. "I don't think so."

"We have a Monday deadline on this, remember? Goes to the printer at noon?"

"I remember. You don't like it; you redo it." She stoops to retrieve a box Jamie hadn't noticed before—shooting a parting comment over her shoulder as she walks off. "Ciao."

Jamie, holding the letter toward the now vacant doorway, simply stares in disbelief.

An hour later, still tense from the exchange with Debra, she raps lightly at the open conference room door—stoic against whatever might face her here. She's half expecting to see Michael; has prepared herself for the ripping open of her own raw wound. Instead, there are but five around the oblong table—Augie and the four male members of the executive board headed now by John Cohen, her longtime ally. Jamie, who has yet to congratulate him on becoming their latest president—the third time in his twenty years with the symphony—shoots a warm smile toward the head of the table which she hopes conveys this, then nods to the others, including the pompous Colin Bradbury, who inadvertently betrayed her to Michael at February's gala. Three of the four men, including Colin and John, are in evening dress, so they've broken from their weekend routines of tennis matches and dinner parties for this. Whatever this is.

John returns her smile with one equally as warm, requesting that she close the door behind her. Shooting a furtive glance across the table at a solemn-faced Augie, she seats herself beside a tuxedo-clad bank vice president whose name momentarily escapes. Augie, she knows, would have used their long acquaintance, their knowledge of each other's body language, to communicate something if Jamie herself were in trouble. This isn't about her, then. Interesting. Out of habit, she's brought along a pen and legal pad, readies now for instructions, alterations in strategy.

John begins. "I apologize for breaking into everyone's weekend like this, but I had rather a lengthy phone conversation with Michael Ryan this afternoon which required immediate action." He pauses, looks to Augie, whose lips are tightly pursed, eyes trained on the center of the table. "Unbeknownst to any of us, Debra Budlow phoned Mrs. Ryan recently with a number of revelations designed to embarrass Michael." John pauses. "And while I'm not privy to all that was said, as much of it was apparently of a personal nature, Michael did tell me that Debra disclosed information regarding his million dollar pledge to this organization—information he had apparently not wished his wife to have." He sighs. "A sticky situation, to be sure."

He pauses a moment to peruse the table of disbelieving male faces. It's then that Augie's gaze meets Jamie's for a split second—the knowledge that Debra has done this out of spite, regardless of the consequences, flashing between them. Funny, Jamie thinks, remembering how Michael once warned her to be careful of Debra. Seems he should have heeded his own advice.

"The fact that Debra was probably not aware of this difficulty between the Ryans is hardly the point," John continues. "There's a pattern here—from all indications an obsessive one. She was observed making advances of a romantic nature to the poor man at some party—advances that I am assured were very firmly discouraged. Michael, himself, assumed that was the end of it."

"Good God." This from Colin, who has thrown himself back against his chair in astonished disbelief.

"As a result of these indiscretions," John continues glumly, "Michael is considering resigning from the board. Much depends, from what I gather, on how we handle the situation. I assured him it would be dealt with immediately and in the firmest possible manner."

Michael has demanded Debra be fired, then. An ultimatum from Molly, no doubt.

With that, John nods curtly toward Augie, who, despite the high level of respect her fifteen years of service affords her, is still an employee of the board and thus remains silent until asked to comment.

"Debra was called in a few hours ago," she says tersely. "She denied nothing and offered no explanation. I dismissed her with two weeks' severance—which, under the circumstances, I consider very generous. At this point, she's cleaned out her desk and returned her keys."

That explains the box, Jamie realizes, and the cavalier attitude about the letter. But why, she wonders, didn't Michael have her fired as well? As Debra's immediate supervisor, she could easily be held at least partly responsible for the woman's actions, her increasingly aggressive behavior. It didn't sit right. Something's wrong.

Beside Augie is a Wall Street accountant who looks as if he'd come directly from the tennis court—shoes and all. Albert-somebody, Jamie thinks. "Surely," he interjects now, "Michael won't resign due solely to the actions of an obviously disturbed employee?"

"Yes, well, you're right—there's a bit more to it than that," John says. "This mess aside, Michael is nonetheless relinquishing his board responsibilities for the foreseeable future. It seems one of his children has become ill. Seriously enough so that he's decided to pull back from his outside obligations and spend more time with the family until things are resolved."

Jamie's heart skips several beats even as she reminds herself that this is no doubt simply another of Michael's games. She's only moderately surprised he'd stoop to using one of his children in an attempt to distance himself from the symphony—another of Molly's demands, no doubt. They'll never see the million dollars, of course. Even in retreat, his strategy is masterful; she has to give him that. No matter what their concerns, a sick child makes his withdrawal understandable, even commendable.

"Ah," the accountant nods. "So the incident with Debra—as distasteful and inappropriate as it was—is only part of the story."

Colin clears his throat. "And the money? What about the money?"

John shrugs. "Who's to say? In any case, we're left now with the imminent launch of a capital campaign whose single largest donor may be about to defect, and with no director of development to implement it." He turns then to Jamie, leaning forward ingratiatingly across the table. "This is where you come in, my dear. We're going to need your assistance in this, more of your time, as well, I'm afraid—at least until someone is hired to replace Debra Budlow. Augie assures me she can get temporary help in, but they'll need training. I hope we can count on you."

"Of course," Jamie says vaguely, automatically. "Whatever you need."

Suddenly, the table is a-buzz with talk, relieved laughter, and she realizes the meeting has ended. John has already risen, and she turns to him with the question no one else has thought to ask— the answer having meaning for no one here but herself. "Which child is ill, John?"

He looks over. "I'm sorry, my dear?"

"Did Michael say which of his children is ill?"

"One of the middle daughters. Begins with an *M*, I think."

"Mia?" Her voice is so quiet she's afraid he doesn't hear her, but his confusion, she realizes with alarm, is due instead to the fact that he doesn't recognize the name. Then, because she must, she asks. "Is it Meghan?"

"That's it—Meghan. Poor child's been sick for several weeks now. No one's sure yet what's wrong, only that it's quite serious. They're seeing specialists, running tests—that kind of thing. Very time consuming, as you can imagine." Turning to Augie then. "Jamie's right. We should send a card, some flowers; mention the little girl by name. It can't hurt, certainly—may just win him back to the fold."

❦

Jamie tosses through the night, reminding herself of the reasons Michael might resort to such a lie—that Molly has demanded he sever ties with the symphony because of Debra, because of the million dollar pledge; or simply—since Jamie now knows just who Molly is—because she can. Perhaps Michael never really meant to make good on the money at all; the idea might simply have been floated as part of a plan to keep her around.

Still, by morning she's decided to call—to try yet again to reach Molly, find out what's really going on. If she can somehow manage it without Michael's interference, she'll simply apologize— wholeheartedly and without equivocation—and hope he hasn't filled Molly in on the rest of it. Anything to keep the door cracked toward the future, the possibility Molly might allow the lessons again someday. At their house, if need be. Willing, now, to let everything else slide if she can just see Meggie again, speak to her, assure her that what happened wasn't her fault. This child with whom, by some magic, she's formed an inexplicable bond— sudden and surprising and certainly inconvenient. But as final and fixed as the stars.

She takes a deep breath and dials their number. Another deep breath as the phone rings two, three, four times. They're at church, of course—it's Sunday morning, after all. Which means Meggie is fine. Perfectly fine. Flooded with relief, she's about to hang up when the phone is picked up at the other end. The voice chills her, killing any hope she'll get a chance to speak to Meggie at all.

"Ryan." He sounds tired, angry.

"I'm calling solely out of concern," she says flatly, surprised to find the hand gripping the phone has begun to shake. "Perhaps I should speak with Molly." She pauses. "I heard Meggie is sick."

A long, cold pause. "Where did you hear this?"

"Emergency board meeting last night."

He snorts. "Molly's at church. With the kids. She wouldn't talk to you anyway."

"Meggie?"

"She's here with me."

"She's all right?"

"You have the nerve to ask me that? I'm going to say this just once. We're not interested in your concern. Don't call here again—ever. Understand?"

Fear in his voice. It was unmistakable.

TWENTY-FIVE

She waits until nine-thirty the next morning to phone the Ryans again, placing the call from her New York office, after she's relatively sure Michael has left the house. If he's like every other lawyer she's ever known, he spends most of Monday in court, so there's little chance he'll be around to screen calls. Thankfully, the need to keep the capital campaign on track in the face of Debra's sudden departure has won her a few extra days here, though neither Peter nor her boss in Nashua are very happy about the prospect. Truth is, if Debra hadn't been so conveniently fired, Jamie would have found another reason to delay heading north. Leaving is simply not an option—not until she's assured herself Meggie is all right.

This time the phone is picked up almost immediately, and by a woman whose voice is clearly an older, deeper version of Molly's own.

"Yes?" An odd mix of fear and hope in the greeting.

"Good morning," Jamie says in her best professional fundraising tone. "You must be Molly's mother. My name is Diana Apollo— Meghan's piano teacher." Rushing ahead against the chance the woman has been warned about her—instructed to brush her off without ceremony. "I was wondering if I might speak with Molly?"

"I'm sorry, my daughter's not here." The composure crumbling quickly. "She left an hour ago for the hospital." And, amazingly, the woman begins to cry.

Five minutes later, Jamie has most of the story—or as much as this woman, eager to vent her anguish, knows. A bout of diarrhea lasting several days; a quick trip to the doctor and an initial diagnosis of some typical childhood virus. Two days later, blood found in Meggie's stool and another visit to the doctor for a culture. No one prepared for how ill Meggie looked the following morning, so pitifully small and helpless. Just a slip of a thing to begin with, Molly's mother reminds Jamie. Alarmed, Molly swept her off to the hospital for blood work, which confirmed what all of them already knew, that something was very, very wrong. And there she remains, having tests—Michael and Molly spelling each other so that someone is always with Meghan, a child who has never once spent a night away from her family.

Jamie knows better than to try and phone the hospital. Her only hope for news is the grandmother, who's promised to call at three with an update.

Somehow she manages to get through the day without going crazy—rewriting the appeal letter and getting all the peripherals off to the printer; familiarizing herself with Debra's files and the status of pending grants and sponsorship proposals, which are far fewer than she would have thought. All of this in a daze, a long day of paper pushing that seems at once trivial and unreal.

Augie stops by in the late afternoon, pausing in the doorway much as Debra herself did a mere two days before—though out of concern, rather than Debra's amused derision. "Everything all right?" she asks, leaning against the door jam. "You've been distracted all day."

Jamie sneaks another glance at her watch. Four-thirty now—the inescapable passage of time sending another jolt of apprehension through her. Still, she manages a quick, business-like nod. "Absolutely."

Augie pauses, then enters the small office. "Do you have time to go through these?" she asks, placing a file on the desk as she seats herself. "I realize it's late in the day, but we should begin preliminary interviews for Debra's position right away."

Jamie gives the folder a cursory glance. "Resumés?"

"We receive them all the time. I pulled these, hoping you'd take a minute to go through them before you leave tonight—hold onto any you think have potential, schedule some interviews. I can do the preliminaries, then have you meet with the top few people when you're down again." She sighs. "You don't suppose there's any chance I could talk you into coming back full time? Convince that husband of yours to relocate?" She smiles at Jamie's astonished look. "I had to ask; I promised the board."

Jamie's smile is wan. "The only way we'd get Peter here is if the city suddenly decided to devote all of New York harbor to growing mussels or cod." She glances again at her watch and looks up with a cheerfulness she doesn't feel. "How about if I take these with me and look at them tonight? We can discuss them in the morning. I'd like to go over the status of Debra's outstanding grant proposals with you then, as well. A number of things are going to need to be addressed before I can get down again."

"We could do that over dinner if you like," Augie suggests. "Why don't you stay in the City tonight? Gaspar is in Vienna this week, and it would be wonderful to have the evening to catch up. Our guest room awaits. You may remember," she adds, leaning back in the chair, "that I make a wonderful Wiener Schnitzel."

"I do remember." It's tempting, certainly—even more so when she realizes Gaspar's trip to Vienna is the one he and Augie have been planning for months, a working vacation built around the premier of his latest opera. Augie should be there, Jamie knows—would have flown out this morning, but for this mess. And while Debra's stupidity might be the immediate cause, in many ways the whole thing traces back to Jamie's own tortured connection to Michael Ryan. "I'm sorry, Augie. You should be in Vienna right now, celebrating with Gaspar."

Augie shrugs. "So we are both without our husbands tonight. You will stay, then?"

Augie, she knows, is offering a chance to redeem their friendship, and she loves her for it. Suddenly, she'd like nothing better than to lose herself for an evening in the warm lighting and softly-cushioned elegance of Augie and Gaspar's West Side apartment, allow herself to be pampered and fed and listened to. If anyone could understand what she's going through, it would be Augie—the only person in her life who was part of all this when it began. She's a breath away from saying yes; then—as if a shadow has moved across her, is reminded again of Meggie, the call that hasn't come. And the apprehension that has been growing all afternoon creeps deeper into her heart.

"I wish I could," she says, avoiding Augie's gaze as she slips the file of resumes into her briefcase. "But I need to be home tonight. Peter and I have some things to thrash out." A non-excuse, of course; another lie to add to the list. Except for the last part, which is unfortunately true enough. Peter was decidedly unhappy this morning with her decision to stay on, wants to discuss what he calls her inability to say no. "I've got to hurry as it is if I'm going to make my train."

It's a little before seven as she climbs the porch steps, rummaging through her briefcase for the house key when the sound of a vehicle turning into the drive draws her gaze. Michael's SUV pulling in behind her—a sight more unnerving than surprising. No doubt he's the reason Molly's mother never called back. Still, things can't be that bad if he's still got the energy to harass her like this. There's that at least.

She remains where she is till he reaches her, his gaze hostile above a wrinkled suit coat as he halts at the bottom of the steps. It doesn't appear he's shaved today. Or that he cares.

She leans against the porch post, shaky suddenly, and puts her briefcase down beside her. "Yes, I called," she says. "And I'll keep calling until someone tells me how Meggie is."

"Gloria didn't know who you were, or she wouldn't have told you anything this morning."

"I asked for Molly. I thought she, at least, would talk to me. We're both mothers, after all—whatever else has happened." Too late she realizes this use of the present tense in relation to herself, girds herself against the way he has of sharpening her words with a choice few of his own, then slipping them into her heart. Surprised when the predictable response doesn't come. "Are you going to tell me how she is, or have you driven all the way over here just to insult me? Christ, why don't you just tell me what's wrong?"

He runs his hands over his face, his exhaustion palpable. "We don't know yet. All these specialists running around, and still nobody's got a handle on it. I'm no fucking doctor, but even I can see she's worse every day."

My God, this could happen so fast? Another thought, then. "What about Matthew and the others?"

"They're fine. Whatever happened, whatever this is, she picked it up on her own." The muscles in his jaw are working now, as if this business of being civil is almost too much.

"What do the doctors say?" Jamie asks. "What can they do?"

He barks a laugh. "Not much. Wait for more tests, manage her fluids, watch her urine output. Hope whatever it is runs its course without too much damage. Sometimes it does." He grins at her then—a nasty smile twisted with bitterness. "You should be happy," he says. "It's what you wanted, after all."

"What?"

"To see me hurt. That's why you came back here, wasn't it?"

Sarcastic and self-absorbed—how unusual for him. "This is why you're here?" Jamie demands. "To turn this into something about you? About us?" She stoops and retrieves her briefcase, heads to the door. "Save your breath." She inserts he key in the lock, then turning asks, "Why *are* you here, anyway?"

"To tell you to call it off." His stance hasn't changed, but his eyes drill into her, the waves of hostility rolling off him thickening the air.

"Call what off? What are you talking about?"

"Don't play fucking dumb with me. You and all your voodoo shit. Whatever it is you've set in motion here—just call it off."

That's it? They can't figure out what's wrong, so it's somehow her fault?

His hands are balled into fists, and she's reminded of his potential for sudden violence. There's danger here, but she's far too outraged to care. She strides toward him, glaring down from the top step.

"I'm sorry—you think I've somehow arranged all this? Called the gods down on your head in retribution? Great idea, actually. I should have thought of it." For the first time she notices the bloodshot eyes, the dark circles. Well, she'd wanted him pushed to the edge—he was right about that much anyway. But not this way. Not this. "And how dare you imply I'd do anything to hurt Meggie. I love her, damn you—how could I not?" Something cracking open inside with the words, a spilling of bittersweet feeling, the urge to beat her breast. Nothing good comes of loving children—too many avenues of potential loss. As Michael, himself, now knows.

She shakes her head at his defiant glare. Never has she seen anyone rocket so fast, so violently, from vulnerability to rage. She could almost feel sorry for him. Almost. "Go home, Michael—

for God's sake. Molly's resolve is a lot stronger than a couple of bacteria. Meggie will pull out of this fine; you'll see."

"You're damn right she will." His voice is brittle and terse as he backs toward the car. "She's my kid; she's gonna beat this."

TWENTY-SIX

Jamie returns to the house two weeks later, determined to ignore the existence of Michael Ryan and his entire family. Resolved as well to close up the property and quietly withdraw from everything she's begun here. Meggie, no doubt better by now and lost to her in any case, will easily find another teacher—Molly will see to that. And Augie, while she certainly won't be happy about it, can find someone else to run the capital campaign. No one is indispensable, after all. There's simply nothing to be gained by staying any longer—though it took physical distance and two agonizing weeks with no word about the girl or her condition to finally convince Jamie of that. Besides, no way Michael or Molly will ever offer up the truth of the day Sam died; she knows that now.

She's considering all this as she makes the turn at her mailbox, only to find Michael, himself, perched on her porch step in the afternoon sun—his SUV parked smack in the middle of the dusty drive. Back for another go at her, it seems. She's so angry at the sight of him sitting there she can barely see to park the car—jerking it around onto the grass so she won't have to move it again when she finishes throwing him off her property.

Michael barely glances up as she pulls in. Elbows parked on his splayed knees, hands cupping a container of coffee, he looks damp and wilted from the heat. Good—she's kept him waiting a while, at least. She's halfway up the walk with her bag, ready to let loose on him about all this goddamn grandstanding, when he finally raises his eyes. Even from fifteen feet away he looks awful—unshaven, tie askew. And nearly crazed, it seems, with exhaustion.

The rage she's been nursing blooms abruptly into visceral, gut-wrenching alarm. "What's wrong?" she asks testily, the anger of a moment ago still in her voice.

He swirls what's left of the coffee and throws it back, avoiding her eyes as he crushes the cup. It's only when she reaches him that she catches the sharp scent. Scotch—at three in the afternoon. Jesus.

"What's happened?" she demands again. Standing before him now, the bag still clutched awkwardly in her grip.

He speaks to the shapeless pile in his hands, turning it over and over as he talks. "She was finally starting to get better; that's the thing." He makes an attempt at his usual defiance, but his voice is strained and raw with whatever has happened over the course of the last few weeks. "Then bang—she starts to crash."

"What is it?"

"We still don't know. They've ruled out cancers, anything genetic. Something bacterial, viral maybe. They think it's hantavirus, then aplastic anemia. E.coli, maybe, which produces a toxin that damages the intestines, blood vessels." He pauses and looks off toward the trees. "Kidneys." he says softly. His mind somewhere else now. On doctors, tests, a little girl lying prone in a hospital bed.

"No," Jamie says, sitting down on the step. Then again, more softly, "No." She looks over, trying to read him. "But how would she get such a thing?"

"Who the fuck knows? A piece of unwashed fruit, a bad hamburger, playing in the dirt where some animal's died…" He trails off. "Could be anything."

They both look up as a yellow school bus rumbles by, the laughter of small children spilling from the open windows. The end of the first week of school. Sam would have been on that very bus, Jamie realizes with a jolt. Meggie on one just like it.

"They think it's one thing, then it looks like something else, then back again—like it's shifting, hiding from us." His eyes remain glued to the bus as it bumps and jounces from side to side along the rutted road. "They've started talking about registering her for a bone marrow transplant, kidney donation. Trying to prepare us for whatever, not to mention the wait—years, sometimes."

He yawns, rubs his stubbled chin, the sunken eyes. "No way my daughter's gonna wait around like that. So I had everybody tested—everyone but Molly. She can't donate because of the pregnancy. We thought maybe one of the kids might be compatible, but the cross matches were all wrong." He stares again at the crushed cup in his hand, the muscles in his jaw working now—looking everywhere, it seems, but at Jamie.

Her mind, shocked to a thick, sluggish pace, stumbles over his words—tested, cross-match, compatible. It requires all her effort just to take it in. Speech utterly fails her.

Michael pauses. "So then Molly gets on this kick about you," he says, flashing a furtive glance her way. "How Meghan likes you so much. The two of you so cozy—your little secrets, pennies in the windows—all that crap. And she still asks about you all the time. Even now. So Molly figures there's a reason you two were so close—that maybe this is it."

"This is what?"

"A match," he snaps, as if she hasn't been keeping up. "That you're a match. In Molly's twisted little brain, it means something. I don't know; maybe she's right. It's a long shot, I know, but if that's what she wants…" His eyes—raw and wounded, and almost desperately earnest—take Jamie in fully for the first time. "We want you to get tested," he says. "You can name your price. Anything—anything at all."

Her first reaction is laughter; even she knows the chance of such a thing is all but nil.

"You can't be serious," she says. But it seems he is; his manner as assessing and vigilant as it would be negotiating any business deal. Fighting for Meggie now, for the life of his daughter. She can see it in his face, in the pain which has somehow altered his gaze. The kind of pain with which she's all too familiar. And wants nothing to do with now.

"Just so I understand," she says. "I can't be trusted to give Meggie piano lessons, but body parts are okay—is that it?"

He says nothing—the lawyer in him no doubt waiting for the anger to pass. Well, screw him.

"Sorry. I'm not interested in giving anything more to your family—I mean, considering you already took my son." She stands abruptly, feeling the heat rise in her face at the reality of what he's asking, the fact he could even make such a request. This, of course, is why he needed the scotch.

In the silence that follows, it dawns on her that this is the exactly what she's been waiting for, has been planning for in one way or another since she opened the house up again ten months ago. Her chance to destroy him. All she has to do is say no. She tries it on, the satisfaction of sending him on his way with the knowledge she might have helped Meggie but turned her back. Both of them knowing why. And as terrible as it was to lose Sam the way she did, Michael's loss will be far worse. At least she was saved the torture of watching a child die.

Her face must reveal something of this, because he shoots her his usual mocking leer. "I suppose you think this makes us even."

"Not at all," she says coldly. "You have any number of children. I only had the one." With this, she picks up her bag and heads toward the door.

"You said you loved her," he accuses, following with his eyes.

"Ah," Jamie says, fumbling for her keys. "But I hate you so much more." She waits for the satisfaction she should feel at this, at her decision to walk away, but actually doing so is proving difficult. It's becoming harder to move with each step, harder to breathe. Because it's really Meggie she's walking away from, not Michael; it's Meggie who's so very ill. Still, she forces herself to reach for the doorknob, its exact location blurred with teary indecision and the burden she carries every hour of every day—the pain and guilt of not having been able to help Sam as he lay dying. And it hits her with sudden and absolute clarity that if she does nothing now to at least try and help this child, she'll be utterly unable to live with herself. Even if it means helping Michael.

She tilts her head back and erupts in a choked half-laugh, half-sob at the incredible, unbelievable irony of it all, then turning, furious, flings her bag the length of the porch. "God damn you!" she screams.

Michael whirls. Fight or flight—he's not sure which.

Pacing now, arms crossed against her chest, Jamie's filled with a sudden, mocking fury. "Wasn't it you who said all this was fated?" she demands. "That you were meant to be thrown into my path that day? Remember that little speech? Because I sure do."

She stops and glares at him, swipes at the tears flowing freely now. "That would mean that this was fated too, then, wouldn't it? Meggie's getting sick, I mean—maybe even dying. Have you thought about that? That this might be part of the plan, too?"

Michael stands as if stricken, arms limp at his sides.

"You think the gods really care about one little girl? After all, they didn't care enough to save Sam."

"I don't know," he says softly, tentatively—as if sensing a possible change of heart. "I hope so."

It seems that even he can love a child, but somehow this baring of his soft underbelly only serves to make Jamie angrier. Determined to make this as hard for him as possible. "This doesn't let you off the hook for anything—you got that? If I do it at all, it will be for Meggie, not you." And how in the hell to tell Peter, she wonders, if comes to that?

"And you are going to pay for it," she says. "Pay dearly."

He nods—trying unsuccessfully to mask his relief, reaching slowly to the checkbook protruding from his back pocket.

He should be so lucky. "Put it away, Michael, " she says—her smile slow and mocking. "We both know what I want, and it's got nothing to do with money. You do remember our little game, don't you? The trading? Only this time I get to ask all the questions. And you're going to answer every single one of them."

Their eyes lock. It's occurred to him then; he may have known all along it would come to this. Again the nod.

She begins her pacing again. "Tell me all of it, then," she instructs. "And if you give me that attorney-client privilege crap just once, you can forget about any of this."

He leans back against the post rail, hands tucked behind him, and looks off toward the street. "This whole thing has pretty much destroyed my marriage; I don't suppose that's enough for you."

"Oh, you haven't had a real marriage in years," Jamie says dismissively. "We both know that. And, no, that's not enough. Nothing," she hisses, her anger rising again, "will ever be enough. The truth will simply be adequate."

Grabbing her elbows to stop the shaking that's begun along her arms, she rests her back against the cool wood of the house. Something to brace herself against the pile of half-truths he'll no doubt throw at her.

He shifts, sighs, looks down for a moment. "You were right about the donations, but they were Molly's idea, not mine—the result of her Catholic guilt. That and her own particular brand of retribution."

Interesting, but it tells her nothing, really. Playing his games, even now. "Don't make me work for this, Michael," Jamie warns. "You've got about a minute to tell me where you were coming from that morning—why you were so upset."

"All right," he says, spreading his hands. Then again, more quietly, after the briefest of sighs. "All right. I'd spent the night before with a woman I'd been seeing for about six months. An artist friend of Molly's. I was coming from her place."

This is supposed to be news? She knew from the moment she met him that he messed around on regular basis. Still, it's low— even for this guy. She shoots him a frustrated, lets-get-on-with-it look.

"We'd planned it so carefully," he continues. "I told Molly I had an early deposition in New York and had to spend the night in the city—then went over to Susan's place. She lived on Porter Street—the bungalow at the end of the road." He pauses, caught up in the memory of something.

Lived—past tense. "So she's not there anymore," Jamie says, realizing she'd been on the right track with the Porter Street research all along, just hadn't gone back far enough.

"No, she's gone." Michael says, looking almost wistful. "Anyway, we fought that next morning as I was leaving. She told me she was pregnant, wanted me to end my marriage. I refused, of course. I'd told her from the start that divorce wasn't an option. I offered to pay for an abortion. She cried, screamed all kinds of threats; she could be overemotional at times. So I bolted. That's when it happened."

It made a certain amount of sense, given what she knows of him, but it doesn't explain why he was screaming into his cell phone—talking to his lawyer, he said—when he careened into her path. About a client, he said. It had to be this woman, this Susan. And then she remembers the woman Debra told them about—the client who filed the complaint against Michael for misappropriating her funds. Stealing from her, when you came right down to it. She was an artist, too—a family friend. And her name was Susan. My God.

"Susan was the woman who sued you," Jamie says.

"Ah." He nods. "Debra's been a busy girl."

"Go on." There has to be more; mere concern over this little indiscretion couldn't account for the level of fear and fury on his face that morning. That phone call was about something else, something else entirely. "None of this tells me anything about why my son had to die."

Michael ignores her. "I was halfway out the door when I turned to tell her I'd call her later—you know, give her some time to calm down, and there she was—a gun hanging at her side. I have no idea when she picked it up; I just remember thinking it looked too heavy for her, and how ironic the whole thing was, because I'd been the one telling her to get one in the first place—it's so isolated out there. I mean, we all knew she could be unstable at times, but there'd never been anything like this before. I kept telling myself to move, to take it from her, but I couldn't. I just stood frozen, wondering when she was going to shoot me, and then she smiled this weird smile and put the gun in her mouth. Just like that, she pulled the trigger. I didn't have a chance to react, to do anything."

Their eyes are locked, but neither speaks for several moments. Jamie's mind is suddenly with this woman—pregnant and desperate and unwilling any longer to be bent to Michael's will. "I see," she says flatly. "So you really killed two children that morning—yours as well as mine."

Something flickers in his eyes. "Not that I particularly care what you think," he says. "But I did love her."

"And stole from her," Jamie says, her voice full of challenge. "Go on, tell me you called the police. That you stayed with her till they got there." She feels sick, suddenly—knowing that's not at all what she's going to hear.

"I couldn't do anything for her; I mean, you can imagine what I had there. I'd have stayed if there was any hope at all. So I went out to my car and called my attorney. He told me to get the hell out of there. We were still on the phone when the accident happened."

Jamie's pacing again in her agitation. "Did your lawyer tell you to do that, too? Drive off with a two year old dying in the road?"

No." His jaw is working now. There's only so much he's going to take, it seems—even for Meggie. "He told me to turn around and go back, but I was panicked. I couldn't be found there—you do see that."

"Tell me why." Michael's head snaps up at the pure venom in her voice. "No, really. I want you to say it."

"There were a number of reasons."

"Molly would find out?" Jamie suggests.

"Among other things."

"Other things—like placing you there at a certain time? The woman once sued you, after all. It might look like—well." It occurs to her then that in not reporting the death, Michael might also have been buying time. Chances were, when Susan was ultimately found, any evidence of their lovemaking would have decayed along with the rest of her. Scandal averted; marriage saved.

"You have to understand," he says. "Bringing me into it wasn't going to help anyone."

"Ah." Jamie nods. "Except us, perhaps—Sam and me. I mean, had you bothered to stop. What a shame someone happened along and got your plate number."

"Yeah," he says softly, looking away—and she's not sure if he's caught the sarcasm or not. "It blew my cover with Molly, of course. The only thing I could do at that point was come clean about everything." He walks to the end of the porch and turns, resting his back against the rail. "It took some doing, but she finally agreed to back me up, tell the police I was at home with her that night. I knew they'd eventually come around. I mean, my fingerprints were all over Susan's place. Easily explained by the fact I was her attorney, of course, and known to be out there on legal matters from time to time. But still. Thankfully the whole thing died down pretty quickly."

Jamie simply stares, incredulous at the callous intellectualizing. Her accident and Sam's death only the tip of the iceberg. "Amazing," she marvels. "None of this seems to bother you at all."

"I've had a long time to get used to it."

"And Molly?" Jamie asks. "Has she gotten used to it as well?"

"Molly has her own way of dealing with the whole thing. She decided exposing me and ending our marriage would hurt the kids more than me—so she hit me where she figured I'd bleed the most."

"The donations," Jamie says—her voice flat.

"The donations. Minimum of seventy-five thousand a year for ten years. To make up to her, to make up to you—to remind me, of course," he adds bitterly.

"To make up to me?" Jamie demands. "You people think throwing a little money around can ever make up for what happened to my son? And then what—you and Molly go on as if nothing has happened?"

"Hardly. On the surface everything seems fine, though nothing's been the same since."

"I should think not. Still, she keeps having children."

"She keeps having children. They're to remind me, too, I'm told. Of all that was lost that day."

Jesus. Even Jamie couldn't have dreamed up anything this twisted. It appears she owes a debt of sorts to Molly—the woman's very fecundity a daily reminder. Children born to punish and shame him—all of which should afford Jamie at least some degree of satisfaction. Strangely enough, it doesn't.

"Does Molly know who I am?" she asks. "The whole Diana thing?"

"She does now." His laugh is tight, brittle. If he's aware how badly he's come off in all this, he's not letting on.

"You told her?" Jamie asks.

"I didn't have to. Debra beat me to it."

Of course. "And Molly wanted her fired for her trouble."

"Molly doesn't like surprises."

"So why not have me fired as well?"

A small smile. "Molly wouldn't hear of it."

Now this is a surprise. "Why not?"

Michael shrugs. "She feels sorry for you; she's still punishing me—take your pick." He waits a beat. "She's convinced herself all this is retribution for what happened that day; that Meghan is the price we're paying for it now. Revenge of the gods—that kind of thing. And that only you can help us now."

"So even your showing up here today was Molly's idea. And confessing all this to me is supposed to break the spell—is that it?"

"Confession is Molly's thing, not mine. But I'll do anything to help Meghan, as you now know."

Almost a minute goes by before he speaks again—a minute in which Jamie finally realizes just why he's worked so hard to keep her around—searching through her things that day during Meggie's lesson; embroiling her in the capital campaign. He had to find out how much she knew, try to keep a lid on it all.

"So," he says. "We're finished here?" He pulls a card from his pocket and lays it on the porch rail. "Our doctor. He'll arrange all the tests."

"There's almost no chance this will work," Jamie tells him as he starts down the steps. "You do know that."

"Probably not, " he agrees. "Right now, it's all we've got." He heads toward the SUV then—no thank you, no good bye. And no apology for any of it. Her cooperation was purchased, after all, and at a price that may just be the highest he's paid for anything in his life.

TWENTY-SEVEN

Hour after hour of punishing trilling exercises—taken on because if Meggie is suffering, she must too—have done nothing to quell Jamie's considerable unease. The doctor has promised the initial test results today, the all-important blood and tissue matching, and so she's waited through the afternoon—a prisoner to all she promised in return for Michael's terrible secret. A secret she thought she wanted, and even, God forgive her, used Meggie to get—sure that having it would change her somehow, make her whole again. Instead, she's simply sad—sad for all of them—sad and guilty and dirty with the knowledge of it. Pitifully aware that on some level she's trying to redeem both Michael and herself with this effort. And not knowing why.

She's had it with the trills, finally, and switches to Bach—the *Fugue in C# minor,* whose almost obsessive adherence to the rules of counterpoint, the seemingly infinite elaboration of a single melody, usually irritates her but now rather suits her mood. Makes life simple when you get it all down to a single crystallizing element. One melody, one thought, one life-defining experience.

But she quickly drops the Bach as too tame. What she needs, she decides, is Scriabin, and she begins pounding her way through the disembodied, percussive *Le Vers de Flame*, its disturbing dissonance at one with her turmoil. Using the music to push away the other painful reality rearing up now as it does each year when fall closes in. Sam's birthday in less than a week. The thought of another of Philippe's increasingly distant letters already on its way from France—its perfunctory platitudes about the loss of their son primed to suck the life from her—makes her want to weep with exhaustion. This chance to help Meggie, she knows, the only thing standing between her and another emotional tailspin.

She raises a tear-streaked face in a silent prayer to her son, whose shimmer she longs to feel—asking his acceptance, forgiveness for whatever part she played in the events of that unthinkable day. Reaching toward him as she opens herself to this, accepts what she's pushed off all this time—her self-reproach recast now as the need sustain another. I couldn't help you, she thinks toward him—but just maybe I can help her. You know her, after all; you spoke to her in a dream. Willing him to understand this joining of forces with their mutual enemy, an enemy on all levels but one— the love of a child. So lost is she in this texture of emotions—a melody in counterpoint to the permutations of the music—that all about her seems illusion, even to Michael's shadow playing now at the very edge of the living room. Until he speaks, that is.

"I knocked, but you didn't answer."

She lowers her gaze to the keys, swipes quickly at her eyes. "Please leave," she says flatly. "I'm expecting a call."

"Yeah, well, he called me instead. I'm the one paying him, after all." Snappish, cold. No sign of the pleading eyes, the gently persuasive technique of his last visit. Telling Jamie all she needs to know.

She draws her hands from the keyboard and lays them in her lap, raising her eyes to him at last. "No good?" she asks quietly, blood pounding in her neck.

The bitter laugh she so remembers. "No, no good. You're not a match."

"Ah." She'd expected as much; still, she's flooded with an almost desperate disappointment. She waits for him to come forward into the living room, to launch the kind of physical face-off they usually have, but he stays where he is—trying, it seems, to work something out.

"I realize why you didn't tell me, of course." His voice taut with rage. "You had to go along with all this to get me to come clean. It was perfectly done, really. I didn't see it coming at all."

Please, God, no more games. She's so tired of the games. "I have no idea what you're talking about," she says wearily.

Drawing nearer, but only so far as the couch where he parks himself casually on an arm. "You couldn't have helped us, helped Meghan, even if you'd been a match. But then you knew that."

"And why is that?"

He leans toward her, exaggerating the pronunciation of each word as if to a dull child. "Pregnant—women—can't—donate. You knew that, too, of course."

It's as if all the air has been sucked from the room. "But I'm not—I can't be."

"Oh, believe me, you are."

Jamie's mind races, trying to remember a time she and Peter hadn't been careful. She can think of none. "It's a mistake," she says weakly.

"No mistake. They double-checked, figuring no one would be stupid or uncaring enough to come forward in such a state. They haven't met *you*, of course."

"Wait," she says, overwhelmed—needing to slow this down. Rising from the piano in agitation—everything registering all at once now. It's simply too much to process—too big an idea to fit here in this room with the two of them at each other like this.

"What," Michael sneers. "You're going to tell me you didn't

know? That this wasn't part of the plan? Save your breath." A shake of the head as he glares toward the ceiling. "I still can't believe you'd use this, use Meghan—who started dialysis this morning, by the way, because her kidneys can't handle whatever this is anymore—just to get what you wanted from me."

"That's because I didn't." Agitated about Meggie and furious now. Stepping from behind the piano but not quite sure where to head. The couch? The window? The kitchen for a knife?

"And setting me up like that, so I'd find out, put it all together on my own. You're good—gotta give you that."

She raises her hands as if to push him away. Push it all away. "That's it. That's enough," she says, moving briskly to the hall. "You're going." Pulling the door open. "Now."

And there, staring back at her from the porch is the familiar bearded face—so out of context that at first she draws a blank.

"Bake?" she finally asks, incredulous—her gaze traveling from the faded green of his Ben & Jerry's t-shirt to the beefy hand poised to knock at a door flung wide before him. "What are *you* doing here?" Other things beginning to register now—the smell of diesel and sweat that precedes him everywhere; Barbara Ann standing sheepishly off to the side. A panicked thought, then. "Is Peter all right?"

Bake glares past her toward Michael. "Who the fuck are you?" he demands.

"I'm sorry," Barbara Ann says to Jamie. "I told him we should call first. We finished with the Long Island thing this morning, and he dared me to find this place." She smacks Bake hard on the arm. "I told you this was a stupid idea."

"No—this is great," Jamie says. "Really. Come in—please." Still struggling to accept the sight of Bake's hairy form looming in her doorway, the sense that her life is running completely out of control. Only then does she realize how all this must look—her agitation, Michael's face flushed with anger and emotion.

No one moves.

"I knew this was what was goin' on," Bake growls, his eyes glued to Michael. Then over his shoulder to Barbara Ann, "Didn't I say this is what was goin' on? Shit." His gaze travels distastefully over Jamie.

"That's ridiculous," Jamie tells him. "Michael's daughter..."

"It's so obvious—you bein' gone all the time and all," Bake says, cutting her off. "I don't know why Pete don't see it, but then he's completely fuckin' blind when it comes to you." He taps the side of his head with a stubby finger. "But I knew. So I said to myself, I'll just swing by an check it out." He glares at Michael, pulls himself up to his full height, which about brings them eye-to-eye. "She's married, you know—to my best friend."

"Well, that's a relief," Michael snaps. "I thought you might be the husband."

Bake nods slowly, taking a step forward to jab a finger at Michael's chest. "You're a twisted fuck, you know that?"

"Oh, for God sake, stop it," Jamie says. "Michael's daughter takes piano lessons from me. That's it."

Bake cocks his head as if listening. "That so? Cause I don't hear no piano." He turns to Barbara Ann. "You hear a piano?"

"Listen, asshole," Michael begins.

"Oh, cut the crap," Barbara Ann says, pulling at Bake's arm now. "It's none of our business, anyway. Let's just go; traffic's gonna be a bitch as it is."

"You better hope Pete's okay with this," Bake warns as he backs away. "Cause he's sure as hell gonna know about it when I get home. Come on," he tells Barbara Ann, his eyes traveling over Michael one last time. "We're outta here."

Jamie watches from the doorway, wanting desperately to protest. But what, exactly—her innocence? That's a laugh. What's worse, she wonders—the kind of betrayal Bake's just accused her of or what she's really done here? Building another life Peter has little inkling of and absolutely no place in. The very denial of his existence central to her strategy. Which suddenly, now, for the first time in almost a year, makes no sense to her at all.

"He's going to make trouble," Michael says.

"Yes," she says, distracted. Slowly shutting the door.

"What will you tell your husband?" A new wariness in his voice.

"Everything. Jesus, what do you think?" There's little choice now—the realization tinged with the sweet flush of relief. Finally, an end to all this, an end she couldn't have foreseen even an hour ago. And the possibility of a fresh start, assuming—well— assuming Peter wants one. This baby possibly the only way she could have found her way back to him, considering everything she's put between them. It hits her again hard, in the pit of her stomach—the idea of this baby. She hadn't wanted another child, would never have consciously opened herself to the potential for such pain, such loss. Still, here it is. She wonders if the irony has struck Michael yet—that he should be the one to bring her this news of a coming child, the way this whole thing has come full circle. She wonders if he still believes in fate. She thinks now that she just may.

She turns to him, then—part of her already working out how long it will take to throw her things in the car and get on the road, whether it's possible to beat Bake back to the boat. "You need to go," she says quietly.

"Whoa—we're not done here."

"Oh, indeed we are."

"We made a deal," he reminds her flatly.

"The deal was I'd get tested. I did. There's nothing I can do for Meggie now, as much as I'd like to—you said so yourself." Edgy now, pacing—needing this to be over, to get out of here.

But Michael has turned inward against her words—hands on hips, regrouping. "Molly doesn't know about your results yet," he says, nodding to himself. "I can handle the doctor; he'll keep the whole thing under wraps if I tell him to." Looking up, eyes tracking Jamie. "So this is what we do. I'll tell Molly you're a match, that you'll help with whatever. You'll keep quiet about the results—that and your pregnancy."

Jamie whirls on him. "Jesus—what for? That's beyond cruel." Shaking her head. "No. This ends here. Now. I won't do it."

"Oh, you'll do it. I'll call your husband, otherwise—tell him this kid isn't his; that it's mine."

"Peter knows me better than that." Hoping to God it's true.

"Right, okay. Must be a hell of a guy, though—I mean to believe you after you told him about our tasty little encounter in the hall. You did tell him about that?"

Jamie laughs. "Oh, for God's sake, Michael. That was never really about us; haven't you figured that out yet?" And it was true. For one brief moment they'd formed a bizarre, twisted kind of union—the mother of Sam's birth, the father of his death. And if there'd been any element of desire in it at all, it was for that mutual connection, fed by hate and pain and longing, as if she might reach through him in a caress of her son.

Besides, she finally has the truth, ugly as it is. She could expose him as well, if he wants to play that game. But Meggie's illness makes it all seem worse than petty now.

"You don't get it, do you?" he asks. "There's no way you're walking away from this."

"You're the one who doesn't get it," she snaps. "I'm already gone."

"Look," he says quietly—trying for reasonable, sincere. "Molly's got this thing about you, okay? She's convinced you have some magic power to fix all this. I mean Meghan talks to your kid in her sleep, for God sake." Watching Jamie's face now, desperate for some in. "Sammy, right?"

He gets her with that, but she shakes her head, fighting the vision this conjures—Meggie lying prone, whispering toward the stars. "I won't do it," she says again. "There's no point."

"The point," he hisses, "is that Molly's a total basket case right now. If she believes you're ready to give Meghan whatever she needs, it'll take the pressure off. Free me up to explore other possibilities."

"Meaning what exactly?"

"There are places overseas..." He trails off, rakes a hand through his hair, tries again. "With enough money you can buy anything—marrow, organs, anything. What the fuck do you care, anyway? Only Molly can't know; she'd never go along. That's why I need you. That's why you're going to do this. Otherwise I make that call. And believe me, your husband will wonder. Every time he looks at that kid, every day of his life—even after that paternity test he's going to demand—he'll wonder." A grim smile. "Your choice."

"Listen to yourself. It's still all about you, isn't it—about keeping things from Molly. Why don't you try being honest with her for a change? She might just surprise you." A pause as Jamie decides, almost hoping he'll go for it—no matter the consequences. "Tell you what—you want to call Peter? Go ahead. He'll know everything ten minutes after I get home anyway."

Michael's only response the flicker of an eye.

"Here," she says, grabbing her cell from the coffee table—no longer afraid of him or of herself or of the raw, unspeakable bond between them. Ready for whatever. "I'll dial it for you." She punches the numbers, extends the phone.

"What's the matter?" she spits when he makes no move to take it. "Change your mind?"

A quick glance towards the floor, then his gaze travels to the window in search of some comeback, something else he can throw at her. And coming up with nothing.

Jamie cancels the call, tosses her cell to the couch and heads for the stairs. Let him find his own way out; she's got packing to do.

"I can't lose her."

The words stop her for a moment—the feeling behind them so close to her own quiet despair, it takes her breath.

"I can't lose her," he says again, his jaw working. "You don't know..."

But of course she does. How hollow it feels to have reached this place. How bitterly sad. And in a sudden and startling epiphany, she realizes that somewhere in all this anger, the fury she's been carrying for almost four years has left her. No idea how or even when; just that she's somehow clear of it. It isn't forgiveness, exactly. It isn't even really empathy. It's just that all at once Michael is nothing more to her than a pathetic, frightened father—as wounded in his own way, as brutalized by what happened as she, herself, was. Is. His part in it just as haphazard, as chance-driven as her own. Christ, she thinks, mounting the stairs with a heavy step. The unbelievable waste of it all.

ɸ ɞ

The elevator doors slide open with a soft ding, the medicinal smell stopping Jamie cold. Pediatric intensive care—the words and all they conjure making her nauseous with memory, the vow she'd once made never to walk a hospital corridor again.

The room number had been easy enough to track down—a quick call got her that much. Coming up with a plan now she's here is proving harder. Molly she can probably deal with, but she stands no chance at all, she knows, if Michael has beaten her here or phoned ahead with news of her defection.

The nurses' station immediately before her is crowded and busy—the very air thick with anxiety. Heart pounding, still reeling from the craziness of the last few hours, she averts her gaze— making a quick right down the corridor toward Meggie's room. Expecting to be challenged, praying she won't be. But it seems a grim face and aching heart speak for themselves here.

The door to the room is open and, miraculously enough, neither Molly nor Michael are in evidence. Jamie's gaze goes immediately to Meggie, on her side in the bed—legs tucked, eyes closed, one arm wrapped around a worn teddy bear. Deeply asleep, it appears—that or medicated. Looking desperately pale and washed out. And so very small.

Only then does Jamie turn her attention to the room itself—the IV cart, the tubes, the various monitors—all of it far too familiar. A soft blue cardigan and open book rest on a chair pulled to the side of the bed.

No telling how much time she has, so she moves quickly. A red, heart-shaped helium balloon bobs above the metal side rail, the muted green wall behind it literally covered with get-well cards. Jamie nudges the balloon aside and bends close.

"Hey there," she whispers, pulling Meggie's blanket to her shoulders.

The sound of running water then, a door opening across the room. And in the split second before the woman sees her, Jamie recognizes an older version of Molly—the same build and fiery coloring—racks her brain for the name Michael let slip when he confronted her about calling the house for news.

"Who are you?" the woman asks, forehead crinkling in confusion.

Good question. Who indeed, now everything is out in the open. Jamie? Diana? Some strange amalgam of the two?

"Meggie's piano teacher," she says quietly, her sheepish smile meant to disarm. "We spoke on the phone several weeks ago." She leaves it at that, unsure how much Molly has shared with her mother about all that's happened. "I'm heading out of town, but I couldn't leave without seeing her." Gloria, she thinks. The woman's name is Gloria.

A nod as the sweater is retrieved, the book moved from the seat. "Meggie talks about you all the time," she says, sitting. "She's always been a such a somber child—well, I'm sure you know. But she so looked forward to her lessons. It's amazing how she's come alive since starting with you."

Actually, Jamie thinks, fingering a lock of hair from Meggie's cheek, it's quite the other way around. She catches sight of it, then—a corner of the thin, black book protruding from beneath the pillow. Meggie's practice book.

She's so swallowed by emotion she can barely resist taking the girl up, crushing her to her chest. "You'll tell her I was here?" she asks, not trusting herself to look up. "That I miss our time together?" Pitifully few words considering all that's in her heart.

"Of course."

"And that she isn't to blame," Jamie adds. "It's important she knows she isn't to blame."

Her head snaps up at the sound of approaching footsteps, eyes darting to the door until the danger is passed.

"They'll be back soon," Gloria says softly, kindly.

Jamie nods, reaching to her pocket and withdrawing her gift. Carefully prying open a hand, she puts the pennies in Meggie's palm—folding the small, warm fingers around them. "For luck," she whispers, kissing the damp forehead before rising.

Turning, then, she strides purposefully from the room—unwilling to let even one of them see her tears.

TWENTY-EIGHT

She reaches the boat just before eleven—the dogs scrambling up the darkened companionway in greeting as she picks her way through the cockpit. She's been coming home late more often than not these last few months, so they know to expect her step and there's no barking—just a lot of begging for attention. Still, if Peter has gone to sleep, he's awake again now.

The dogs jockey around each other as they whine their way to where she's slipping off her sneakers—Lucille's round sausage body quaking with excitement, Gus stretching and yawning as he nuzzles his way beneath Jamie's hand. "Okay," she murmurs, rubbing the profusion of ears and listening anxiously for any evidence of Peter below. "Yes, yes, okay." Another clattering of nails as they precede her back down the companionway.

Jamie settles on the top step while the dogs sort themselves out—peering into the quiet dark of the boat's interior for some sign of Peter. Then she spots him. He hasn't gone to bed after all, but is sitting fully clothed at the small table, the light from the oil lamp so dim it's hard at first to make him out. Waiting for her, it seems—not as he usually does with music playing and dinner bubbling on the stove, but waiting in the dark, in silence. A silence he doesn't break now.

"Hey," she says—picking her way down the steps, her eyes moving over the galley where what would have been dinner sits congealing in the pots, the counter beneath his row of cookbooks looking greasy and cluttered..

Peter says nothing. There's a bottle on the table before him and he reaches for it now, filling the shot glass beside it.

She drops her bag inside the door to the aft cabin, resting her back against the bulkhead. "Never knew you for a scotch man," she says, recognizing the bottle as one his graduate students gave him a few Christmases back and which has gone untouched—until now.

Peter throws the liquor back, reaches again for the bottle.

"Okay, so Bake's been here and told you a bunch of lies. He's the one who finished the rum, right?" Still no response. She sighs, sheds her sweater and tosses it on the settee. "This all you been doing since he left?"

"I been to the doctor... he said I'm all right," Peter sings softly as he pours himself another shot. *"I know that he's lyin'... I'm losin' my sight. He should have examined the eyes of my mind... twenty-twenty vision and walkin' 'round blind."* He laughs and shakes his head—tossing back the drink. Pours another.

Reaching to the small cabinet housing their bar, Jamie pulls out a second shot glass and places it on the table beside the bottle. Trying to remember the name. Jimmy somebody. Not Jimmy Vaughan, brother of Stevie Ray. Jimmy, Jimmy...

"Jimmy Martin," she says, finally pouring herself a shot, since Peter has made no move to do so. "You want to tell me what he said? Bake, I mean—assuming you're sober enough to talk about this."

"One is the loneliest number that you'll ever do," Peter sings. *"Two can be as bad as one; it's the loneliest number since the number one."*

She sits opposite him and, with apologies to whoever is growing inside her, takes a small sip. Nothing after this, she promises.

We're going to do this right. She reaches for the bottle, locates the screw top at the edge of the table and begins thumbing it on. "Three Dog—"

"Fuck. Off." Wrenching the bottle from her hand.

She freezes. "Peter, I didn't have an affair with Michael Ryan."

"Michael Ryan. The million-dollar man. Man with a plan." He laughs, tosses back the scotch. "Did you know," he says, leaning forward suddenly, "that a lobster will tear off its own claw in order to save itself? Never," he says, pointing a finger at her, "ignore your instincts."

"Okay," she says, half-laughing. "What…"

"Because," he says, cutting her off. "When that asshole—Mr. Smooth, Mr. Man-with-a-Plan—called here that time asking all those questions, I had a feeling about it. But then I thought no, not Jamie. Not my Jae. But I had that feeling, see. So don't fucking tell me you aren't, that you didn't…" He lets a flick of the wrist finish his thought and stares morosely at the empty shot glass.

"I didn't," she insists quietly.

"And what does that mean anyway—*having an affair*? People should say what they mean. *Fucking, shagging, screwing.*" He jerks forward aggressively again. "*Cheating.*"

"I didn't sleep with him."

"Ah! *Sleeping.* Like that's what we're really doing when we say we're *sleeping with someone.* Christ. All this evasion, hiding behind words. Bake's right. That's what you do—hide behind words."

She winces. She'd debated how much to tell him, of course. All the way home in the car. Finally deciding the only thing she wouldn't tell him, couldn't tell him, was what happened between Michael and herself that night in the hall. She'd take that one to her grave.

He starts in with the singing again. "*Back field emotion… I'm gonna have to penalize you—ooh-ooh.*"

Shit. He better be sober enough to hear this, to understand what she's about to say, because she doesn't want to have to go through the whole thing again in the morning.

"Even if I weren't married to you," she tells him—taking the bottle again and capping it firmly. "Even if I didn't love you," she emphasizes, "there are other reasons why I could never get involved with Michael Ryan." She turns and places the bottle of Scotch in the locker, snaps the door shut.

"*Involved with*," Peter sneers.

"If Bake knew any of it," Jamie continues, "if he'd bothered to stay around and listen to me this afternoon instead of just running off when he thought he had it all figured out, he'd never have shown up here and done this to you."

"Oh, yeah?" He's even sounding like Bake now—cocky, belligerent. Still, she's started this, and she's going to get through it somehow.

"Michael's the man who ran me off the road the day Sam died."

He looks up quickly, then, and she gets a flash of the old Peter—loving and concerned, and for a moment thinks she might actually stand a chance. If nothing else, this bit of information seems to have sobered him a little. "I went down there in the first place to find out who he was," she tells him. "Why he never took responsibility. Things—well, things got out of control."

He nods slowly. "Let's see if I understand this," he says reasonably. "You weren't really screwing this guy Ryan; you were screwing your dead kid?"

Jamie's jaw drops, tears springing to her eyes. Reaction noted, Peter returns his gaze to the table, where he's begun scribing little circles with the glass. Trying to hurt her, as terribly and as unforgivably as she's hurt him. He's a scientist, after all; it's in his training. For every action, there's an equal and opposite reaction—Newton or somebody. All right, then, if it will help him get past all this, let her in again.

"You gonna drink that?" he asks, as if he hadn't just ripped her heart out.

It's all she can do to shake her head no.

"I mean, help me out here," he says, throwing back the scotch and placing her shot glass down beside his own. "Make me understand. Because I really don't. What were you trying to do, exactly—I mean all this time when I was so completely in the dark? When I trusted you?"

She considers a moment. "I wanted to ruin his life. The way he ruined mine."

Peter nods. "Something you've gotten good at lately—hurting people, screwing up lives." A pause. "And did you? Ruin his life?"

She wanted to; she tried. But something happened along the way. She opened her heart to a child again—an almost desperately thin, nervous little girl who reminded Jamie oddly of herself. A girl who happened to adore her father.

"No," she tells Peter. "I stopped it." But had she really? After all, hadn't fate stepped in and dealt him an even crueler blow? Tears threaten at the thought of Meggie, tears she'd been shedding all the way home. Thank God the lighting in the cabin was low; she hardly needed something more to explain. "Anyway, the whole thing's over now. All of it."

"All of it." As if he doesn't believe her.

"I phoned Augie before I left—told her I was withdrawing from my position effective immediately. She was surprisingly nice about it. Understood it must be very difficult for us—you and me, I mean." A conversation that took almost an hour. That call, and the detour to the hospital, putting her on the road much later than she wanted. Still, telling Augie most of the story was the least she owed this woman.

"I'm back for good now. Assuming…" You can forgive me? Still love me? She looks off toward the shaft of moonlight streaming down the companionway, not trusting herself to finish, afraid of his response. Aware suddenly of how wrong it might be after all—how terribly unfair—to tell him about the baby before he'd had the chance to decide about her. On her own.

"Thing is, Jae," Peter says, "I could always count on you being straight—a hundred percent. It made up for a lot, you know? It was one of the best things about you—about us. Now I don't know who the fuck it is I married."

She reaches to him, placing her hand on his, and is flooded with relief when he doesn't pull away. "Me. You married me." A hundred percent straight. Okay, then. No more keeping things back. After all, she's a package deal now—two for the price of one.

He shifts in his seat. "What are you doing about the house?"

"Selling it. Why, you want it?"

"God, no. What would I do with a house?"

Jamie looks around the main saloon, the cluttered galley; glances again toward the small aft cabin where Gus is already snoring, and tries to imagine raising a child here. An idea fraught with complication—ludicrous really, but suddenly and almost overwhelmingly appealing. They'll name her Meghan, Jamie decides, assuming it's a girl—a fragile sliver of hope easing into her with the thought.

"Besides," he says, still not meeting her eyes. "The Shoals project is officially on hold, thanks to Barbara Ann and her buddies. Got the word this afternoon. Nothing holding me here now. Nothing left to do but go sailing."

"Oh, Peter—after all your work."

He shrugs. "Doesn't bothers me as much as I thought it would. Kind of freeing, actually. Take a year or so off, then head over to Spain—to Hawaii, maybe—some place people are a little more forward-thinking."

"Sounds great." A pause. "When do you leave?" Wanting to say *we*, needing desperately to say *we*, but sensing he's not yet sure of her. Won't be, maybe, for some time to come. She can live with that, though—long as there's a chance.

"Well," he says. A small smile—finally. "There's next week to get through first."

"Next week. Yes." Is he talking about Sam's birthday, she wonders, or is there something else she's promised to be part of and forgotten about, as she has so many other things these past months? She takes a chance. "But it'll be all right, I think. Now."

"Yeah, well, Philippe's letter hasn't arrived yet."

She gets up then and moves to his side of the table, sliding in beside him. "What if we don't open it this time—just tear it up and toss it over the side?"

"Better yet, mail the goddamn thing back to him. Return to sender."

She nods, laces her fingers in his. "There's something else we need to talk about, too."

"Christ, there's more?"

No more holding back. "We can't talk about it out here, though," she says. "We have to go to bed first."

"Are we going to bed? Or are we *going to bed*?"

Tell you what," she says taking his hand and pulling him to his feet. "I'll lay it all out, then you can decide."

ACKNOWLEDGEMENTS

I owe a great debt to the many books I've read on death and the grieving process. Dealing with the rage and anguish that accompanies the loss of a small child and still managing to come through it somewhat emotionally intact has to be the hardest thing anyone will ever do. I'm in awe of every one of you.

Many thanks to Skip Small, MD, who helped me with the details of Meggie's illness—walking me through a variety of medical scenarios and prognoses. I'm also grateful to Chris Jackson, PhD.—friend, fellow writer and classical pianist—who explained some of the not-so-basics to this non-musician, then kindly vetted the technical portions of the manuscript; and to Ms. Judith Cudhea, piano teacher to small children, who opened my eyes to the magic music holds for the very young and pointed me toward Jamie's use of the Bastien Primers and the Burnham Preparatory Series as teaching aids.

Thanks, also, to Steven Brigandi, Beth Walker and Mike Brown—all of the State of New Hampshire Department of Transportation—for taking me under their collective wing and sharing anecdotes about toll tending on the Big Road; to Sally Kim and Kelly Skillen for their invaluable feedback on early drafts, and to my incredibly patient readers: Roxanne Turner, Barb Yoder and Bob Ellrich. Finally, a huge, huge thank you to everyone at Snowbooks for taking a chance on me.

ABOUT THE AUTHOR

Darcy Scott is a former symphony orchestra marketing director, who works as a marine industry publicist when she's not off adventuring. An experienced ocean cruiser, she's sailed to Grenada and back on a whim, island-hopped through the Caribbean, and been struck by lightning in the middle of the Gulf Stream. She currently lives with her husband on their sailboat in Maine. This is her debut novel. Learn more at www.darcyscott.net.

QUESTIONS FOR DISCUSSION GROUPS

Darcy Scott is available for live e-chats during Book Club discussions of *Hunter, Huntress* when time and scheduling permit. Feel free to email your requests to her at www.darcyscott.net.

The following are a few questions to get things rolling.

1. Consider the unspoken accommodations made in Jamie's and Peter's marriage as well as that of the Ryans. How important is emotional honesty in a relationship? When is it acceptable to hold back from one's partner, if at all?

2. Jamie is obsessed with the idea of Michael's guilt, consumed with the need for answers, but she herself made decisions the morning of the accident that contributed to Sam's death. Is one more responsible than the other? Why?

3.   Though she initially fixates on Michael's two-year-old son, Matthew, Jamie finds herself drawn to Meghan—a relationship that ultimately disarms her. Despite this, she willingly uses the girl as a pawn in her plans for revenge. What does that say about her? Is morality absolute, or is it a fluid thing, dependent on circumstance?

4.   Discuss Michael's physical aggression the night he forces himself on Jamie in the hallway of her home. Was this sexual assault, or does her response and its complicated implications make it something else?

5.   Michael's interest in Jamie seems to intensify once he learns her true identity, as if he's increasingly drawn by the risk she poses. Discuss this from the standpoint of addiction.

6.   Consider the role of Orion's myth in the novel, the ways in which the paranormal intervenes in the course of events. Have you, yourself, ever experienced this kind of divine or otherworldly intervention?